"Doss's trademark humor keeps Charlie and Scott wise-cracking as the plot spins smartly along to an unpredictable ending . . . Moon mysteries still charm us with Western voices and ways."
—*Rocky Mountain News*

STONE BUTTERFLY

"The Moon series deftly blends traditional mystery elements with Native American mythology—a surefire read-alike for Hillerman fans."
—*Booklist*

"Droll, crafty, upper-echelon reading."
—*Kirkus Reviews* (starred review)

"Style, pathos, enthusiasm, and humor to spare."
—*Mystery Scene*

"A clever plot . . . will keep readers turning the pages."
—*Publishers Weekly*

SHADOW MAN

"Doss likes to toss a little Native American spiritualism and a lot of local color into his mysteries. Fans of the series will be well pleased."
—*Booklist*

"Fans of Daisy Perika, the 80-something shaman who brings much of the charm and supernatural thrill to James D. Doss' mystery series, should like *Shadow Man* . . . nice reading."
—*Rocky Mountain News*

THE WITCH'S TONGUE

"With all the skill and timing of a master magician, Doss unfolds a meticulous plot laced with a delicious sense of humor and set against a vivid southern Colorado."
—*Publishers Weekly*

"Doss's ear for Western voices is remarkable, his tone whimsical. . . . If you don't have time for the seven-hour drive

from Denver to Pagosa, try *Witch's Tongue* for a taste of southern Colorado."
—*Rocky Mountain News*

"A classy bit of storytelling that combines myth, dreams, and plot complications so wily they'll rattle your synapses and tweak your sense of humor."
—*Kirkus Reviews*

DEAD SOUL

"Hillerman gets the most press, but Doss mixes an equally potent brew of crime and Native American spirituality."
—*Booklist*

"Lyrical and he gets the sardonic, macho patter between men down cold. The finale is heartfelt and unexpected, and a final confrontation stuns with its violent and confessional precision."
—*Providence Journal-Bulletin*

THE SHAMAN LAUGHS

"Harrowing . . . suspenseful."
—*The New York Times Book Review*

"A mystery that combines the ancient and the modern, the sacred and the profane, with grace and suspense."
—*Publishers Weekly*

THE SHAMAN SINGS

"Stunning."
—*Publishers Weekly* (Starred Review; named Best Book of the Year)

"Magical and tantalizing."
—*The New York Times Book Review*

"Gripping . . . Doss successfully blends the cutting edge of modern physics with centuries-old mysticism."
—*Rocky Mountain News*

A Dead Man's Tale

JAMES D. DOSS

St. Martin's Paperbacks

Epigraphs that appear throughout *A Dead Man's Tale* are taken from the Western folk song known variously as "Bury Me Not on the Lone Prairie" and "The Cowboy's Lament."

This is a work of fiction. All of the characters, organizations, and events portrayed in this novel are either products of the author's imagination or are used fictitiously.

A DEAD MAN'S TALE

Copyright © 2010 by James D. Doss.
Excerpt from *Coffin Man* copyright © 2011 by James D. Doss.

Cover photo of cattle at dawn near Clinton, Ontario, Canada © Radius Images/Getty Images. Cover photo of pink sky over Monument Valley © Fuse/Corbis. Cover design and illustration by Danielle Fiorella.

All rights reserved.

For information address St. Martin's Press, 175 Fifth Avenue, New York, NY 10010.

Library of Congress Catalog Card Number: 2010032509

ISBN: 978-0-312-54889-6

Printed in the United States of America

Minotaur hardcover edition / November 2010
St. Martin's Paperbacks edition / November 2011

St. Martin's Paperbacks are published by St. Martin's Press, 175 Fifth Avenue, New York, NY 10010.

10 9 8 7 6 5 4 3 2

For

Barry Carithers
Arvada, Colorado

and

Rob Meekins
Houston, Texas

PROLOGUE

ELSEWHEN IN A FUZZY CHRONOLOGY

When times get hard, most of us manage to cinch our belts up a notch or two and tough it out until the dawn of a brighter day. But on those moonless nights when chill winds moan and groan under the eaves and starving rats gnaw in the walls, keeping body and soul together is easier for some than for others. While our hardest-hit neighbors face home foreclosures, extended layoffs, and diets heavy on maca-roni, beans, and rice, better-off citizens cut back on steak-and-lobster dinners, sunny Caribbean cruises, and other benefits that fall into the category of sugar and spice and everything nice.

Then, there are the high-end outliers—those fortunates who thrive in good times and bad.

Among that envied latter category, one such privileged soul is Samuel Reed, Ph.D. The former professor of physics, apparently sound of mind and limb, is happily optimistic about his future. And why shouldn't he be? This prime-of-life alpha male has a top-of-the-line trophy wife who is about to celebrate her thirtieth birthday. Is the fellow well heeled? Very much so and then some. The scientist-turned-entrepreneur has sizable accounts squirreled away in several dozen banks and credit unions, and every dollar and dime is federally insured. Floating atop that radiant lake of liquidity is a fleet of lucrative investments. The remarkably success-ful financier owns more prime real estate than a Wall Street

shyster could shake a crooked stick at—including that upscale
habitat where Sam Reed hangs his hat in Granite Creek,
Colorado. As a sideline, he also turns a nice profit by placing wagers on major sporting events.

When envious friends inquire about the secret of his
success, a cold-sober Sam Reed will assert that the process
required years of detailed study of the ins and outs of in-
vesting, and recommend patience to those who aspire to
accumulate an unseemly share of earthly treasures. After a
double shot of rye whiskey, he might admit (with a sly
wink) that he has benefited from "two or three lucky
streaks," the first of which transformed him from Chevrolet to Mercedes within a few weeks. Neither explanation is
wholly satisfying.

So what is the truth of the matter—how did a university
professor with no prior record of accumulating filthy lucre
manage to acquire a massive fortune? Therein lies the ker-
nel of a sinister mystery, which has to do with the subject
of Sam Reed's remarkable *memory*. It's not just that the
gifted man can recall detailed market data for stocks and
commodities and recollect practically everything there is
to know about high-strung jockeys, wild-eyed quarter horses,
and cool-as-ice NFL quarterbacks—plenty of aspiring
millionaires have excellent memories and end up flat broke.
If Reed is to be believed, he has the uncanny ability to
remember—

But we get ahead of ourselves.

Perhaps it will be better to let Professor Reed describe
what it is that he does. As it happens, the obstinate fellow
won't do that until he is so disposed, and at present he is not.
In a little while, as his options become limited, he might be.
We shall see.

In the meantime, let us reconsider our earlier query:
"And why shouldn't he be?" (happily optimistic about his
future).

Because the fourth of June has arrived, that's why. This
is the day when Samuel Reed's coconut-cream pie in the sky

is destined to turn decidedly sour. As it happens, he has an appointment with that gloomy, cloaked personage who totes an oversized scythe on his bony shoulder.

Blissfully ignorant of his looming misfortune, the wealthy man is in for a big, bad surprise. At this very moment, Irene Reed's faithful husband is homeward bound with an eighty-dollar box of birthday chocolates for his comely spouse. We find him in a gay, almost whimsical mood. We know this because Dr. Reed is crooning a happy tune. ("Lida Rose.")

Look out, Sam. Mr. D is about to enter, stage left.

Being something of a showman, the hollow-eyed performer appeared with a touch of fanfare—right on cue, a massive bronze bell dolefully began to toll the eleventh hour.

Samuel Reed's lighthearted crooning was not dampened by this discordant downbeat. Oblivious to the timely omen that was booming off his final seconds, the victim stepped into the abyss. It was not to be a peaceful, painless passing, as when a saintly aunt falls asleep to awaken in another, brighter world.

As a plump lump of spinning lead drilled its way through his chest, Sam's happy life was terminated in a searing agony—his heart and spine mangled beyond any hope of repair. About one and a half missing heartbeats later, another heavy projectile exploded from its brass casing to enter his left eye, and—there is no delicate way to put this—his cerebellum was transformed into a substance resembling lumpy oatmeal.

A classic instance of overkill.

Citizen Reed had kicked the proverbial bucket.

His chips were cashed in.

Curtains for certain.

End of the trail.

Why this seemingly excessive emphasis on the permanence of Samuel Reed's condition? Because—if one accepts the victim's testimony—his absence will prove transitory.

Seems unlikely in the extreme? Agreed. But in the interest of clarification and fair play, we shall allow the dead man to have his say. For which purpose, we must turn the clock back some thirty-two days.

CHAPTER ONE

10:54 P.M., MAY 3
PLAY IT AGAIN, SAM

Samuel Reed is every bit as cheerful as he had been (and would be again) on the evening of his untimely demise. As the jolly fellow slips along Shadowlane Avenue in his sleek gray Mercedes, he sings at the top of his fine tenor voice. ("Sweet Adeline.")

Without missing a beat, our happy crooner turns into a graveled driveway that snakes its way through a small forest of spruce and aspen before looping around his two-story, nine-bedroom, twelve-bath brick residence.

SOME STRANGE GOINGS-ON

Having activated a radio-frequency device on his key chain to open a twenty-foot-wide door, Sam Reed pulled into the spacious garage under his so-called guest house. Because Mr. and Mrs. R. rarely entertained overnight visitors, the up-stairs apartment served as the businessman's at-home office. But even that designation was not entirely accurate; in actual practice, the quarters over the detached garage provided a quiet sanctuary upon those occasions when Irene was in one of her snarling-snapping moods. As it happened (and not by accident), Sam's spouse did not have a key to the guest house, nor did she have need of one. His better half kept her pink Cadillac in the attached six-car garage, where that symbol of GM's pre-Chapter 11 days was alone except for the lady's shiny new ten-speed bicycle.

Sam Reed parked his superb German motorcar beside his buff black Hummer and closed the garage door with his remote. Before getting out of his automobile, he reached across the seat to pick up the—

Pick up the *what*?

There was nothing on the passenger seat for his gloved fingers to grasp.

The driver blinked at the empty space. *Now what did I expect to find there?*

This reasonable question triggered the recollection of a chain of seemingly mundane events, which began with Reed's usual routine after a long, tiring day of turning tidy profits. He remembered locking the door of his downtown office over the Cattleman's Bank and clearly recollected walking down the stairway to emerge onto the parking lot.

So far, nothing remarkable.

Then . . . *The moment the cold air hit me in the face, I remembered that I had something important to do before driving home. Something to pick up for Irene . . . but what was it—something from the supermarket? No. I don't think so.* Like a big-mouth bass breaking water to gulp up a plump insect, the memory surfaced abruptly: *Oh, of course— I walked a few blocks down to the Copper Street Candy Shop and arrived just minutes before their ten thirty P.M. closing time.* Reed could still taste the delicious double espresso he'd tossed back while the proprietor was wrapping a box of gourmet chocolates in shiny silver foil. This latter recollection was particularly significant: the purchase of absurdly expensive sweets for the lady of the house occurred only once each year. *And then I walked back to the parking lot, got into my car, and placed the box of chocolates on the passenger seat.*

This explained his reaching for a box of chocolates. Sort of. His brow furrowed into a puzzled frown. *But the choco-*

lates are not there. And Reed knew why: *Because I did not stop at the candy shop this evening.* Why? *Because Irene's birthday is a month away.* Which raised a relevant question: *What the hell is going on?* As trained scientists are wont to do at the drop of a beaker, he postulated a plausible theory: *I've been working too hard; my mind is playing tricks on me.* Even when endowed with a superior intellect (he reasoned), a minor malfunction was bound to occur from time to time.

Shrugging it off, Reed emerged from the Mercedes with his ivory-knobbed cane in hand and exited the garage by a side door facing the rear of his residence. He paused for a sweet moment to inhale a breath of the invigorating night air and treat his eyes to the silvery aspect of a half inch of late-spring snowfall. *What I need is a glass of wine and a good night's sleep.*

Alas, the prescription for what ailed him was to be found in neither bottle nor bed.

As he trod along, tugging a foreshortened moon shadow toward his home, a chill breeze wafted by to cool his face. Endowed with an exquisitely sensitive imagination that could be triggered into delightfully whimsical visions by the slightest suggestion, the closet romantic was instantly transformed into a lean, hard-eyed mountain man—leaning into a blinding blizzard. To enhance the dandy fantasy, Sam Reed commenced to croon a few lines of "Bury Me Not on the Lone Prairie," adjusting his pace so that the crunch-crunch of his pricey Florsheim Kenmoor shoes in the snow provided a synchronized rhythm to the melancholy old cowboy song. He was just about to bellow out the good part about *where coyotes howl and the wind blows free* when his shoe crunching was accompanied by a distant downbeat.

From somewhere miles and weeks away, a half-ton bronze bell began to count off the eleventh hour.

Uh-oh?

No. Not tonight. This was not that dreaded End of the Trail.

But the dreadful tolling (which not another mortal soul could hear!) was suddenly accompanied by an extremely unpleasant phenomenon.

Samuel Reed's initial sensation was that a white-hot poker had been thrust through his chest. This assault was instantly followed by an agonizing pain behind his forehead. Believing that he was suffering a heart attack or a stroke or both, the stricken man staggered and almost fell. *This is it—poor Irene will find my frozen body here in the snow.*

Not so.

At the seventh peal of the imaginary bell, his pains began to diminish. At the eleventh and final gong, after a half-dozen rib-thumping heartbeats and half as many gasping breaths, they were gone. Professor Reed was fully recovered. A most welcome development, indeed—and one that should have been entirely gratifying.

But, by some means or other, he had become aware of a stark new reality: *Before much time has passed, I am destined to reside among the deceased.* And not due to natural causes.

Enough to make a man stop and think. Which he did.

I'm a goner unless I do something about it. Which he would.

In the meantime . . . *I'm glad this creepy experience is over.* It was not.

The first indication of *more to come* was a slight buzzing at the base of his skull. This was followed by a giddy sensation of weightlessness . . . as if the slightest breeze might blow him away like a dead cottonwood leaf.

What's this? The expectant fellow cocked his ear as if listening for something. Or perhaps *to* something.

Then . . . *Oh my goodness!*

Samuel Reed was suddenly bedazzled by a stunning jolt of mental clarity that would have felled a lesser man. As he looked up to see the moon's pockmarked face staring blankly back at him, his mouth curled into a grin that was a notch or two beyond silly. An uncharitable observer might have described the expression as teetering right on the ragged edge of *idiotic,* and concluded that the unfortunate fellow was suffering from an attack of lunacy.

Sam would have disagreed with that diagnosis, and asserted that he was experiencing a wonderful epiphany. But it is worth noting that the fellow is an authentic specimen of that gender whose members are frequently mistaken—but rarely in doubt.

What is the truth of the matter? We do not know. The jury is still out.

But right or wrong, the man grinning at the earth's silvery satellite was convinced that he understood precisely what had occurred. He threw back his head and enjoyed a hearty laugh.

This was—in a very real sense—a new beginning.

CHAPTER TWO

MRS. REED FIDGETS AND FRETS

Having heard Sam's Mercedes arrive a few minutes earlier, Irene Reed was wondering what was keeping her husband. Desirous of finding out, she pulled on a black silk robe, slipped her bare feet into a pair of black velvet house slippers, and padded from the parlor into the dining room to peek between the curtains at the snowy backyard. The lady's pouting lips carried on a conversation with her petulant thoughts.

"Oh, there he is." *But why's he standing in the snow like some dodo that don't know where to go?* "And what's Sammy laughing about?" *Probably some stupid joke.* The humor critic arched a penciled-on left eyebrow. "Now he's talking to himself!" *What next?* (She is about to find out.)

Samuel began to sing. Loudly. ("Just the Two of Us.")

"Oh, I hope the neighbors don't hear!" The embarrassed wife shook her head in dismay. "That's what happens when a man doesn't get enough rest and relaxation." *But working long hours is how he makes so much money.* Irene's eyes got as big as silver dollars. "Would you look at that—it's cold enough to freeze an Eskimo and he's taking off his overcoat—and his jacket!" *Well if that ain't goofy, I don't know what is.* "Now he's rolling up his shirtsleeve." *Maybe Sammy's started taking dope again.* "First it was popping pills, now he's about to stick a hypo into his arm." *Oh, I can't look!*

The delicate creature beat a hasty retreat into the parlor.

* * *

Not to worry, Mrs. Reed. Your husband is not about to insert a hollow needle into his arm; the mere thought of puncturing his flesh makes Sam cringe. Whenever he needs a specified fluid injected under his skin, a shady lady in town performs that disagreeable task for him. What is the eccentric man's purpose in baring his forearm? Professor Reed plays his cards close to his vest, so it's hard to say. But sooner or later, he's bound to give himself away.

As her chilled silk-stockinged toes were getting all comfy-cozy on the warm brick hearth, Irene Reed scowled prettily at the crackling fire. *Soon as I get warmed up, I'll go to the back door and yell at the silly bastard*. The lady of the house turned her cold backside to the fireplace. "But I won't let on that I know he's started pumping drugs into his veins." *I'll be all sugary-sweet*. "That's what Sammy likes." She poured herself a stiff shot of Tennessee sour mash whiskey and tossed the fiery liquid down her throat.

As Samuel Reed rolled his sleeve down, refastened the cuff, and slipped into his jacket, he was experiencing a conflicting mix of emotions that combined to a near-zero sum. The downside was a violent death that awaited him around some dark corner. But such an outcome need not be inevitable, and it was counterbalanced by an opportunity. Make that a *once-in-a-lifetime* opportunity. The irony of the descriptor produced a thin little smile under the dapper man's immaculately trimmed mustache. So absorbed was the scientist-entrepreneur in his thoughts that he was startled by his spouse's shrill screech from the back door.

"I've been waiting up for you, Sammy—don't stand out there in the cold like a silly old goof." Irene added a shiver and a "Brrrr!"

Buttoning his woolen jacket, her husband called out, "I'll be right there, dear."

"Well hurry up—I've got something *special* waiting for you!" With this enticing invitation, his gorgeous wife disappeared inside, leaving the door open wide.

Still a bit giddy from his extraordinary experience, Samuel Reed needed to get a fix on his temporal coordinates. He entered through the rear of his home and stepped into a little-used game room that was provided with all manner of entertainments, from computerized tests of manual and mental skills to old-fashioned amusements like a Ping-Pong table, a 1950s-era pinball machine, an antique Reno Sally slot rigged to fleece the occasional guest who could not resist feeding it quarter-dollars. Oblivious to these garish furnishings, he switched on a century-old Tiffany floor lamp and peered at the Cattleman's Bank calendar, whereupon—every morning without fail—he crossed off the previous day. The last date with an X through it was the second of May. *Which makes this the third.* Reed's eyes goggled, his mouth gaped, and he heard himself say, "I have a month and a day left!"

Again he was distracted by his spouse's summons—this time from their spacious parlor. "Don't dillydally, Sammy—come in here by the fire."

He smiled at the girlish pout in Irene's voice. "I shall be there directly."

"I've got something sweet and yummy—come to Mummy and get some while it's hot!"

Reed inhaled deeply, put on his happy-face mask, and marched into the parlor, where piñon flames snapped and crackled merrily in a fireplace large enough to roast a side of prime beef flanked by a half-dozen tender piglets.

His darkly attractive wife, wearing a black silk negligee and a sly smile, was stretched out on a midnight-blue velveteen couch. Irene raised a smallish glass that was half filled with an aromatic amber fluid. Smiling seductively at her husband, the lady gestured to draw his gaze to a crystal pitcher perched on the hearth. "Would Daddy like a nice hot toddy?"

The husband sighed. "Mommy always knows just what Daddy likes."

This is an appropriate time to leave Mr. and Mrs. Reed to enjoy the privacy of their luxurious residence.

Tomorrow morning, we shall pay a call on another sort of man altogether. Charlie Moon does not have a wife to come home to, and his bankroll would not choke a garter snake or grubstake a frugal silver prospector searching for "sign" in the badlands on the yonder side of Pine Knob. No, sir—not for a week, on a menu of moldy old corn pone, cold navy beans, and sour stump water.

CHAPTER THREE

" 'O bury me not on the lone prairie.'
These words came low and mournfully
From the pallid lips of the youth who lay
On his dying bed at the close of day."

MAY 4
HARD TIMES ON THE COLUMBINE

Though you wouldn't have guessed it from the hearty breakfast in the ranch headquarters. Eighteen-year-old Sarah Frank, who was serving it up on big platters, also provided nonstop cheerful chatter. The winsome lass was fairly bubbling over about how much she was enjoying her second semester at Rocky Mountain Polytechnic University in Granite Creek.

Every now and then when he could slip a slender word in edgeways, Charlie Moon contributed a remark or two.

Whenever Sarah finally ran out of breath, Charlie's aunt Daisy commenced to entertain those present with her customary early-morning organ recital, which began with the composer's well-known "Overture to an Aching Left Kidney," followed by her lighthearted "Waltz with a Leaky Bladder," and finally the big finale—an untitled fugue dedicated to Daisy Perika's troublesome colon.

What a great way to start a day—and break an overnight fast with a feast.

After Moon had finished off three fried eggs, a Texas-size chicken-fried steak soaked in thick brown gravy, and enough crispy fried potatoes and made-from-scratch buttermilk biscuits to feed slender little Sarah for a week, the Ute rancher politely inquired whether anyone had a hankering for that last piece of beef in the cast-iron skillet. The ladies did not, so the tall, lean man helped himself to the lonely piece of meat, smothered it in a ladle of hot gravy, and made short work of the combination.

With all that cooking, talking, eating, and whatnot, the Columbine kitchen was already a mite warmish and it was about to heat up by a few extra degrees that cannot be measured on any Fahrenheit, Celsius, Kelvin, or other temperature scale that you might care to mention.

Watch the girl do her stuff.

While Sarah helped Charlie with the dishes, the willowy youngster's left hip just happened to bump him from time to time. It was enough.

These small intimacies inspired Mr. Moon to get out of the kitchen and onto the east porch first chance he got, which he did, leaving Sarah to sigh and Aunt Daisy to shake her head and wonder where all this foolishness was going. *Sarah has her cap set for my nephew but that silly girl is like a daughter to Charlie and what he wants for a wife is a grown-up woman and there's a half-dozen brassy hussies just waiting to be asked and I wish one of 'em was a nice Ute girl but every one of 'em is a* matukach *but I'd just as soon he stayed single as marry one of them pale-skinned women because if that mixing keeps up for two or three more generations the whole tribe'll look like they was from Norway and won't that be a big joke on us Southern Utes but at least I won't live to see it.*

The old woman does tend to think in run-on sentences, but when you boil it all down to the dregs, Daisy Perika's analysis of the edgy relationship between Charlie Moon and Sarah Frank was not so far from being right on the mark—and such tensions in a household raise a pertinent question: when a hardworking man is pursued by a romantic teenager and vexed by a testy aunt, what does he need from time to time?

A rejuvenating dose of rest and relaxation, that's what.

But managing an outfit the size of Charlie Moon's Columbine Ranch doesn't leave much time for a fellow to enjoy the finer aspects of life, like angling for rainbow trout, dancing with a pretty girl who's at least thirty years old, picking an old-time tune on his Stelling's Gold Cross banjo, or just taking a long, peaceful walk in a shady forest of aspen and fir. Mr. Moon would dearly love to set aside a few hours for any one of these activities, but if it ain't one danged thing that interferes with a man's plans it's half a dozen more. Here are a few f'r instances.

Purebred cattle falling like flies from the latest highly contagious and mysterious malady that perplexes even those folks with Ph.D.s in cow-ology.

The three wa-hooing Columbine cowboys that busted up the Harley's Bad Boys Bar last week and "borried some fancy motorsikkles." It was all just for fun, to hear them tell it. (The unrepentant sinners are locked up in jail, impatiently waiting for the boss to go their bail, and that'll happen when cottonwoods leaf out in twenty-dollar bills.)

Over and above and on top of miscellaneous cattle diseases and pesky personnel problems, there are plagues of ravenous range worms and clouds of famished locusts that devour every last blade of grass on twenty sections in twenty minutes, and don't even talk about broken-down windmills and wheezy bulldozers hitting on maybe two cylinders and hungry cougars who've acquired a taste for Columbine prime beef. Such problems tend to nibble away at a stockman's razor-thin profit margin.

Which is why Charlie Moon looks forward to that happy time when he'll be flat-out retired, and those sweet mornings when he can sleep in until 7 A.M. and never have to look a homely Hereford in the face again or a bronc in the other end. Sad to say, like energizing the nation with nuclear fusion or solar power or wind, that longed-for day always seems to be twenty years away. In the meantime, the owner of the cattle operation is obliged to set a good example for his employees, which is why the Ute Indian was up well before the sun yawned and cracked a bloated fireball of an eyeball over the jagged Buckhorn Range.

It helped that most every morning on the Columbine could be rated somewhere between fine and fair, but this particular May 4 dawn had outdone itself. The eastern sky started off by showing off a pale, dusty blue that bloomed into a soft rosy hue, and just about the time Charlie Moon figured it'd done about all it could do, an armada of wispy cloud-ships sailed by to fill his eye with pearly pink that made him think of cotton candy and the cherry-flavored lips of the first girl he'd ever kissed.

But back to the heavenly display.

On the blue, rosy, pink background someOne had painted misty wisps of scarlet and also brushed on a few swirls of royal purple, which made a rainbow so pretty that it fairly made a man's eyeballs ache. Imagine Moon's surprise when the Artist struck flint to steel, making a white-hot spark that set the entire sky afire—what a fine show! For an encore, molten gold rolled off the snowy mountains like lava, threatening to sweep trees off the foothills and flood the deep Columbine Valley right up to the brim. Like most celebrations, the fireworks were over too soon, but the performance left a fellow thinking that life was about to dish out a dandy treat.

For a struggling stockman situated on the high, rolling prairie between the Buckhorn and Misery mountains, the hoped-for blessing might amount from anything to a boost in beef prices that'd been sliding down a slippery slope since last October, to an all-night root-soaking rain that'd revive sixty sections of parched pasture.

Fat chance.

Charlie Moon might as well hope that his aunt Daisy would settle down and behave like a normal woman of her advanced age. Or for that matter, that sweet little Sarah Frank would find herself a young man who was worth his boots and saddle, and thereby stop giving Mr. Moon the big-eye, which was downright embarrassing for a man that was old enough to be the Ute-Papago orphan's daddy.

Odds were, this would be another run-of-the-mill day, much like a thousand others. The price of beef on the hoof would slip a little or maybe level off, and there would be no sweet rainwater to refresh the Columbine's thirsty earth, Daisy would commit a fresh outrage sufficient to shock a deranged Nazi storm trooper, and Sarah would flutter her eyelashes at him and drop hints about how she was of an age to consider matrimony and had been for about three years now.

Charlie Moon figured he'd have to settle for what he had. These were hard times, and a man should be grateful just to make his way through one day and into the next. But one way or another, the Columbine's bills would have to be paid. Which reminded him that there was another side to that coin—the rancher had a few unpaid debts he could call in. But after thinking it over, Moon realized that all his debtors were worse off than he was.

Except for the notable exception.

If I could figure out some way of collecting the back wages the county owes me for standing in as Scott Parris's deputy now and again, that'd be a big help. Intending to call Chief of Police Parris, Moon made a reach for the telephone. He hesitated. Even though this was county money, it didn't feel right—leaning on his best friend. *Scott has troubles enough without me shoveling on some more.*

On the other hand . . .

The county does owe me the debt—and some of it's for work done two or three years ago. This would be hard, but times were tough all over and the thing had to be done. Charlie Moon pulled the telephone out of his jacket pocket, found the programmed number, his finger was on the button . . . the stubborn digit refused to press it.

The rancher shook his head. *I can't do this.*

Not to Scott.

CHAPTER FOUR

LAYING DOWN THE LAW

About six seconds flat after Charlie Moon had almost called him, Chief of Police Scott Parris—who knew about his Ute friend's financial troubles and was well aware of the back pay the county owed his part-time deputy—made up his mind to do something about it. And *right now*.

About two hundred heavy boot-stomps later, the angry chief of police marched into the County Council Chamber, where the mayor was conducting a breakfast meeting with a half-dozen cronies. This six-plus-one committee, whose average weight was in excess of two hundred pounds, was known derisively by disappointed voters as the Seven Dwarves.

Scott Parris was not present to play Snow White. The big-shouldered cop raised a meaty palm to command silence. "I don't have any time to waste, so I'll have my say and hit the bricks." He waved a finger at the mayor and six council-persons. "Every mother's son of you knows that Charlie Moon—with verbal approval from the mayor—has served as my deputy on several occasions during the past several years. You also know that despite all the paperwork I've filed to make things 'legal and proper,' and all the hours I've spent reminding you fine community leaders that it ain't right to let Charlie go unpaid for his efforts in keeping the citizens of this county safe from murderers, burglars, arsonists, *grafting politicians,* and other felons—you still ain't paid him one thin dime!" Seeing the mayor about to open his mouth and make another in a long line of inane protests that would make his blood boil, Parris—who was getting madder with every racing heartbeat—snapped, "Shuddup, Bruce!"

The mayor shudduped.

The chief of police gulped in a deep breath. "Now here's the deal. Either you cut Charlie a check for full payment right away, *or else*. You guys hearing me clear?"

A recently elected councilman, who had a Yale law degree mounted on his office wall, was not intimidated. Not yet. He cleared his throat. "That sounds very much like a threat."

"You're damn right it is!" Parris banged his big fist on the table, spilling six cups of coffee and the new councilman's green tea. His red face inches from the lawyer's gray mask, the burly cop bared his big teeth in a wolfish grin. "If you politicians don't do the right thing, there's gonna be ten kinds of hell to pay. You want to hear the one that'll really make your day?"

It was clear that not one of the Seven did.

Which was why the chief of police enjoyed telling them. Parris watched seven pale faces blanch chalky white, arteries thumpity-thumping on seven flabby necks. When he'd had his say, the Dwarves got down to some serious business. There were concerned murmurings, hoarse whisperings, exchanges of knowing nods.

Bottom line?

A solemn promise was made that sometimes-deputy Moon would be paid in full. (The county's top cop asked when.) Not to worry. The check would be cut right away. (Parris demanded specificity.) Sometime today. Tomorrow at the latest.

"Tomorrow is not an option," he roared—and stormed out of the room.

As he hit the street, the chief of police realized that this was probably the latest in a long line of broken vows. *But if they don't keep their word this time around, I'll get even with every one of those miserable egg-sucking sons of bitches!*

An overdose of anger tends to distract a man from what's going on around him, and the furious chief of police took no notice of those citizens he met on the sidewalk. Including the soft-spoken pastor of the Wesleyan Methodist Church, who said, "Good morning." Also Ms. Janey Bultmann (owner of Bultmann Employment Services), who was already lighting her twenty-fourth cigarette of the day.

Scott Parris was also unaware of the dapper middle-aged man in the three-piece suit. The one with the thin mustache who carried an ivory-knobbed cane. Like the kindly cleric and the chain-smoking businesswoman, Samuel Reed could not help but notice the big, buffalo-shouldered cop with blood in both eyes and murderous mayhem brewing in his heart. *My—the brutish fellow looks like he's anxious to strangle someone with his bare hands.* It occurred to him that if push came to shove, a man would want Scott Parris on his team—which idle thought planted the germ of a notion in Professor Reed's fertile mind. Within a few minutes it would produce a tender green sprout that would leaf out and bloom. Though pleasing to Samuel Reed's biased eye, the blossom would not be especially fragrant.

CHAPTER FIVE

WHERE SAM REED MAKES HIS MILLIONS

The third floor of the Cattleman's Bank building consists entirely of offices leased to local businesses. The current occupants include two insurance representatives, three realtors, a thriving partnership of dental surgeons that specializes in endodontics (a euphemism for root canals), a dispensing optician (her logo is a yard-wide pair of spectacles suspended over the door), a defunct crisis-intervention center whose automated telephone message advises anxious inquirers to "call back during our regular business hours." A short hallway on the northern side terminates in a solid oak doorway which has neither printed sign nor mail slot. Most who notice the unmarked entrance assume that it conceals the janitor's storage room, an electrical closet, or the like.

Behind the door is an L-shaped inner sanctum that comprised three rooms and a full bath. One of the smaller rooms serves as Samuel Reed's kitchen, the other as his occasional bedroom. The kitchen and bedroom are satellites to a strikingly spartan corner office. The hardwood floor is uncarpeted; the room's sole furnishings are a knotty-pine desk, a comfortable armchair, a maple floor lamp with a green velvet shade, and a wicker waste basket.

When the office is unoccupied, the desktop is bare. On those occasions when serious business is conducted, a laptop computer is placed on the oiled surface.

A pair of large plate-glass windows face north; their

twins look to the west. These are the views that the lessee prefers, and Professor Samuel Reed never settles for second best. The desk is positioned so that the man seated behind it can enjoy a panoramic view of blue-gray granite mountains snugly capped with last winter's snow.

This space is occupied by a venture incorporated under the name Do-Wah-Diddy Investments, Ltd. The corporation's semilyrical moniker was selected because the owner-manager of the firm sometimes muses about retiring to that mythical southern community that is neither town nor city, and also because he likes Phil Harris's lively song.

The enterprise has no clients, but not to worry. D-W-D-I, Ltd.'s net income exceeds that of any ten businesses in the county, and by a comfortable margin. Aside from a few tight-lipped employees of the Internal Revenue Service, the sole owner of the "small business," and Reed's Denver accounting firm, no one knows that Do-Wah-Diddy's scrupulously accurate federal returns document the fact that his annual tax payments are *never* less than seven figures.

The entrepreneur also turns a nice profit by placing bets on sporting events, and this aspect of Sam Reed's business has its own peculiar hazards. More about that in due time.

The burning question of the moment is: how does he do it?

To those country-club cronies who dare ask him outright, Reed merely smiles and taps a finger against his temple. This gesture is generally interpreted as "I'm smarter than you are" or "I know more than you do." How smart the entrepreneur is remains to be seen, but the latter is certainly true. Reed does know more. Not a few of his envious peers are convinced that D-W-D has access to insider information. Perhaps. But is it the usual kind? Those SEC investigators who have tried to untangle some clue from Reed's activities have noted something odd. For longish periods of time, Do-Wah-Diddy is virtually inactive. For more than a month of Mondays, only a few thousand dollars' worth of stocks and bonds are bought or sold. Perhaps a dozen bets are placed. During the hiatus, D-W-D may make a modest profit, or dip into the red. Then, for no apparent reason, Samuel Reed will suddenly begin working like a demented beaver, which is when he sleeps over in his in-town office bedroom and prepares all his meals in the well-stocked kitchen. Just as suddenly, the feverish activity will cease. The office will remain quiet until the next frenzied session begins. During these lengthy downtimes, Sam Reed will catch up on *Physics Today,* read fabulous tales about lusty mountain men and crafty Indians, sing frequently and loudly with the local barbershop quartet, and polish his impressive mandolin skills.

On this morning, Sam Reed is gearing up for the first day of an extended buying-selling, bet-placing session. If he appears not to be enjoying his work with the usual gusto of a man who believes that life is The Game and the player's bank balance is his score, it is understandable. The entrepreneur is somewhat distracted from the pleasure of his sport by the knowledge that Death is waiting.

THE COUNTDOWN

The digital clock that Samuel Reed had programmed on his laptop was refreshed every ten seconds on the upper-left-hand corner of the screen:

> 31 Days, 14 hours, 21 minutes, 50 seconds
> 31 Days, 14 hours, 21 minutes, 40 seconds

And so on.

After signing off from the Las Vegas Online connection, Reed blinked at the readout, which was ticking his life away.

> 31 Days, 14 hours, 20 minutes, 10 seconds

Suppressing a cold shudder, he pushed himself up from the cushioned chair and approached the north window. The fact that he had made a profit in the pleasant neighborhood of thirty-six thousand dollars in less than thirty minutes did little to cheer the investor. He could have made three times as much, but Sam Reed was one smart cookie and he knew that if a man in his line of work was *too* successful, the Securities and Exchange Commission might take an intense interest in his activities. Not to mention those hard-eyed, coldhearted characters who ran the casinos. Unlike the SEC attorneys, the gaming kingpins who had mob connections neither launched formal investigations nor sought indictments. Mess with those bad boys and they dispatched Guido the Knuckle Dragger to stop your clock permanently. Which was why—to balance his sure-thing wins—Reed always placed a bet or two that would lose. Likewise, in hope of keeping the SEC off guard, he would buy a couple of stocks that would take a dive tomorrow.

Sam Reed watched a chill breeze whip the budding trees. With the comfy satisfaction of one who is snug inside, he enjoyed the out-of-doors entertainment. Pedestrians holding on to skirts and hats. Vehicular traffic buzzing along this way and that.

A raven settled expertly on a nearby maple branch and cocked her head. The rakish creature looked Reed straight in the eye and made a rude *gaaawwwking* croak. As if to say, "Your number's about up, bub."

Samuel Reed smiled at his morbid feathered friend. "Perhaps." While he had been buying, selling, and placing wagers, Reed's subconscious had been hard at work on the urgent issue of how to keep body and soul together. This subliminal effort had not been wasted. The owner of Do-Wah-Diddy Investments, Ltd., was a man with a plan.

He addressed the wind-ruffled raven thusly: "I shall approach the authorities and request their assistance in protecting my life."

The blue-black bird cracked her horny beak and made a series of cackling sounds. The imaginative entrepreneur interpreted this response as a chuckle. A *derisive* chuckle.

If the raven was suggesting that Reed's plan was a rather mundane result for an investment of considerable subconscious cerebration, her conclusion would have been understandable. After all, asking the cops for help is a remedy that even the meanest intellect is capable of. A person who believes every word they hear on "talk radio" knows enough to call 911 when a three-hundred-pound maniac with a bloody machete is hacking his way into her (or his) flimsy dwelling.

But do not underestimate that most remarkable thinking machine on the planet. When a keen human intelligence is pitted against a mere bird-brain, the wingless biped will come out on top. Well . . . more often than not.

Say seven times out of ten.

CHAPTER SIX

A WELCOME WINDFALL

Columbine Ranch and personal business took Charlie Moon to town two or three times a week, and after the rancher had paid calls on Jeppson's ABC Hardware, Pine Mountain Lumber & Building Materials, and Fast Eddie's Barbershop, he dropped by the GCPD station to visit his best friend on the surface of this rocky planet. After saluting dispatcher Clara Tavishuts, who was taking a call about the latest big brouhaha over at the Mountain Man Café (where a two-hundred-pound waitress who called herself Momma Sha-Na-Na was beating up a couple of long-haul truck drivers), the long-legged Ute ascended the stairway to the second floor, opened the door to Scott Parris's corner office and poked his head in. "Please tell me I'm disturbing some serious police business so I'll know I didn't come all the way over here for no good reason."

The chief of police allowed as how it was *fortuitous* that his Indian friend had dropped by. Scott Parris's girlfriend had given him a list of one hundred respectable expressions. She had urged him to pick a word that he liked, use it till he owned it, and then proceed to a new challenge. "I just called the Columbine to let you know I had something you'd be happy to see."

Happy wasn't halfway there; when the town cop pushed a rectangle of blue-green paper across the top of his desk, the Indian caught his breath.

"There it is, Deputy Moon." Parris glowed like a 120-volt bulb plugged into a 240-volt socket and about to pop. "You're paid in full."

A long moment passed before the hard-up rancher got the words past the lump in his throat. "Thank you."

"You're welcome as spring rain." The beefy cop snorted. "You earned every dime and then some."

Moon stared at the numbers on the check. "How'd you manage it?"

"I was hoping you'd ask." Parris's toothy grin split his big face. "I hinted to the mayor that if the county didn't pay up, my buddy Charlie was going to sic his junkyard-dog lawyer onto them." The way Parris saw it, this had been one of those occasions when a plausible falsehood was preferable to the truth.

Charlie Moon laughed at the thought of turning Walter Price loose on the mayor and his town-council cronies. "Nothing like a terrorist threat to galvanize the local government into action."

"Damn right." The overweight public servant enjoyed a belly-shaking chuckle. "Most fun I've had since my eighth birthday, back in Indiana."

"If I recollect correctly, that's when your daddy gave you a Red Ryder BB gun."

"Yes it was. Also when Mom made me a three-layer chocolate cake with pink candles, and Granddaddy took me fishing on the banks of the wide O-Hi-O and I landed me a five-pound carp."

Moon had heard the story a half-dozen times. "What'd you use for bait?"

"Granddaddy's secret-recipe bacon-grease doughballs on treble hooks. That was the worst-tasting fish I ever put in my mouth." Almost overcome by nostalgia, Parris enjoyed a wistful sigh. "But Miz Carp was a beauty and the biggest fish I'd ever caught."

"I appreciate the back pay, pardner." Charlie Moon folded the check and slipped it into his shirt pocket. It wasn't a fortune, but the years-overdue payment would be enough to take care of the Columbine's electric and telephone bills and about six months of back taxes. Nothing to sneeze at.

A MAN OF ACTION

Feeling about as tip-top as a man looking Mr. Death in the empty eyeball sockets can, Samuel Reed kicked off phase one of his daring plan by barging through the GCPD headquarter's front door. The sprightly fellow sprinted up the stairs two at a time. Like Moon, who had preceded him, Reed's destination was Scott Parris's office, where the grumpy boss-cop could generally be found during the midmorning hours.

Approaching the closed door marked CHIEF OF POLICE, Reed raised his ivory-knobbed cane to rap—and paused. He heard voices behind the door. The loudest words boomed from Scott Parris's lungs, but who was the other fellow, who spoke so softly? *That sounds like the Indian cattle rancher.* It was common knowledge that Charlie Moon and Scott Parris were close friends, and that from time to time the tribal investigator dabbled in matters of serious crime. Samuel Reed, who had intended to speak privately to Parris, paused to consider the pluses and minuses of the situation. Though loath to delay his dramatic entry into the lawman's office, he realized that the town cop and his Ute friend might well be discussing some highly confidential matter. *It would be rude to break in on a meeting in progress.* A gentleman had no choice. *I must wait until an opportune time to knock.* Fortune tends to favor the courteous soul, and Reed's impeccable good manners would provide a fine opportunity to eavesdrop on the cops.

Quiet as a church mouse wearing tiny sheepskin house slippers, he moved closer to the door. And listened.

As it happened, Samuel Reed would hear no succulent secrets, merely run-of-the-mill conversation. But for an inquisitive fellow such as himself, no tidbit of information was deemed entirely worthless. As he often reminded his lovely wife, the mark of a successful investor was the ability to recognize value in the seemingly commonplace—and to spend that coin to his advantage. The extraordinarily successful entrepreneur enjoyed another advantage. One that he did not share with his spouse.

Charlie Moon leaned back in his chair and crossed one long leg over the other. "So what's going on in the local law-enforcement business?"

"Nothing that'd interest you." Parris turned in his chair to gaze at a live motion picture of downtown Granite Creek that was neatly framed in this office window. "Some halfwit is roaming around town at night, prying people's back doors open." He shot a sideways glance at the Southern Ute tribal investigator. "But I suppose you've heard all about that."

The busy stockman shook his head. "I've haven't been paying much attention to the local news."

"You're better off." Parris watched a scruffy-looking raven settle on a sycamore limb. (Yes. The very same uncouth bird who had carried on a conversation with Samuel Reed. Such coincidences are not so remarkable in a small town.) "Local rag's calling the perp 'the Crowbar Burglar.' He doesn't steal all that much, but once he gets inside, the rascal vandalizes the house."

"Anyone hurt so far?"

Parris shook his head. "But it's only a matter of time." *With a little luck, somebody'll shoot the bastard stone cold dead.*

Moon read the hopeful thought on his friend's face.

A worry frown furrowed the white cop's sunburned brow. "Last night, Mr. Crowbar broke into a residence that was occupied by an eighty-year-old widow. Scared the poor old soul half to death, but she got out the front door with her walker and hobbled over to a house next door. The neighbor called the cops, but by the time we got officers on the scene, the bad guy was long gone."

Charlie Moon realized that his friend had not heard the footsteps coming up the stairway. The tribal investigator would have given a shiny 1959 silver dime to know who was loitering outside the office door. "The elderly lady get a look at the burglar?"

"Yeah, but all she remembers is the crowbar." Scott Parris grunted. "She describes the suspect as about average height, neither short nor tall, and she wouldn't classify him as either fat or thin. Age? Oh, somewhere between thirty and sixty." He was tiring of this dismal subject. "How're things out yonder on the range, where the buffalo roam and the antelope canter about?"

Moon shrugged. "Tolerable."

"From what I hear, half a dozen ranchers in the county have been forced to sell off their herds at rock-bottom prices." This remark provoking no response from the Ute stockman, he added, "There's talk that the Columbine's about to dump a few hundred purebred Herefords."

"Bad news sure travels fast."

"That's a fact." Parris scratched at his itchy left ear. *Momma always said that meant somebody was about to knock on the door.* "I guess times is tough all over."

"That's what they tell me."

Scott Parris noticed that the raven was no longer in the sycamore. The feathered creature had taken up a precarious perch on the cop's windowsill. Cocking her head this way and that, the bird was apparently taking in every word.

The men jawboned about one thing and another until their conversation was interrupted by something that might have gone unheard.

A gentle rapping.

A mere *tappity-tapping.*

Parris arched a bushy eyebrow. *Must be the plumbing acting up.*

Moon grinned. *I guess our spy has heard enough.*

A portentous silence, then—

A tentative rapping.

Rappity-rap-rap.

The Ute pictured a tiny peckerwood pecking on the office door.

Scott Parris was not amused. "What'n hell's that?"

A voice in the hallway responded crisply, "The properly framed question, is—'*who* in Hades is that?'" The knob turned and the door opened just enough for a well-peeled eyeball to peek inside. "The longed-for answer is, 'It is my own jovial self, come to pay a courtesy call on the finest chief of police in Granite Creek.'"

The object of this dubious flattery rolled his eyes. "Sam Reed."

"Indeed." The scientist-entrepreneur entered the office with a flourish of his ebony walking stick. He tipped his gray homburg to salute the Ute. "Greetings and salutations, my good man—and if I may paraphrase Leigh Hunt's "Abou Ben Adhem," 'May your tribe increase and prosper.'"

The Indian nodded a hello at the jolly fellow.

"You working-class stiffs are no doubt wondering, 'Why are we blessed with a visit from such a distinguished and beloved citizen as Professor Samuel Reed?'" He tapped his cane on the hardwood floor. "I will not keep you in undue suspense. It's like this: from time to time I respond to an overwhelming urge to apply my considerable talent to some admirable civic service. Last week, I helped an elderly nun jaywalk across our fair city's busiest thoroughfare. Never mind that the old darling did not hanker to get to the other side; that is an immaterial detail. The point is that I was motivated to do good unto one of my fellow human beings. And today"—he aimed the cane at Parris—"you will be pleased to know that I have come to do my favorite constable an enormous favor."

"*Pleased* don't even come close, Sam." Parris drilled his visitor with the gimlet eye. "I am thrilled plumb to death."

"As you should be! And do not assume that I am here on some such pedestrian objective as to assist you in the capture of the notorious Crowbar Burglar. Perish the petty thought. On the contrary, I intend to add some essential spice to the insipid broth of your dreary life." Sensing some slight doubt, Reed proceeded to flesh out his intentions. "What a jaded fellow like yourself needs now and then is a fresh challenge. A blinding flash of cerebral stimulation, a heady rush of adrenaline. Given your chosen vocation, the specific remedy for your doldrums is as obvious as the bulbous nose on your face." He fixed Parris with a benevolent gaze. "What you need is an interesting crime to solve."

The lawmen exchanged glances. And thoughts.

PARRIS: *The guy's a nutcase.*

MOON: *Maybe. Maybe not.*

PARRIS: *No maybe about it. I'm going to kick him outta the door and down the stairs.*

MOON: *Don't go making a boot print on his butt before he's had his say.*

PARRIS: *Okay. But you'll be sorry.*

Having a facility for reading expressions, Reed nodded his thanks to the Ute. Straightening his red bow tie, he said, "I do not think a warehouse arson would be quite right for what ails you. On the other hand, a brazen, broad-daylight bank robbery by a carload of brutish thugs would surely do the trick. Or the kidnapping of a rhinestone-studded rock star whose gaudy tour bus just happened to be passing through Granite Creek. But, sad to say, arranging such events would press even my considerable resourcefulness to the uttermost limits. So what *can* I do to help you?" Reed tapped his cane against the toe of his immaculate shoe. "Oh, here's a nifty idea." He smirked. "How about I deliver up a cleverly planned homicide?"

The Ute slipped on his high-stakes-poker face and reached for the peanut jar on Parris's desk.

GCPD's top cop got up from his chair and glared at the impertinent man through slitted eyes. "Read my lips, Reed. In this neck of the woods, we don't make jokes about any kind of crime. Armed robberies get our dander up. Kidnappers get strung up on the nearest cottonwood. And there ain't *nothing* funny about murder."

"I quite agree, Chief Parris." Samuel Reed nodded with vigor. "And if you do not wish to accept my assistance in preventing a homicide, that is certainly your prerogative. I will detain you no longer from your urgent official duties, not the least of which is chasing after some slope-browed misfit who is bent on vandalizing local real estate with a crowbar."

Reed was putting the handsome hat on his head when the bulldog cop bristled and barked, "Siddown!"

Standing ramrod straight, the professor of physics assumed the role of grade-school teacher addressing a slow-witted seven-year-old. "Let us be clear about something, Mr. Parris. You do not intimidate me. Not in the least. One more snappish order to sit and you will see the back of me!"

Oh boy, this'll be good. Moon helped himself to another handful of peanuts. Munch-munch.

Sam Reed and Scott Parris stood eyeball-to-eyeball.

The dapper dandy stroked his neatly clipped mustache.

The brawny ex-Chicago cop glowered. Ground his bicuspids.

The clock on the wall ticked.

Something had to give.

The wall clock tocked.

Charlie Moon was enjoying the face-off. *My money's on Mr. Fancy Pants.*

Parris blinked. "Now what's all this bull-hockey about a homicide?"

Raising his nose in the air, the visitor twirled the fancy walking stick. "If you wish to question me in a civilized manner, I am prepared to cooperate. Otherwise, I advise you not to waste your onion-scented breath—or my precious time."

Parris directed his why-me-lord expression at the ceiling fan.

From somewhere up there . . . *Why not?*

"Well?" Reed rapped his stick on Parris's desk.

"I apologize for *snapping* at you." The defeated chief of police collapsed into his chair. "And I'm sorry as all get-out that I'm not civilized enough to suit the likes of you." He glanced at his wristwatch. "In about an hour, I'll have my second meeting today with the town council, where a half-dozen halfwits elected by a collection of village idiots is gonna tell me I've got to figure out a way to run my department with a thirty percent budget cut." He shot a bitter look at the annoying visitor. "But excuse me for bothering you with my piddlin' little problems. Please feel free to sit down—or stand on your head if it'd make you more comfortable—and tell me anything that happens to pop into your so-called mind about a potential homicide."

"Thank you. Though somewhat lacking in sincerity, your apology is accepted." Sam Reed cleared his throat. "And please accept my sincerest regrets for referring to your fetid breath." The entrepreneur seated himself. "Now that we have cleared the air, I trust that there will be no further unpleasantness."

"My sentiments exactly." The chief of police managed a toothy smile that suggested a bad-tempered alligator about to pounce on an unwary mallard. "I promise to put you on my Christmas-card list, and I hope . . . I mean to say I'd consider it *fortuitous* if you'd drop by my place some evening for crumpets and tea."

"Ah!" Reed clapped his gloved hands. "You have more wit than I gave you credit for." *But not much more.* He assumed a painfully sober expression. "Modesty compels me to confess that one of my few failings is this—I have a regrettable tendency to underestimate my inferiors."

Parris's face reddened like an overripe tomato.

Moon choked on a peanut.

Seemingly oblivious to these impacts of his confession, the modest man addressed the affronted chief of police. "Are you prepared to accept a challenge which will radically alter the course of our tightly intertwined destinies?"

The disgruntled lawman had no ready reply.

Samuel Reed was smugness personified. "Ah, I see by your semiconscious expression that you fairly salivate at the thought of a stimulating adventure."

Scott Parris cocked his head as if to say, *I'm listening.*

Charlie Moon was too.

Also the raven on the windowsill.

CHAPTER SEVEN

"He had wasted and pined 'til o'er his brow
Death's shades were slowly gathering now
He thought of home and loved ones nigh,
As the cowboys gathered to see him die."

PROFESSOR REED'S PECULIAR PROPOSITION

Samuel Reed removed his calfskin gloves with exaggerated care, aligned them palm-to-palm (suggesting disembodied hands in prayer), and placed them on the lawman's desk. "Chief Parris, I propose a wager."

The magic word? You bet.

Scott Parris's pulse rate picked up.

Charlie Moon's ears pricked up

"Make that a *once-in-a-lifetime* wager." Reed's eyes sparkled at Parris. "Here's the deal. I will provide you with pertinent information about a homicide which certain unsavory 'person or persons unknown' will attempt within your jurisdiction. Now for the *good* part—" He paused and cupped a hand to his ear. "What was that—did you fellows hear something?"

Parris shook his head.

Charlie Moon smiled.

"Egad—there it goes again." Reed put his hand in his

jacket pocket. "Well bless my soul, boys, it's true—money does talk! At this very moment, my chatty little bankroll—an intimate friend whom I refer to as Miss Lucre—is attempting to make herself heard." He removed a banded cylinder of banknotes and addressed the currency thusly: "You have rudely interrupted my conversation with the chief constable, Miss L. Please have your say and be done with it." He placed the currency close to his ear. "Ah, yes. Would you mind repeating that for Mr. Parris?" He extended the cash money over the lawman's desk, and with no discernible movement of Reed's lips, a shrill, little-girl voice said, " 'This hick copper could not prevent a jaywalking if he was informed about it a month in advance.' "

"How dare you insult our honorable chief of police!" Reed glared at the discourteous bankroll. "Now apologize this very instant."

"I will not!" Miss Lucre squeaked. "That doughnut muncher could not find a felon if the malefactor was delivered to him in a laundry bag."

"That does it." Reed shook his head. "You shall be punished for your insolence—and most severely. But do not think that I shall invest you in dodgy municipal bonds or deposit you in a Nigerian National Bank savings account at ten-thousand-percent interest. No such lenient chastisement awaits *you,* Miss Lucre. I shall dispose of you in an utterly absurd wager which I have no chance whatever of winning."

The greenbacks shrieked, "Oh, the *horror*! Please—anything but *that*!"

Moon laughed out loud.

Despite a lingering sting of chagrin, Parris could not suppress a grin.

Gratified by this response, Reed proceeded with his performance by addressing Scott Parris: "Am I talking even money? Check the blank by 'NOT A CHANCE.' I am an obscenely wealthy man and a bodacious high roller. Why, if I smoked Havana cigars, I would light those stogies with hundred-dollar bills."

Parris eyed the annoying citizen.

"Don't think you can fool me with that blank expression. You're just *dying* to know the odds."

The chief of police did not deny this assertion.

"Would I propose a mere two to one that you cannot prevent the homicide I have in mind? Hah! Such a mediocre proposition would be unworthy of a man of my caliber." Samuel Reed beamed upon the butt of Miss Lucre's insults. "I propose *ten* to one!"

Scoot Parris blinked.

Charlie Moon too.

"Yes, Chief Constable Parris—you heard me correctly. You slap down a hundred dollars on the barrelhead, I will see you with a thousand happy clams. You hock your creaky boots, tattered hat, and scuffed saddle down at Pinky Dan's Pawn Shop and come up with a thousand bucks, I will see you with ten thousand of the same." The fastidious fellow paused to brush a minuscule smidgen of lint from his cuff. "That is my self-imposed limit, however. I am a modest man, and anything over ten grand would be unseemly and ostentatious. And I daresay, a thousand would be more than you could afford to lose." Reed retrieved his gloves and pulled them on until the fingers were comfortably snug. "Fascinated, aren't you. And I still have not gotten to the *really* good part."

Parris was eager to go there with him.

As was Charlie Moon.

"You will not believe this." (They wouldn't.) "But it is my most fervent hope that you will win the wager. And I promise—on my word of honor as a remarkably successful investor, a member of the American Physical Society, and a gentleman of the first order—that I will provide you with every assistance toward that happy end." Reed eyed the chief of police. "I believe that this is a propitious time for you to ask the critical question."

Parris stared dumbly at the eccentric citizen.

"Ah, this is too difficult for you." The uninvited guest assumed a pitying expression. "Never mind, I shall help you along. The question is—'Who is the intended victim, Dr. Reed?' "

"Okay." Parris mimicked the meticulous man's crisply enunciated speech: "Who is the intended victim, Dr. Reed?"

The one addressed tapped his walking stick against his vested chest. "Myself."

The chief of police brightened at this good news. "Yourself, huh?"

"None other. So you understand why it is in my interest that you succeed in preventing the homicide, thereby winning the wager."

This guy's a loopy goofball. But the cautious lobe of Parris's brain whispered this warning: *Be careful. If it turns out that Sam Reed is on the level, you're gonna look like a big dope.* "So where are you gonna get knocked off, and when?"

"Ah, now you are beginning to make noises very much like a competent policeman. As to the where, I cannot specify the precise location of the homicide. The unseemly event might occur anywhere between Copper Street and my residence. I sometimes stop at the Conoco station to top off my tank, or at Sunburst Pizza to pick up a late-evening take-home snack. As to when, the attempt will be made on the first Friday of June, which is a month away. I will be working late at my office on the third floor of Cattleman's Bank building, and my death will not occur before ten thirty P.M."

Whether triggered by the mention of pizza or the suspicion that Samuel Reed was deadly serious, Parris experienced a searing surge of what medical professionals refer to as acid reflux. After the pain subsided, he asked, "So how d'you know it'll happen on the evening of June fourth?"

"Ah, that would be giving entirely too much away— and what good is a heinous crime without some element of mystery?"

"Look, Reed, if you don't intend to level with me—"

"Oh, very well. Just for the sake of advancing superstition, let us assume that my mother was a full-blooded Armenian Gypsy queen and that I am her seventh son—in which case I can foresee the future with crystal clarity."

Parris's expression suggested that he was the only son of cynical Hoosiers who knew when a seventh son of a Gypsy was blowing smoke in his eyes.

Undeterred by the cop's glare, Reed placed a pair of gloved fingers lightly on his left temple and closed his eyes. "Ah, the veil between Now and Then is being lifted—and there I am, enjoying a late-evening stroll down Copper Street, which is my common practice after a long day's work. Look, I am opening the door and entering the candy store where I invariably treat myself to an invigorating dose of caffeine." A puckish smile. "Here comes the good part: whilst sipping my coffee, my exquisitely sensitive nostrils detect the delicious scent of dark chocolate—which reminds me of a husbandly obligation. I summon the clerk and purchase a box of handmade truffles for my sweet wife."

Parris remembered that holiday that he always forgot. "Valentine's Day?"

Reed cracked one eye long enough for it to twinkle at the chief of police. "I am reliably informed that the lovers' holiday invariably occurs on the fourteenth day of February."

"Oh, right." *I ought to write that down someplace.*

"Please excuse me while I continue to foresee my future on the evening of my demise." Reed reclosed the eye. "My, how time does fly—I have hardly finished my double espresso and tucked the red-ribboned candy box under my arm, when the manager—no doubt eager to go home herself—commences to lock the front door."

Scott Parris could practically smell the chocolate and coffee. "The Copper Street Candy Shop shuts down at ten thirty P.M. every night of the week."

Samuel Reed nodded. "On the proverbial *dot*."

"And you get popped sometime later?"

"Indeed." Reed had opened both eyes. "And if you ask me nicely, I might tell you precisely when the calamity will occur."

This guy is giving me big-time heartburn. "How'll you know that—will you check your wristwatch?"

"An excellent notion, but the opportunity will not present

itself. Nevertheless, immediately prior to the violent event, I will hear the bell toll."

"Bell?"

"Certainly. The bell tolleth not only for me, but also to summon the faithful members of St. James Episcopal Church to eleven P.M. Compline for a half hour of soul-stirring plain-song."

"Sounds to me like you're a goner," the cop growled. Parris's hand found half a roll of Tums in his shirt pocket.

"It would seem so." The energetic man sprang up from his chair. "But I am no fatalist. Let those Gloomy Guses among us believe that their future is chiseled in marble, but not me, sir! I say the die is not yet cast on my fate, nor the bullet molded which cannot be avoided. With the expert assistance of you and your plucky chaps in blue"—Reed made a slight bow—"I intend to avoid that unhappy outcome. I simply refuse to become a crime statistic."

Parris popped a minty antacid in his mouth and crunched it like candy. "If any of this is on the level, you must've turned up some convincing evidence that somebody's gonna kill you." As the medication's soothing effect kicked in, his humor improved. "I won't even ask about motive. I can think of a half-dozen reasons why I'd be more'n glad to take on the job myself." The dyspeptic cop forced a grin that made the corners of his mouth ache. "But just so I'll know who I should send a thank-you card to, who's the dude who's gonna do the deed?"

"I do wish I could help you." The tip of Samuel Reed's gloved finger caressed his beloved mustache. "But that, my clever copper, is for you to find out. Despite my best efforts to treat all of my neighbors and business associates with utmost courtesy, a successful fellow like myself is bound to have his enemies—though I daresay very few would go so far as to make arrangements for my untimely demise. Even so, if any stray thought should occur to me which might aid you in identifying the potential assassin, you may rest assured that I shall inform you." The entrepreneur removed a wafer-thin gold pocket watch from his vest pocket. "I am due for a manicure in nine minutes." He flashed a foxy grin at the edgy lawman. "Do we have a bet?"

Six heartbeats thudded under Parris's ribs.

Reed gave his red bow tie a one-handed tweak. "Well—what say you to the proposed wager? Can you keep me alive and free of serious injury until the dawning of June fifth—is it yea or nay?"

The hard-up public servant pulled a slender wallet from his hip pocket and examined the contents. Sixty-four dollars.

Realizing that his friend needed encouragement, Charlie Moon dished out a helping: "Go for it, Scott."

Grateful for this neighborly support, Sam Reed nodded his thanks to the Indian.

Scott Parris wanted to go for it. But . . . *I'd be out of my mind to bet a dime if this slicker gave me a million to one that tomorrow would never come.* (Very sensible. Tomorrow is always a day away.) But when did Reason ever prevent a man from yielding to a practically irresistible temptation—especially with his best friend egging him on? Parris laid a precious twenty on his desktop. Then another.

Reed tapped his walking stick on the currency. "Good for *you,* sir!" He pulled the talkative bankroll from his jacket pocket, peeled off four hundred-dollar bills, and added them to the pot. "With your permission, Mr. Parris, I will ask the president of the Cattleman's Bank to hold the cash until June fifth, which is the day following my expected demise. If I am alive and healthy on that day, Fred Thompson will render the winnings unto our local chief of police. If I am either no longer among the living or grievously injured, the cash will be contributed to a charity of Fred's choice."

Widely regarded as a fair-minded man of utmost integrity, Fred Thompson—a fellow who made a wager himself now and again—often acted on behalf of gamblers by holding cash, bank drafts, real estate deeds, or other properties until the outcome of a wager was determined.

No objection being immediately forthcoming, the wealthy

man put the four hundred and forty dollars into his jacket pocket. The self-proclaimed high roller regarded Charlie Moon with an expression that suggested something approaching affection. "To show my appreciation for your encouraging words, I will pass on a tidbit of information that should prove useful to a person of your chosen vocation as a husbandman of malodorous bovine creatures."

"Go right ahead," the rancher said.

"I understand that you are under pressure to make a major sale of beeves. I advise against any precipitous action on your part." To emphasize this warning, Samuel Reed wagged a finger.

"I don't have much choice," Moon said. "Some major bills have to be paid." *And the check in my pocket won't cover half of what I owe.*

Reed shook his head and made a *tch-tch* sound.

Intrigued by the investor's self-assurance, the stockman put the query bluntly: "What do you know that I don't?"

Too good to pass up. "An astute question, and one which deserves a candid answer. But how to put it?" Reed stared at the ceiling as if lost in deep thought. "Compare the Library of Congress to a rickety bookmobile; or towering Mount Everest to a tiny anthill. Professor Einstein to—"

"Okay, you've had your say." Parris glowered at the smart aleck who was teasing his buddy. "If you've got some hot information about the beef market, spit it out!"

"There's no need to get miffed." Reed straightened his immaculate tie. "I was merely having a little innocent fun. I am certain that Mr. Moon was not in the least offended."

The Ute smiled to show that this was so.

Before *spitting it out,* Reed feigned a cough and cleared his throat. "It just so happens that within a few weeks, prices for American beef will take a steep rise." He read the *Why would that happen?* expression on Moon's face. "The reason for this turnaround will be a rumor—which will prove to be all too true—of the outbreak of a dreaded bovine malady. This misfortune will occur on a major cattle operation in

Argentina." Aware that gestures oftentimes speak louder than words, Reed touched the tip of his cane lightly on the toe of his polished shoe, the knobby end to his lower lip.

The gesture was entirely transparent to the Ute rancher: Reed was alluding to the worst horror of the cattle industry. *Hoof-and-mouth disease.*

Scott Parris also got the message.

Sam Reed was pleased to see the effect of his dreadful gesture. "You two gentlemen—I use the term loosely in one instance [he arched a brow at Parris] and without *reservation* in the other [he grinned at the Indian]—have truly made my day." With this, the happy man removed his homburg, bowed again, donned the spiffy hat, turned away with a twirling flourish of ivory-knobbed cane, and was gone.

The lawmen sat still as stones while the wall clock ticked and tocked, neither uttering a word.

As was customary in such circumstances, the white man broke the silence. "Charlie, what'n hell just happened here?"

The tribal investigator unfolded his lean frame from the chair. "I'm not sure, pardner." Moon strode to the window and took a long look at the raven, who gawked back at the man on the inside of the pane.

"From what I hear, Sam Reed's got enough hard cash to buy up the whole county." Parris fixed a perplexed frown on his friend's back. "How d'you figure that sneaky little slicker has built up such a fortune?"

Moon smiled at his reflection in the glass. "Forty dollars at a time."

"I expect you're right." Parris shook his head and grinned. "But I feel a helluva lot better than I did before that fast-talking rascal showed up."

"So do I." *Which is a likely sign we've been flimmed and flammed by a first-class flimflam man.* Charlie Moon winked at the raven. *And I don't have the least notion of what Reed's up to.* But ten-to-one odds was enough to tempt an ordinary man, and the Ute would bet on anything you might happen to mention, and that at the drop of a hat. The compulsive gambler straightened his black Stetson. "I've got a thing or two I need to attend to, so I guess I'd best be getting on down the road."

"See you later, Charlie." After his best buddy's departure, Parris suffered a sudden attack of inexplicable loneliness. His insides felt as hollowly empty as his office, where the only sounds were the rusty-raspy creak-creak of the ceiling fan and the gasping-gurgling of the plumbing that sounded like a drowning man. It was enough to make a fellow start up a conversation with any dull-witted creature who happened by, so the tough cop turned his sunburned face to the window and cracked a grin at his feathered friend. *What do you say to a crow?* "I ain't got any bird food to pass out, ol' Double-Ugly, so you might as well hit the road."

Scott Parris heard the raven's throaty chuckle before that irascible descendant of dinosaurs launched herself from the second-story windowsill. The dark lady winged her way gaily through the bright sunshine and circled the Methodist Church's soaring white steeple twice before disappearing into the soft, cool shade of U.S. Grant Park.

CHAPTER EIGHT

CONDUCTING SOME FUNNY BUSINESS

As he emerged from the GCPD building, Samuel Reed paused on the concrete steps to reflect on what had transpired upstairs. *That business with Scott Parris and his Indian friend went pretty well.* The thoughtful man reviewed his performance. *Did I forget anything of consequence?* Thinking not, he stepped onto the sidewalk. *I may have overplayed my hand a bit, tipping Mr. Moon about the pending surge in beef prices.* He immediately dismissed the self-criticism; in a singular situation such as this there were more important matters to concern himself with. Right at the top of the list: *I must pay a call on Lily.*

In the mood for a brisk walk, Reed left his flat-black Hummer parked on Copper Street in front of the police station and strode purposefully along Granite Creek's main drag for six blocks. As he was approaching the Sugar Bowl Restaurant, Reed felt the skin prickle on the back of his neck. *Someone is staring at me.* The edgy pedestrian paused, made a pretense of reading a menu posted on the window, and glanced in the direction whence he had come. He saw nothing remarkable. Merely the usual midmorning shoppers. Vehicular traffic zipping along this way and that. *Nothing's amiss; I'm imagining danger where there is none.* Smiling ruefully at the thought of this epitaph sandblasted into his tombstone, the man who was living on borrowed time resumed his vigorous walk.

After turning the corner off Copper onto a shady side street aptly designated Spruce Lane, Sam Reed slowed his pace to enjoy on the tranquility of a neighborhood comprised of brick apartment buildings and a scattering of small businesses. Ignoring signs that attempted to attract passerbys' attention to shops providing Expert Spinal Manipulations, Handmade Toys for Men and Boys, and Quality Pre-Owned Apparel, the determined pedestrian approached his destination in a single-minded fashion. His business was of a highly personal nature—and with a citizen of dubious reputation. The moderately prosperous lady conducted her trade in a small ground-floor apartment at 21B Spruce Lane. The sign over the door proclaimed the nature of her public business.

LEADVILLE LILY'S TATTOO PARLOR
Body Art Applied by Hygienic Electrical Applicator
Or upon Special Request by
Japanese, Samoan or Thai Technique

Samuel Reed knew that the name on the proprietor's driver's license was not Lily. He was also aware of the fact that she'd never spent a minute in Leadville, but this small deceit served only to enhance her mystique as a somewhat shifty character. Whatever Lily was up to "on the side," she was a capable craftsman in her stated vocation. If someone was in the market for for a first-class piece of skin artistry, the so-called Lily was the person to see. Not that there was much call hereabouts for epidermal ornamentation. The bulk of Lily's trade was with out-of-towners, though not those tourists one typically encounters in gift shops crammed with Chinese-made souvenirs of Colorado landmarks, Old West museums that provide gunfights thrice daily during the season, and noisy restaurants that cater to the average American family, which is comprised of a pair of harried adults and 2.6 pint-size terrorists. The dispenser of tattoos depended primarily upon shifty-eyed passersby. Also furtive passers-through. And, on occasion, a local citizen who had a hankering for one of her services, advertised or otherwise.

Samuel Reed had already forgotten about the skin-prickling premonition that someone on Copper Street was displaying an inordinate interest in him. If he'd had the least inkling that he had been stalked all the way from his parked Hummer by a sinister-looking character, the cautious entre-preneur would have walked past the tattoo parlor without so much as giving it a glance. Regardless of the hoary old prov-erb, what a man doesn't know certainly *can* hurt him, and in this instance Reed's ignorance would come back to bite him.

After trying the knob and finding Lily's door securely latched, the man of business tapped his ivory-headed cane lightly on the thin glass pane. He waited expectantly for her appearance, expecting that this transaction would be much like all the times before.

Sure enough, the tattoo artist pulled a dusty lace curtain aside and scowled at him with a wrinkled face. Her throaty voice was barely audible, but her lips said, "Whatta you want?"

As he had expected . . . *The poor old soul doesn't recog-nize me.* Reed tipped his homburg at the frosty countenance. "Open up, madam—you have a customer who is eager to part with some hard cash."

The magic words.

There was a click of the latch, a quick twist of the knob. The proprietor's leathery face regarded the self-assured man with a half measure of suspicion. *I guess he's okay.* She stepped aside to admit the potential client. "Okay, big spender. C'mon in."

Samuel Reed stepped inside, watched the lady lock the door, then followed her to the back room. Which was where all of Lily's serious business was conducted.

Neither the no-nonsense businesswoman nor her eager client noticed the shadowy presence that momentarily blocked the soft glow of filtered sunlight from her glassed front entrance, then vaporized like a puff of fairy dust—as if it had never been there.

CHAPTER NINE

THE SHADOW

His important business at Lily's Tattoo Parlor successfully completed, Samuel Reed was both relieved and gratified. Twirling his cane and whistling the lively tune to "Goodbye, My Coney Island Baby," the happy man retraced his steps along Spruce Lane to Copper Street, which thoroughfare he followed back to the GCPD building, where he had left his Hummer parked at the curb.

Reed's shadow?

The hombre who had killed more men than he cared to remember lurked nearby. (Though highly adaptable and able to improvise on the spot, he reputedly leaned toward head shots.)

As Reed slipped inside his gas hog, he experienced that eerie, tingling sensation again. The one where hairs stand up on the back of a paranoiac's neck to confirm his deep suspicions that . . . *Someone is stalking me.* He looked this way and that at dozens of locals who were busy with their various errands. None of them was taking the least notice of the rich man in the flat-black SUV. It occurred to Samuel Reed that his murderer might have hatched a new plan. *I could be shot down like a dog in broad daylight.* The potential victim squinted at the murky entrance to Burro Alley. *Perhaps from a littered alleyway.* The well-bred man curled his lips at the distasteful notion. *That would be extremely vulgar.* A professional assassin with any sophistication would conceal himself behind barely parted curtains in a third-story window and watch his victim through a telescopic sight. The jumpy fellow in the presumed crosshairs imagined a silenced, 8-mm Czech BRNO Vz24 Mauser rifle, a steady finger already taut on the trigger. Reed's wide eyes scanned dozens of windows above Copper Street. Any one of them might be concealing a cold-hearted (but tasteful) killer. The potential victim attempted to convince himself that his fears were groundless: *This is merely a leftover emotion from last evening's unsettling experience.* But from deep down in that part of his brain that simply *knows,* Sam Reed was getting the message that something extremely unnerving was about to occur and there was not a thing he could do to prevent it. Which, in light of his current location, was extremely vexing. *Here I am, parked right in front of the police station.* But where was a cop when you needed one? *A hired killer with a pistol could simply walk up to my automobile and shoot me through the—*

Bang-bang! (Within six inches of his left temple.)

"Yiiieee!" (Reed's shriek.)

"Hey!" (Charlie Moon, who had rapped his knuckles on the driver's-side window.)

Samuel Reed lowered the Hummer window and glared at the Ute. "What?"

"Just wanted to ask you a question." Moon eyed the nervous man. "That bet you made with Scott at ten-to-one odds—I wondered whether I could have a piece of the action."

"Well . . ." Reed's angry glare faded to a sheepish stare. "I don't see why not. How much action can you stand?"

The destitute rancher flipped a folded piece of paper into Reed's lap. "That's my back wages for serving as Scott's part-time deputy. It's made out to Fred Thompson at the Cattleman's Bank."

Reed blinked at the paycheck. "This amounts to quite a substantial wager, Mr. Moon." His mouth made a wan smile under the meticulously trimmed mustache. "Are you sure you can afford to lose this much?"

"I can't afford to and I don't plan to." The man who

couldn't pass by a bet without saying "howdy" reflected the smile back at Reed. "One way or another, I figure Scott'll keep you alive through the fourth of June—and I'll end up in the chips."

Reed nodded slowly. *And with that happy prospect in mind, you will be bound to provide your friend with every assistance on my behalf.* "Consider yourself a partner in the wager."

"You can take it to Fred with the rest of the pot." Moon squinted in the bright sunlight. *If I take that check to the bank, all the way there it'll be whining: "You're a fool, Charlie—you should've used me to pay the back taxes and electric bill."*

"Very well." Reed started the Hummer engine. "I shall see to it forthwith."

As he watched the wealthy investor pull away from the curb, make an illegal U-turn, and head straightaway for the Cattleman's Bank, the destitute rancher took a deep breath. *That may be the dumbest bet I ever made, but the thing's done so I might as well stop thinking about it.*

But he didn't.

As Samuel Reed eased his heavy vehicle slowly along Copper Street, he was startled to feel the warning sensation. His skin began to prickle again. He was absolutely certain that someone was still back there somewhere. Watching.

Someone was. That same man who had followed him to Leadville Lily's Tattoo Parlor.

Imagining a spinning 8-mm Czech bullet shattering the safety glass and his skull, the man marked for death swallowed hard. *I'll never make it to the bank.*

But he did.

CHAPTER TEN

A JOB OF WORK

After going over the Columbine books in his upstairs office, Charlie Moon returned to the parlor, feeling lower than a snake's belly button. But don't start feeling sorry for him; your sure-enough cowboy is not about to sit around the house and mope.

First, he defines the problem: *Until I win the bet with Sam Reed, what I need is some extra cash money.*

Okay, a no-brainer. But essential to the process.

Now the cowboy figures out how to deal with his problem and jumps right on it. *I'll pick up the telephone and call my cattle broker and tell him to make the best deal he can and*— The stockman grimaced at a sharp pain under his belt buckle. The very *thought* of selling off prime beeves at rock-bottom prices had knotted Moon's guts. Especially in light of Reed's tip that beef prices would soar in a few weeks.

But what else could he do? The hardworking brain under the black John B. Stetson hat came up with another notion: *I'll find a way to earn some extra money on the side.*

Doing what? (He is about to tell us.)

I could sign on as a guard at the tribe's casino. Pay would be minimum wage. *But a few bucks an hour beats no income at all.* But not if it all got spent on gasoline for driving back and forth between the ranch and Ignacio.

Here comes notion number three.

I still have my Southern Ute investigator's shield, so I'll

*call up Oscar Sweetwater and see if there's some police work
I could do for the tribe.* Before he could think of a reason not
to, Moon got up from his favorite rocking chair, snatched up
the parlor telephone, and dialed a number he knew by heart.
After the fourth ring, he heard the tribal chairman's gruff
"Hello." For an instant, Moon hesitated. Asking for work
wasn't going to be easy. "Hello yourself, Oscar."

"Well, it's Charlie Moon." Oscar Sweetwater seemed
pleased to hear the part-time tribal investigator's voice.
"Funny you should call this very minute. I was just about to
pick up the phone and ring your number."

Charlie Moon felt a surge of hope. Sweetwater never
called to see how he was doing or talk about the weather or
how the two of them ought to get together for lunch at Angel's Café next time the busy rancher was in Ignacio. The
chairman was a strictly business sort of fellow, who rarely
contacted Moon unless he had an assignment in mind.
"What'd you want to talk about, Oscar?"

"Oh, it's nothing much. A little job of work." Sweetwater
sounded sly as a fox trying to talk his way into the hen-
house. "We can talk about that when I get up to see you,
maybe in a day or two. What'd you call me about?"

"It'll keep till you show up at the Columbine." Charlie
Moon said goodbye and hung up. *Well that turned out pretty
good. With what I make off Oscar's "little job of work,"
maybe I can keep my nose above water for another couple
of weeks.*

CHAPTER ELEVEN

ONE CRAFTY OLD INDIAN

It doesn't take a lot to disturb Daisy Perika's sleep. The night wind whistling thorough the eaves will do it, the plaintive yip-yip of a lonely coyote, or simply thinking about what she intends to do tomorrow. Which, in this instance, was to visit her home on the Southern Ute reservation. Not that there was really that much to think about. Sarah Frank would load her red F-150 pickup and drive the tribal elder to her snug house at the yawning mouth of *Cañón del Espíritu*. But Daisy had a talent for finding things to worry about. Such as: *Did I get everything packed in my suitcase or did I forget to remember something important?* Also: *Maybe we should just make it a day trip and come back tomorrow evening and have supper with Charlie.* And then . . . *Maybe it would be best to stay overnight so I could enjoy sleeping in my own bed again.* A worried squint at the beamed ceiling. *I wonder if Sarah will miss any classes over at the university.* And worse still: *What'll we do if Sarah's pickup breaks down and her cell phone don't work?* A moaning groan. *I won't get a wink of sleep.*

After tossing and turning in her Columbine headquarters bedroom for much of the night, just short of daylight Daisy Perika was finally drifting off into a deep, peaceful sleep—when she was jarred awake by a raucous squawking. The horrid, grating sound salted her already-raw nerves. (Imagine the Wicked Witch of the West dragging sharp, dry fingernails along a dusty chalkboard, and cackling evil laughter all the while.)

The Ute elder got out of bed, mumbled a guttural expletive in her native tongue, jerked the window curtain aside, and glared at the ruffled raven who had so rudely disturbed her sweet slumbers. "Hit the road, you half-wit loudmouth, before I borrow Charlie's twelve-gauge shotgun and blow you to a bunch of flindered feathers and stinking bird guts!"

The raven cocked her head, and this is (more or less) what she said: "Awrrk—haawrrk—whaawrk!"

Any bespectacled professor of Advanced Communication Theory that you happen to meet on the street will tell you that very little information can be contained in a statement that consists of a mere three "bits." How much? About three bits' worth.

Any practitioner of Daisy Perika's arcane trade could (if she would) tell you that there are barely perceptible undertones, subtle intonations, and understated accents that accentuate the Western American Raven vocabulary. The combination of these components, particularly when used by a skillful conversationalist, tends to enrich the seemingly sparse statement with considerable content. In this specific instance, enough to cause the elder to suspect that this particular member of the crow family was someone she knew. Her glare faded to a hopeful stare. "Are you who I think you are?"

A rather open-ended query, but it did not ruffle the visitor's feathers. She nodded as ravens do, with an affirmative croak and several rapid jerks of her head. To prove the truth of what she had said, the talkative creature languidly stretched one black wing, then the other—which meaningful gestures removed any doubt about the matter. Daisy Perika concluded that this was definitely Delilah Darkwing, who dwelled within a half mile of the tribal elder's reservation home. Delighted to be visited by her neighbor from *Cañon del Espíritu,* the shaman apologized for her earlier curt remarks and asked what was on Delilah's acorn-size mind. Had her old friend brought urgent news from the Canyon of the Spirits?

"Awrrk—awrrk—haaarwrk!" Obviously excited, the presumed Miss Darkwing shifted her slight weight from one spindly leg to the other. Then back again. "Awrrk—waawrrk—sqwaawrk!"

As she listened intently to these remarks, Daisy learned that the answer to her question was No. And Yes. The subject of the compulsive gossip's report had nothing to do with *Cañón del Espíritu* or that motley horde of ghosts who were fated to haunt the ancient canyon until the voice of the final trumpet awakened all the dead. But urgent news it was, and of no mean import.

After the raven had had her say, she took to wing and flew away without waiting to hear the bemused "thank you" mumbled by the elderly Ute. Daisy Perika returned to the bed, laid her head back on the pillow, sighed, and closed her eyes. *Well. That does give a person a lot to think about. When I get home, I'll check things out.*

This peculiar episode naturally raises a trio of pressing questions.

First, was Daisy's early-morning visitor really her old friend Delilah Darkwing from the shadowy canyon between Three Sisters and Dogleg mesas?

Perhaps. One hesitates to speculate.

Second, was this the selfsame raven who had spied on Samuel Reed and perched on Scott Parris's office window-sill?

Hard to say. (Ravens look and talk much alike.)

Third, how did a scruffy-looking creature come to have such a remarkable name? It is gratifying to have a question that one can answer. Daisy had given the name to her. For reasons that the shaman has never confided to her closest friend or next of kin, she is firmly convinced that the feathered creature is *possessed*. Yes. And by no less than the spirit of a young Ute woman who died a few years back. The deceased person's first name was Delilah—but her surname was nothing nearly so impressive as *Darkwing*. That embellishment was Daisy Perika's invention.

CHAPTER TWELVE

TWO MORE CRAFTY OLD INDIANS—ON A MISSION

The shiny new Dodge pickup transporting the pair of elderly Native Americans had just passed through the Columbine Ranch front gate and was bumping along the miles-long graveled road toward the headquarters where, only a couple of hours ago, Charlie Moon's aunt had carried on an intense conversation with a raven.

The driver glanced at the sullen Chickasaw, who was hunched forward in the passenger seat. *Lyle looks like he's asleep.* From Oscar Sweetwater's perspective, it was hard to tell. Lyle Thoms's left eye tended to droop. Moreover, the Chickasaw elder had said precisely nine words since they left Ignacio more than an hour ago. The words (repeated three times) were: "We there yet?" The passenger startled the Ute by suddenly jerking his head erect and peering through the windshield at the Misery Range peaks, which were wreathed in swirling gray clouds.

"Look's like it's snowing up there," Sweetwater said. "Honest-to-goodness spring comes late in this high country and lasts maybe a month. After that, there's about two weeks of real summertime."

The Chickasaw glanced at the Southern Ute tribal chairman. "We there yet?"

"We're on Columbine property, but it's a few more miles to Charlie Moon's big log house."

Thoms leaned back and closed his eyes. "This Moon fella—he half as good as they say?"

"He's *twice* as good and then some." The Southern Ute chairman raised his chin in a stern gesture of tribal pride. "Charlie Moon *always* gets the job done."

The passenger grunted.

Gripping the steering wheel with both hands, Sweetwater scowled at the winding road ahead. *If Charlie don't get this Chickasaw's business taken care of right away, there'll be sure-enough hell to pay.* He swallowed a sigh. *And I can't even afford the interest.*

Some twenty minutes later, the Dodge pickup rolled past the foreman's residence, then immediately crossed the Too Late Creek bridge. As the Columbine Ranch headquarters loomed into view, Lyle Thoms craned his neck to get a look at the two-story log structure.

Oscar Sweetwater parked the dusty truck under a budding cottonwood. "Wait here a few minutes, Lyle." He set the hand brake. "I'll go find out if Charlie's in the house."

The Indian from Oklahoma responded with a shrug.

MR. TWICE AS GOOD IS SOFTENED UP

Charlie Moon had heard the pickup rattle across the bridge. He was waiting on the headquarters west porch when the tribal chairman braked the vehicle to a stop under the cottonwood. In the cool shadows, and unnoticed by his visitors, he watched Oscar Sweetwater say something to a passenger whose face was unfamiliar. The tribal investigator was mildly surprised when the man who signed his occasional vouchers for services rendered got out of the truck and left the other man inside.

When the elected leader of Moon's tribe discerned the slender form in the shade of the porch roof, he raised his right hand. "Hey, Charlie."

"Good morning, Oscar." It would have been impolite to

inquire about the old man in the truck. If and when he was of a mind to, the chairman would identify his passenger. Moon invited the shrewd politician inside and asked whether he would like a cup of hot coffee.

"That'd be nice," Sweetwater said. "And maybe something to chew on while I drink." He looked hopefully toward the kitchen. "Has Daisy made any of them fried fruit pies that I like so much?"

Moon shook his head. "She's busy packing her suitcase." *For maybe the third time this morning.*

"Where's that fussy old woman going?" *Someplace a long ways off, I hope.*

"Daisy and Sarah leave for the res later today. Every week or two, my aunt visits her home to make sure everything's shipshape."

Sweetwater snorted. "If I know Daisy—and I do—she'll be wandering around in Spirit Canyon, talking to animals and ghosts and . . . whatnot."

Moon understood that "whatnot" was Sweetwater's code word for the *pitukupf*. Withholding comment on that sensitive subject, he opened the porch door for his guest.

A minute later, Sweetwater was seated at the kitchen table. "I brought an old friend with me." He gestured with a jerk of his head. "He's out in the pickup."

Moon turned up the flame under the percolator. "Maybe he'd like some coffee and a bite to eat."

"That can wait. First, I want to tell you something about him."

Their conversation was interrupted by Sarah Frank's hurried entry into the kitchen. She exchanged a quick greeting with the tribal chairman, but avoided eye contact with Charlie Moon, who watched in bemused silence as the young woman snatched a matched pair of mugs from a cupboard and a brown paper sack of stale pastries from the breadbox.

After tending to their distinguished guest, Sarah poured the apple of her eye a cup of black coffee. She also stirred in a tablespoon of Tule Creek Honey, and then—without a word—she rushed away.

Oscar Sweetwater glared at the empty space the girl left behind. "Does she ever stop to catch her breath?"

Moon smiled at his edgy guest. "Young folks are generally brimming over with energy they need to burn up."

"Well I wish she'd burn it up somewhere else; it tires me just to see her buzzing around like a ninety-pound mosquito." The grumpy old man frowned at the glazed doughnut in his hand. "What was we talking about?"

Moon took a sip of the sweetened brew. "You were going to tell me about the gentleman who's waiting in your pickup."

"Oh, right—his name is Lyle Thoms. First thing you need to know is that he's one of them hard-nosed Chickasaws from Oklahoma." He shot Moon a look that said, *And you know what they're like.* "Long time ago, Lyle did me a favor." Significant pause. "A really big favor." He waited for the tribal investigator to ask what.

Moon took another, longer drink of coffee.

The old man made a gnarly fist with his right hand and stared at it. "Did you know I had a sister?"

"No." The chairman could still surprise him.

"Well, ain't you gonna ask what her name was and what happened to her?"

"What was your sister's name, Oscar—and what happened to her?"

Sweetwater opened his mouth, shut it when he heard the peg-peg of Daisy Perika's walking stick.

Charlie Moon's aunt ambled in and took a look at the tribe's ablest politician. "What're you doing here, you old renegade—stirring up trouble for us good Indians?"

The chairman raised his chin. "With you on the job, there's no need for that."

After an appreciative chuckle, Daisy addressed her nephew: "I can't find my blue shawl."

Moon pointed with his coffee cup. "It's on the hat rack in the hall."

"Oh." The old woman with the oak staff turned and peg-pegged away.

Sweetwater watched her go. "What was we talking about when she butted in?"

Moon smiled at his guest. "Your sister."

"Oh, that's right. Her name was Sophie." Like a little boy about to swallow a dose of castor oil, Sweetwater hesitated and made an ugly face. "What happened to Sophie was . . ." He blinked away a pair of tears. "It's been over sixty years, but I can remember it better than what I had for breakfast this morning."

Moon put his cup on the table.

The old man raised his chin again. "One night, while my folks was away in town and me and Sophie was playin' out in the front yard, this fella pulled up in a big, shiny black car and started asking questions like 'How far is it to Durango?' and 'Can I talk to your daddy?' and 'Are you two kids home alone?' "

Seeing what was coming, the tribal cop closed his eyes to the dark vision the old man was summoning up.

"I can't hardly talk about it, even after all these years." Sweetwater coughed. "Let's just say that I got beat almost to death—and I was the *lucky* one." The silence ticked away a dozen old-man heartbeats. "The bastard took Sophie with him. Every able-bodied man in the tribe and about two hundred *matukach* searched for my little sister. They found her body over by Flint Hill."

A full minute of silence followed.

A soft breeze sighed under the eaves.

Finally, Sweetwater was able to speak again. "Based on what I told the cops about the man and his motorcar, the state police was able to find him. The arrested the devil up over by Las Animas; he was headed toward Kansas. I don't want to go over the whole nasty business, Charlie—but he was indicted by a grand jury, and tried. I was the only witness that could identify him, but when I got on the stand, I was so scared I couldn't hardly say a word. And the defense attorney—some slicker from Denver—made me out to be a fool kid who couldn't tell one *matukach* from another." Silence. "The jury found him not guilty."

Moon shook his head. "I bet I can guess the rest of the story."

"I imagine you can."

"Your father put the word out about the killer, who probably ended up in Oklahoma." Moon gestured with his chin. "And that old Chickasaw hard case who's biding his time in your pickup—he saw to it that justice was done."

"I'm not saying he did." For the first time that day, Sweetwater came very near smiling. "And I'm not saying he didn't." There was a hard look in the chairman's eyes. "But that bad man ended up dead, and he didn't die easy." He glared at the Southern Ute warrior. "Lyle Thoms did me and my family a special favor." Sweetwater sucked in an oversized helping of high-country air. "And now he's asking me for one."

"I'm guessing this isn't official tribal business."

"You guess right, Charlie. This is personal—and a favor to Lyle is a favor to me." The chairman took a sip of his now-tepid coffee. "But don't worry about working for nothing. Lyle's got deep pockets. He'll pay you."

"Pay me for doing what?"

Oscar Sweetwater pushed himself up from the straight-back chair. "I'll let my friend tell you that."

Charlie Moon listened to the old man's boots clomp away down the hallway.

The Southern Ute tribal chairman sent the Chickasaw elder into the Columbine headquarters but decided to remain outside.

"To enjoy the fresh air," Oscar Sweetwater told Lyle Thoms.

Also to distance himself from any legal entanglement in the Chickasaw's grim business. Charlie Moon was a man you could depend on to get the job done. But there was always a chance that something would go wrong.

CHAPTER THIRTEEN

THE CHICKASAW'S PROPOSAL

Charlie Moon ushered his guest to the place where important business on the Columbine was generally conducted. Lyle Thoms seated himself at the tribal investigator's kitchen table, in a chair that was still warm from Sweetwater's recent presence.

Figuring he knew more or less what was coming, Moon waited. *Best thing is to let the old man have his say, then figure out how to handle things.*

Lyle Thoms got right to the point. "I want a man killed."

Moon didn't blink. "That's all?"

"No." Not given to subtleties, Thoms was immune to sarcasm. "I'll need proof that he's dead. You can scalp him or cut off his private parts—whatever suits you. Just send me something so I'll know you got the job done." To facilitate the mailing, Thoms recited his four-digit post office box number in Tishomingo, Oklahoma, which—and this was one of those peculiar coincidences that is bound to occur from time to time—also specified the day and month of Daisy Perika's birthday.

Which naturally intensified the old woman's interest.

Yes, Charlie Moon's inquisitive auntie was enjoying her favorite pastime.

DAISY GETS AN EARFUL

From the Ute elder's self-centered point of view, her practice of eavesdropping on other folks' private conversations did not represent a character flaw. She was merely pursuing an interesting and enlightening hobby. And it was great fun to sneak around and find out things you were not supposed to know.

Which was why Daisy had slipped out of her slippers, left her walking stick in her bedroom, and managed to creep along the hallway without creaking a single board in the thick oak floor. *This time, that sharp-eared nephew of mine won't know I'm here.*

CHARLIE MOON PLAYS ALONG

"So who is this fellow that needs killing?"

"Posey Shorthorse." Lyle Thoms pulled a wallet from his hip pocket and removed something from behind a thick wad of greenbacks. He pushed it across the kitchen table to his host.

Moon picked up the snapshot of a muscular young man. *He looks mean as a stepped-on rattlesnake.*

"That's Shorthorse." Thoms's thin lips twisted into a distasteful grimace. "He's a Chickasaw—one of our bad ones." He pushed another item across the oilcloth.

Moon looked at the blank rectangle of paper. He turned it over to discover a stylistic representation of a lizard. *That looks like something you might find painted in the bottom of a Mimbres pot.* The reptile's tail was curled around its body three times.

"That's my business card," Thoms said. "This year, I'm head man of the Blue Lizard Clan." He looked searchingly at the Ute. "Shorthorse got my fourteen-year-old granddaughter pregnant, then beat her up so bad she lost the baby. After that, he went off and left her alone." He exhaled a deep sigh. "Poor little girl went stone crazy. Soon as she was able to walk, she went down to the creek and drowned herself." Thoms thumped his knuckles on the table. "I want Shorthorse killed." He thumped it twice. "The clan wants him killed." A triple thump. "And we'll get it done one way or another." A thoughtful pause. "Problem is, Shorthorse knows we're after him." He raised his knuckles again, paused. "Late last year, we got word that he was bumming around out in Los Angeles, living off women. We sent a Chickasaw warrior out there. Our young man never came home." Thoms took a sip of strong black coffee and made a face as he swallowed. "We figure Shorthorse must've killed him and then left L.A. I figured the bastard was gone for good, but just last week I got word that he'd been seen in Granite Creek."

From long experience, the tribal cop realized that chances were no better than one in ten that the man who'd been spotted was the Chickasaw that Lyle Thoms wanted killed. *And even if it was Posey Shorthorse, he was probably just passing through.* But Oscar Sweetwater's old friend had to be treated with faultless respect. "Do you have any other information that might help me find him?"

Lyle Thoms stared at the Ute. "Would it help if I gave you his address?"

"Well . . . that might come in handy."

"If I knew where Shorthorse hung his hat, I'd have already shot him dead." The Chickasaw's face was like stone.

The Ute could not suppress a grin.

"You'll take care of him, then?" There was a steely glint in Thoms's eye.

"I'll look into it." *First chance I get.* A bad apple like this was probably wanted for several felonies. *If I find out the fellow's in town, I'll turn Scott Parris loose on him.*

"Good." Thoms helped himself to a deep breath. "That's settled, then."

THE SPY BARELY AVERTS DISCOVERY

She did it with two fingers. It happened like this: Daisy
Perika felt a sneeze coming on. A great big one. The kind
that can blow the ham and eggs right off your plate.

Did she panic? Not a chance.

The tough old lady pinched her nostrils shut and held her
breath until she thought her head was going to swell up like
a balloon and explode all over the place.

But it didn't.

And the "ah-choo!" gave up before Daisy did.

MOON IS SNOOKERED

The head man of the Chickasaw Blue Lizard Clan drummed
his fingers on the kitchen table's red-and-white-checkered oilcloth for a moment, then paused. "Let's talk about your fee."

The needy rancher waited in respectful silence.

"I've thought about it." The Chickasaw studied the Ute's
best poker face. "If I was to pay you for swatting a fly buzzing around my head, that'd be worth maybe fifty cents. If I
needed you to kill a rabid dog on my front porch, I'd pay . . .
say, fifty dollars. Then, if I wanted you to get rid of a man,
that'd be worth more."

Moon's poker face slipped a half smidgen. *How much
more?*

A fair hand at seven-card stud, Lyle Thoms read Moon's
expression and answered the question. "Let's say . . . twenty
thousand dollars cash money."

The tribal investigator blinked. "That's a fair price."

"Yes it is, for a killing a *man*." Thoms leaned toward
Moon and spat the words across the table at the Ute. "But
Posey Shorthorse ain't no man. He ain't even a green snake
or a dung beetle."

Charlie Moon wondered where this was going.

Lyle Thoms told him. "For ridding the world of a *nothing* like that, I'll pay you twenty-five cents."

The supposed assassin cocked his head. *Did he really say—*

"I know you'd be glad to do it for free—but it's an insult, see?" Realizing from Moon's bemused expression that he wasn't quite getting through, the Chickasaw elder put it this way: "Before you execute Shorthorse, make sure that low-down bastard knows you're doing the job for *two bits*."

After barely suppressing a disastrous sneeze, Daisy Perika came very near giving herself away by laughing out loud. Deciding on a tactical retreat, the tribal elder withdrew to her bedroom, where she let the chuckle out—and then busied herself with packing for the drive south in Sarah Frank's pickup.

CHAPTER FOURTEEN

THERE IS ABSOLUTELY NO PLACE

Like home, of course.

When Sarah Frank and Daisy Perika arrived at the tribal elder's remote dwelling for an overnight stay, tears formed in the old woman's eyes. There could be no doubt about it, everything was better here than on the Columbine—including the sky, which was of a deeper hue of blue. And those half-hearted birdsongs on Charlie's ranch couldn't hold a candle to the crooning of robins and bluebirds in *Cañón del Espíritu* and . . . *The air here makes me feel twenty years younger!* Before going inside, Daisy took time to inhale a dose of that vaporous elixir. After shivering in those chill winds that whistled on her nephew's ranch, the warmth of this sweet afternoon breeze felt ever so welcoming. Indeed, the moist breath exhaled from the mouth of Spirit Canyon carried delectable hints of an early summer, and familiar scents of savory herbs and enticing spices that Daisy gathered to concoct everything from arcane medications to tasty soups and salads.

Fine as they were, the sky, birdsongs, air, and flora were just for openers.

At the instant she stepped over her threshold, the homesick woman was almost overwhelmed by the inexpressible joy of . . . *being back where I belong again!*

Daisy's creaky rocker by the parlor hearth was miles more comfortable than any chair in Charlie Moon's log house, and the tired old soul knew that tonight she would sleep like the blessed dead . . . *and in my very own bed*!

But what is home without a neighbor? Daisy will say, "Just the way I like it!"

But even for this cantankerous old lady, it depends upon the personality of the nearby resident, and after Mrs. Perika has been abroad for a while her standards tend to become relaxed. So much so that even a formerly detestable face can be a welcome sight.

Which explains why Daisy was eager to pay a call on the only more or less mortal soul within an hour's walk. Even though the Ute shaman was not particularly fond of the dwarf, the *pitukupf* was a singular resident in a community populated primarily by such run-of-the-mill society as wild animals and spirits of dead people. The eccentric citizen whom she aimed to visit was a remarkable little man who had spent the better part of his thousand or so years within the shadowy sanctum of *Cañón del Espíritu*—most recently, as the sole occupant of an abandoned badger hole.

There were two reasons for Daisy's desire to see the wily *pitukupf*.

The first was friendship. Though their relationship had been checkered by the occasional misunderstanding, the little man was (excepting the raven) Daisy's only friend in the vicinity. But that term of endearment can be misleading. They were friends only *after a fashion*—in the sense that aged warriors David and Goliath (had the oversized Philistine not perished during their initial encounter) might have become jolly comrades after the wars who would (whilst tipping pewter mugs of mulled ale) debate the relative merits of shepherd's slings and gigantic spears. The relationship between Daisy and the dwarf was, to put it simply—complex. Not so very long ago, the annoying little trickster had vexed the volatile old woman to the point that she had very nearly *beaten her tiny neighbor to death*.

Please don't ask. It was an embarrassing incident, best forgotten.

Daisy's second reason for desiring an audience with the

dwarf had to do with the recent visit to the Columbine Ranch by one Delilah Darkwing, who had urged the tribal elder to arrange a meeting with the *pitukupf.* Needless to say, urgings by ravens are ignored at one's peril. Minutes earlier, when Sarah pulled her red pickup into Daisy's front yard, that feathered personage had been perched expectantly on the topmost branch of a juniper. In the Ute-Papago girl's presence, the shaman and the raven had limited their exchange to meaningful glances.

Daisy deposited her suitcase in the bedroom and advised Sarah that she was going to "take a little walk."

Stiff from the long drive and brimming over with pent-up energy, the eighteen-year-old was ready for a hike. "Where to?"

"Oh, I don't know." The elder avoided the youth's hopeful gaze. "I just want to go have a look at things."

"What things?"

Daisy bristled at this cross-examination. "Rocks. Trees. Skunks. Centipedes. Whatever I happen to come across!" The edgy old woman leaned against her stout oak staff, took a deep breath—and explained so that even a teenager could understand: "I want to be *by myself* for a while and enjoy some peace and quiet." She jutted her chin in a defiant gesture. "While I'm gone, you can fix us some supper."

Sarah arched a doubtful brow. "Well . . . okay." *I guess.* "What do you want to eat?"

"I'm not picky." Charlie Moon's aunt shrugged. "Anything that don't smell bad or try to bite me back."

DAISY'S TIME ALONE

That was her intention, but she was never entirely without company.

Miss Darkwing was never far from Daisy Perika's side; the gossipy raven flew from huckleberry bush to aspen sapling to mossy boulder to aged ponderosa—all the while updating the tribal elder on recent events such as births, deaths, feuds, mysterious disappearances, and newcomers in the canyon. Not to mention dreadful omens, thunderous rumblings from Cloud Woman, fiery night-sky portents, and the like.

As Daisy trod her breathless way into Spirit Canyon along the slightly upgrade deer path, she also encountered a lonely disembodied soul who was determined to bend her ear, a cheeky chipmunk who demanded a handout *or else,* and a cheeky little rattlesnake who coiled under a winterkilled Apache plume—all of whom she pointedly ignored. In addition to these residents, not a few pairs of unseen eyes watched the aged woman's progress with considerable interest—and not all of them belonged to such common residents as mule deer, squirrels, cottontails, badgers, and ghosts.

With much huffing, puffing, grunting, and groaning, Daisy finally arrived at her destination. She was in for a disappointment. After tapping her walking stick on the ground by the badger hole and calling out several times, she was forced to conclude that the dwarf was not at home. *It's just like the ugly little wart not to be here when I want to talk to him.* The disgruntled visitor kicked a stone into the entrance of the *pitukupf*'s underground dwelling, but this did not satisfy. Charlie Moon's annoyed aunt looked around for someone to complain to, but the raven—who presumably had some pressing business to attend to—was nowhere to be seen.

Daisy's feet ached liked she'd walked ninety miles. *Before I head back to my house, I'll sit down and rest for a while.*

The familiar ponderosa log was within a few yards of the badger hole, where it had fallen years ago. She seated herself on the rotting trunk, gazed at the twilighting sky, and commenced to wonder where on earth the *pitukupf* might have gone. But not for long.

"Yikes!"

Someone or some*thing* had tapped a finger on Daisy's shoulder.

A smallish finger.

The startled woman turned to see the little man, who was standing on the log beside her. The *pitukupf*'s wicked grin enraged the shaman, and she was about to brain the impudent rascal with her oak staff when she remembered the reason she'd come to visit her after-a-fashion friend. Knocking the dwarf's head *clean off* (in B'rer Bear fashion) would not materially enhance her chances of finding out why the dwarf had dispatched Delilah Darkwing to summon Daisy Perika to an urgent meeting.

CHAPTER FIFTEEN

"O bury me not on the lone prairie
Where coyotes howl and the wind blows free
In a narrow grave just six by three—
O bury me not on the lone prairie."

DAISY'S SELF-APPOINTED GUARDIAN

Daisy Perika was not half as surprised by the dwarf's appearance as was Sarah Frank, who had followed the shaman into *Cañón del Espíritu*.

Sarah had not visualized the entirety of the *pitukupf,* but she had seen the lower portion of his anatomy with crystal clarity, and the sight of a pair of spindly little legs standing on the log beside Aunt Daisy was enough to send chills rippling along the Ute-Papago orphan's spine, constrict her throat so that speech was impossible, make the delicate hairs on the back of her neck stand up like porcupine quills, plus other physiological responses too numerous to enumerate. Staring fixedly at the disembodied limbs, she opted for denial. *That can't be real.* That being the case, she was obliged to provide a satisfactory explanation for the apparition. *I haven't had anything to eat since breakfast and my blood sugar's low so I'm having a hallucination.* Sarah closed her eyes and prayed for the vision to go away. She cracked her left lid. The horrid little legs were still there and Aunt Daisy was talking to the empty space above them! The girl reclosed the eye, clasped her cold hands, and prayed *very hard*. When she opened both eyes, Daisy was talking to completely empty space. Greatly relieved, Sarah thanked God and her guardian angel. To restore her dwindling supply of glucose, the girl unwrapped what she thought was a candy she'd found in her pocket—and popped a mentholated cough drop into her mouth. Sarah made a face and a promise to herself: *As soon as I get back to Daisy's house I'll eat some chocolate-chip cookies and strawberry ice cream.*

But something else was about to happen that would make the girl feel distinctly uneasy. Something that all the sugar in Colorado wouldn't help.

Here it comes.

Watch the coal-black raven flutter down from *somewhere up there* and settle lightly on Daisy's left shoulder. This sudden appearance was enough to spook the eighteen-year-old, but in addition to the dramatic entrance—the bird put her beak very close to the old woman's ear and began to gabble.

Sarah Frank was goggle-eyed with astonishment. *Oh, my—that crow looks like it's* talking *to Aunt Daisy!*

Indeed it did. But what made the effect *perfectly eerie* was that the Ute elder was obviously listening to every word, even nodding now and again.

The girl began to harbor the hopeful suspicion that . . . *I'm not really here and this isn't actually happening.* Then what was going on? *It's a bad dream and I'll wake up in my bed at the Columbine and laugh about it. Ha-ha.* But she knew better.

After Delilah D. had had her say, she unfolded her dark wings and flap-flapped away.

As if nothing out of the ordinary were transpiring, Daisy Perika resumed her conversation with the dwarf, which (according to the little man's custom) was conducted in an archaic version of the Ute dialect.

What did they talk about? The usual. How the weather wasn't like it used to be years ago. Olden times when everything was better. Long-gone friends and enemies who had passed on. And, in closing, the critical subject.

Without saying why, the dwarf sternly advised his aged Ute neighbor to *steer clear of Chickasaws*.

Daisy Perika realized that the *pitukupf* must be referring to Lyle Thoms, the crotchety Chickasaw elder who had offered Charlie Moon twenty-five cents to kill a man by the name of Posey Shorthorse. She waited to hear the rest.

There wasn't any more. That was it.

Well. Talk about your anticlimax.

Daisy was furlongs and miles beyond disappointed. *I can't believe I went to all this trouble to hear that.* But touched to realize that the little man was concerned about her welfare, the tribal elder did not complain. Not explicitly. Daisy merely assured her diminutive companion that while she appreciated his good intentions, she was in no need of such advice. As the Ute elder saw it, Chickasaws, Choctaws, Navajos, and Apaches were pretty much birds of a feather, and each in kind was to be avoided. "The next time you want to tell me something I already know, send me a penny postcard."

The *pitukupf,* who was a sensitive soul, got her drift. And he was more than a little miffed.

She turned her gaze to the darkening sky. "I shouldn't have set here so long—I'm stiffer than this pine log." Pushing herself erect with the sturdy oak staff, the creaky-jointed old woman brushed bits of rotten ponderosa bark off her cotton skirt, bade the sullen dwarf a polite goodbye, and began to retrace her trek along the deer trail.

As Daisy Perika slowly made her way to the mouth of Spirit Canyon—every step bringing her ever nearer to hearth and home—did she have the least notion that the Ute-Papago orphan had been spying on her?

Well of course she did.

How did Daisy know?

Miss Delilah Darkwing had told her so.

CHAPTER SIXTEEN

THE EMERGENCY

When Mrs. Irene Reed was picking up the parlor telephone to place an urgent call to the local constabulary, the lady was at home alone.

Which raises that ages-old question: where is a husband when a woman has need of the brute? The query is somewhat too general for a meaningful response, but in this particular instance Samuel Reed was miles away from both his home and his spouse. Moreover, the absent helpmate was enjoying himself immensely.

Do not judge the fellow too harshly. As wives gather with one another to chat about this and that, husbands must also occasionally have some time off for manly recreation and conversation, and Professor Reed was no exception. On the evening in question, he was in a private dining room at the Silver Mountain Hotel with three hairy-chested friends who shared his love of a cappella vocals that are characterized by consonant four-part chords (for every note, and in a predominantly homophonic texture). They call themselves the Velvet Frogs. No, not the chords, notes, or homophonics.

We refer to the happy male foursome.

Having tucked away succulent slabs of prime rib, buttered baked potatoes, melt-in-your-mouth apple pie, and splendid Bishop's Blend coffee, the barbershop quartet was tuning up its fourfold voice for a practice session. The program included such favorites as "Down by the Old Mill Stream," "Wait Till the Sun Shines, Nellie," "Goodbye, My Coney Island Baby," and "Sweet Georgia Brown." That wasn't all, and the V-Frogs always saved the best for last. Their big finish and surefire crowd pleaser was "Shine On Harvest Moon." It is difficult to imagine a more innocent, wholesome gathering of menfolk.

There is yet another reason to cut Sam Reed some slack. Even though his spouse is at home without her husband, and about to place a 911 call, Irene Reed is as calm as an alpine lake on one of those still days when there is no breeze to make the slightest ripple on its glassy surface.

And why shouldn't she be calm? The lady has nothing whatever to fear, save being charged with *making a false emergency call*.

THE COPS

It had been a busy evening for GCPD dispatcher Clara Tavishuts. In addition to the usual complaints about barking dogs, howling drunks, and a low-flying saucer-shaped UFO whose uncouth occupants had allegedly abducted an enraged senior citizen's favorite tomcat, three citizens—all nervous women at home alone—had called 911 to report suspicious activity. Each of them was convinced that the notorious Crowbar Burglar was prowling about her neighborhood, and one lady was certain that she had seen the malefactor skulking in her rose garden with evil intent. GCPD units were duly dispatched, but without turning up any sign of the fellow whose nighttime pastime was prying his way into residences and scaring the daylights out of those householders he encountered.

The first and third calls had been taken by Officers Eddie Knox and E. C. "Piggy" Slocum.

The former was in the passenger seat riding shotgun. Literally. Sawed-off Savage 20-gauge. Over-and-under double barrel. Loaded with buckshot. Officer Knox addressed the driver as follows: "Wanna know what I think, Pig?"

The plump cop with the swinish nickname grunted.

Being familiar with the tonal content of his partner's

abbreviated replies, Knox recognized this as an affirmative response. "I figure the odds against us taking this pry-bar guy alive to be about twenty to one."

Another grunt.

"Why? Well it's plain as the nose on your face—this Gomer's been lucky so far, but his pocketful of four-leaf clovers is just about used up. It's all a matter of statistics, Pig." Knox set his jaw in that manner which signaled that he was about to educate his partner. "Did you know that four out of every five homes in Colorado contains at least one loaded firearm?"

Recognizing a rhetorical question when he heard one, the driver did not waste a grunt.

"This night-crawler has already broke into six homes that was occupied. It's a wonder he ain't been shot already by some feisty old granny with a big horse pistol." Knox jutted his chin at Slocum. "You mark my words. Before the month is over, Mr. Crowbar will break into the wrong house and get his nasty self pumped full of Pb." *That'll rattle his cage.*

E. C. Slocum blinked at the windshield. "Pumped fulla *pub*?"

Eddie Knox spelled it out: "P-B." He grinned at his partner. "Which, as any ten-year-old with a big forehead knows, is lead—which is used for making sinkers, toy soldiers, and bullets."

Slocum coughed up a derisive grunt. "I never heard of any such a thing." *Eddie's making that up.*

"I don't mean to be overly critical, Pig—but when you're not busy turning the pages on Spiderman comic books or watching Donald Duck cartoons on TV, you might want to take a gander at the periodic table."

This reference suggested victuals to the perpetually hungry man. "Where's that at?"

THE FOURTH CALL

Officer Knox was about to tell him when the dispatcher's voice interrupted their conversation: "Unit 242—proceed to

1200 Shadowlane Avenue. Prowler report. See the lady. Mrs. Irene Reed reports that someone is in the process of breaking into the rear entrance of her residence."

Eddie Knox barked into the microphone, "We're on it, Clara." He grinned at his partner. "Step on it, Pig—maybe we can get there before the lady stops ol' Crowbar's clock!"

Slocum had already pressed the pedal to the metal.

"But no emergency lights or siren," Knox said. "I don't want to scare this varmint away. Let's go in dark and silent and nail his hide to the barn door."

"We can't do that." Slocum shook his head and quoted from The Book: " 'When a citizen is in imminent danger, standard procedure is to use emergency lights and siren in hopes of diverting a potential assailant from doing serious bodily harm.' "

"Dammit, Pig—we'll never catch this guy by goin' by the stupid rules!"

E. C. Slocum's grunt was an eloquent and final statement. The issue was closed. He turned on the flashing red-and-blue lights and flipped the siren switch.

All their noisy way to 1200 Shadowlane Avenue, Eddie Knox sulked.

Officer Slocum hit the Reeds' driveway in a sliding turn that kicked up buckets and bushels of white gravel. That, and the screaming siren and flashing emergency lights sent a lone coyote loping away like all the hounds of hell were nipping at his tail. The driver slowed enough for Knox to eject himself from their sleek black-and-white Chevrolet. Slocum sped around the circular drive and braked the GCPD unit to a lurching halt behind the Reeds' guest house.

After Eddie Knox circled the brick house and met Slocum in the Reeds' backyard, he sullenly announced that there was "no sign of any burglar, as might be expected the way you came a-roarin' in like a Texas twister on steroids. If Mr. Crowbar was in the vicinity, he's probably in the next county by now."

The amiable Slocum took no offense.

Having heard them coming from some two miles away,

Mrs. Reed opened the back door of her home and waved at the cops. Slocum holstered his sidearm, and Knox propped the shotgun over his shoulder as they approached the citizen, who was already yelling at them. "You must have frightened him away, but he was here—trying to break into this door!"

Both cops aimed black five-cell "skull crusher" flashlights at the specified door.

Slocum grunted twice.

Knox interpreted his partner's observation for the civilian: "There's no evidence that anybody was attempting a break-in, Miz Reed." He gestured with the flashlight. "See? Not a mark on the door, or the frame."

"Oh." She stared vacantly at the uniformed cops. "Maybe it was a different door."

"Maybe so." Knox tipped his hat. "Don't you worry about a thing. Me'n my partner will check out all of your doors and windows."

"Thank you." She hugged herself and shuddered. "This whole business has been very unnerving."

"Yes, ma'am. We'll knock on your front door before we leave and get a statement about exactly what you heard and saw—the whole ball of beeswax."

Irene Reed nodded and closed the door.

Knox arched an eyebrow at his partner. "Nice-lookin' lady, wouldn't you say?"

Considering his partner's observation unprofessional, E. C. "Piggy" Slocum did not respond.

A LAWMAN'S HUNCH

At ten minutes past nine the following morning, Scott Parris was seated at his desk with a cup of coffee, perusing last night's duty reports. It was dull, tedious work, but part of what the chief of police got paid to do. When Charlie Moon's best friend saw the caller's name on a terse report filed by Knox and Slocum, his brow furrowed as if it had been plowed for planting corn. *First, Sam Reed shows up in my office predicting his murder. A few days later his wife places a 911 call about a prowler.* The cop reread the report, focusing on those phrases that practically jumped off the page:

> *. . . caller reported sounds of someone breaking into rear entrance of residence . . . responding officers found no evidence of attempted forced entry on doors or windows . . . no evidence that a trespasser had been present outside residence prior to officers' arrival . . .*

Staring unblinkingly at the routine call report, Parris forgot all about the warm coffee mug in his hand. Somewhere deep in the lawman's instincts, a tiny alarm bell started to ring—and a plausible scenario began to take root in the fertile imagination under his freshly plowed forehead. His lurid imaginings were accompanied by a haunting suspicion. *Maybe Sam Reed ain't a nutcase after all.* Which worrisome possibility called for an appropriate course of action.

Right off, Scott Parris knew what to do.

He left his office, got into his black-and-white, and went and did it.

Then he placed a call to his best friend and advised Charlie Moon that he was on the way to the Columbine.

CHAPTER SEVENTEEN

HOW THE CHIEF OF POLICE SEES IT

Scott Parris did not devour the free lunch with his usual manly gusto. The Columbine victuals were first-rate as usual, but the cop picked at his medium-rare T-bone steak with the sated appetite of a gorged vulture. He showed no interest in the huge baked-and-buttered Idaho potato. Rather than eat his pinto beans, the discomfited diner preferred to line them up in neat, straight rows like little brown soldiers. The problem was, the Granite Creek chief of police had expected to have lunch with his best buddy—not the Southern Ute tribal investigator's entire family, which included Charlie Moon's irascible aunt Daisy and the effervescent Sarah Frank. The tribal elder's black eyes seemed to see through him, and the enthusiastic youth was practically overflowing with an enthusiastic monologue about how much she was enjoying her freshman semester at Granite Creek's Rocky Mountain Polytechnic University. There seemed to be no end to the scholar's accounts of fascinating classes in American literature, American history, introductory calculus, and that perennial crowd pleaser—elementary computer science.

After the foursome had worked their way past peach cobbler and vanilla ice cream, Parris gave Charlie a shifty-eyed look and suggested that they go upstairs to the rancher's office and talk about a thing or two.

Were the women offended?

Apparently not.

Daisy offered to percolate a fresh pot of Folgers finest, and Sarah graciously volunteered to bring the men a tray of coffee and cookies.

PARRIS'S SUSPICIONS

As Charlie Moon closed his office door and booted his way across the oak floor, he recalled the visit from Lyle Thoms and the offer of twenty-five cents to assassinate Posey Short-horse. *Maybe I ought to ask Scott to be on the lookout for this rogue Chickasaw.* But, for some reason or other, the timing didn't seem quite right. "What's on your mind, pardner?"

Scott Parris perched his hefty bulk on the edge of an oak-framed leather armchair and clasped his knobby hands to make a massive double fist. "I'm beginning to think maybe Sam Reed ain't entirely crazy."

The man of the house eased himself into the chair behind his desk. "I never figured he was."

"I mean about his wild-eyed story that somebody intends to do away with him on the fourth of June."

"What's happened?" The tribal investigator frowned at the town cop. "Has somebody taken a shot at our imaginative friend?"

"Well . . . no." *Not yet.* "But a few minutes after ten last night—while her husband wasn't home—Mrs. Reed placed a 911 call and told the dispatcher somebody was breaking into her house. Knox and Slocum responded to the complaint. But—" the storyteller paused for dramatic effect, "when they got there, there wasn't no prowler."

During those yesteryears when Charlie Moon had served as a uniformed tribal policeman, he had answered dozens of such calls. But, knowing that his friend had probably responded to just as many mistaken reports, he figured Scott must be going somewhere.

The chief of police was. "Not only wasn't there no prowler—there wasn't the least indication one had been there. Mrs. Reed had claimed somebody was prying her back door open, but there wasn't a mark to support her story. Not on the rear entrance or any other door—or on any of the windows."

"So the lady was mistaken." Moon leaned back in his chair. "She's been reading those scary stories in the local paper about the so-called Crowbar Burglar and was nervous about being home alone. Mrs. Reed probably heard the wind blowing a tree branch against the house and jumped to the wrong conclusion."

"That's pretty much what Knox and Slocum figured."

"But you don't."

"I'm not absolutely sure, Charlie." The dyspeptic cop felt a burning churning in his stomach. "But when you add this groundless 911 call to Sam Reed's conviction that somebody is gonna shoot him dead—well, it's just a little bit worrisome."

"You figure Reed's wife might mistake him for a burglar?"

"That can't be ruled out." Parris unclasped his double fist and examined networks of blue veins on the backs of his hands. "It might even be worse than that."

Charlie Moon responded with a slow, thoughtful nod. "She might have deliberately placed a false prowler call to lay the groundwork for *deliberately* shooting her husband when he comes home late some night—and then claim she thought it was the Crowbar Burglar come back again to break in."

"That's the way I see it, Chucky." Parris drummed the fingers of his right hand on the arm of the chair. "Shootings that're honestly due to mistaken identity happen all the time. And when it's cold-blooded murder, it's damn near impossible to prove—especially in a case where the shooter has called in a previous report of a prowler. Our mealymouthed DA not only wouldn't prosecute—he'd tell me to lay off the unfortunate widow. Pug Bullet is more concerned about political repercussions than seeing that justice is done."

"Maybe so. But all you have is a possibly false prowler report—and you can't even prove that." The tribal investigator clasped his hands behind his neck. "I hate to be the one to say it, pardner—but that's more than a little thin."

Prepared for this gentle rebuff, Parris grinned. "You remember how Sam Reed said he'd get killed on his way home from the candy store? And that it'd happen about the time he heard the eleven P.M. church bells?"

"I do."

"Think on this: the Copper Street Candy Shop closes at ten thirty P.M., which is when Reed claims he'll leave with his wife's box of birthday chocolates." Parris paused for the expected response.

Moon was immediately forthcoming. "Unless I disremember, the man didn't say anything about his wife having a birthday on the fourth of June."

"That's right—he didn't. But she does." Scott Parris was immensely pleased with himself. "I found out when I checked the info in Mrs. Reed's driver's license."

Moon mulled this over. "Seems odd he didn't mention her birthday being June fourth." He grinned at his friend. "So Sam Reed leaves the candy store with the chocolates—what then?"

"The candy store's about an eight-minute walk from Reed's office upstairs over the Cattleman's Bank, where he parks his car. Let's say Reed pulls out of the bank parking lot at about ten forty P.M. I checked before I left town this morning: give or take a little, it'll take him about fifteen minutes to drive from the bank lot to his residence in the suburbs, a couple more minutes to park in his garage."

"Which puts him at his back door pretty close to the eleventh hour."

"Right!" The cop slammed his big fist on the oak chair arm.

The wooden-faced Indian winced inwardly. *I hope he don't splinter my chair.* "So what do you intend to do?"

"There's not much I can do." GCPD's top cop scowled under bushy brows. "Before I could say a word to Sam Reed about his wife being a potential suspect, I'd need more information. Like do they keep any firearms in the house? Does Mrs. Reed carry a pistol in her purse?" Seeing the doubtful look on Moon's face, he pressed on. "And there's the question of motive; this might not be entirely about Mrs. Reed inheriting her husband's money. When I checked her driver's license data I found out that Irene Reed is about half Sam's age, and even on her license snapshot she's pretty as one of those flashy ladies you see on magazine covers. We both know Sam Reed ain't much to look at, which naturally raises the question—does the gorgeous young married woman have herself a good-looking young boyfriend? And with that possibility in mind, where does Mrs. Reed go when her husband ain't home?" Parris paused. "I need to know all that kind of stuff." The chief of police blushed as he prepared to drop the heavy hint on his friend. "But you know how thin my budget is. I not only don't have the manpower to shadow Mrs. Reed—my officers aren't exactly what you'd call detectives."

The tribal investigator got the message. *Scott wants me to look into this business for him. But not as his deputy— unofficially. That way, if the Reeds get wind of what's happening, it can't be tied to GCPD.* Coming from his best friend, this was not an unreasonable request. Then, there was the bet Reed had made with both of them—a ten-to-one wager that Scott Parris couldn't keep him alive past June 4. Keeping Reed among the living was not only in Parris's financial interests but also in Moon's. *Problem is, I just don't have the time to take on any more work.* It was hard to turn his friend down flat, so Moon settled on a noncommittal reply: "Yeah, I see what you mean."

Misinterpreting this vague response as an "I'll look into it," Parris allowed himself a half smile. *I hoped you would.*

Sarah Frank, who was standing in the carpeted upstairs hallway outside Moon's office door with a tray of coffee and homemade chocolate-chip cookies, had also gotten the message. No, the girl was not a deliberate eavesdropper cut from the same cloth as Daisy Perika. She had merely paused when she heard the men's voices discussing a serious matter, and wondered whether she should withdraw with the refreshments until a more opportune moment or announce her presence.

Choosing the latter course, the girl cleared her throat. "Excuse me." Behind the closed door, Scott Parris's voice stopped in midsentence. Sarah felt her face burn. "I'm sorry to interrupt, but would you like some fresh coffee and warm-from-the-oven cookies?"

Of course they would.

Parris opened the door, thanked the eighteen-year-old, and took the tray. After she had departed, he placed the coffee and cookies on Moon's desk. "Sarah's a very nice young lady." He cocked his head at the memory of all those years gone by, and sighed. "Makes me wish I had a daughter."

"A man with girlfriends who aren't old enough to drive a car don't need any daughters."

Parris popped a hot cookie into his mouth and chewed. "Eu're jub jebbus."

"I'm not a bit jealous." Moon arched a brow at his friend. "I'm concerned about the reputation of this county's finest public servant."

The cookie fancier washed the cookie down with scalding coffee, made a face. "Ouch!"

The sharp-eared Ute, who had not heard the girl's approach, wondered how much of their private discussion Sarah Frank might have heard. *I hope she's not picking up bad habits from Aunt Daisy.* The tribal elder would go to almost any length to spy on her nephew and his guests. But when he noticed that Sarah had placed a small pitcher of Tule Creek honey on the tray *just for me,* Charlie Moon dismissed the uncharitable thought. Stirring a spoonful of the amber sweetener into his steaming coffee, he reminded himself that Sarah was a sweet kid. And, unlike his mischievous aunt, she was sensible. The girl didn't make trouble for him. Well, hardly ever. And never on purpose.

As Sarah Frank made her way down the stairs one deliberate step at a time, the willowy young lady was mulling over that tantalizing snippet of conversation she had overheard between the chief of police and Charlie Moon. The Ute-Papago orphan paused at the landing to gaze down into the spacious Columbine headquarters parlor. Her expression could fairly be described as *thoughtful*.

When thoughtful women pause to meditate upon vexing problems that are plaguing their favorite men, it often happens that the naturally supportive gender figures out a way to help—and jumps right in.

It happened again.

CHAPTER EIGHTEEN

SARAH SLEEPS ON IT

But only in a manner of speaking. The poor thing got barely a wink of sleep. All night long, the agitated girl turned from one side to the other. And back again. She also tried lying flat on her back. As is common among insomniacs, the same thoughts circulated through her mind: *Mr. Parris needs someone to find out whether or not Mr. Reed's wife has a boyfriend, but the chief of police doesn't have the manpower to keep an eye on Mrs. Reed.*

It was almost inevitable that Little Miss Womanpower would get a great notion. (She already had, while making her way down the stairs from Charlie Moon's closed-door office meeting with Scott Parris.) Back to her left side to consider it in some detail. *I don't see why that wouldn't work.* (Another apt epitaph.) After turning onto her right side for about the forty-leventh time, she is about to describe the notion, more or less in the proverbial nutshell:

I only have one late-afternoon class tomorrow and none on the weekend. It would (she thought) be great fun to skip fifty minutes of American literature and follow the married woman around for two or three days. Sarah rolled onto her left side. *I might find out something important that would help Mr. Parris.* In which event, Charlie Moon would be very proud of her. *Then maybe he would stop calling me "kid."* Oh, how that put-down rankled! The kid hammered her fist into the pillow. The fact that Charlie Moon's references to her

youth were virtually unconscious and that he didn't have a
mean bone in his body served only to enhance the affront.

About an hour before dawn, the sleepless girl finally
made up her mind. *If I'm going to do this, I need to get out
of here before first light.* Out of the bed she bounded. In two
minutes flat, Sarah was dressed. In three more, she was in
the headquarters kitchen, percolating a pot of coffee, stuffing bread and sliced ham into a brown paper bag. The whole
point was to be away before Charlie Moon got out of bed
and started asking questions. Such as: "Where're you off to
so early?" Straight-arrow Sarah could not lie to a stranger,
much less to the man she loved more than life itself. If she
merely evaded his direct question, Charlie would suspect
that she was up to something. And when the Ute's suspicions
were raised, her heartthrob had an uncanny way of finding
out what was going on. *And he might come downstairs any
second now.*

But so far, so good.

Sarah was reaching for the kitchen door when—

AUNT DAISY INTERVENES

"What're you doing up so early?"

Sarah had her hand on the doorknob. "I'm going out."

"Well a blind jackass could see that." The old woman
smirked. "You might as well tell me where you're off to"—
Daisy pointed—"and what you've got in that paper bag."
She sniffed. *Smells like ham.*

The girl glared at the snoopy old woman. *It's none of
your business.*

"Oh yes it is." Daisy chuckled.

Sarah rolled her eyes and sighed. *How does she read my
mind?*

"You've got a face like a comic-book cover." Daisy, who
in her youth had dabbled in games of chance, added this sage
advice: "Don't ever get into a poker game with Charlie Moon;
you'd lose your last dime on a pair of deuces."

Sarah looked the tribal elder straight in the eye. "It's a secret."

"Well of course it is. If it wasn't, why would I want to know?"

The girl stiffened her back. "I don't intend to tell you."

"That's why it's so much fun *making* you spill your guts."

Oh, she makes me so mad I could just spit! "You can't make me say a single word."

"Hah! Just watch me."

The girl watched in wide-eyed terror as Daisy took a deep breath, opened her mouth—"What are you going to do?" Sarah already knew.

Daisy confirmed her suspicions. "I'm going to holler loud enough to wake up all those dead people in the Pine Knob graveyard—and Charlie Moon. Soon's he comes to the top of the stairs and yells, 'What's goin' on down there,' I'll tell him you're sneaking off with a picnic lunch and won't take me along because you're up to *no good*!"

"You wouldn't!" Sarah knew she would.

"Don't talk silly."

Sarah shook her finger in the old woman's face. "If you come along, you'll end up getting both of us in trouble. You always do!"

Daisy glared at the cowardly digit shaker. "So what d'you want to do—live forever?" She rudely brushed the accusing finger aside. "Take if from somebody who knows, young lady—getting old as the hills ain't what it's cracked up to be."

Foolishly, Sarah fell back on an ethical defense. "But what you're doing is—"

"Blackmail, pure and simple." The wicked old woman chuckled. "And don't you be telling me what I *won't do*." She gave the girl a look that chilled. "In my time, I've done things that'd make your hair curl and stand on end!" Daisy set her jaw. "Ask me how many men I've killed."

The innocent stared in horror and shook her head.

"Well I'll tell you anyway. It was three." Daisy paused, shook her head. "No, that's not right." The tribal elder began to count on her fingers. "It was four." She smiled and nodded. "I almost forgot that nasty old Navajo—"

"No no no! I don't want to know!"

"Okay, but you're missing a dandy story." The elder bared her peg-shaped teeth in a hideous grin. "The tribal police never found but one piece of his body and that was his—"

"No!" Sarah meant it and Daisy knew it.

"Oh, all right." *Kids these days are so squeamish.* Daisy tapped a finger on the brown paper bag. "You have enough lunch in there for the both of us?"

Defeat staring her in the face, Sarah nodded dumbly.

After they closed the kitchen door ever so softly behind them, and made their way ever so quietly along the south porch, the women were joined by Sidewinder, the official Columbine hound. When the rangy old dog made it clear that he was determined to come along on the outing, Sarah didn't put up an argument.

Charlie Moon was in the parlor, watching through a west window. Amused by their semistealthy early-morning getaway, he watched the trio get into Sarah's pickup. *I wonder what this is all about.* Aunt Daisy was always planning something or other, and there was no telling what specific mischief she might be up to at a given minute. The sleepy man yawned. *Sarah should be able to keep the old woman out of any serious trouble.* While his elderly relative seemed to be slipping back into a sinister version of her youth (when Daisy had allegedly done some seriously bad things), the kid was developing into a responsible young adult.

In earlier, happier times, when he could spare a few hours, Charlie Moon might have followed the red pickup and found out what kind of new trouble his aunt was getting into. Nowadays, the busy rancher had way too much on his plate to go chasing after the old woman. And even if he didn't have a thing to do, a man would be a fool to deliberately serve himself a helping of Daisy Stew, which was bound to give him a serious case of heartburn.

CHAPTER NINETEEN

DAISY WHEEDLES

Sarah Frank was capable of red-hot anger and could fight like a tigress when sufficiently provoked—but the kind-hearted youth could not hold on to a grudge with both hands. By the time they had passed through the Columbine gate, leaving the painfully bumpy ranch lane for the pleasure of rolling along on miles of smoothly paved highway, the driver had entirely forgiven the old blackmailer seated beside her in the pickup.

Aware of this act of Christian charity, Daisy Perika was slightly miffed. The aged woman needed spice in her life, and there was nothing like a good fight to make an otherwise bland hour savory with flavor. Though pretending to nap, she was trying to think of some way to enliven an already promising day.

The honest hound on the floor at Daisy's feet was truthfully asleep. In dog years, Sidewinder was almost as old as the tribal elder and he needed his rest.

The clever old conniver continued to cogitate. *Whatever's got Sarah so excited probably happened yesterday, after Scott Parris showed up for a free meal.* The most interesting remarks the chief of police had made at lunch were "Please pass me the bread" and "No, I don't need any more beans." But after the meal, Charlie and the white cop had gone upstairs to her nephew's office. *And it wasn't long after that, that Sarah took some coffee and cookies to them. And now that I think about it, she had an awfully peculiar look when she came back to the kitchen.* Daisy spent a mile or so "hmm-ing" about that factoid. *Sarah must've heard something up there. Something the men didn't want her to hear. Something that wasn't any of her business. Police business.* Daisy figured there was nothing to lose by making a probe or two to test her hypothesis. Without opening her eyes, she muttered, "Listening at keyholes can get a person into serious trouble."

Startled by this sudden insightful observation, Sarah ran her red pickup onto the shoulder.

I knew it! The sly old woman smiled.

Sarah struggled to get the vehicle back onto the blacktop. *How does she do that?* "I thought you were asleep."

"Just like you thought those two men didn't know you was listening outside Charlie's office door." Daisy opened her eyes and wagged a finger at the driver. "Take it from someone who knows—Charlie Moon can hear a chigger sneeze a mile away. And for a pale-skinned *matukach,* Scott ain't an easy man to fool."

"I didn't intend to listen, I—" *Oh, I am so stupid—why did I say that?*

"Well of course you didn't." Daisy barely managed to conceal her pleasure at this confession. "But don't apologize, there's nothing wrong with a woman finding out what the menfolk are up to." Her crackly old voice cackled a wicked laugh. "Even if she goes out of her way to do it." *Now, I'll give her some time to think about it. Sooner or later, she'll tell me what she's up to.*

Sarah had clamped her mouth shut.

Daisy Perika waited for a full minute.

The girl was as silent as the hound.

She needs a little nudge. "Getting mixed up in police business can be tricky." The manipulator counted ten telephone poles. "And dangerous to boot."

"That's why I didn't want you to come along and—" *Oh, no. I've done it again.*

"That's very sweet of you. But now that I'm here, you

might as well tell me what kind of trouble you're about to get me into." The devious old hypocrite grinned like a possum with a ripe pawpaw. "You owe me that much."

Field Marshal Daisy had won the battle.

Sarah surrendered. Unconditionally. She told the tribal elder everything she knew (which was admittedly only a fraction of the big picture), closing with: "Mr. Parris needs to find out whether a Mrs. Reed is cheating on her husband."

"So you're going to spy on this married woman?"

"I'm not going to *spy* on anybody. All I'm going to do is . . . well . . ." Sarah frowned as she searched for a face-saving euphemism. "I'll keep an eye on her."

Daisy chuckled. "Call a skunk a lilac, it stinks just the same."

The greenhorn detective responded in a professional tone. "I'll make notes about where Mrs. Reed goes and who she talks to and somehow or other find out whether or not she has a boyfriend and if she *does,* what the boyfriend's name is and where he lives." The producer of this lengthy statement paused for a breath of air. "That sort of thing."

"Well if you ask me, that's an awfully low and sleazy line of work—following a woman around, prying into her private affairs. No decent person would do such a thing." The tribal elder beamed upon the scowling youth. "So you can count me in!"

CHAPTER TWENTY

SARAH AND DAISY'S (AND SIDEWINDER'S) EXCELLENT ADVENTURE

A bloodred sun was floating about five diameters high in a misty-blue sky when Sarah Frank drove slowly past 1200 Shadowlane Avenue, which address was identified by shiny brass numbers on a cedar post by the driveway entrance. This was not going to be as straightforward as she had hoped. *I can't even see the Reeds' house from the road.* The amateur detective was dismayed and discombobulated, but not defeated. She rolled about twenty yards down Shadowlane before turning her spiffy F-150 onto a ten-acre vacant lot. The combination of the tight right turn and the abrupt transformation from smooth-as-glass asphalt to a rutted dirt lane jolted a napping Daisy Perika wide awake just in time to see the For Sale by Owner sign.

Ditto the snoozing Columbine dog at her feet.

Make that a half ditto. Sidewinder had been rudely awakened, but the dog had not noticed the For Sale sign. The creature's gaze was firmly fixed on the driver, his sad, houndish eyes clearly conveying the accusative query: *Why did you do a mean thing like that?*

The tribal elder did not limit herself to a silent complaint. "What're you trying to do, you Papago wildcat—jar my back teeth loose?"

"I'm sorry." And the Ute-Papago orphan was sorry. But

not a whole lot. Sarah shot the cranky old complainer a glance that was salted with an unspoken snappy rejoinder: *If you'd stayed on the ranch instead of nosing your way into my business, you'd still be in bed.*

"I know what you're thinking," Daisy mumbled.

Good! Shifting down to Low, Sarah left the dirt lane to bumpity-bump her way onto a broad, rocky crest of a heavily treed section of the expensive real estate. Ignoring the hound's protesting groans and Daisy's painful moans, the Miss Papago Wildcat eased the pickup to a stop under a bushy juniper. "This'll do just fine."

"Do fine for what?"

"For the stakeout."

"Oh, right." Daisy would never have admitted that she had completely forgotten where they were and why. Not for all the succulent green chili in Hatch, New Mexico.

After slipping on a pair of Dollar Store plastic sunglasses and pulling a droopy-brimmed straw hat down to her ears, Sarah dug into a black canvas shopping bag and came up with a brand-new Pilot G2 ballpoint pen, a small Student Memo Pad, and a pair of Sears binoculars (her late father's), which were several decades older than her youthful self.

Pleased to witness such childish whimsy, Daisy smiled at the girl. "You look like a sure-enough snoop."

"This is what professionals do." The novice gumshoe adjusted her shades. "I make notes on my pad, and I need the binoculars so I can see the *target* that I'm shadowing without that person realizing that I'm nearby. But just in case somebody does get a look at me, the hat and sunglasses will help conceal my identity."

"Hah!" The old woman punctuated that remark with a snort. "Nobody out here in this ritzy neighborhood would recognize the likes of you or me."

Not so, Miss D. As we shall shortly see.

The young lady and the elder are unaware of the stealthy approach of a pair of armed and dangerous men.

But Sidewinder's nose knows; watch it sniff and snuff.

*And so do his long, droopy ears; see how they vainly attempt
to prick. Listen to his low, guttural growl.*

"Aaaiiieeeeee!"

No. That was not a growl.

Neither was the "Eeep!" *emitted by Sarah Frank about
forty milliseconds later.*

The aforesaid "Aaaiiieeeeee!" *was Daisy Perika's terrified screech.*

The startled Ute elder glared at the round, pink, smiling face
framed in the passenger-side window. "Piggy Slocum—I
ought to beat you to death with my walking stick for scaring
me half to death like that, and I will, soon as I get this window down!" As she attempted to lower the glass barrier between her and the chubby, good-natured cop, Officer Slocum
advised her that the window button wouldn't work with the
ignition in the Off position. This helpful advice served only
to further agitate the Southern Ute elder.

"Hmmph!" (Officer Eddie Knox.)

"Eeep!" (Sarah again, louder this time.)

The girl had been startled by Cop Number Two, whose
scowling, bushy-browed face appeared at the open driver's-side window, Knox's bulbous nose close enough to be
tickled by the droopy brim of the girl's hat.

"Well I should've known," Daisy said. "If Tweedledee
shows his silly face in public, Tweedle*dumb* can't be far behind."

Seemingly oblivious to this affront from Sarah's testy
passenger, Knox queried the driver, "What're you doin'
parked on private property, Sarah?"

Humiliated to the core, the girl behind the sunshades
could not get a word out.

Unencumbered by the least propensity toward humility,
Daisy raised her chin in an impudent gesture. "What's it to
you, Peg-leg Eddie?"

From the squinty-eyed look that Eddie Knox aimed at
Daisy, one might conclude that the valiant police officer who

had lost a leg in a shootout did not appreciate this rude reference to his high-tech prosthesis.

Her oak walking staff gripped in both hands, Daisy was eyeing Knox. *I bet I could knock Big-mouth's teeth down his throat before he could dodge.*

Sensing that things were about to get out of hand, Slocum piped up in a conciliatory tone. "I betcha they're gatherin' a basket of last season's piñon nuts."

"I don't think so, Pig." Knox pointed his nose at the binoculars. "My guess is, they're doin' some bird-watching." The cop grinned at Sarah. "How about it, kid—you spotted any mountain bluebirds?"

"No," Daisy snapped. "But we did run into a pair of blue-coated jackasses!"

Officer Knox had had that portion that is commonly denoted "just about enough." *If that nasty old witch makes a jab at me with her stick, I'll slap the cuffs on her so fast it'll make her head spin—and then I'll charge her with assaulting an officer.*

Licking her dry lips, Sarah was opening her mouth to explain when she was interrupted by Daisy.

"Since when is it against the law for a couple of honest, taxpaying citizens to check out some land that's for sale?"

This tactic by Charlie Moon's unpredictable auntie caught Knox off guard. *The old girl's foxy as ever.* He grinned in genuine appreciation. "You telling me you're interested in buying property out here on Shadowlane Avenue—a *ten-acre* lot?"

Daisy assumed her ultrahaughty Queen of the Utes expression. "If that's the biggest they've got." She sniffed. "Thirty acres would be more to my liking."

Believing the old woman was serious, the innocent Slocum shook his head and said, "Daisy, these lots go for a hundred thousand an acre!"

Though startled by such an obscene price, the prospective buyer affected an indolent shrug. "Does it already have water and electric and telephone?"

"Yes'm," Slocum said. "Natural gas too, and it's all underground." He pointed at what *wasn't* there. "That's why you don't see no 'lectric poles."

"Well with all that, it'd be a bargain at twice the price." Pointedly ignoring the cops, Daisy Perika directed her next remark to Sarah. "Our tribe makes tons of money with gas leases and casinos and whatnot, and the chairman's my first cousin. If I said a word to Oscar Sweetwater, why, he'd likely buy up this whole end of town—and pay cash money on the barrelhead."

Realizing that he wasn't going to get anywhere with Daisy, Knox ran up the white flag. "I s'pose these two suspicious characters ain't violated any county ordinance, Pig. Let's you'n me hit the road and get some serious police work done."

Slocum tipped his hat at the ladies and withdrew with his partner to their unit, which Knox backed off the ten-acre lot and onto the street.

With the aid of her venerable 8X binoculars, Sarah watched the GCPD unit beetle its way north along Shadow-lane Avenue until the sleek Chevrolet black-and-white was out of sight. Relieved to the point of wanting to cry, the girl satisfied herself with a sigh. And a silent prayer of thanks as she turned her binoculars on the Reed driveway.

Highly satisfied with herself, Daisy smirked. *This is turning out to be a fine morning.* And the day was still young.

"Oh!" Sarah frowned as she adjusted the optical instrument for a better focus.

"What is it?"

"A man driving a black Hummer. It must be Mr. Reed."

It must be and it was. He turned south, and before you could whistle your favorite Chopin nocturne or "Chattanooga Choo-Choo" he was down the avenue and out of sight.

Daisy yawned.

Minutes passed. (Eleven of them.)

"Oh!"

"What's it this time?" The old woman stifled a second yawn.

"A pink Cadillac coming down the driveway. A lady's driving it."

"Probably be one of them Mary Kay cosmetics gals, making calls on all the rich, wrinkled old white women who live out here." *I bet they buy cold cream by the gallon.*

Sarah shook her head, which caused her to momentarily lose sight of the expensive automobile. "It must be Mrs. Reed." As the car exited the driveway and turned north, she dropped the binoculars into the canvas shopping bag, started the pickup's engine, and backed up so fast that Daisy and the hound were (respectively) yelling rude imprecations and howling bloody murder.

Your budding detective is not deterred by such distractions. Picture cold springwater running off a mallard's back.

But Sarah was going overly fast in Reverse, and as she roared toward the curb, the F-150's rear bumper caught the edge of the For Sale by Owner sign and twisted it by about ninety degrees.

A few heartbeats later, she was zooming down Shadowlane Avenue like Casey Jones in Ol' 97 rolling down Tennessee's Copperhead Mountain at full throttle with a good head of steam—and no brakes.

There is nothing quite so exciting as *the chase*!

It would have been even more so, had the young woman realized that Officers Knox and Slocum had completed a wide circle and were now about a half mile behind her. What with the suspicious cops on her tail and Charlie Moon's wild-eyed aunt seated beside her, Sarah Frank's initial fling at amateur detection seemed destined to terminate abruptly.

CHAPTER TWENTY-ONE

THE FATEFUL NUDGE

Sarah Frank had slowed her pickup to the respectable velocity of thirty-five miles per hour, which was not excessively
above the posted speed limit of twenty-five mph, which was
about right for an avenue that had abruptly morphed from
a straight-as-an-arrow thoroughfare to a twisty-turny two-
lane that now wound its serpentine way around dry, juniper-
studded hills and dipped through shallow arroyos where
thirsty cottonwoods and willows had put down roots.

As she enjoyed the picturesque scenery and delightful
scents of springtime greenery, Daisy Perika noticed a familiar geographical feature. Nudging Sarah in the ribs, she was
pointing out how "you can see Black Frog Butte clear as day
from here and over there to the west you can see a mountain
shaped like a—"

What Daisy saw in a westerly direction must remain un-
reported.

The tour guide's informative commentary was interrupted
by a loud exclamation from the driver, who was startled by
both the unseemly elbow nudge and what it had distracted
Miss Frank from seeing until she was almost on top of it.

"YIIEEEEEK!"

Which is what Sarah shrieked upon rounding a tight Shadow-lane curve to encounter that avenue's intersection with Sixteenth Street, where those county officials so empowered had thoughtfully placed traffic signals, which not a few local senior citizens referred to as stop-and-go lights. The operative command at this instant was Stop, which Mrs. Irene Reed had obeyed in her pink Cadillac, which expensive vehicle was directly in Sarah's pickup's path, with the distance between them closing fast. The alarmed driver's instincts sent an order marked IMPERATIVE to her right leg, which immediately responded by jamming the F-150's brake pedal *to the floor.*

A quartet of rubber tires squealed like scalded pigs.

Daisy Perika ducked. *Oh my God we're all going to be killed!*

Blissfully unaware of the pickup that was bearing down upon her, the rich woman in the sissified GM luxury sedan wondered: *What is that awful screechy noise?*

With teeth clenched, knuckles white, Sarah summed up the situation in one word: *There'snowayIcanstopintime!*

True. 'Twas do-or-die time.

While shifting her foot from brake to accelerator pedal, the plucky youth jerked the steering wheel hard to the left and zoomed around the pink Caddie like it was standing still (which it was), and ran the red light like a wild-eyed outlaw (which she was) being pursued by a carload of armed coppers that was gaining fast (which the carload was). While roaring through the intersection, Sarah's shiny red F-150 pickup missed being T-boned by an oncoming Mack truck by *this much*!

Like so many of life's gut-wrenching events, this one was over in a moment. (For Sarah, Daisy, and Sidewinder.)

Officers Eddie Knox and E. C. Slocum arrived just in time to see the Lopez & Sons cement truck screech to a halt in front of the pink Cadillac, which latter vehicle had the right-of-way because the light for Mrs. Reed and the GCPD cops was now green for go. But they could not.

Annoyed at the cement-truck impediment, Mrs. Reed tooted her horn at the cursing truck driver, who had stalled his vehicle in precisely the right spot to block both the intersection and the cops' view of the fleeing red pickup.

The situation was apparent to the experienced officers. The cement-truck driver had obviously run a red light, thereby almost causing a collision with the lady in the pink luxury automobile. Neither the French-Canadian trucker's angry shouts (he spoke nineteen words of English, fourteen of them vulgar) nor his insistence (in flawless French) that the &%$# idiot in the red pickup had run the light—served to set things right.

SAMUEL REED'S DISTRACTED WIFE

Why did Mrs. Irene Reed not send the cops chasing after Sarah Frank's pickup truck? Because the driver of the pink Cadillac had not seen the red F-150 approach, or flash by on her left. Why not? Because, with the aid of the rearview mirror, which she had turned to a convenient angle, the lady had been touching up her pink lip gloss. (Meticulous attention to color coordination was a skill Irene took pride in.)

An irate Irene Reed was detained by Officers Knox and Slocum just long enough to have her say, which included: "I heard brakes screeching and at first I thought someone was trying to stop behind me but then I realized it was that monstrous truck." The woman who detested commas pointed an elegantly manicured pink fingernail at the offending vehicle, and kept right on with her monologue.

Recognizing the pretty lady who'd placed the 911 call about a prowler, Officer Eddie Knox nodded politely and interjected a "Yes ma'am" at appropriate intervals. His ears heard but his brain did not register a word of Irene's nonstop, ninety-mile-an-hour prattle about how she ". . . simply *must* be going because I have a *thousand* things to do and really *can't* just sit here all day while you fellows try to figure out what has happened when it is so *glaringly* apparent that this half-wit truck driver ran a red light and might have killed me if I had not seen him coming and refrained from proceeding . . ." And so on. Until she finally ran out of breath.

As she gasped for air, Eddie Knox uttered his final "Yes ma'am" and tipped his hat. "We'll be in touch with you later for a formal statement." The cop returned Mrs. Reed's driver's license and sent the upper-crust citizen on her way, which required a circuitous detour around the cement truck and an exchange of glares with the operator of that formidable vehicle.

Having rid himself of the nonstop chatterbox, Officer Knox turned his entire attention to the frustrated driver of the Mack truck, who, having gotten the engine started, was attempting to communicate to Officer Slocum the fact that he did not speak *Anglais,* and this with the enormous distaste of one whose lips are accustomed to mouthing musical phrases of the world's only civilized language.

THE IMMIGRANT'S REVENGE

Jean-Henri Dubois had suffered several outrages during the past few hours, such as a girlfriend who had fed him watery scrambled eggs for breakfast. Not to mention her dyspeptic spaniel, which animal (during the wee hours) had vomited in both of Jean-Henri's expensive fleece-lined boots. When the GCPD cops put a big ticket on him, the French-Canadian truck driver decided that he'd had quite enough and *then some,* thank you very much. Right on the spot, he made up his mind to return to Saint-Jean-sur-Richelieu, where a girlfriend knew how to prepare a proper omelet and the gendarmerie treated citizens with due respect. But he would not depart for civilization before getting even with these &$*#% Americans! To this end, Jean-Henri backed his umpteen-ton vehicle up to the immaculate GCPD black-and-white and proceeded—calm as you please—to dump the entire load of cement onto it.

After a moment of stunned disbelief, Eddie Knox

commenced to jump up and down and curse all foreigners (especially truck-driving foreigners) and threaten to shoot the driver. Thankfully, he did not, but out of utter frustration the furious cop did pop some lead into the big truck's diesel engine and left rear tire. Neither verbal abuse nor misuse of his official sidearm produced any noticeable effect upon either the sturdy Mack truck or the deadpan driver.

Officer E. C. "Piggy" Slocum simply stood and shook his head in wonder at such goings-on, which would be something to tell his grandchildren about. *If I ever was to get married and have childurn and then they was to grow up and get married too and have grandchildurn for me to tell stories to.* Mr. Slocum was a complex soul.

Having immensely enjoyed the benefits from this wonderfully cathartic experience, Jean-Henri was in a fine mood when he pulled his big rig out of the intersection. So much so that he was inspired to sing a somewhat sinister little ditty from his childhood: "*Les yeux bleus vont aux cieux,*" which in honest, unitalicized speech is rendered "Blue Eyes to Heaven Rise." After crooning his merry way to the Lopez & Sons Sand, Gravel & Cement headquarters, the cheeky French-Canadian drew his last paycheck and departed, never to be seen again or henceforth in these parts, or anywhere else south of the border. As he mounted his gray motorbike and pulled his goggles down, Jean-Henri Dubois bid Granite Creek *adieu* and *au revoir,* and as he sped out of town let loose with another lusty song: "*À Quebec sur mon petit cheval gris*" ("To Quebec on My Little Grey Horse"). Farther on down the road toward Salida, tiring of children's songs, he bellowed out the nineteenth-century French-Canadian composition about his legendary namesake—the hardworking folk hero with the big hammer in his hands. Couldn't no steam drill outdo *him*—Jean-Henri was a sure-enough *steel-driving* man.

What fun!

And Daisy's and Sarah's excellent day was just getting started.

CHAPTER TWENTY-TWO

DAISY BARELY RESTRAINS HERSELF

To Daisy Perika's eternal credit, the genial elbow nudger refrained from criticizing the youthful driver for an asinine blunder that came ever so close to creating indescribable carnage at the intersection. Not aloud. *If that eighteen-year-old Papago girl don't learn to drive right, she'll never live to see nineteen.* (When chagrined with Sarah, Daisy tended to overlook the fact that the teenager was half Ute.) Barely a block from the intersection, the charitable old woman offered this sage advice to the rattled girl: "You'd better find someplace to get out of sight."

"What for?" Poor Sarah had forgotten what they were doing in Granite Creek.

"To wait for that woman to pass by." Daisy sighed. *Kids nowadays need everything explained to them.*

What woman? The driver managed to get her mind in gear. *Oh, right—Mrs. Reed.*

Daisy pointed a gnarled finger at a shady side street. "There's a good place to pull over. She'll be showing up before you know it, and we'll want to get behind her again."

And so they did, and Mrs. Reed did, and they did. •

But this time around, Sarah was the very soul of caution. Ever so wary, she stayed well behind her quarry and slowed for every blind curve.

THE CLANDESTINE RENDEZVOUS

It was unfortunate that Irene Reed had departed a minute too soon to witness the dramatic spectacle wherein the GCPD cops' spiffy black-and-white was buried under tons of cement dispensed by the aforesaid "monstrous truck." This woman, who appreciated both dark humor and slapstick comedy, would have enjoyed the entertainment.

But harbor no regrets, Mrs. R.—Fate has a way of evening up the score.

Indeed, Professor Reed's missus would soon be involved in another twisted melodrama, one whose plot would be conceived, produced, and staged by a cunningly devious mind. The vain author of the tasteless farce would also serve as the star of the piece.

Unaware that she was destined to be an unwitting player in a one-act, one-minute production—or that she was being tailed by a pair of highly unlikely sleuths (and a hound) in a red pickup truck—the pretty lady in the pink Cadillac turned in at the Sand Hills Country Club gate and gaily waved her way past the stern-faced security guard who knew every member on sight. After parking her sleek automobile in the velvet shade of a stately blue spruce, Irene slammed the door and strode off with the purposeful gait of a woman who knows exactly where she is going, precisely whom she expects to meet when she gets there, and that . . . *the handsome rascal damn well better show up on time if he knows what's good for him.*

SARAH MAKES HER PLAY

After a glance at the uniformed gatekeeper at the golf-club entrance, Sarah Frank decided to pass. This despite a derisive snort from Aunt Daisy, who let the cautious girl know that "no make-believe *matukach* cop would keep *me* from going where I wanted to. Why, in my grandfather's day, us

Utes owned everything you can see in all directions!" Being a more or less charitable soul, Daisy refrained from adding that when the Utes were Lords of the Shining Mountains and feasting on buffalo and elk, Sarah's Papago ancestors were eking out a miserable living in the Arizona desert by dining on cactus apples, flint-hard beans, and collared lizards. But she could not help *thinking* it.

Oblivious to the tribal elder's bragging, Sarah was looking for a good location to spy from and found it. She turned into the parking lot at the Wesleyan Methodist Church, whose immaculately landscaped six acres adjoined the three square miles of Sand Hills Country Club real estate. It was beneficial that the church was situated on a small hillock that overlooked the golf course by about fifty feet. As the house of worship was unoccupied at this hour, Sarah had her choice of 260 places to park her pickup. She selected a spot where the view of the golf course was relatively unobstructed, and behold—barely a hundred yards away, standing on a narrow blacktopped pathway, was the lady who had piloted the pink Cadillac. The paved strip where Sam Reed's wife stood was similar to those provided for members' golf carts, but no such traffic was likely to disturb her. First, the ribbon of blacktop was too narrow. Second, it meandered off the edge of the course to dead-end at a small structure that looked to the imaginative Ute-Papago orphan like one of two things: the minuscule residence of a reclusive old man who made a meager living selling pilfered golf balls, or—a tool shed. Sad to say, it was the latter.

"Mrs. Reed looks like she's waiting for someone," Sarah said. The better to use her binoculars, she removed her floppy-brimmed hat and sunglasses and tossed both aside. The shades landed where she had intended (on the seat between them) but the hat sailed onto Daisy Perika's lap. Sarah's casual discard of that personal item onto the tribal elder's person irked the feisty old woman quite a lot and then some. *What am I, just someplace to put things she don't need right now?* Being one of those Christians who was inclined less toward the Sermon on the Mount and more toward Eye for

Eye, Tooth for Tooth, the Latter-Day Pharisee decided that she would get even with the thoughtless teenager. *Tonight, after I get undressed and put my nightgown and house slippers on, I'll walk into Sarah's bedroom and say, "My closet is too full for this stuff," and then toss my clothes and shoes onto her bed.* That ought to make the point. *So that's what I'll do.* The senior citizen grinned wickedly. *Unless I can think of something better.*

Blissfully ignorant of the irritable auntie's silent subplot, the honest young woman continued to think aloud: "Oh, I wish I could get close enough to find out who she's here to meet—and hear what they talk about." *But you don't want the target to know you're watching them and there's just no way I can get close without being spotted.* Addressing Daisy, she pointed. "I'm going down there where I can see a little better. But don't worry, this'll just take a few minutes."

"Take as long as you like." Her venom seemingly spent, Daisy patted the hound's head, yawned, and closed her eyes. "I feel a nap coming on."

After smiling at the sleepy old woman, the girl got out of the pickup and took a brisk walk off the edge of the parking lot, then downhill to vanish in a narrow grove of young aspens that had sprouted along the border between the church and the country-club property. Once in position, the hopeful spy raised the instrument to her eyes. After fine-tuning the binocular optics, Sarah searched until she framed the shaky figure of Irene Reed. Steadying the binoculars against a sapling for a more stable view, the delighted detective whispered to herself, "She's looking at her wristwatch. Whoever she's supposed to meet must be late." The young woman figured it was twenty to one that the tardy person was a man. A boyfriend. Who else would a married woman meet in such a lonely place?

One minute passed.

During which period Sarah Frank thrice recited the seven lines of Miss Dickinson's "If I Can Stop One Heart from Breaking."

While the Rocky Mountain Polytechnic University student paid lip service to her American literature course, Mrs. Reed uttered a string of unseemly obscenities, and checked her wristwatch three times.

Two minutes.

Sarah had completed the wood-cutter's song in Whitman's "I Hear America Singing" but got stuck trying to remember what the ploughboy was up to.

As she continued her vigil, Irene Reed appended unspeakable blasphemies to her obscenities. Her platinum wristwatch was consulted five times.

Sarah had dismissed the ploughboy and said goodbye to Mr. Whitman. Continuing to peer through her Sears & Roebuck binoculars, our scholar had a go at Longfellow's "The Day is Done." But it was not. Not by a long shot.

A few tick-tocks into Minute Number Three, when Irene was beginning to seethe with the volcanic anger of an attractive, vain, upper-crust female who has been stood up by a hairy-legged person she considers beneath her station, a young man with a dark complexion and a bright, toothy smile appeared. The fellow with the rake over his shoulder waved at Mrs. Reed. He appeared (to Sarah) to be well over six feet tall (he was six four), thirty inches wide at the shoulders (an amplification by the impressionable teenager), and superbly muscular, in which latter assessment Sarah was not guilty of the slightest hyperbole.

There was more.

The darkly handsome man had long, curly locks that fell to his shoulders. Long, curly, *blond* locks that (this was Sarah's opinion) ruined the eye-popping effect of this otherwise virile specimen with just the slightest hint of . . . how to say it? *Femininity.*

And there was still more.

As Sarah watched the almost-flawless example of young manhood approach the married woman and gather her into a breathless embrace, something extraneous to the scene caught the exuberant spy's eye.

Enter (stage left) another player.

Sarah Frank's brow furrowed behind the binoculars. There

was something eerily familiar about the hunched, sunglassed senior citizen under the wide-brimmed straw hat. The elderly person was being tugged along the paved pathway by a dog on a leash. A leash that resembled the orange nylon towrope that Sarah kept in the bed of her pickup. *And those look like my sunglasses and that looks like my hat and that old dog looks a lot like Sidewinder— Oh, no!*

Oh, yes.

Behold the shameless scene stealer—the star of this seamy little melodrama.

CHAPTER TWENTY-THREE

PITIFUL OLD LAME, BLIND WOMAN
(THE PROMISED ONE-ACT,
ONE-MINUTE PRODUCTION)

While Daisy Perika and the hound had tarried just out of sight of the married woman and her muscle-bound boyfriend, sheet lightning flashed over mountain peaks that were veiled by a lacy gray smoke of swirling snow. As soon as the couple had decoupled and begun to use their lips to form syllables, the tribal elder was eager to hear as much as she could of the conversation. Alas, the noise of the gathering storm frustrated Daisy's intrigue; the boom-and-rumble of thunder and the ploppity-plop of plump raindrops on new ash and aspen leaves was drowning out most of their verbal exchange. When a snoop can discern only one word out of three, the delicious novelty of eavesdropping quickly wears thin, and when it did, the Ute elder decided upon a tactical withdrawal.

As often happens with animals, the Columbine hound had other ideas. Sidewinder was loath to depart before he had crashed the couple's intimate party, and so off the odd pair went—this time, the dog taking the reluctant old woman for a walk.

As the curious figure approached with the oak walking stick in her right hand and the taut dog rope in her left, the bemused twosome parted to make way for the senior citizen and her determined dog to pass.

It seemed that they would do just that when Sidewinder

stopped abruptly, apparently to sniff at an intriguingly disgusting scent upon the paved pathway. Daisy was unable to arrest what physicist Samuel Reed would have referred to as her "forward momentum," which was equal to the product of Daisy's mass and velocity. The poor old soul stumbled, almost tumbled, and would have fallen flat on her face had she not managed to make a successful grab for something to hold on to. The nearest sturdy object was the young man with the curly blond hair.

"Yikes!" Daisy yelped.

"Whoops!" saith Mr. Goldilocks.

"Oh!" Irene Reed instinctively reached out to help.

"I'm sorry." Daisy held on. "I'm just an old stumblebum—can't get around like I used to when I was eighty-five."

Weary of this tired old joke, the hound snorted contemptuously.

The desperate comedian kept right on holding on to the golf course assistant groundskeeper. "It's not just my limbs that don't do what I want 'em to, I've almost lost my sight." The sly deceiver blinked behind Sarah's cheap sunglasses. "Just a few minutes ago the lady on the radio said it was almost noon, but things look so dark to me that it might as well be midnight."

Sidewinder—a canine who *could not abide a lie*—rolled his eyes.

As she assisted her boyfriend in the embarrassing task of unclasping himself from the clumsy woman's embrace, Irene Reed's forced smile hurt her face. *Dotty old people shouldn't be allowed to roam around in public. Not without a designated guardian.*

After exchanging a few inane remarks with Mrs. Reed and her man-friend, Daisy brushed a crisply green little aspen leaf off her sleeve, turned in the direction whence she had come, and departed with the hound, who (apparently humiliated by the encounter) was pulling his embarrassing burden in the general direction of the Wesleyan Methodist Church parking lot and an eighteen-year-old novice detective who was extremely alarmed and also greatly vexed with Charlie Moon's outrageously zany aunt Daisy

But despite Sarah's fertile imagination, her intimate knowledge of several of Daisy's previous misadventures, and the fact that she had been an eyewitness to this latest escapade, she was not fully aware of what had transpired at the lovers' rendezvous.

Fortunately, neither was Irene Reed. Nor her boyfriend.

What the hound knew must remain a matter of conjecture.

While Daisy was being towed uphill by the Columbine hound, Sarah Frank watched Mrs. Reed and the young man embrace again to enjoy a parting kiss, then go their separate ways. After a brisk walk back to the members-only parking lot, the married lady slipped into her pink Cadillac and exited the Sand Hills Country Club gate with a perfunctory wave at the uniformed guard. Sarah took no interest in Irene Reed's departure. Her entire attention was focused on the young man, who, after stopping to get a raincoat from a Chevrolet Camaro, had headed toward the Sand Hills Pro Shop. After he had pushed through the door and vanished inside, Sarah hurried back to her red F-150, arriving just in time to meet Daisy Perika, who was huffing and puffing from the dog-assisted hill climb. The Ute elder presented the floppy hat and cheap sunglasses to the girl without a word. But not without a self-satisfied smirk.

Knowing that it would be pointless to complain to this habitual malefactor who took considerable pride in her misdeeds, Sarah Frank urged Charlie's aunt and Sidewinder to "get into the truck as fast as you can—we might have to leave in a hurry."

Daisy and the dog complied without dissent. But once in the pickup cab, one of them said, "That rich *matukach* hussy's already gone; I saw her drive away."

Somewhat frostily, the neophyte detective informed her critic that there was no further point in tailing Mrs. Reed. "We know where *she* lives." Sarah asserted that she intended to follow the boyfriend home.

Grimacing at the aches in her legs, the grumpy old woman grunted. "He might hang around for hours."

"I don't care—we're staying here until he leaves." Sarah set her chin, pressed the binoculars against her eyes, and scanned the employees' parking lot until she spotted the Camaro. *Good—his old car is still there. I'll watch it until he shows up, then I'll follow him.* But "follow" was a rather pedestrian descriptor, suggesting a seedy gumshoe.

What the youthful sleuth hankered for was a modish sense of style. An elegant air of flair. Even a classy dash of panache.

Sarah Frank whispered, "I'll *tail* him."

CHAPTER TWENTY-FOUR

IT TAKES A FELON TO KNOW ONE

Whether or not this maxim is true in a general sense, it certainly applied to Mrs. Irene Reed's favorite country-club groundskeeper—and to Daisy Perika. About a minute after the aforementioned tribal elder (henceforth designated Felon Number One) got settled in Sarah's pickup, Felon Number Two slipped into his souped-up classic 1982 Chevrolet Camaro and pulled out of the Sand Hills County Club employees' parking lot. As he motored along the boulevard, the driver was troubled about his meeting with the enigmatic female. No, not Irene Reed. The wealthy married woman was (he believed) entirely predictable—putty in his hands.

It was his encounter with the blind woman and her Seeing Eye hound that bothered him. For some reason or other, the young man couldn't purge the elderly woman's jarring appearance from his thoughts.

SARAH STICKS DOGGEDLY TO THE TRAIL

Her earlier misadventure at the intersection still fresh in her mind, Sarah Frank remained cautious on this sinuous road. Her rule of thumb was to stay about a block behind her target. *That way, I won't be spotted.* And no way was she going to take a chance on rear-ending the spiffy Camaro when it stopped (just around a bend) at a stoplight.

And she didn't.

But when she saw the classic Chevy approaching a signal light that had just turned yellow, our novice sleuth knew what was going to go wrong, and it did. The boyfriend's vehicle accelerated, passed under the light about two heartbeats after it turned red, and she was torpedoed. Scuttled. Sunk. And any other nautical description of disaster one might summon up. There was nothing for Sarah to do (with a state policeman not far behind her) but to brake to a full stop at the red light and wait. Except to chew the fingernail of her left thumb and bang her right hand on the steering wheel and wail, "Oh, turn green, please-please-please turn green!"

After some sixteen hours, the traffic light complied.

IRENE REED'S BOYFRIEND

As the young man drove along the tree-lined boulevard, the autopilot portion of his brain was intently focused on the road ahead. But what the assistant golf-course groundskeeper saw in his mind's inner eye was a definitely old, supposedly lame, allegedly blind woman being pulled along by a homely hound—the pair mutually attached by a length of nylon tow-rope. The eccentric had seemed so pitifully helpless, so charmingly harmless.

But, by some deep inner instinct, he knew this was a sham. *There's something wrong about that old hag.* He tried to put his finger on what didn't fit. For one thing . . . *She wasn't confused or stupid; that was all a big act.* His subconscious took a glance at the rearview mirror. And for another thing . . . *The way she turned up right out of nowhere, it was almost like* . . . The pair of bushy black eyebrows under his yellow hairline bunched, and behind the brow with the worried frown, his lurid imagination completed the chilling thought: *It was almost like she was a witch.*

In his culture, like Daisy's, *brujas* and *brujos* were ubiquitous. Why, if a fellow were to throw a half-dozen bricks into a crowd on any busy street corner in any town in the US of A, he was bound to hit two or three female or male witches. Not one of them would suffer a scratch or a bruise, but you could bet your last dime that they'd put the Evil Eye on you!

About three minutes and a mile after the superstitious young man had deliberately run the red light, he made a stop at a busy Conoco station to fill the Camaro's tank—and made a rather unpleasant discovery.

What the hell—

As the puzzled motorist stood by the gas pump, the red pickup his subconscious had noted in the Camaro's rear-view mirror came creeping along the street. He got a glimpse of the slender girl behind the steering wheel and a good look at the old *witch* in the passenger seat. The young man squinted to get a better look—and did. Chico Perez's lips whispered the numbers on the license plate as he memorized them.

JUSTIFIABLE FRUSTRATION

Neither Daisy Perika nor Sarah Frank noticed the furious yellow-haired man glaring at them or the low-slung Chevrolet. Both the frowning biped and the sleek motor vehicle were almost entirely concealed by a row of gas pumps and other vehicles.

"Oh!" Sarah banged her small fist on the steering wheel again. "Where did he go?"

"Well, unless that old low-rider can sprout wings and fly, he either went straight ahead, or he turned left or right." Following this uncalled-for sarcasm, Daisy's snort was of the derisive sort. "Either way, you've lost him." Her chuckle could be filed under "self-satisfied." "We might as well head back to the Columbine."

"Oh, *shoot*!" Yes. That is precisely what she said. And like the straight arrow she was, Sarah went straight ahead. Within less time than it takes to think about it, her F-150 was out of sight of Mrs. Reed's muscular young boyfriend.

JUSTIFIABLE HOMICIDE?

That's how the owner of the Chevrolet Camaro saw it. But despite his slowly growing anger, the dangerous man could not help but smile. Even a casual passerby with one glass eye would have noticed that there was more anticipation than mirth in his twisted grin. Like Daisy when Sarah's hat was tossed into her lap, the party who had suffered the offense was determined to get even. He was already beginning to savor the sweet foretaste of vengeance. But the disciplined young man knew that a fellow shouldn't start slicing his cake before it was baked. The first order of business was to find out who owned the pickup.

Chico Perez hoped it would turn out to be the girl he'd seen driving it.

TEMPORARILY THWARTED

Sarah Frank continued for almost two miles before she gave up her futile effort to locate the Camaro. But the Ute-Papago orphan was not about to abandon her effort to assist Scott Parris in his investigation of Mrs. Reed, thereby earning the undying gratitude of the chief of police and eternal admiration of Charlie Moon. *All I have to do is ask somebody at the country club who the big guy with the curly blond hair is and then I'll look him up in the phone book.* Very sensible.

Except for a few minor issues.

For starters, Sarah was not acquainted with that stratum of society that could afford membership in the exclusive club.

For another, the assistant groundskeeper's number was not in the telephone directory.

Last—and this was a very serious issue—any inquiries Sarah Frank might make at his place of employment would almost certainly help Mrs. Reed's angry boyfriend find out *who she was* just that much faster.

HOMEWARD BOUND

During the long drive back to Charlie Moon's cattle ranch, Sarah—who was occupied with a multitude of regretful thoughts that all began with *Oh, I wish I had*—had nothing whatever to say to Miss Daisy.

Which was fine with the Ute elder, who was busy reliving her delightful little adventure, recalling every word she'd said to the cheating married woman and that ridiculous young man with dark skin and curly blond hair. *That was more fun than I've had since last year when I finished off that half-naked excuse for a man who tried to—*

But that particular felony (committed with considerable malice aforethought and substantial enthusiasm, that had resulted in serious and permanent physical and psychic injuries to a fellow human being) is best left in those not-so-dim mists of recent history. Let it simply be said that despite her well-deserved reputation for creative mischief, upon that occasion Daisy had truly outdone herself. Within a few days, she will upstage that singular accomplishment with another record breaker.

But we must not anticipate; this eventful day is not yet over.

With a clearing of her throat as a preamble, Daisy Perika said something that astonished her youthful companion: "I'm sorry about messing up. All I wanted to do was take a nice little walk with the dog." She made a big show of patting the hound, who was resting his homely head on the seat between them. The astute old canine cracked his left eye to glare suspiciously at the elderly hypocrite. As she addressed the girl, Daisy smiled sweetly at the animal. "After we walked for a little piece, I got all turned around and couldn't find my way back to the truck. And before I knew what'd happened, me'n this lop-eared old fleabag walked right up on that white woman and her boyfriend." She added in a contrite tone, "I shouldn't have poked my nose into your business." Apparently overcome by her confession, Daisy wiped at dry eyes. "I should've stayed at the ranch this morning and let you take care of this spying all by yourself."

All this from a testy old woman who never, ever apologized. Sarah Frank was obliged to forgive Daisy's multitude of trespasses. "Oh, that's all right."

"No, it's not." The repentant sinner shook her head. "Except for almost getting us killed at that red light, you did a fair job today and you ought to get all the credit when you tell Charlie Moon what you found out about that married woman and her boyfriend." Daisy shot the girl a sly sideways glance. "And if it's all the same to you, I'd just as soon my nephew didn't know how I made such a fool of myself when I took the dog for a walk."

"All right, I won't tell him." But good-hearted as Sarah Frank was, and loath to attribute less-than-charitable intentions to another person, she could not help being just the least bit suspicious of the old woman's motives.

CHAPTER TWENTY-FIVE

SARAH MAKES HER REPORT

But not during suppertime at the Columbine, when she was seated conveniently at Charlie Moon's right hand. Though the tribal elder's beady little black eyes sparkled with anticipation, Sarah Frank said not a word about what she had accomplished.

Sarah also kept mum while drying the supper dishes that Charlie had washed.

Daisy Perika took her time clearing the table, wiping imaginary spots off the red-and-white-checkered oilcloth and tending to any unnecessary task that would keep her within earshot of her nephew and Granite Creek County's youngest private eye.

It was not merely Daisy's expectant hovering that unnerved the girl. During supper, Sarah had been thinking over her adventure. After considering the risks she had taken, how the pair of snoopy GCPD cops had almost spoiled everything, how close she had come to having a terrible automobile accident, not to mention (which she couldn't) how Aunt Daisy had come within a hairsbreadth of turning her stakeout of Mrs. Reed and her boyfriend into a humiliating fiasco—the amateur detective began to feel very amateurish indeed. Sarah seriously considered concealing the entire matter from Charlie Moon. On the other hand . . . *I did find out something that might help Mr. Parris.* On the *other* other hand . . . *Charlie might get upset if he finds out what I did.*

No matter. What it all boiled down to was—*I have to do what's right.*

Sarah waited until the man of the house had withdrawn to his upstairs office and shut himself inside to tend to some business. When she tapped a tentative knuckle on the door, Moon was busy copying receipts that documented operating expenses he would deduct on next year's tax return. If there was a next year for his cattle operation. Leaving his Canon PC copier to shut itself down, he opened the door to smile at his favorite teenager.

Avoiding his direct gaze, Sarah spoke barely above a mumble. "I'm sorry to bother you, but I thought you might like some after-dinner coffee and something sweet."

"A cup of something hot will hit the well-known spot." Moon winked at the winsome lass with long dark locks draped over her thin shoulders. "But besides yourself I don't see anything sweet."

He thinks I'm sweet? Indeed he did, but the man she firmly intended to marry had never, ever paid her such a compliment. The confused girl glanced at the tray and felt her face burn. "Oh—I forgot the cookies. I'll bring them to you later."

"That'll be nice." He reached for what she had brought.

When Sarah refused to let go of the tray, Moon got the message. "You can put it on my desk." When she did, and showed no sign of leaving, Moon got it again. "If you don't have anything better to do, have a seat." He pointed his chin at the ninety-year-old leather couch. "You can keep me company while I get some work done."

Sarah seated herself primly. Pointedly ignoring Moon's curious gaze, she rubbed a barely perceptible wrinkle from her blue denim skirt.

Figuring it was going to take some time for the girl to decide to say what she had on her mind, Charlie Moon restarted the Canon and copied a receipt from the company that had repaired the remote-control opener on the Columbine front gate for the fourth time in three years. *If those guys would fix it right, it'd save me two or three hundred bucks a year.*

His pensive guest exhaled a long, wistful sigh.

Moon ignored the signal.

Sarah upped the ante with an "ahem."

The rancher copied a receipt for a $1,240 payment to a local veterinarian. *Vaccinations get more expensive every year.*

"Charlie?"

"Yeah?" Unconsciously imitating his aunt, Moon shot the girl a sideways glance. *She looks kinda nervous.*

"There's something we need to discuss."

The rancher switched off his copying machine. "Okay, let's discuss."

"I did something today." Sarah repeated the wistful sigh. "Something that I suppose you won't be pleased about." The girl clasped her hands in prayerful fashion and offered up a hopeful big-eyed look that would've melted a glacier. "I hope you won't be really, really mad at me."

He smiled. *She's cute as a spotted puppy.*

He doesn't look *mad.* Sarah tried to smile back.

Moon swallowed the smile and replaced it with a fair-to-middling scowl. "So what'd you do, run your pickup into one of my prime Hereford bulls and make a big dent in his fender?"

"Oh, no." Sarah shook her head. Recalling her close call at the intersection in Granite Creek, she felt her face warm again. *I've got to tell him straight out.* Getting started was the hard part. In preparation for her confession, the girl cleared her throat. "You remember how you and Mr. Parris were talking about Mr. Reed's wife?"

So you were listening outside the door. Moon's phony scowl was transformed into a genuine frown. *The kid's picking up bad habits from Aunt Daisy.* "Yes, I do."

"And how Mr. Parris said he'd like to keep a close eye on Mrs. Reed—if only he had the officers available?"

"I remember that too." Moon seated himself beside Sarah on the couch.

"Well, I thought I might be able to . . . to help."

Sensing that she was about to burst into tears, Moon

looped his arm around the slender girl's shoulders. "That's very thoughtful of you."

Her eyes moist, she turned to smile at this man she would gladly have died for. "You can guess what I did, can't you?"

"When it comes to the ladies, I generally don't have a clue. But let me try some wild speculation and see how close I can get."

Entranced by his light embrace, she waited.

Moon "hmmed." Scratched his head. Then: "I bet you turned on your snazzy little laptop and got on the Internet and did one of those searches to find out whether or not the lady has a criminal record—"

Sarah was shaking her head.

The tribal investigator "hmmed" again. Stared intently at a sizable knot on the pine-paneled wall. "Okay, how about this. When you and Aunt Daisy went pickuping into town this morning, you started talking over what you could do to amuse yourself. After considering one thing and other, you two decided it might be fun to follow Mrs. Reed and find out if she was up to something. And so you drove over to her neighborhood."

Sarah nodded.

"Lemme see now. What would've happened when you got there?" The Ute continued to gaze at the pine knot. "Okay, here's how I see it. You decided to park your truck someplace where you could eyeball the Reed residence, but you needed some cover so if Mrs. Reed happened to zip out of her driveway, she wouldn't spot you."

She nodded again. *He is* so *clever!*

"Hold on a minute, I think I'm getting the picture." It was evident that Mr. Clever was pleased with himself. "Right, I can see how the whole thing unfolded. You parked your fine Ford pickup on a vacant lot across the street from the subject's home. And while you were waiting for Mrs. Reed to drive away in her pink Cadillac, a couple of GCPD bluesuits showed up in their black-and-white and tried to hassle you, and Aunt Daisy told 'em she had every right to be there because she was thinking about buying the real estate you was parked on and— Ouch!" (Sarah had elbowed him in the ribs.)

"Oh—you knew all the time!"

Despite the sharp pain in his side, Moon laughed.

She glared at the fun-loving tribal investigator. "Those two gossipy cops must've told you."

"Not directly." Moon gave her a quick hug before unfolding his lean frame from the couch. Now out of elbow-gouging range, he towered over the seated girl. "Eddie Knox gave the chief of police the lowdown and Scott called me on the phone. He said, 'Tell Sarah she'd better leave police business to them that knows how to do it.'" Moon cocked his head. "He didn't give me any advice to pass on to Aunt Daisy, because everybody knows she don't listen to a single word I say."

This was *so* embarrassing. Sarah's face felt hot as a flapjack sizzling in a skillet. "So what else do you already know?"

"Only that Knox and Slocum followed you after you took off after Mrs. Reed, but they lost you when they got involved in an accident at an intersection."

Sarah went ice cold. "Accident?"

"Nobody was hurt, but it was a close thing." Moon grinned at his recollection of Parris's narrative about how the hapless cops got a whole load of cement dumped on their unit. "I figure I've said about enough." He grinned at the girl, who was particularly pretty when she was angry. "It's your turn, now. Tell me what you found out about Mrs. Reed."

Sarah got up from the couch, smoothed her skirt again. "Oh, I don't think I found out anything you'd want to hear about."

"Try me."

"Well . . . she has a boyfriend."

A frown found its way to Moon's brow. "Is that a fact?"

Sarah's head bobbed in a perky nod. While Moon listened intently, the debut gumshoe provided a quick summary of what she had witnessed at the Sand Hills Country Club. Except, of course, for Aunt Daisy's dog walk where the old woman had stumbled and practically fallen into the muscular young man's arms. After pausing for a breath, she added, "I tried to follow—to *tail* Mrs. Reed's boyfriend when he left the golf course, but I lost him."

Charlie Moon tried to think of what he should say. At the moment, there was no purpose in reminding Sarah of what she already knew. If there was no danger in playing at detective, it wouldn't be any fun. Later on, when she was calmed down, he would have a long talk with her about how it wasn't smart to mess around in other people's private business. In the meantime, he would take it easy on the teenager. "You'll need to tell Scott about this boyfriend."

"You two apparently like to talk about what I've been doing." The girl lifted her chin in an impudent gesture. "Tell him yourself." Sarah marched out of Moon's office, closing the door behind her. It would be an exaggeration to say that she slammed it. But not by much.

And despite the fact that Charlie Moon spent the next ten minutes on the telephone updating Scott Parris on what the Ute-Papago youth had found out about Mrs. Reed and her boyfriend—during which interval he could have benefited from a boost in his blood sugar—Sarah Frank did not bring him a single cookie.

CHAPTER TWENTY-SIX

THE CHIEF OF POLICE SEIZES THE DAY

Scott Parris spent a mostly sleepless night wondering whether Sarah Frank's titillating discovery was of any importance. *Ten to one, the boyfriend will turn out to be a dead end. A waste of time. A snipe hunt.* Like a gristmill waterwheel churning up stream-bottom muck, the questions would surface for consideration, sink into the murky depths—only to rise again and recirculate through his consciousness. *Does Mrs. Reed's romance with the golf-course groundskeeper have anything to do with Sam Reed's conviction that he'll be murdered on his wife's birthday?* June 4 was getting closer with every sunrise. *If so, is Professor Reed aware—or at least suspicious—of his wife's fling with this employee of the Sand Hills Country Club?* The dapper scientist-turned-investor was something of an enigma to the down-to-earth cop, and also something of a plain pain in the butt. *And if Reed does know his missus is messing around, why didn't he tell me about it right up front?* Because he was a proud man, and embarrassed to talk about it? *Or does he want me to uncover the dark family secret on my own?* Then, back to square one. *One'll get you ten, this boyfriend will turn out to be a dead end.* With this gloomy assessment, the insomniac's internal dialogue would start all over again.

When the cold gray glow of dawn began to evict the darkness from his bedroom, Scott Parris rolled out of the brass four-poster, shaved his sunburned face, and showered while singing the lines he could remember from "Tennessee Stud" loud enough to wake up the neighbor's dog. The man who was pushing the far side of middle age combed his thinning hair in thoughtful silence. After a breakfast of oatmeal seasoned with blueberries and walnuts, GCPD's top cop called in to advise the dispatcher that he would be out of the office for most of the day. Before leaving his home, the ex-Chicago policeman paused at the hallway mirror for a last-minute inspection of his person. He started at floor level, admiring a new pair of Roper boots, approving the knife-edge creases in his black dress slacks, skipped the slightly bulging belly and homely face, and made his way up to the cherished brown fedora he had inherited from his father.

Considering the nature of his destination, Parris fastened the top button of his white cotton shirt and straightened the glistening gold shield clipped to his morocco belt. Last, he checked to make sure that the beige nylon shoulder-holster harness was tastefully concealed under his powder-blue corduroy jacket. On most days, the longtime lawman was barely aware of his sidearm, which was merely part of his attire. Today's business should be entirely peaceful, but on this particular morning the cop was oddly comforted by the cold, heavy presence of the snub-nose Smith & Wesson .38 nestled snugly under his left armpit.

As Scott Parris watched the balding, somewhat overweight fellow in the mirror reflect a frown back at him, he knew perfectly well what his two-dimensional counterpart behind the looking-glass was thinking. *Be careful out there, chum. A man in our line of work never knows what he's liable to run into—or the day when he'll draw his last breath.*

Not so very far away, another, younger man was also grabbing the day by the gullet.

GRANITE CREEK MUNICIPAL BUILDING

It was 8:02 A.M. when Chico Perez strode though the door to find the office occupied by three employees who were beginning another day's work. A sleepy little bureaucrat was setting up the coffeepot and mumbling something to himself about the damn *rat race*. An energetic lad of twenty had opened a white box of assorted doughnuts, turned on the copy machine, and was happily filling a half-dozen hardwood trays on the countertop with various and sundry forms to be filled out by citizens who had business related to the operation of motor vehicles. Perez headed directly for the third public servant, who was giving him the big-eye. Irene Reed's boyfriend leaned his elbows on the Formica-topped counter and flashed a smile at the middle-aged woman. "Hello, Phyllis."

"Good afternoon, Mr. Perez." The lonely woman stared through rose-tinted spectacles that magnified her eyes, giving the impression of one who has been frozen in a state of perpetual surprise. "So what brings you here—did you misplace your driver's license again?"

Goldilocks laughed. "I dropped by to see your pretty face."

"I bet." She smiled. *I wish.* "So what's on your mind?"

"Official business." Perez rapped his knuckles on the counter. "I'd like to buy me a dandy used pickup."

"Not a problem. Bring the owner with you, and make sure he's got the registration and title—"

"That's the problem, Phyllis. I don't know who owns this nifty little F-150—which is just what I've been looking for. I spotted it in the Smith's supermarket parking lot, and there was a For Sale sign taped onto the rear window. I was on my way to get a closer look at the truck—and damn my bad luck—the guy drives it away before I can find out who he is."

"I don't see how I can help you." Phyllis tapped her ballpoint pen on a stapler. "There are probably a thousand Ford pickups in the county, and lots of them are red."

"But only one of 'em will have this number on the license

plate." Perez pushed a small square of lined yellow paper across the counter.

The clerk looked through the bottom of her bifocals at the number, then rolled her brown eyes up to gaze at the handsome young man. "I'm sorry—I can't help you."

"But it's in your computer."

"Well . . . yes. But I'm not allowed to give you that information." Darting a wary glance at her co-workers, Phyllis lowered her voice to a whisper. "I could lose my job."

"No way we'll let that happen. But I'd *really* like to buy that pickup." He leaned closer and winked at the flustered lady. "You busy tonight?"

She held her breath for several heartbeats. *Oh, what the hell—nobody'll know but me and Chico.*

THE SAND HILLS COUNTRY CLUB

As was his customary practice, Howell Patterson arrived right on time at precisely 8:58 A.M., to back his Prius into the space marked MANAGER. Unaware that he was being shadowed by an impulsive and dangerous man, the thin, gray-suited, black-tied emigrant from Maryland emerged from his efficient automobile, closed the door with just sufficient force to latch it, and—key ring in hand—aimed his distinguished face toward the sprawling brick building where Granite Creek's privileged elite enjoyed the company of their peers. The senior administrator was turning the key in the door lock when he felt the weight of a massive hand on his shoulder. A lesser gentleman than Mr. Patterson might have cursed, yelped, or at the very least stiffened slightly at the unexpected touch. This man from Glen Burnie was made of sterner stuff. Ignoring the intrusion for the moment, Howell Patterson removed his key from the door and pocketed the key ring. Ready to face down anything from a hardened criminal to the village idiot, he turned his head just enough to raise a critical left eyebrow at the man with the heavy paw. "Oh." There was a feigned trace of disappointment in the "Oh"; the merest hint of a sneer curled his upper lip. "It is *you*."

Whom did he see?

John Law.

THE CHIEF OF POLICE IS SUBTLE

Scott Parris grinned at the snootiest man in Granite Creek County. "G'morning, Howie."

Duly distressed at being addressed in this manner, the manager of the Sand Hills Country Club raised his nose at the affront and sniffed like a pedigreed French poodle appraising a back-alley mutt. "To what do I owe the dubious distinction of an early-morning visit from the township's chief constable?"

The chief of police chuckled. "I'm here to do you a humungous favor."

"Indeed?" Howell Patterson placed his right hand over the left side of his chest, whereunder he firmly believed his blood pump to be located. "Oh, be still my racing heart!"

"Ha!" The big cop slapped him on the shoulder. "I like to drop in on you, Howie—you always cheer me up. And you don't fool me—under that uppity exterior, you're a regular, ordinary snob."

The Marylander arched his brow again. Under it, his left eye emitted a minuscule twinkle. "When I update my résumé, may I use you as a reference?"

"Sure." Parris pushed the battered fedora back from his forehead. "But only if you're applying for a job a long ways east of the muddy ol' Mississip'."

"I will be delighted to comply with that condition." The manager opened the door. "Please come inside. While I prepare a fresh pot of English breakfast tea and warm up some scrumptious homemade crumpets which I have in my briefcase, we can continue to exchange asinine remarks which in these parts pass for witticisms."

Parris accepted the invitation and was surprised—nay,

astonished—to learn that Mr. Patterson was serious about the tea and not kidding about crumpets in his valise. After waving off a sterling silver cream pitcher, downing the steaming black tea in two gulps, and making short work of a couple of crunchy crumpets, the cop broached the business that had brought him to Howell Patterson's office so early on a fine May morning. "Here's the deal—I need some information that'll help me protect and serve the citizens hereabouts. But do I go to the DA and ask for a warrant—which I'd get in a Colorado minute—but which would cause a big stink here at the country club and embarrass my friend Howie no end?" Parris shook his head. "I do no such thing. To spare you the humiliation of anything that might look the least bit like a potential scandal, I drive all the way over here to provide my favorite country-club manager with the opportunity to tell me what I need to know *right up front*. That way, we avoid all the nasty rumors that'd keep rich folks' tongues wagging around here for months on end, maybe even weeks."

After removing an immaculate linen napkin from his lap, Howell Patterson clasped his hands together. "What, precisely, do you wish to know?"

"Now that's the spirit." It was essential to avoid raising any suspicion about a particular groundskeeper, whom Howell P. might already know was enjoying clandestine meetings with Mrs. Reed. Parris leaned forward and lowered his voice to a discreet whisper. "The names and addresses of all your employees."

Howell's left eyebrow arched for the third time in one day, which was practically unprecedented. "May I assume this has something to do with the groundless allegations that someone—presumably a club employee—has been pilfering unlocked vehicles in the members' parking lot?"

This is too easy. Grateful for the unexpected gift, GCPD's top cop assumed a deadpan expression that hinted that Patterson was right on the mark. "At the moment, I'm not in a position to respond to that question." The chief of police attempted one of those semi-sly shrugs that is intended to be interpreted as *meaningful.* "But I will go so far as to say that you're nobody's fool, Howie."

"I am entirely undone by such high praise." The manager unlocked a desk drawer, removed a leather-bound loose-leaf notebook, and placed it on the precise center of the glassed desktop. Both eyes twinkled at Parris. "As it happens, I am not authorized to release such information without a warrant." With a practiced flick of the finger, Howell Patterson opened the notebook at a green plastic separator labeled CONFIDENTIAL EMPLOYEE INFORMATION. He consulted his Rolex Oyster. "If you will excuse me for—let us say a quarter of an hour—I shall leave my office and attend to some unspecified business." He got up from his chair. "Please feel free to help yourself to whatever may tempt your fancy . . . among the remnants of our light breakfast." Before departing, he thoughtfully turned on his copy machine.

Twelve minutes later, Scott Parris left the Sand Hills Country Club with a napkin-wrapped crumpet in his jacket pocket and, for dessert—the name, birth date, and Social Security number of Mrs. Reed's lover, also a slightly blurred facsimile of the muscle-bound man whose curly yellow locks hung to his broad shoulders.

When the time was right, the chief of police figured he would pay a courtesy call on the boyfriend and offer the reckless young fellow some sage advice about how it was inadvisable to mess around with another man's wife, especially in a county where ninety-eight husbands out of a hundred packed six-shooters and the other two used razor-sharp bowie knives to get the point across.

But that public-service work was somewhere near the bottom of Scott Parris's to-do list. It would have to wait until the busy cop had a few minutes to spare.

CHAPTER TWENTY-SEVEN

THE COUNTRY CLUB MANAGER'S SMALL VICTORY

Before the chief of police was quite out of sight, Howell Patterson had returned to his office, checked the 990-gigabyte cache memory on his high-end copy machine, and determined that the coarse policeman had copied only one page from the Confidential Employee Information. His suspicions verified, the savvy manager of the Sand Hills Country Club made an instant decision. Seating himself behind his immaculate desk, he paused to purse his lips in anticipation of the pleasure he would derive in lording it over a lesser soul. Thus prepared, Mr. Patterson lifted his cordless telephone from its cradle and made the call.

BACKFIRE

This was not a time to mess with Janey Bultmann. Testy on her best days, the lady was (for the sixth time this week) attempting to quit smoking before she left on her annual vacation. Busy at her cluttered pine desk, she wore three nicotine patches (don't try this at home!) and was chewing a disgustingly sweet cherry-flavored nicotine gum. When her plastic Walmart telephone jangled, Janey lurched and yelped. Being a marvelous multitasker, simultaneously with the lurch and yelp, she spat the medicinal chewing gum into a cup of tepid black coffee, threw a Cattleman's Bank ballpoint pen across her small Copper Street office, and glared with heartfelt malice at the offending instrument. "Who the hell is that!" The answer to this reasonable question was provided by the helpful caller ID on her telephone. "Oh, it's that prissy little country-club creep." Pretending not to know who was calling, she greeted the man she detested in the vivacious tone of a nineteen-year-old receptionist on her first day at work: "Bultmann Employment Services. How may we help you?"

"This is Howell Patterson, Ms. Bultmann."

Janey B.'s minuscule supply of vivaciousness was already exhausted. "This is *Miss* Bultmann, Mr. Patterson." She snatched a half-smoked cigarette off a filthy ashtray, lit it up, and took a puff. *Oh, that's soooo good.* "What's up?"

Howell Patterson smiled at the unexpectedly apt straight line. "Mr. Perez's tenure as assistant groundskeeper at the Sand Hills Golf Course."

"What?" She coughed and tossed the cigarette butt aside, missing the ashtray by a yard. "What's the problem?"

"The first problem, *Miss* Bultmann, is that you have evidently forgotten our arrangement, which is that I decide when the services of one of your clients is no longer required at Sand Hills Country Club—without the necessity of explaining my reasons for reaching such a decision to you or any of your dubious ilk." He paused for her response, which he planned to interrupt.

Bastard. "Oh, I remember what's in our contract. But you know, I thought maybe you might let me know what'd gone wrong so I could make sure that . . . you know—"

"The *second* problem is your execrable habit of using the phrase *you know* as a byword, as it were." Patterson's self-satisfied smile bordered on a smirk. "The third is that you seem incapable of providing temporary help which meets even a modest benchmark of quality, much less the high standards of Sand Hills Country Club."

Dirty rotten stinking bastard! Janey ground her teeth. "Don't worry about Chico Perez. I'll let him know right away that—"

"In addition to not requiring his services as assistant groundskeeper, be advised that I do not want to see your temp on club property. Immediately after this delightful conversation, I shall inform Club Security that Mr. Perez is not to be admitted at the front gate."

He had pushed the frantic woman too far.

Janey Bultmann's eyes appeared to bulge halfway from their sockets. "Not even if he arrives as the guest of one of your members?" *Hah! That'll shut his mouth.* Her mouth twisted into an ugly sneer. "From what I hear, Chico is popular with some of the rich bitches who pass for high class through your fancy front gate."

"Take care what you say, Miss Bultmann." Howell Patterson paused to give this monotone warning time to sink in, and to clear his throat. "Several of your clients are still drawing pay at the club. I would hate to think of letting those unfortunates go, and taking our business to your competition. But it might become necessary if you do not learn to bridle your venomous tongue when addressing me—"

"Don't threaten me, you two-bit cross between a fussy old maid and a brass horse's ass!" *Oh, my—I shouldn't have said that!* But in for a dime, in for a dollar. "I know a thing or two about you that the president of the club's governing board might like to hear about—and he's a good friend of mine. So if you dismiss another of my clients without due cause I'll nail your nasty hide to the barn door and charge your fancy-pants club members a dollar a pop to shoot bullet holes in it!" Janey Bultmann cut the connection before Howell Patterson could reply to this concoction of outrageous bravado and sinister innuendo. Getting in the last word made Janey feel better than she had when she gave up smoking after breakfast this morning. "Ha-hah!" She picked up the noxious butt, which was busily burning a small brown hole through the cover of *Time* magazine, and popped the deadly pacifier between her lips. "That'll give that mean little bastard something to think about!"

It did.

Pale with rage and nauseated with stomach-curdling fear, the austere manager of the Sand Hills Country Club placed the telephone gently into its cradle without exhibiting the least outward evidence of his emotions. *What an odious woman.* He frowned at the lovely view framed by his office window. *She's bluffing, of course.* As was his habit when vexed, Mr. Patterson pulled at the lobe of his left ear. *That vicious harpy knows nothing of my past.* For the cautious soul, there is always a But.

But what if she's not bluffing?

THE LADY'S LAST-MINUTE BUSINESS

After allowing herself a full four seconds to calm down, Miss Janey Bultmann looked up her client's cell-phone number and placed a call.

Chico Perez was saying hello when the woman's raspy voice shouted in his ear.

"This is Janey, sweetheart. Bad news, baby. You're fired. Pink-slipped. Canned. Sacked. Laid off. Made redundant." She listened to Perez's response. "No, the silly little prig didn't say why, but we can guess, can't we?" The smoker paused to cough. "You've been messing around with one of those married women at the club again, haven't you? No, don't tell me, let me guess. I bet the lucky chicky is that good-looking Mrs. Reed." Janey took another puff before lighting a fresh cancer stick with the butt. "Okay, don't tell me if you don't want to." The busy businesswoman glanced at her wristwatch. "Look, I'm getting ready to hit the road on my vacation but I'll cut you a paycheck and get it in the mail before I close up shop and— What?" She shrugged. "Okay, sweetie. Just this once, I'll pay you in cash. But you'll have to sign a receipt. And I can't wait all day; I'm about to close so I can go home and pack for my trip." Another puff. "Okay, honey-bun. Yeah, that'll work fine. See you then, big guy."

ROUTINE POLICE PROCEDURE

Scott Parris barged through the doorway into his second-floor corner office, seated himself behind his desk, and started tapping on the computer keyboard. After accessing a familiar site, touching the Return button, and waiting for a dozen seconds, a Chico Perez with a matching Social Security number and birth date popped onto the screen. According to an appended note, less than seven months ago Mr. Perez had reported losing his Social Security card and applying for a new one. The cynical lawman snorted. *I bet he's also got himself a forged birth certificate.* The cop clicked on another link and performed a routine criminal-background check. As Parris had expected, this preliminary search turned up nothing of importance. *Either the guy's clean as a whistle or he's hiding his past with faked ID.* His mouse finger decided to click on the box next to a line that read TRAFFIC VIOLATIONS. After an annoying delay while the sizable .pdf file downloaded, he leaned close to the screen to squint at a facsimile of a speeding violation issued in Bloomington, Indiana. The infraction was no big deal. . . . *But wait a danged minute.*

A curious detail had caught the cop's eye. He did some mental arithmetic. *That ticket was issued thirty-five years ago. Which would make Mr. Perez at least fifty years old.* He grinned. *Maybe I ought to take a closer look at Mrs. Reed's boyfriend.* Parris promised himself that when he had a few minutes to spare, he would fax a form to the FBI requesting detailed information on the Chico Perez with the Social Security number listed in the country club's employment records. *Unless I forget to remember—I'd better make myself a note right now.* The harried public servant was looking for something to write on when he was distracted by the musical warble of his desk telephone.

"Parris here."

"Hiya, Scott. It's me—Pug. I wondered whether you could join me for lunch?"

The chief of police rarely got an invitation from the district attorney. "Sure, if you're buying."

"That all depends on you." DA "Pug" Bullet's chuckle might have been a death rattle. "If you can come up with some official business we gotta talk about, I'll put both our meals on my expense account."

Scott Parris decided that this call fell under the heading Providential. "Well, as a matter of fact, there might be a thing or two we need to discuss."

"Okay, fellow grafter. See you the Silver Mountain main dining room in twenty minutes."

CHAPTER TWENTY-EIGHT

SAMUEL REED'S MYSTERIOUS RENDEZVOUS

No. Resist the temptation to leap to an unwarranted and uncharitable conclusion. In contrast to his wife's frivolous affair, Sam Reed's clandestine meeting was *not* with an attractive member of the opposite gender. Quite the opposite.

As he piloted his sooty-black Hummer along a mountain road nine hundred feet above Granite Creek, Professor Reed was mildly apprehensive about what might transpire at this remote encounter. But, being the plucky fellow he was, the wealthy investor plugged right along on all eight cylinders. Slowing at the designated turnoff, he shifted down and hummed along a narrow forest road shaded by a gloriously green clone of freshly budding aspens. The winding lane emerged into a small pasture frequented by deer and elk. When it dead-ended abruptly at the edge of a precipitous bluff, Reed cut the ignition and set the emergency brake. The punctual fellow checked the dashboard clock against his wristwatch and was pleased to have two reliable witnesses to the fact that he had arrived right on the minute for his appointment. Expecting the other party to show up late, he was prepared for the wait, and the panorama presented to him was so lovely as to be soul satisfying. *It is so wonderfully silent here.* Sam Reed inhaled a deep breath and sighed it out again. *I'll sit still as a stone and enjoy the quiet—*

Boom! (A five-pound meteorite falling onto the Hummer's steel roof? No.)

"Ho!" (A startled Sam Reed, who was not as cool a customer as Howell Patterson.)

"Hah!" (An enthusiastic Scott Parris, who enjoyed banging his big fist on top of other people's motor vehicles.)

Reed lowered the driver's-side window and shot a nasty look at the chief of police. "You are beginning to try my patience."

"Ah, don't be such an old poop, Sammy. What you need is some R and R." The happy cop opened the Hummer door and patted the angry citizen gently on his padded jacket shoulder. "Tell you what. Let's you and me go for a little walk so you can unwind some. We'll sniff the smelly wildflowers, commune with Ma Nature—all that baloney."

His ivory-knobbed walking stick in hand, Samuel Reed tagged glumly along behind the big, beefy man who was leading him along a deer path. Despite his initial annoyance, the scientist-investor was feeling quite at ease when they paused under a soaring old pink-barked pine that might have been the great-granddaddy of ponderosas. It was Parris's penultimate favorite spot in Granite Creek County, the top honor being reserved for the pebbled shore of alpine Lake Jesse on Charlie Moon's Columbine Ranch. From here, a man could see just about everything worth seeing and from a perspective generally reserved for the Deity. Granite Creek gleamed like the most perfectly civilized village in the world, and in every direction of the compass, misty-blue mountain ranges reclined like gigantic enchanted creatures dreaming of a mystical past that never was but should have been. Hovering protectively over all this, a stunningly turquoise umbrella that faded to a far rosy horizon.

To render the effect absolutely perfect, a regal pair of bald eagles circled overhead with impeccable dignity and grace.

After a minute or two of awed silence, Sam Reed realized that he was feeling wonderfully relaxed. *Peaceful* was the word. No, even more than that. *I feel absolutely serene.*

Like I could lift my wings and fly across yon valley and soar higher and higher until I reach that distant place where the sun sinks into the vast western sea. This was an absolutely perfect spot. But when a human being is present, he will invent a downside. The fact that Scott Parris was indirectly responsible for his joy was distinctly irksome to Reed.

"Aaarrgh!"

Jolted by what sounded like a bear's growl, Reed inquired, "What was that?"

"Me." Having cleared his throat of some unmentionable impediment, Parris spat on a pine cone and slapped Samuel Reed between the shoulder blades. "You've had enough R and R to last you for a fortnight. Let's you and me get down to some serious business."

"Oh, do go on!" Reed turned his full smirk on the cop. "I am practically quivering with feigned anticipation."

THE CHIEF OF POLICE IS
DEVILISHLY DEVIOUS

"Okay, here's the deal." In an unconsciously sinister gesture, Scott Parris pulled the fedora's brim down to shade his eyes from the sun. "After thinking over what you told me and Charlie Moon about how you figure a person or persons unknown are gonna do you in on June fourth, I've had a powwow with the district attorney. Me and Pug Bullet have decided that when a distinguished local citizen such as yourself requests help from the police, he's entitled to some consideration."

"Just like that?" Reed stared suspiciously at the cop. "What's happened—have you uncovered evidence of a threat against my life?"

Parris turned his blushing face to avoid the man's penetrating gaze. "Oh, maybe a thing or two. Nothing worth mentioning." He tilted his head to watch one of the eagles take a dive into a thermal, then soar heavenward to merge into the sun. *That sure does look like fun.* "But with you so sure your number's about up—and despite the fact that you haven't told me *why* you think somebody's gonna shoot you—it's my duty to provide whatever protection I can."

"Balderdash," Reed said. "Something has happened, and you might as well tell me."

Parris shot a sideways look at the suspicious citizen. "Well, there's one thing that's bothering me some, but you already know about it."

Reed arched an eyebrow. "Please remind me."

"Last Friday evening while you were singing with your barbershop-quartet buddies, your wife reported an attempted break-in."

"I am aware of that fact." The husband gazed at the chalky trunk of a soaring aspen whose equally pale branches were uplifted as if greeting some unseen Presence. "I am a busy man, Mr. Parris, so let's cut to the chase. What's the bottom-line purpose of this meeting?"

"I'd like to take some routine precautions, but I'll need your cooperation."

"Such as?"

"First thing, I'll need your permission to mount two or three of my night-vision TV cameras on your property. That way, if the rascal shows up again—and he might—we'll catch him on video."

Reed shrugged. "Go right ahead."

"Great." *Now for the ticklish part.* "Second thing I'll need is permission to tap your telephones."

Reed's arching eyebrow set an altitude record for the week. "Is that absolutely necessary?"

The cop nodded. "Before they make their move, bad guys who're planning break-ins commonly call the target residence to verify that no one's home."

"Ah, I see."

Pleased that this was going so well, Scott Parris added in a chillingly ominous tone, "And sometimes, they want to make sure somebody *is* at home before they bust in."

"Oh, my."

"First priority is a tap on your landline." Before taking

the final bite, Parris licked his lips. "But just in case the presumed bad guy has managed to get one of your cell-phone numbers—either yours or Mrs. Reed's—I'd like to cover those too."

"Well, I suppose that could be arranged. Except that—"

"Except that you can't give us permission to tap your wife's cell phone, and neither one of us would want to scare the lady."

"Ah, yes." Reed twirled his elegant walking stick. "Which does pose a dilemma."

Parris assumed an innocent expression. "Unless your wife happens to misplace her telephone."

"I'm afraid I don't see how that would—"

"My girlfriend, now she's sharp as a tack—has a Ph.D. in something or other. But Amber's always losing things. Her Visa card, her compact, and just last week she left her teensy little electric-blue telephone at the Sunburst Pizza Restaurant. It was lucky for her that a waitress who likes me picked it up before some lowlife got hold of it." He grinned at Reed.

"Are you suggesting that I—"

"Not me." The sworn officer of the law raised both palms to ward off the accusation. "But just on the off chance that Mrs. Reed does happen to misplace her mobile phone, you could give her yours to use while you took your time getting her a new one."

"Oh, now I see. And my phone would already be tapped."

"Right. That way, we could keep tabs on any felon who happened to call the lady of the house—without her knowing that there might be a threat against her husband's life. It's not only better for Mrs. Reed to be protected from any unnecessary worries—and I don't mean to denigrate the fair sex in any way—but a married man such as yourself is bound to know that the ladies do tend to talk to one another. And this investigation has to be done strictly on the Q.T."

"Yes. That makes perfect sense. But it does occur to me that I—"

"That you'll be without a mobile phone for a few days, which is a serious problem for a busy man of business such as yourself." Another grin. "Please ask me if I have a solution to that problem."

"Very well. Consider yourself asked."

"Thank you kindly." Parris removed a small object from his jacket pocket, which smelled faintly of Howell Patterson's crumpets. "This is a brand-new TracFone that I picked up during my lunch hour at Walmart."

Appalled, Samuel Reed accepted the instrument. "Surely you're joking—you actually dined at *Walmart*?"

"You should try it sometime, Sammy." The well-fed cop managed a modest burp. "Best green-chili cheeseburger and crispiest danged Tater Tots I've had in six months of Mondays."

A thin smile creased Samuel Reed's face. "You are not fooling me for a second, Mr. Parris."

Scott Parris returned a blank stare that might easily have been interpreted as a first-rate poker face. "What?"

"I daresay you know very well." Reed added a disdainful "hmmph" that spoke volumes.

The burly cop shook his head.

"As it happens, my dear wife misplaced her cell phone sometime yesterday." Samuel Reed sighed. "I would not care to speculate about *who* might have had a reason to arrange this beneficial mishap."

Parris shook his head more vigorously. "If you're thinking I had anything to do with Mrs. Reed losing her phone—"

"Such an unseemly thought would never cross my mind." Reed reflected Parris's deadpan expression. "But considering the remarkably coincidental nature of your sordid proposal and Irene so conveniently misplacing her mobile phone—how would you characterize the situation?"

Scott Parris thought about it awhile before grinning like a sinister jack-o'-lantern. "I'd call it *fortuitous*."

CHAPTER TWENTY-NINE

"It matters not, I've been told,
Where the body lies when the heart grows cold
Yet grant, o grant, this wish to me
O bury me not on the lone prairie."

A GENERAL SENSE OF UNEASE

A willful person who has survived to a ripe old age is likely
to suffer remorse when remembering errors made along the
way. From time to time the more sensitive souls will awaken
in the middle of the night to recall a particularly egregious
sin of commission or omission, or at the very least regret a
wrong turn made along life's journey.

Daisy Perika, who took pride in being considered ex-
ceptional, was an exception to this rule. The tribal elder had
blundered along her crooked pathway for decades, hardly
ever giving a thought to the harmful effects of her words or
deeds. If she woke up worrying about something, it was likely
to be an opportunity she had missed to feather her own nest or
get even with some pest who had crossed her path. Which was
why her recent sleeplessness was so frustrating to the callous
old soul.

As Daisy lay in her Columbine four-poster from late Saturday night until Sunday's first light, she stared at the shadowy
beamed ceiling. The insomniac also fretted, fumed, and ra-
tionalized. *There wasn't anything actually wrong with what I*

did—and I didn't even mean to do it. From the corner of her eye, she saw a moth shadow flit along the ceiling. *The whole thing was nothing but an accident.* Was that merely a shadow cast by a moth, or was it a huge spider about to drop down besider? *I was just trying to help Sarah.* Preparing herself for an encounter with an oversized arachnid, Daisy reached for a magazine on the bedside table. *If I didn't lend her a hand from time to time, that silly half-Papago girl wouldn't know which way to turn.* Hoping that the hideous creature would not fall onto her face, she rolled the magazine into a formidable spider swatter. *I don't know why I'm letting that silly business with the married woman and her boyfriend bother me so much.*

But of course Daisy did know.

What she had done had not helped Sarah Frank. More to the point, the Ute-Papago orphan was unaware of Daisy Perika's latest mischief, which was labeled TOP SECRET for the simple reason that the Ute elder had committed a serious crime—the kind for which a person can do hard time. And the worst was yet to come.

The innocent moth settled lightly on the quilt, just over Daisy's right knee.

Wham!

"Hah!" *That's what you get for pretending to be a spider.*

GUILTY AS CHARGED

After breakfast, when Daisy attended Sunday-morning Mass with Charlie Moon and Sarah Frank, the youthful priest delivered a homily that was deeply painful to the old sinner. His subject was "Why the Ten Commandments Are Relevant Today."

During her earthly sojourn, this particular pilgrim had dealt frivolously with most of them—with two exceptions. Let it be noted on her behalf that the Ute woman had honored her parents. Moreover, never in all her life had Daisy made an idol to bow down to—not literally. And it would be uncharitable to assert that this apparent virtue was merely an oversight—that fashioning an object of worship from wood or stone had never occurred to a woman who was so busy with other mischief.

What made Daisy cringe with barely concealed shame during the earnest priest's sermon was not an introspective examination of her many years of missing the mark. The guilty secret that gnawed at her vitals was that very recently she had broken the Eighth Commandment as surely as if she had shattered Moses's stone tablet personally and with malice aforethought. She was, as a Baptist minister might have said, "convicted of sin."

Which was an unpleasant and unfamiliar experience. So much so that the lifelong Catholic Christian did not dare approach the altar for Holy Communion. *If I went up there, lightning might come down from heaven, blow a big hole in the church roof, and strike me dead!* Remaining behind in an otherwise empty pew while Charlie and Sarah went to the altar to receive the precious gifts, the backsliding old soul knew what the solution was. *I'll have to go to Confession.* Daisy groaned. *It's been so many years since that last time, I don't know if I'll remember how to do it.* Surely there must be another way. The optimistic reprobate hoped that she would shed the sense of guilt after leaving church. *What I need to do is get out of here and forget about sins and all that gloomy stuff.*

What she got was just the opposite.

Even as they drove though the pleasant suburbs of Granite Creek, the remembrance of many long-forgotten misdeeds came back to haunt her. Like that time when a seven-year-old Daisy used leftover Easter-egg dye to tint her younger brother's face a fine shade of green and then scared her mother half to death with a story about how the little fellow had eaten half a bar of lye soap. This and many other regrettable instances of misbehavior (too numerous to enumerate) served to put the old woman in a repentant mood. Her maternal grandmother had told her that God kept two books for each of us, a fragrant golden-leafed volume listing our good deeds, a filthy old pulp paperback for recording our sins. The size and heft of the books increased with the entries, and when that Final Day came, one book would be weighed against the other and a fateful decision made.

Having no doubt about the outcome, Daisy decided that she ought to add some weighty stuff to the good side of the balance and . . . *Considering how close I am to the grave, the sooner I get it done, the better.* She nodded. *First chance I get, I'll do something nice.* Recalling a favorite proverb ("There is no time like the present"), she beamed a smile at the back of her nephew's head and tried to think of something sweet to say. It wasn't easy. What Daisy finally came up with was: "It's very kind of you to drive me to church this morning."

Charlie Moon, who took his aunt to church about nine Sundays out of every ten, told her she was welcome. *I wonder what that's all about.*

As well he might.

Astonished to learn that merely *trying* to be nice made a person feel good, Daisy wanted more. "Stop at that nice little candy store, the one on Copper Street where they sell homemade ice cream."

Moon grinned. *So that's it.* "You hankering for some butter pecan?"

The old woman nodded. "A half gallon ought to be enough." Daisy fished around in her purse and found a twenty-dollar bill. "I'm buying."

When the miserly old soul reached over the front seat to stuff the greenback into her nephew's shirt pocket, Charlie Moon came very near to arching an eyebrow.

Sarah Frank, who witnessed this unprecedented event from the passenger seat, did not shy away from such a display.

MAKING AMENDS

While the senior citizen was waiting in the Expedition for Charlie and Sarah to return from the Copper Street Candy

Shop, she could imagine—almost *see*—her pretty little golden-leafed book increasing in volume and heft. The calculating old soul estimated that it should take only two or three more acts of selfless kindness for it to get as big as a battleship and blow the ugly book right out of the water. Above all things, your moral philosopher hates to be interrupted while involved in the happy pastime of self-congratulation, but that is precisely what happened.

Daisy was rudely jarred from her blissful reverie by the appearance of a pimply, unshaven face at the window.

"God bless you," the young man said—his beer-and-onions breath washing over Daisy's face.

"Who're you and what do you want?" the blessed one snapped.

One direct question would have confused the youth; two queries were over the top. The befuddled fellow stared blankly at this testy mark. "Uh . . . I wondered if you might have some spare change."

She pointed a crooked finger at his runny nose. "If I did, I'd invest it in U.S. savings bonds. Now hit the road, riffraff—before I jab my thumb in your eye and gouge it out!"

Boy, this is some tough town. The panhandler backed off and ambled away. *I'd better thumb me a ride up to Boulder.*

While the ice cream was being spooned into two quart containers, Charlie Moon happened to notice that Sarah was eyeing a tiny box of chocolates with a big price tag. The tall man with the thin wallet nodded to the clerk, who got the message.

While her nephew was merely doing what came naturally, Daisy was recalling another proverb. Something about how by being kind to strangers, a person might end up doing a favor for an angel in disguise. Not that she thought that the repellent young man could possibly have been concealing wings under his tattered shirt. *But it'd be a smart move to do something nice for a heavenly messenger. Why, that'd be worth giving spare change to a dozen no-good bums.* Deep sigh. *But I'd never be so lucky as to—*

What had interrupted Daisy's thoughts? She had noticed a bewildered-looking woman limping down the sidewalk. *She looks wet as a drowned catfish; probably got drunk on rotgut whiskey and fell into the gutter. I bet she don't know where her next meal's coming from.* This was clearly no angel, but a person had to start someplace to have any hope of hitting the big score. Daisy stuck her head halfway through the car window and yelled, "Hey—Boozy Betty."

The middle-aged woman slowed, stared suspiciously at the wrinkled face in the SUV. "You talking to me?"

"Sure." Daisy nodded. "Come over here."

The pathetic figure approached. "What d'you want?"

"Are you one of them homeless persons that wanders around eating out of trash cans?"

"I guess so, but I don't remember eating anything lately."

Pitiful little thing. For the first time in ages, Daisy felt a surge of genuine compassion. "What's your name, honey?"

A listless shrug. "I don't remember."

This was almost too good to be true. *Homeless and a lunatic.* The tribal elder grinned. *I'll rack up points like Minnesota Fats on a roll.* Saint Daisy assumed an expression that was intended to be beneficent. "I'd like to help you."

"Oh." The gray face brightened. "That's awfully nice of you."

Damn right it is. "Now what do you need?"

"A smoke."

"I don't have any tobacco."

"That's too bad." The woman got a hard, glittery look in her eye. "I'd *kill* for a cigarette."

"You look like you need something to eat." Daisy pointed. "My nephew's over there in the candy store; his name's Charlie Moon. Tall galoot, skinny as a garter snake. Tell you what—you go inside and tell Charlie that his aunt Daisy said to buy you a nice big chocolate bar."

"Chocolate makes my skin break out."

Daisy sighed. *Being nice is hard work.* But, undaunted, she opted for some cheerful small talk. "Where do you live—in a big cardboard box somewhere?"

"I don't live anywhere." Another shrug. "When it's daytime, I like to hang out here on the street."

"That's nice." *She's not too bright.* "But where do you *sleep,* dearie?"

The pale, pitiful figure pointed. "You want to see, go around back—in the alley." Evidently warming to the old lady, the woman leaned closer.

As she did, Daisy caught a whiff. *Oh, my—she smells like she crawled out of a sewer.* That put an end to her experiment in charity. Before closing the car window, the aspiring Good Samaritan gave the unfortunate person directions to the Salvation Army shelter. "You stink like an outhouse in July, so first thing you should do when you get there is take a hot shower. And use a whole bar of soap!"

Without a word, the dismal soul turned away and wandered off as if in a stupor.

Try to be nice to people and what does it get you? Daisy treated herself to a melancholy sigh. *Not even a thank-you.*

By the time Charlie Moon and Sarah Frank returned, the nephew with ice cream and a big smile on his face, Sarah with a little box of chocolates in her hand and a warm feeling in her heart, the tribal elder had reverted to form.

As the amiable man got into the big automobile, Daisy Perika inquired in a peevish tone, "So where's the change from my twenty-dollar bill?"

CHAPTER THIRTY

THE GRIM WAGES OF SIN

As on every evening since Daisy Perika had committed the theft, she entered her bedroom with this thought uppermost in her mind: *I didn't do anything wrong, because I didn't actually mean to take it. Before I knew it, there it was in my hand and all I could think of was to hold on to it and hide it.* Desiring a peaceful night's sleep above all other blessings, the strong-willed woman made herself this firm promise: *Tonight, I won't look at it.* She jutted her chin. *I won't even think* about it.

Her mind was made up.

But the gradual transformation of gray twilight into blackest night began to work its dark magic on the tribal elder's psyche. Her fingers, which evidently had minds of their own, turned the latch to lock her bedroom door. She sighed. *Now what did I do that for?* Simple privacy, she told herself. *It's not like I'm afraid that somebody might walk in here and find me with it in my hands.*

But one misstep generally leads to another.

I guess it wouldn't hurt to make sure it's still where I put it.

Bending her aged back, Daisy grunted and pulled a shoebox from underneath her bed. She seated herself in an armchair and placed the box in her lap. *I know it's still in there, so there's no reason to take the top off the box and have a look.*

Her fingers removed the cardboard lid.

Her eyes peeked in.

The *thing* was there.

As if it were endowed with eyes, the purloined property seemed to look back at her. As if it had a mouth, it seemed to whisper . . . *Go ahead—pick me up.*

Who could resist such a temptation? Not Miss Daisy.

I'll check to make sure all the goodies are still inside.

And so Daisy's evening went, a mix of gloating and fretting over her ill-gotten treasure. Finally, she placed the object back in the shoebox and shoved it under the bed with her foot.

Minutes later, after Daisy had gotten into bed and pulled the quilt up to her chin, she addressed God with this solemn promise: *That's the very last time. Tomorrow I'll do something about it.*

The grandfather clock in the parlor began to sound the hour, which was a big one.

Daisy Perika counted twelve gongs and two hoots from an owl. *It's already tomorrow.*

Her bedside clock continued to tick and tock.

The owl in the cottonwood continued to announce her presence.

When the sleepless woman heard the gong that announced the half hour, she muttered, "This won't do." Foreseeing another sleepless night ahead, Daisy Perika got out of bed, slipped on her house slippers and robe, and dialed a telephone number in Granite Creek. As soon as the sleepy lady on the other end picked up, the Ute elder snapped, "This is Daisy and I know how late it is but I need to talk to you. But not on the phone so I'll get Sarah to drop me off at your place tomorrow afternoon."

"Very well, Daisy." Millicent Muntz yawned. "Good night then, and sweet dreams."

Daisy Perika did not enjoy a good night and her dreams were anything but sweet. But between brief episodes of fitful sleep, she was comforted by the thought that . . . *One way or another, I'll get this business settled.*

CHAPTER THIRTY-ONE

OLD FRIENDS

Old in the sense that Millicent Muntz and Daisy Perika were both well along in years; the period of their acquaintance was (as we shall soon see) not comparable to their longevity.

As the women sat in Miss Muntz's immaculate kitchen, sipping weak green tea (Millicent), strong black coffee (Charlie Moon's aunt), and munching almond cookies warm from Miss M.'s oven, the soul mates engaged in chitchat about this and that, and their reminiscences naturally included the adventure that had brought them together two years earlier, when the Ute elder had hatched a plan that (despite being somewhat harebrained) had resolved a dodgy dilemma that the white woman had found herself enmeshed in.

As a result of that dangerous escapade, the fragile maiden lady was convinced that she owed her life to Daisy. Millicent Muntz was not one to let a debt go unpaid; she tended to fret until the score was evened up. This aspect of her impeccable character (in addition to her natural curiosity) was why Miss M. was so eager to hear what kind of trouble Daisy was in, so that she could help her Ute friend. But being a keenly intelligent octogenarian, she knew better than to press. *When Daisy is good and ready, she will tell me what's on her mind.*

Now, whether Daisy would ever be *good* remains an unsettled issue (she is a work in progress), but by and by she signaled (by clearing her throat of cookie crumbs) that she was *ready*.

DAISY'S CONFESSION

As the Ute woman turned the translucent china cup in her hand, she assumed the offhand tone that one of her advanced years might use when discussing the unseasonably dry weather or how the print in newspapers and magazines is so small nowadays that a person can hardly read a word of it. "D'you remember that skinny little Ute-Papago girl—the orphan who moved in with me three or four years ago?"

"Yes, dear." *Poor Daisy is getting awfully absentminded.* "I spoke to Sarah when she dropped you off here this afternoon."

"Oh. Right." *Some morning I'll wake up and not remember my own name. And the day after that I'll wake up dead.* "Well, a few days ago Sarah got this notion that she should help Charlie Moon and Scott Parris with some police business." Daisy added, "Charlie's my nephew and Scott's the chief of police."

Her host nodded, but graciously refrained from reminding her forgetful guest that she knew both men quite well.

"Scott needed to find out whether a particular married woman had herself a boyfriend, but he couldn't spare a cop to snoop around and dig up some dirt. So Sarah decided she'd follow the woman and find out what she was up to."

"Really? How delightfully exciting!"

What Daisy was getting to would be difficult, so she decided to make her way there gradually. She began by making a minor confession: "I know you believe I'm sweet as honey in the comb, Millie—but you don't know me as well as you think you do. Truth is, from time to time I can be a little bit pushy."

The polite white woman concealed her smile behind a teacup.

"When I found out what Sarah was up to, I kind of bullied her into taking me along."

"I'm sure that you had the girl's best interests in mind."

Daisy shook her head. "All I cared about was getting out and having a good time."

Miss Muntz laughed. "And did you?"

The storyteller nodded. And grinned.

"Tell me all about it." So as not to miss a word of what promised to be juicy gossip, Miss Muntz leaned forward.

Daisy launched into her story, leaving out Irene Reed's identity. As the narrator approached the *good* part, she hesitated. "I couldn't see much, what with wearing Sarah's big hat and her silly sunglasses. And when those two got through clutching each other like a couple of silly teenagers and started gabbing, the thunderstorm was making so much noise I couldn't make out what they were talking about. I was thinking about sneaking away when Charlie Moon's stupid dog gave me a yank like an Arkansas mule pulling up a pine stump. And off he dragged me—in the one direction I didn't want to go!"

"Oh!" Miss Muntz set her teacup aside. "How perfectly terrifying for you."

"You can say that again." But Miss M. didn't, and Daisy continued her account of the harrowing encounter. "Well, here me and Sidewinder go, right up to where those two was standing. I didn't know what to do, so—bold as brass—I made up my mind to pretend like I was blind as a bat and half deaf and too addled to know where I was."

The white-haired lady clapped her hands. "What a *madcap* thing to do—how wonderfully clever of you!"

The elder of the pair paused for a moment to bask in the well-deserved praise. "Things might've turned out pretty well, except that dopey dog stopped on a dime and I took a tumble. I would've fallen flat on my face if I hadn't made a grab for the young man."

"Oh, my. How embarrassing for you."

Daisy groaned inwardly at the memory. "I would've gotten hold of the woman, but I was closer to him than her. Anyway, when I got my arms around him, my right hand just naturally ended up where it didn't belong."

Miss M. blushed. "Oh, *dear.*"

"That ain't the half of it." Avoiding the white woman's reproachful gaze, Daisy blinked at her coffee cup. "He had one of them long wallets that sticks out of a man's pocket."

Daisy's host was beyond blushing, even oh-dearing.

Setting her face like flint, the Ute elder made her confession all in one breath: "First thing I knew, the young man was helping me back to my feet and his wallet was in my hand and I knew he'd think I'd picked his pocket deliberately so I hid it under my shawl and got away from there as quick as I could." Which was not entirely true. A part of Daisy had been thrilled to have the wallet.

Miss M., a retired schoolteacher who had heard any number of naughty students tell everything from outright lies to poorly constructed half-truths, could read the deceit in Daisy's face. She was also a practicing Catholic who knew that a weak confession was little better than none at all.

The white woman's brittle-as-ice silence unnerved Daisy, who insisted, "I've been meaning to mail it back to him, but you know how things are when a person gets busy with one thing and another. Hard as I've tried, I haven't managed to get around to it."

"What was in the wallet?"

"Nothing much. Usual stuff."

"A driver's license?"

Daisy nodded. "And some pictures of women." *All of 'em probably married.*

"Pictures—that's all?"

"Well, there was some credit cards and stuff."

"No cash?"

"Uh . . . now that you mention it, I think maybe there was."

"How much?"

Daisy shrugged. "About four hundred and twenty-eight dollars."

Her friend drew in a long breath and let it out with a sorrowful sigh. "Daisy, dear—I know that you are a Christian." *Not an outstanding example, but one of God's children nevertheless.* "You must go to Confession."

Having been there, done that, Daisy shook her head. "Them priests are as alike as peas in a pod. If I told one of 'em what I'd done, he'd say, 'Daisy—you can't have Holy Communion till you've given that man his property back— and *apologized*.' " She banged the china cup on the kitchen table hard enough to make Miss Muntz wince. "And I ain't gonna grovel and say, 'I'm so sorry I picked your pocket,' to a lowlife rascal who messes around with married women!"

"Very well." Miss Muntz turned up her nose and sniffed. "If your mind is made up on the matter of a confession and apology, I shall not press you. But the essence of this matter must be dealt with forthwith." The former schoolteacher was not in the habit of mincing words. She told Daisy Perika exactly what had to be done and when.

The old sinner shuddered at the thought. "I have to take the wallet back to him *tonight*?"

"Immediately. I will drive you to his residence." Seeing the stubborn expression hardening on Daisy's face, she smiled as if addressing a fractious child. "But you need not confront the fellow. We'll put his wallet in a manila envelope, which you will place in his mailbox, where he'll find it on the morrow."

"I'd like some time to think about it and—"

"Out of the question." Miss M. shook her head. "If you wait for even a few minutes, you will come up with an excuse to avoid the ordeal and then you'll be right back where you started from." Practically oozing compassion, the well-meaning lady patted Daisy's hand. "But don't worry—I will be with you to provide moral support. Now where does the owner of the purloined property reside?"

Daisy fished the wallet out of her voluminous purse and squinted at a Colorado driver's license that had been issued barely three months earlier. "It says 686 Sundown Avenue."

"That doesn't sound familiar, but we shall find it. I have a detailed map of the county." Miss Muntz popped up from her chair like an impetuous teenager about to begin an adventure. "Get your coat on, Daisy—we must make hay while the sun shines!"

"I don't need any hay and the sun's already about to settle down behind the mountains," the pickpocket grumbled. But, overwhelmed by the white woman's enthusiasm and her bare-knuckled approach to matters of ethics and conscience, Daisy Perika could see no way out. *And I did come here for Millie's advice.* There was this consolation: *Once we get this done, at least I'll be able to sleep nights.* Which prospect brought on a deep sigh and a worrisome doubt. *Unless I lay wide awake thinking about how I had four hundred and twenty-eight dollars in my hand and tossed it into the wind like so much corn silk.*

Millicent looked down her nose at the dawdler. "Let's get a move on!"

"Oh, all right." Daisy heaved herself up from the chair and followed Miss Muntz into the attached garage, where the white-haired woman's Buick awaited them.

CHAPTER THIRTY-TWO

MISS M.'S PLAN GOES SOMEWHAT AWRY

The search for the place where Chico Perez hung his hat had taken them almost a mile outside the Granite Creek city limits and into a shabby neighborhood that had few street signs and no streetlights at all. The elderly white lady eased her venerable Buick slowly along the narrow strip of potholed blacktop that boasted the presumptuous title Sundown Avenue. "Ought to be called *Run*down Avenue," Miss M. murmured as she took a sideways glance at a dilapidated double-wide on a half acre littered with all manner of junk. "I realize that some people do not have the means to live in a nice neighborhood, but you would think they might at least have the pride to keep refuse from accumulating."

"One person's trash is another one's treasure." Daisy was watching mailboxes slip away behind them.

As if to accentuate an already dismal outing, a cold rain began to pelt the windshield. This unwelcome treat was followed by sheets of wind-driven sleet. "Oh my." Miss Muntz's gloved hands gripped the steering wheel tightly. "We had better find the address before the inclement weather renders our mission impossible."

The aged Indian was indifferent to meteorological phenomena, and more alert than the driver. "We just passed a mailbox 684, so 686 should be the next one."

Miss M. applied the brakes as the sedan slipped past a narrow, weed-choked driveway that provided access to a slatternly old clapboard house that was almost concealed in a grove of sickly elms and thirsty junipers. "That must be it." Uncertain of what to do next, she stopped. "I mustn't park here on the road, but there is no suitable place to pull over and— Oh, here comes a big truck behind us!"

"Take a run around the block and pick me up on your way back." With her big purse looped over her left shoulder and the walking stick in her right hand, Daisy Perika was already getting out of the car. "This won't take a minute."

Miss M. cringed as the truck looked like it might knock her beloved automobile aside like a toy car a child had discarded on the road. "But—"

Her "but" was drowned in the roar of a diesel engine as the huge flatbed roared past her sedate sedan.

The Ute woman had already slammed the car door and was toddling away toward the driveway entrance, where she expected to find a mailbox.

Miss Muntz was all in a dither. "Oh dear—what do I do now?" The storm was darkening the sky like there would be no tomorrow, and a furious hail of sleet began to pepper her windshield. The driver decided to proceed per Daisy's suggestion. "I'll drive around the block and pick her up."

Alas, in these environs there were no "blocks" to drive around, but rather a maze of meandering lanes with bewildering forks where either choice delivered the unwary tourist to an unseemly destination. And there was nary a road sign to be seen. Within three minutes flat, Miss Millicent Muntz was completely bewildered. But not discouraged. *This will take a little while longer than I estimated, but if I just keep turning right I'm bound to circle around and find Sundown Avenue again.* A reasonable plan. Unless one happens to turn right into a blacktop lane that, after a country mile, dead-ends at a long-abandoned cemetery.

With the chill wind at her back, Daisy quickly made her way to the driveway, where she found a mailbox post with yellow numbers painted on it. She leaned close to see the numerals. Whether you read the address from the top to the bottom or vice versa, it came out 686. *This is where Chico Perez lives, all right.*

But there was a minor problem, which had to do with what was missing from the post. The mailbox.

Like her friend who was piloting the Buick upon stormy seas, Mrs. Perika was not disheartened. *I'll find some other place to leave Perez's wallet where he's bound to find it, like in his car if it's not locked.* But she could not see a vehicle in the driveway. Daisy Perika turned her face toward the sad-looking little house and applied logic to the situation. *There's no lights on in the shack and no car so he's not at home.* Which suggested a straightforward course of action. *I'll leave his wallet on the front porch, then hurry back here to wait for Millie, who'll be showing up any time now.*

As we are apt to be when we make unwarranted assumptions, Daisy was dead wrong on four counts.

Millicent, of course, would not be returning "any time now."

Chico Perez habitually parked his Camaro behind the low-rent house where it could not be seen from Sundown Avenue.

All the lights *except the forty-watt bulb in the bathroom* were turned off.

But these were minor little flea-bite errors compared to Daisy's Number Four—i.e., her conclusion that Mr. Perez was not at home.

At this very moment, the muscular young man was stepping out of the shower stall and reaching for a towel to dry himself. How Perez sensed the unwelcome presence is unclear. He might have heard Daisy step on something in the front yard, or perhaps it was one of those inexplicable hunches. By whatever means, Chico Perez felt a sudden shiver of apprehension and the certain knowledge that . . . *Somebody's out there.*

By the time Daisy Perika was approaching the front porch steps, Perez, with the towel tied around his waist, was watching her from one of the squalid hut's filthy windows. *Well what's this?* He recognized the hunched form. *The old witch has come to pay me a visit.* But why would she do that? *I bet she's come to break in and steal something.*

To make her task all the easier, Perez unlatched the front door. Opened it a crack.

The chill breeze did the rest.

As Daisy was painfully climbing the front porch steps, the door was swinging back and forth. She shook her head at such carelessness. *The dope didn't even close his front door when he left.* As she leaned on her sturdy oak staff, Daisy's already wrinkled brow furrowed deeply. *I could just pitch his wallet inside the house, then close the door.*

Gesturing to her, as it were, the swinging door called out a squeaky-creaky invitation: *Come in . . . come in . . . old friend . . .*

From somewhere deep inside her own inner sanctum, a small voice urged Daisy not to enter therein. On the contrary—to *leave this place in utmost haste.*

Another (louder) voice assured her (in the vernacular of her childhood) that there was no reason to be a silly old scaredy-cat.

And that was that.

Daisy Perika stepped into the abyss.

CHAPTER THIRTY-THREE

"I've always wished to be laid when I died
In a little churchyard on the green hillside
By my father's grave, there let me be,
O bury me not on the lone prairie."

NO WAY TO TREAT A LADY

Once inside, Daisy Perika paused to lean on her walking stick. *It's awfully dark in here.* The old woman blinked. *And quiet, too.* But not for long.

BANG!

When the door slammed behind her, Daisy almost swallowed her tongue. When her heart started beating again, she assured herself that . . . *it was probably just a draft.* Whereupon she heard a raspy clickity-clatch. What was that? The door latch.

Uh-oh.

Then, a whispery ripping sound.

A shadowy form was pulling a window shade down.

Big uh-oh.

Chico Perez switched on a spindly brass floor lamp.

Daisy found herself standing face-to-face with a scowling savage garbed in a towel.

The man of the house was brandishing a butcher knife. He took hold of her with his free hand. "What's your game, you sleazy old pickpocket—you come to steal the few dollars I've got left?"

The old woman was unable to utter a single syllable. It is difficult to speak when a muscle-bound brute of a man has your neck gripped tightly in his hand.

"I ID'd the girl who drives you around in her red pickup." He curled his lip. "But I haven't gotten around to learning your name." He gave the tribal elder a shake that rattled her teeth. "So spit it out—who'n hell are you!" He gave her another, harder shake. Daisy's purse slipped off her shoulder, thudding onto the floor.

All his victim could get past her lips was a raspy "Aaarrrk."

Perez laughed, then spat in her face. And had a second thought. *Maybe she didn't come to swipe anything.* As a terrible alternative occurred to him, the young man eased his grip on her neck. "You figured you'd catch me sound asleep and . . ." He fought back the sudden chill of fear. *And put some kind of awful spell on me.* The possibilities were horrifying. *She might make a nest of tapeworms grow in my belly . . . or cause my eyes to dry up like prunes and fall out!*

Daisy was attempting to find her voice.

"Save your lies, old witch—I'll do all the talking. Here's what's going to happen next." Perez thumped her left earlobe with the butcher knife's cold steel blade. "First, I'll slice off your ears and nose and make you eat 'em." A pleased smile split his broad face. "And then you know what I'm gonna do?" Feeding on the fear in Daisy's eyes, the sadist delighted in telling her. "I'll cut out your tongue and stuff *that* down your gullet."

Daisy gulped.

He gave her a moment to digest this horror. "After you've flopped around on the floor for a while, I'll slit your throat."

The aged woman knew he wasn't bluffing.

"But while you're still breathing, I want you to know what'll happen *after* you're dead." He pricked her nose with the tip of the butcher knife. "Your friend Sarah takes an evening class over at the university. Some dark night when she's heading for her pickup truck, I'll be waiting for her in the parking lot. I bet she'll be glad to see *me*!" As he anticipated this encounter, Perez's face twisted into a hideous grin. "So what do you want sliced off first, granny—your pointy little rat ears or your shriveled-up pig snout?" He cocked his head. "Can't make up your mind? Then I'll decide for you."

Daisy Perika closed her eyes. *God help me and Sarah!*

She had never uttered a more heartfelt prayer. What she wanted was for Charlie Moon to step through the door and shoot her assailant stone cold dead.

Not a chance.

What she got was a near-death vision.

From some unfathomable depth in Daisy's memory, a recollection bubbled up of her favorite movie star. But not a jittery old back-and white flick on a TV; we're talking sure-enough Technicolor filling a mile-wide silver screen. And Mr. Newman (bless his sweet, blue-eyed soul) was performing one of her favorite scenes. (The one where Paul is confronted by a muscle-bound oaf about twice his size who is about to beat him to a pulp and then some.) The Newman solution had been a fine remedy for a limber-limbed movie star working from a carefully crafted script, but the aged Miss Daisy suffered from a serious handicap: *I couldn't get my foot that high if my life depended on it.*

And it did.

But if the tribal elder could not manage a vicious kick, she did carry a big walking stick—and knew what to do with it.

And she did.

As is so often the case, the element of surprise was of paramount importance. That and the fact that Daisy's oak staff caught Mr. Perez squarely in the spot where he was most vulnerable.

The butcher knife slipped from Perez's hand. The brutal bully went down with a groan, hitting the filthy oak floor like an ox felled by a nine-pound sledgehammer.

Knowing that felled oxen are apt to get up and gore a person, Daisy got a good two-handed grip on her walking stick. *I'll give him such a whack . . .*

Then . . . fade to black.

Daisy blinked. *Oh no—I've gone blind!*

Not so.

Chico Perez had yanked the lamp cord from the wall socket.

On Daisy's second blink, the young man made a grab for her leg. As Perez's fingers touched her ankle, the startled tribal elder shrieked like a banshee prodded with a hot poker— and began to flail wildly with her oak staff. There was a yelp from Perez as the club struck a glancing blow to his skull. The stunned man began to mumble incoherently.

The sensible part of Daisy's mind screamed, *Run!*

The other 99 percent was inclined to disagree. *Don't leave till you've finished the bastard off.*

Sensible never had a chance.

Her eyes now partially adjusted to the twilight in Perez's parlor, the crusty old woman raised her wooden club and laid into the task with gusto.

Wap! (Another one on the noggin.)

Being old-fashioned, Daisy Perika was not one to leave a job half done.

Wap! (Across the back of his neck.)

Wap! (Noggin again.)

This exercise went on for quite some time, but the seemingly excessive violence was not unwarranted. Daisy knew that if the young man ever got onto his feet again while she was within his reach, she would be done for. Which is not to suggest that the club wielder did not enjoy her work. When she eventually ceased wapping her victim (because she was out of breath), Daisy leaned on her stick to rest from her exertions. While getting her wind back, the tribal elder evaluated the results of her work. *There's no need to hit him another lick.*

She bent over with a painful grunt to pick up her purse, and was about to loop it over her shoulder when a potential difficulty occurred to her. *Maybe I ought to leave his wallet here.* A lady never knew when a nosy cop might show up and tap her on the shoulder and . . . *I don't want to get caught with a dead man's property.* On the other hand . . . *My fin-*

*gerprints are all over his wallet and I don't have time to
clean them off.* After weighing these pros and cons for about
two seconds, she decided to take the late Chico Perez's
property with her. And would have left straightaway, except
for the fact that she was no longer afraid. Moreover, as her
fear had gradually subsided, a white-hot fury had filled the
vacated space. As she considered the dead man's dreadful
threat against Sarah Frank, Daisy fairly burned with righteous anger. The scared old woman had been transformed
into something truly frightful—a bloodthirsty victim bent
on vengeance. *I almost wish he wasn't quite dead yet, so I
could kill him all over again—this time with his own butcher
knife!*

Which deadly instrument was on the floor by her feet.

Which circumstance gave her a fine notion.

In addition to his wallet, the furious old soul decided to
take some additional items. And so she did.

In the interest of delicacy, the personal property purloined from Mr. Perez shall be designated as keepsakes. Or,
if you prefer—mementos.

A Ute warrior would call them battle trophies.

Daisy Perika departed in the comfortable certainty that
Chico Perez was dead, and with the cheerful expectation that
his rotting corpse would not be discovered before swarms of
rats had gnawed all the flesh from his bones.

Tough old lady.

CHAPTER THIRTY-FOUR

HARD WORK MAKES HEARTY APPETITES

When Miss Muntz eventually found her way back to the spot where she had left Daisy Perika, the sleet-spitting storm clouds had drifted away. The tribal elder was waiting beside the road, her hunched form bathed in silvery moonlight. As soon as the flustered white woman pulled her Buick to a stop, the Indian opened the door and grunted her way into the passenger seat.

"I'm terribly sorry to be so long in getting back, Daisy—I realize you must've wondered what happened to me. Well, you would not *believe* the adventure I've had." Miss M. proceeded to give an account of her unnerving journey along unmarked and sinister rural roads and how she had ended up at a "horrid cemetery all grown over with weeds" where she had heard "a whole pack of feral dogs howling for blood—or perhaps it was wolves—they all sound much the same to me!" On and on, her story went by mile and by minute until every detail was duly recited for her silent passenger. Eventually, the talkative lady remembered the original purpose of the night's mission. "Oh, I'm so sorry—I almost forgot to ask—did you manage to take care of your little task?"

Daisy nodded.

Miss M., who was an ever-so-careful driver, turned her face briefly to beam on her friend. "Now that you've done the right thing, don't you feel much better?"

The woman with the trophies in her purse admitted that she did.

"Good for you! Even though I merely played a supportive role, I suggest that we celebrate our mutual accomplishment." She pondered the possibilities. "Shall we stop someplace for an evening snack?"

Famished by her exertions, Daisy suggested that they take their business to Sunburst Pizza. "I'll get me one with pork sausage and double cheese and green chili."

"An excellent choice, my dear. I shall order a medium calzone with Italian sausage. No bell peppers, if you please."

This reference to calzone was a private joke, and both women laughed.

Just like old times.

NOT EVERYONE IS HAVING A PLEASANT EVENING

Chico Perez had never been a fan of Paul Newman and he had no taste whatever for Westerns. The brutal fellow's favorite movie was the original *Terminator*—and like that remarkably resilient android, Perez was hard to kill. At the very moment when Daisy Perika and Millicent Muntz were about to chow down on greasy pizza and succulent calzone, the severely injured fellow uttered a low, painful groan.

Mr. Perez was flat on his back—staring dumbly at the cobwebbed ceiling. *What the hell happened to me—I feel like I was run over by a truck.* Even in his stupefied state, he realized that such an event was unlikely to have occurred inside his living room. He strained to come up with a better explanation. *Somebody must've beat me up.* But the man who'd never been bested in a fight also dismissed that explanation as improbable. Gradually, in bits and snatches, the events of the evening began to come back to him. *It was that mean old woman—the pickpocket witch.* Perez concluded that the thief had cast some kind of spell on him. *Maybe she called down lightning and I got struck.* Rubbing a hand over his face, he felt sticky blood on his forehead.

Groaning pitifully, the muscleman got to his knees. Grasping the brass floor lamp, Perez pulled himself erect. After staggering, tripping over the lamp cord, and tumbling over a coffee table, he got up again, stumbled into the bathroom—and switched on the light to see what damage had been done.

Several of Chico Perez's neighbors—two of them almost a quarter mile away—heard the mutilated man's horrified screams. Not one of them thought of calling the police.

It was that kind of neighborhood.

Miles away, in a corner booth at the Sunburst Pizza Restaurant, Miss Millicent Muntz tapped a paper napkin at her lips. "The calzone was very tasty."

"My pizza's awfully greasy." Daisy belched. "But that's the way I like it." One small piece remained on her plate. *I'm full, but I'll wash this last bite down with some coffee.*

Pleased with her success in reforming the aged sinner, Miss M. waved at the waiter. "This meal is on me, Daisy."

The words *Oh no, I'll pay for what I ate* were almost out of Daisy's mouth, and her fingers were already unsnapping her purse—when she remembered what was inside it. The Ute elder withdrew her hand and smiled sweetly at her *matukach* friend. "Why thank you, Millie—that's very kind of you."

CHAPTER THIRTY-FIVE

HARD TIMES BLUES

There was no pretty way to put it: the Columbine Ranch was going under.

Charlie Moon had seen this black day coming for weeks, but the steely-eyed man who'd faced down snarling mountain lions, gun-toting hardcases—and even his aunt Daisy—had managed to find all manner of semiplausible reasons and farfetched excuses to avoid doing what had to be done. His most recent hope had been Samuel Reed's forecast of an increase in the price of beef. But even if the successful investor's insider information about a hoof-and-mouth outbreak in Argentina was right on the mark—and Moon figured that was a hundred-yard shot at a gnat's eye with a slingshot—there were bills and wages that had to be paid *today*. After he attended to that grim task, there would be about enough left in his account at the Cattleman's Bank to buy groceries and gasoline for a few weeks. The compulsive gambler was feeling like the village idiot for having bet his county back pay on the wager Reed had proposed to Scott Parris, but ten-to-one odds had been too enticing to pass up. And it seemed highly unlikely that Professor Reed would be dead or all bunged up when the sun came up on June 5. Problem was, by the time the rancher collected his hoped-for winnings, the Columbine cattle operation would be history.

A few minutes after sharing breakfast with Daisy and Sarah, Moon retreated to his upstairs sanctum with a third cup of coffee. While standing at the window, he turned on the FM radio and listened to the Gawler Family "Shinglin' the Roof." The music from Maine was fine and dandy, the splendid view of snow-capped granite peaks also lifted his spirits, and the flood of golden sunshine streaming inside hinted that Good Times were right around the corner. *Maybe I should wait for another day or two before I break the bad news to my employees.* But after he'd heard the *Morning Farm and Ranch Report,* the troubled stockman realized he was all out of reasons and excuses. Cattle prices had taken still another hit and it didn't take a razor-sharp wit to read the proverbial handwriting on the wall.

Whether a man is pulling an abscessed wisdom tooth with rusty wire pliers or castrating a wild-eyed bull calf with a Case pocketknife, he gets the job done *quickly.*

Moon downed his last gulp of honeyed black coffee, snatched up the telephone, and put in a call to his foreman. As soon as he heard Pete Bushman's gruff "Hello," Moon barked back, "I want every man on the Columbine in the bunkhouse at ten A.M. sharp. No exceptions except for the half-wit who's in jail for throwing another drunk through a barroom window, the bronc rider who's laid up in the hospital with a busted pelvis, and that pair of West Texas outlaws that're five miles away riding fence."

When the boss of the outfit used that flinty tone, his brash, backtalking second-in-command cleared his throat and rasped, "Yessir, I'll see right to it." *He's gonna do it.* The foreman returned the telephone to its cradle and turned to his plump wife with a bad-news expression that hinted of deep, dark depression. "I told you this was comin'. He's shuttin' the ranch down."

The woman sighed and closed her eyes. "Oh, Lord help us all."

Dolly's bushy-faced husband patted her on the shoulder. "Now don't you worry, ol' girl—you'n me'll be all right. Why we're safe as . . . as . . ." *As snowballs in hell.* Pete turned abruptly, jammed a faded felt cowboy hat down past his ears, and booted his way across the parlor. He was out the front door and stomping across the porch before Dolly could sense the cold fear that twisted his entrails. *If I have to, I'll get me a job fryin' hamburgers.* He blinked bleary eyes at the Too Late Creek bridge. *If anybody in his right might would hire an old geezer like me for work a boy can do.* "Damn!" The eighty-year-old man kicked one of Dolly's dead potted plants off the porch.

This served to boost Pete Bushman's morale by a notch or two, but did nothing to help his big toe, which was already sore from being deliberately tromped on yesterday by a mare with a mischievous sense of humor.

10:03 A.M.

The bunkhouse slept forty, but rarely all at once because the men worked in twelve-hour shifts and a few were generally out tending to sick cattle, hunting predators, or raising bloody hell in Granite Creek saloons and then spending a few days (without pay) in jail. A privileged few (Foreman Pete Bushman, top hand Wyoming Kyd, and the burly blacksmith) had private quarters.

Charlie Moon, who breathed higher-altitude air than the tallest of his employees, stood like a lone pine at the east end of the crowded shotgun-style building. The Ute waited patiently for the murmuring of some fifty-five toughs to die down. When it didn't, the owner of the outfit raised his hand. The effect was instantaneous silence.

"I expect you fellas know what this is all about," Moon said.

They did. More or less.

"Times are tough. I won't waste my breath telling you how foreign beef is eating our lunch and operating costs keep on going up. You know all about that."

Somewhere near the rear of the gathering, a Mexican cowboy spat into a galvanized bucket of sand provided by the management for that purpose.

A grizzled old hand from Montana spat a salty expletive.

Moon ignored these pithy comments. "Here's the deal. I've got to sell twelve hundred head of prime stock—and at prices so low it'll be like slitting my throat." From the rancher's grim perspective, Samuel Reed's hopeful forecast had dropped all the way from *long shot* to *daydream*. "With most of the purebred stock trucked out, there won't be much work to do around here. And even if there was, I couldn't meet payroll."

Fifty-five pairs of eyeballs burned holes in the boss.

"I don't know of any fair way to decide who goes and who stays," Moon said. "You're all worth your pay and more."

Several snorts greeted this exaggeration. There were three notorious malingerers on the Columbine, a couple of drunks who could barely roll out of their bunks, and then there was Six-Toes, a ratty-faced lowlife detested by one and all.

"So here's the deal. This'll be handled more or less like you fellas had yourselves a union. The employees with highest seniority stay on the payroll." *For a couple of weeks.*

This was greeted with several sneers and a few moans and groans. Everyone present knew that Six-Toes had been on the Columbine almost as long as Charlie Moon, and a few months longer than the Kyd.

The man who boasted an extra digit on each foot displayed a satisfied smirk.

Moon had to steel himself against an overwhelming temptation to punch the mean cowboy senseless. Which, considering the fact that Six would have had to enroll in a five-year correspondence course to work his way up to moron, seemed more than a little redundant. Realizing that his hands were rolled into fists and weren't of a mind to unwind, the Ute concealed the pair of knucklear weapons behind him. "Excepting a few of you who have special skills, the forty men with the shortest time are laid off." Moon passed a sealed envelope to his foreman. "Pete'll read the names off and see that you get paid off in cash." After clearing the lump from his throat, Moon managed a few more words. "You're all welcome to stay on the Columbine until you find another job, or until things pick up here and we need more help, or . . . till hell freezes over." *This is even harder than I thought it'd be.* "You can sleep in the bunkhouse and you're welcome to all the coffee and biscuits and pinto beans you can choke down." *Until that runs out too.* The longtime poker player couldn't read their stares. Moon took a deep breath. "I'm sorry, men. If I was a better rancher, this wouldn't be necessary. But I'm not, and it is." He turned on his boot heel and left the bunkhouse.

This was very close to being the hardest thing Charlie Moon had ever done—which was wrapping his mother's frail corpse in an old blanket and laying her to rest in *Cañón del Espíritu.*

Inside the Columbine headquarters, Moon collapsed onto a chair by the hearth. *I never expected to get rich selling beef on the hoof.* He watched the last amber embers die in the fireplace. *All I wanted was to be a cattle rancher.* Well, a little more than that. A *successful* cattle rancher. It never entered his mind to blame the five-year drought, the annual scourge of range worms and locusts, the Argentines and South Africans who were underselling American beef, or hard times in general. The buck stopped here and the bottom line was that Charlie Moon was responsible for what happened on the Columbine.

The on-the-wagon alcoholic who attended AA meetings almost every week got up, took nine long strides across the parlor, and stomped through the headquarters dining room and into the kitchen, where he poured himself a stiff drink that would've stopped a runaway freight train on a dime, or a charging buffalo on a nickel.

No. Not *that.*

A man-sized mug of Aunt Daisy's brackish black coffee. Unsweetened and cold as a Yukon toad-frog's toes.

After the last gulp, the heartsick rancher set the mug aside, made a grab for the kitchen telephone, and dialed the number of a cattle broker in Denver. Moon listened to the drawling voice mail message that invited him to "tell me what's on your mind after the tone, podner—and I'll get back t'you soon as I can." When the signal beeped in his right ear, the stockman cleared his throat and heard himself say, "Hello,

Roy—this is Charlie Moon. Except for a few head of prime breeding stock, I'd like to sell off my whole herd. I'll be in and out of the headquarters, so if I don't pick up on the Columbine landline call me on my mobile number." *Well, that takes care of that.* He returned the telephone to its wall-mounted cradle. *By this time tomorrow, the Columbine'll be out of business.* The rancher felt himself getting numb all over.

But not enough to anesthetize the big hurt.

Charlie Moon wanted to go away for a while. *To some quiet place where I won't have to talk to anybody.* Or look a laid-off cowboy in the eye. *Maybe I ought to saddle up Paducah and go for a long ride in the mountains.* That sounded like just the right medicine. *I'll find a stream where nobody's fished for a hundred years or more.* The Ute sighed. *Sleeping on the ground for a few nights would do me a world of good.*

Without a doubt. But he was not about to enjoy an interlude of peaceful solitude.

Dr. Fate had written an alternative prescription for this soul-weary man who sought a few hours of peace.

Call it a diversion.

CHAPTER THIRTY-SIX

COMPANY'S COMING

For men like Charlie Moon, the old saying that misery loves company does not apply. The Ute found his healings in solitude. If the troubled rancher had made a list of what he least wanted at the moment, visitors would have been right up there with turpentine in his coffee, an enraged scorpion in his sock, and a registered letter from the Internal Revenue Service. Matter of fact, if Mr. Moon had known that the unlikely pair of hombres was headed thisaway, he would've already been straddling his favorite horse and headed for the lonely wilderness north of Pine Knob.

Most likely because he was distracted by his problems, the keen-eared Ute did not hear the approach of the familiar automobile until it rattled over a half-dozen loose redwood planks on the Too Late Creek bridge—and they don't call the stream that for nothing. There being no ready escape, Moon was obliged to go to the west porch and greet his best friend and—as it turned out—the grinning citizen the chief of police was hauling in the passenger seat of his sleek GCPD black-and-white.

Why was Samuel Reed's happy face split practically ear to ear?

We are about to find out.

Braking to a stop under a gaunt cottonwood, Scott Parris addressed his companion. "You stay put while I go talk to Charlie."

"Very well." Professor Reed clasped his hands behind his neck. "Whilst you convince the Indian sleuth to provide his expert assistance, I shall entertain myself by enjoying the picturesque ruralosity of our surroundings and"—he sniffed—"the earthy fragrance of an aromatically authentic cattle ranch."

"You do that." *Silly little twerp.* On the hour-long drive from Granite Creek, which had taken a week, the no-nonsense chief of police had grown bone-weary of Reed's incomprehensible witticisms, effete affectations, and other annoying mannerisms. Craving the company of a sure-enough man, Parris slammed the car door and marched across the yard toward the genuine article. "Howdy, Charlie."

The melancholy Ute greeted his *matukach* friend with a nod.

The white cop bounded up the steps. "I brought somebody to see you."

"I noticed."

"You have a calendar on your kitchen wall, so you may've also noticed that this is the first day of the month that generally follows May."

Moon reached out to shake his friend's hand. "And on Friday the fourth of June—which is Mrs. Reed's birthday and only three days away—Sam Reed figures somebody's gonna shoot him dead."

"He does, Charlie—and he just might be right." After reminding Moon of his suspicion that Mrs. Reed's 911 call about a break-in was a phony, the chief of police described his routine background investigation of Mrs. Reed's boyfriend. "Whoever this joker is, he ain't Chico Perez. That name's bogus as a Lincoln penny dated 99 B.C."

"You figure you're dealing with some kind of outlaw?"

"Oh, Perez is a bad apple, all right." By force of habit, the town cop turned to glance at his sleek squad car. "At the very least, the bastard's probably got a wife and kids somewhere that don't know where their next meal is coming from."

"So who do you figure for pulling the trigger on Reed—the wife or her boyfriend?"

"Could be either one of 'em." Parris heaved his big shoulders in a shrug. "Or maybe it's a conspiracy. They might be working as a team."

"Does Sam Reed suspect his missus?"

"Nah. The guy's smart about lots of things, but where his pretty wife is concerned, he's got a blind spot a mile wide." Parris briefed Moon on how he'd persuaded Samuel Reed to loan his wife a tapped mobile phone to replace the one she had misplaced.

"And this TracFone that you gave Professor Reed—is that one tapped too?"

"Sure. And before you insult me by asking, he agreed to both taps." The white cop gave his Indian friend a pleading look. "Bottom line is this—we gotta find some way to keep this guy alive."

Moon returned a puzzled expression. "We?"

"Sure. That's why I'm here." The white cop turned his sunburned face away to avoid the part-time deputy's earnest gaze. "I don't have to tell you how shorthanded I am." He waved off an imagined protest. "And don't remind me how long it takes the county to pay you." Now Scott Parris was prepared to beam his blue eyes on Moon, and he did. "But not to worry, my friend—I've taken care of both problems." He shot another sideways glance at his patrol car. "Or maybe it'd be more accurate to say that Sam Reed has."

That was a no-brainer. "So he's agreed pay my wages."

"Damn right, Charlie." Parris's broad face had the beginnings of a grin. "And the man's no cheapskate. Wait till you hear—"

"I'd like to help you, pardner." Moon squinted at the pale blue sky and sighed. "But I've got a lot on my plate right now."

"Hey, I knew you'd say that. But don't tell me you're too busy fattening up beeves to help me save Sam Reed's life— tell *him*."

"Okay." Moon's tone was grim. "Bring him on."

Parris waved a come-on gesture at the wealthy investor, who got out of the police car and strutted across the yard like (Moon thought) *a banty rooster about to pick a fight with a forty-pound bobcat.*

After exchanging nods with Samuel Reed, Moon accepted the man's outstretched hand and gave it a shake.

Releasing the tribal investigator's big hand, the dapper little man jerked his head toward Parris. "Our highly esteemed chief of police refuses to share the results of his investigation with me. But your bosom buddy is apparently convinced that I am destined to die just as I have predicted, which big event is scheduled for this Friday evening."

Despite his gloomy mood, Moon could not help but smile at Reed. "For a man who's about to be murdered, you're in a pretty good mood."

"Destiny," Reed replied with a wink, "is transformed by strong-willed men such as we three. With expert assistance from you two bold fellows, I hope to live to—no, permit me to amend that." He puffed up his chest. "I am *determined* to live to a ripe old age."

"C'mon in," Moon said. "I'll brew us a fresh pot of coffee." The problem was figuring out a way to say no without revealing how the expert investor's failed prognostication about beef prices had created a situation where the rancher didn't have time to *think* about Sam Reed's serious problem. For once, Scott Parris would have to work things out without any help from his Indian friend. Unless . . .

FATE TAKES A TWIST

And it was about to.

While the coffee was percolating in the kitchen, Moon's mobile phone vibrated in his pocket. After glancing at the caller ID, he said hello and drifted off into the dining room for a private conversation with his cattle broker.

"Wow, Charlie—it's a good thing I wasn't able to take the call when you left that message about selling off your herd."

"Is that a fact?"

"Well of course it is." A puzzled silence. "Say, haven't you heard?"

"Heard what?"

"You are probably the luckiest man I ever met." Roy Bivvens chuckled. "But Luck's a fickle lady, Charlie, so if you want to survive in a rough-and-tumble business like ours, you gotta learn to pay attention to what's goin' on."

Moon was beginning to get a glimmer, and his hopeful suspicions were making his skin prickle. "Spit it out, Roy."

"Hell, Charlie—you must be the only stockman in the state who don't know that the price of American beef has gone *right through the roof* during the past couple of hours. New orders from Japan and Mexico alone are gonna make you enough money to buy yourself a sixty-foot yacht and one of them executive jet airplanes and build yourself a five-mile-long runway on the Columbine and—"

Moon interrupted the absurd hyperbole: "Does this have anything to do with an unmentionable bovine malady somewhere south of the equator?"

"Dammit, you knew all along about that outbreak of hoof-and-mouth in Argentina." The broker snorted. "What kinda game are you playin' with me, Charlie—you tryin' to make a fool of ol' Roy?"

"I'd never do that." *Looks like I'm the fool.* The rancher stared through a north window, where a chill late-spring breeze was briskly sweeping away last October's dead cottonwood leaves. "I'm right in the middle of something, Roy— I'll call you back in an hour or two and talk to you about selling maybe half of my herd." He pushed the button while the broker was protesting and turned to see Samuel Reed's slight figure framed in the arched doorway between the dining room and the kitchen.

"Sell within three days," Reed said. "By next week beef prices will begin a gradual decline."

"I'm much obliged." And Moon was. The Columbine not only was saved but would turn a healthy profit for the first time in several years. Feeling light and carefree as a feather on the wind, the rancher ushered Reed back into the kitchen. "Now tell me what I can do for you."

He did.

Whatever Reed left out, the chief of police filled in.

When the dust had settled, Charlie Moon and Samuel Reed shook hands on the deal.

And some fine deal it was. The tribal investigator would be paid a flat fee that would have made a paler face blush rose-petal pink. The cash was paid up front and right on the spot, which (no barrelhead being readily available) was on the kitchen table. The Ute was also given a key to the guest house over the Reeds' detached garage. And if Parris and Moon could keep Sam Reed alive until the day after Mrs. Reed's birthday, the tribal investigator would walk away with the pot from a ten-to-one wager that would be the second-largest of his career as a bet-on-anything gambler.

Charlie Moon's biggest win some years back? There are a half-dozen rumors, a couple of them almost plausible—but the gambler has kept mum about that one. Anyway, that was way back when and this is *right now* and, starting tomorrow, Moon will be camping out on Sam Reed's ten acres, where (Scott Parris is convinced) the wealthy investor is supposed to meet his untimely end.

The bottom line was that Charlie Moon was determined to keep his benefactor alive, and when a flinty-faced Ute makes up his mind to do a job of work, rolls up his sleeves, spits on his hands, and gets right at it—the chore flat-out *gets done.*

Most of the time.

CHAPTER THIRTY-SEVEN

JUNE 2
AN ANNOYING DISTRACTION

Nineteen out of twenty stakeouts were about as interesting as watching grass wither during a long dry spell, but a lawman never knew when number twenty would pop its ugly head up and make his life excessively interesting. With this possibility in mind, Charlie Moon prepared himself for whatever he might encounter during his visit to Samuel Reed's suburban estate. Before leaving the Columbine headquarters, he strapped on his Ruger .357 Magnum revolver, dropped a small flashlight into his jacket pocket, checked the battery in his mobile phone, and, as an afterthought—slipped a couple of Almond Joy chocolate bars into his pocket to keep the flashlight company. Finally, the Catholic crossed himself and whispered a prayer for protection and guidance. Thus fortified, he stepped outside to greet a new day, cranked up his trusty Ford Motor Company SUV, and rolled away.

As he headed to the public highway, Moon proceeded slowly. Not only because the spine-jarring road needed grading; driving along at barely above a snail's pace gives a man time to think, which opportunity he used to mull over various matters. At the top of his list was the stakeout. Whether it turned out to be as dull as dirt or as wild as an 1875 Saturday night in Tombstone or Dodge City, he had to be ready to deal with whatever might come up. Such as: *What do I do if*

*Mrs. Reed's boyfriend comes gunning for Sam Reed and
there's no chance to disarm him and make an arrest—do I
shoot this so-called Chico Perez character dead or just wing
him?* Killing a man, even to save another one, was an unpleasant task. On the other hand, injured felons coupled with
shyster lawyers could create a world of trouble for a lawman.
I'll shoot him dead.

Charlie Moon also entertained some happier thoughts.
*With Sam Reed's tip on cattle prices panning out, things are
looking up.* And how he'd like to have a wife. During the
last few years, the rancher had made a go at matrimony a
couple of times but for one reason or another things hadn't
worked out. More recently, Miss Patsy Poynter had been
haunting Mr. Moon's daydreams and night dreams too. *It's
not like she don't like me.* Indeed, they were good friends.
But therein (he believed) lay the problem. *Patsy probably
sees me as a big brother.* Having suffered bitter disappoint-
ments in prior involvements with the tender gender, the county's most eligible bachelor was wary about sticking his neck
out for another potential axing.

The prospective groom would have been stupefied to
know how many fine, in-their-prime women figured he was
just about the best thing since sliced bread. Or that Miss
Poynter had set her sights on the tall, lean Ute since the time
she had first laid eyes on him. The clueless Moon thought
that Patsy brought him home-baked bread and cookies because she was a kindly young lady who knew he appreciated
such delicacies. It's a good thing the stockman understood a
lot more about cattle, quarter horses, cowboys, cougars, and
such than women.

As Moon approached the intersection where the Columbine lane terminated at the paved highway, his thoughts
about how a loving wife would take some of the rough edges
off his life were displaced by a more immediate issue. Operating expenses.

The front gate was wide open and Pete Bushman's pickup
was parked on the highway side, behind a panel truck with

GRANITE CREEK ENGINEERING, LTD. painted on the door. Bushman was watching the GCE technician remove a gray steel panel from the gate-control box, where a two-wire line from the foreman's residence was used to open the gate when someone called to request admission. The several miles of copper wire had been installed by the previous owner (now deceased), who had been almost as wealthy as Samuel Reed. *What now?* Moon pulled up beside his foreman and the young man in crisp, new blue coveralls. Lowering the window, he repeated the two-word query to his foreman: "What now?"

"Same old same old." Bushman chewed on a tobacco-stained strand of his bushy beard. "The damned—the *dad-burned* thing has stopped workin' again." At his wife's insistence, the crusty old man was trying to clean up his language. "Yesterday, I had to drive all the way out here to let the UPS truck in. After that, I just left the damned—the *danged* thing open."

Moon eyed the fellow with the digital multimeter. "What is it—a bad connection?"

"Don't know for sure. An intermittent, most likely." The technician assumed an upbeat tone. "But don't you worry, Mr. Moon. Before I leave, I'll have it working fine as frog's hair."

"Before you leave, I'll be five hundred dollars poorer." The rancher glared at the offending gate-control box. "And it won't be a month before the thing'll fail again."

Unaware of the thin ice he was standing on, the Granite Creek Engineering, Ltd., employee figured that this was prime time to make a sales pitch. "If you don't mind me saying so, what you need is a modern, up-to-date, remote-control gate opener." He turned his plump face to present a comical gap-toothed smile to his potential customer. "Nobody uses these hardwired controllers anymore. And I'm not talking about those RF devices you folks use to open and close this gate when you're within a hundred feet or so—that part of the system is working just fine." Having planned to make this pitch to the foreman, the technician just happened to have a four-color brochure in his coveralls hip pocket. "This is what you need."

Moon shook his head. "I'm not interested in sinking any more money into—"

"I got one of our System 400 remote-control units in the truck, and it ain't all that expensive if you sign up for our three-year payment plan. What you get for your money is the ability to *telephone* a command to operate your gate. Hey, you could be in China and phone in an instruction to open your gate or shut it. And you can take my word for it, Mr. Moon—the job won't be considered finished until I make your brand-new telephone-controlled installation one-hundred-percent reliable."

"This job is finished right now." The boss gave his foreman a flinty look that cut right to the bone. "Pay this young man for the time he's spent here and send him on his way."

The technician was goggle-eyed with despair. "But I'll have this thing fixed in five minutes flat and—"

The Ute glared at his crusty old foreman. "You heard me, Pete."

Pete Bushman knew when not to talk back. "Yessir."

"Oh, one more thing." Moon shifted his gaze to the sand-blasted windshield. "How many laid-off hands are still hanging around the bunkhouse?"

"All but a half dozen or so." Bushman prepared himself for the worst. "What d'you want me to tell 'em?" *No more free beans and coffee?*

Charlie Moon grinned. "Tell 'em that with beef prices on the rise, I'm only selling off about half the herd—and at a nice profit. Put 'em all back on the payroll." The rancher drove away, throwing up a cloud of dust before the rubber tires hit the paved highway.

Relief flowed over Pete Bushman like a waterfall. *I knew all along that things'd turn out all right!* The foreman also knew who the real boss of this outfit was, and when to take the bull by the horns. As soon as Charlie Moon's automobile was out of sight, Bushman grinned through his tobacco-stained whiskers at the dejected technician. "You go right ahead and fix that [coarse expletive deleted] gate."

GOING TO TOWN

About a mile and a minute before he rolled into Granite Creek, Charlie Moon placed a phone call to Scott Parris. "So how's our friend doing?"

"Sam Reed just had a haircut at Fast Eddie's," the chief of police said. "He's still in our favorite barbershop, getting a straight-razor shave."

Moon grinned. "I hope Eddie doesn't let that blade slip."

"You and me both. We've got a lot riding on ol' Sam seeing the sun come up over the mountains on Saturday morning."

The Ute's concerns were focused on Friday. "What're Reed's plans for his wife's birthday?"

"A midday feast in the Silver Mountain main dining room—where they'll waltz to the romantic sounds of Denver's Bavarian String Quartet, hired for the occasion by the man who makes money so fast he can't count it with both hands. After that, Sam'll apologize for having to work late that night—but he'll tell his wife that come hell or high water, he'll get home at eleven P.M. *on the dot.* Damn!"

"What?"

"Fast Eddie just nicked Reed on the gullet."

"Our lives hang by a silver thread, pard—we're here today, gone tomorrow, forgotten next week." As a black Corvette convertible zipped pass his Expedition at ninety miles an hour, the Indian philosopher caught a glimpse of the driver. The pale woman's long red hair was blowing in the wind like flames on a white tallow candle. "What's Mrs. Reed up to today?"

"Sam wrote her schedule down for me. Lemme see . . .

Shopping for m'lady's summer hat. Midmorning coffee at the Sugar Bowl. Shopping at Mimi's Antique Glassware. M'lady's weekly manicure. Shopping for this and that. Oh, and get this: 'Luncheon at Phillipe's Streamside Restaurant'—la-de-dah!"

Moon was making mental notes. "What're her plans for this afternoon?"

"Big surprise. Mrs. Reed will be shopping for silver candelabras."

"The variety will be good for her."

"Then she'll be having supper at the country club and after that she'll be playing cards with some of her snooty lady friends. Sam figures she won't be home until at least nine P.M., more likely ten."

"That'll give me plenty of time to get settled in before the lady shows." But there was another player. "What's the latest on the boyfriend?"

"The guy who calls himself Chico Perez don't work at the country-club golf course anymore. Also, there's no vehicle parked at his place and nobody answers when I knock on his door. His nearest neighbors haven't laid eyes on him for at least two or three days. Not only that, his rent's overdue." Parris's smile brightened his voice. "Looks like the lowlife's skipped town."

Good news was always welcome. "Have there been any telephone conversations between Perez and Mrs. Reed?"

"Nary a one. Gotta go, Charlie. Sam's out of the chair and paying for his haircut and shave." Parris brayed a mulish laugh. "Our well-heeled friend must be pretty ticked off about getting his Adam's apple sliced—he just flipped Eddie a two-bit tip!"

This reminded Charlie Moon of the token fee Lyle Thoms had promised him for assassinating Posey Shorthorse. "Every quarter dollar counts. G'bye, Scott." As he pocketed his mobile phone, the tribal investigator reminded himself that he'd made Thoms a promise, and that . . . *soon as this business with Sam Reed is behind me, I'll see if I can track down that renegade Chickasaw.* A hopeful thought occurred to him. *If Shorthorse ever was in Granite Creek, maybe he's left town too.*

The prospect was not entirely implausible. From time to time, those things that plague us do go away of their own accord.

CHAPTER THIRTY-EIGHT

THE STAKEOUT COMMENCES

After a number of stops in sections of Granite Creek that he was more familiar with, Charlie Moon arrived in Samuel and Irene Reeds' upscale neighborhood at about two hours before sundown. The tribal investigator made several passes of the residence at 1200 Shadowlane Avenue. When there was no traffic to see him enter the Reeds' driveway, he made a quick turn. Using the remote-control device on the key ring provided by Sam Reed, he opened the door on the guest house garage, pulled his Expedition inside, and immediately lowered the segmented steel plates behind him.

After waiting for his pupils to dilate in the darkness in the windowless space, Moon climbed a steel stairway, where he used a shiny brass key to unlock the door to the guest quarters that served as the scientist-entrepreneur's at-home office.

The first thing that caught his eye was a magnificent pool table positioned at the precise center of the parlor. Moon rubbed his fingers over the green felt. *I'd sure like to have one of these at the Columbine.* A softly cushioned leather couch long enough for Moon to sleep on dominated the windowless wall. An immaculate cherry desk facing the west wall was apparently where Reed conducted his lucrative business affairs. Moon continued his inspection until he was familiar with every detail in the room, including the thick woolen curtains that he would keep tightly closed so that light wouldn't leak out and alert someone to the fact that he was staked out in the guest house. Someone such as Mrs. Irene Reed—or her boyfriend. Moon didn't think there was much chance that Chico Perez would show up. *I expect that rascal's in another state by now.*

The kitchenette tucked away in a corner of the room did not escape the hungry man's attention. The refrigerator was stocked with a variety of delicacies, including a three-pound plastic tub of Hoke's Famous Barbecue (chopped beef brisket), a quart of Ben & Jerry's chocolate ice cream, a half-gallon of cold-brewed coffee, mustard potato salad, coleslaw, thin-sliced deli ham and beef—and that was just for starters. But a snack would have to wait.

The tribal investigator entered the cozy bedroom. Unlike the spacious parlor, it was permeated with that crisp "new" scent of a space that has not been lived in. The sleeping quarters was furnished with a maple bedstead, a matching dresser and chest of drawers, a single leather armchair, and, most tantalizing of all to the rancher—a well-stocked bookcase. Dozens of volumes waited invitingly behind spotless glass doors. Charlie Moon yielded to the temptation and the avid reader was pleased with what he found there. Unless someone made an early move on Sam Reed, he had a lot of hours to while away in this place.

Charlie Moon approached a window that he knew would provide a view of the rear of the Reeds' residence. He parted the heavy woolen curtains a finger's width and eyed the back door, which Mrs. Reed had reported as the site of a break-in attempt. He reserved judgment about whether the lady had made an honest mistake—or (as Parris believed) was setting up an excuse to shoot her husband for a prowler. Moon needed an effective observation post, and this window would serve as the primary lookout. With that in mind, the bedroom lights would not be turned on for the three-day duration of the stakeout. To ensure that no error was made, Moon unscrewed every light bulb in the room from its socket and concealed them under the bed.

Checking out the full bath off the bedroom, the cash-poor

rancher marveled at the hand-painted tiles that covered the floor, walls, and every square inch of the bathtub and shower stall. Moon recognized the work of the Angel Fire artist who had produced the tiles and knew what the talented lady charged for her work. *I could buy me a new F-350 pickup for what this job cost Sam Reed.* He also noticed that the wealthy man's fixtures were Moen's finest—and gold plated. *The upper 1 percent lives pretty high on the hog.*

Satisfied with the guest house, he descended the stairway and exited the garage by a rear oak door that opened into a covering cluster of dwarf pines and juniper. The Ute ascended a thickly wooded ridge onto BLM land behind the Reeds' ten acres. It took him about half an hour to locate an elevated spot that provided a suitable view. With patience and concentration his ancestors would have approved of, Charlie Moon studied every feature of the landscape until a three-dimensional map was engraved on his brain.

He waited.

A sweetly soft concert of twilight and moonshine was beginning to fill the evening with a pearly gray prelude to night when—at the nearby call of a robin-size saw-whet owl—the tribal investigator got one of those inexplicable hunches. Without knowing *how* he knew, Charlie Moon was certain that Mrs. Reed was on her way home. *And she's not a mile away.* The diminutive owl hooted again and he saw a pair of headlights top another ridge about five hundred yards to the north. Not quite a minute later, he watched Irene Reed's Cadillac turn off Shadowlane and heard the big machine crunch its way along the graveled driveway. As the sleek automobile circled the guest house, it glowed pink in the silvery moonlight. The blushing Caddie slowed as the driver remotely opened the door on the garage attached to the residence and pulled inside. Moments after the door lowered behind the luxury automobile, lights began to go on inside the large brick dwelling.

Silently as a panther padding along a mossy forest floor, the Ute circled the Reeds' home. After satisfying himself that all was well, the lawman returned to the guest house and made a fresh pot of coffee. Positioning himself at the bedroom window, where he could keep an eye on Mrs. Reed's back door, it was inevitable that Moon would begin to muse about the man he was trying to keep alive until June 5. The scientist-turned-investor was more than merely interesting. Professor Reed was a curious contradiction. Practically an enigma.

Moon considered a for-example: *That morning in Scott's office, Reed told us he had to hurry away to get a manicure.* And as it happened, Samuel Reed had apparently lied about having an appointment that no other self-respecting Granite Creek County man would have admitted to—not if you held the muzzle of a cocked and loaded .44 Colt revolver to his head. After Reed had admitted to his shameful intent, the man under the homburg had made a beeline to Leadville Lily's seedy establishment. Charlie Moon knew this because he had followed Reed there. And whatever other unseemly activities the proprietor might occasionally engage in, Lily had her standards. She would never stoop to clipping a grown man's fingernails. Moon couldn't imagine a fellow like Sam Reed paying Miss Lily to decorate a patch of his skin. Which raised one of those questions that tends to nag at a fellow's mind and keep him awake nights: why would Reed lie about getting a manicure and then slip off to a tattoo parlor? *Because he was up to no good.* Okay. But what particular category of "no good"? There were persistent rumors of drug dealing at Leadville Lily's business establishment, but Scott Parris hadn't been able to uncover any substantive evidence to lend credence to the gossip. *Which don't prove Lily's not dealing.* One thought daisy-chains to another. *So maybe Reed has a habit.* The simplest explanations were generally right on the mark.

Even so, Charlie Moon was entertaining another, more compelling notion: *From what I hear around town, Sam Reed's one-man investment business is a lot more successful than the law of averages allows.* The Ute's dark brow furrowed into a thoughtful frown. *So how does he manage that?* Again, the obvious explanation was that the dealer in real estate, stocks, and commodities benefited from insider information. But considering the range of Reed's investments, that would require a sizable network of paid informers. *An operation like that would be extremely risky.* Sooner or later, Sam Reed would get nailed by the SEC. *Chances are, they're already onto him, just biding their time until they've made a solid case.* The best evidence would be incriminating conversations between the investor and his informers. But Reed would know this, and a sensible felon would go to considerable lengths to conceal his communications from the feds. *Maybe he pays Lily to use her telephone.* Moon shook his head. Federal attorneys fairly salivate at the thought of recorded conversations, where voices and telephone numbers can be identified. *Reed might use Lily's computer for sending and receiving coded e-mails.* Not exactly bulletproof, but solid evidence would be harder to come by. *And computer files are not the sort of proof that easily convinces a jury.*

Moon sighed his way back to the simplest explanation: *I'm probably way off base. Chances are, Sam Reed went to Lily's for the same reason most folks do—to get a tattoo.* The rancher grinned as he imagined the middle-aged married man with a coiled rattlesnake inscribed on his chest. The grin begot a barely audible chuckle. *Or maybe a girlfriend's name on his arm . . .* But that didn't make much sense.

Where on his body could a man hide an incriminating tattoo from his wife? Moon decided that a fellow's options would be severely limited and did not bear thinking about. Realizing that his thoughts were meandering around aimlessly like a horse browsing on a sparse prairie, he decided to rein his ruminations in. And succeeded. More or less.

With the intention of distracting himself from pointless musings, Charlie Moon removed the small flashlight from his pocket and began to examine the contents of the bedroom bookcase. On each of the four shelves, the volumes (with one notable exception) were arranged so that the spines were perfectly aligned. It was apparent from the titles that Sam Reed had selected all the books himself; there was hardly anything here that was likely to suit a lady's taste. The Indian cowboy was delighted to spot a copy of J. B. Gillett's *Six Years with the Texas Rangers*. The ardent reader's trusty right hand was reaching for that delightful treasure when his gaze was pulled to another volume. Yes, the one that protruded ever so slightly from the neatly arranged row on the top shelf. The volume by David Deutsch spoke to him.

No, really.

This is what it said: *You've already read that dusty old cowboy-and-Indians tale a half-dozen times, pardner. Have a gander at what's between my covers—you'll be mighty glad you did!*

Whether or not he would (be mighty glad) remains to be seen, but such a beguiling invitation is utterly compelling. Abandoning the trusty Gillett, Charlie Moon's fingers left a gap where *The Fabric of Reality* had resided. After retiring to the parlor, seating himself in a comfortable armchair, turning on a small floor lamp, and turning two or three pages, the reader was hooked. After a few more, Moon was mesmerized. This was (he thought) the sort of reading that would elbow insignificant thoughts out of a man's mind.

Perhaps. It all depends on the man and the kind of mind he has—and which thoughts can properly be classified as insignificant.

As Charlie Moon read the last few lines of the second chapter, he was beginning to feel uneasy. Now perched on a spruce branch just outside the guest apartment, the lonely saw-whet owl screeched her shrill *whoop-whoop-whoop* at the Ute. The reader was assaulted by an unseemly thought. One of those unsettling notions that comes from nowhere, like summer thunder booming from a clear-as-crystal sky. He attempted to dismiss the absurdity but could not quite let go of it. The pesky thing was trying to take him somewhere. Mr. Moon could not see around the dark corner and didn't want to go there. He turned off the lamp, opened the window curtains, and tried to concentrate on the foam of a moonshine-twilight concoction that was flowing lightly through the window glazing and washing over the carpet.

A wasted effort.

The sinister possibility tiptoed its way back into the tribal investigator's deliberations. It was one of those highly unlikely what-ifs, which was less like a thought than an insistent whispering in Moon's ear: *Here's something to think about—what if Reed had his body tattooed so it could be positively identified?*

Moon shook his head. There were all sorts of ways for an ME to identify corpses. Like fingerprints, dental records, and DNA.

Again, the whisper: *Forget about medical examiners. Someone might need to ID Sam Reed's carcass without the aid of modern forensic technology.*

Moon's brow furrowed. *Who?*

That's for me to know and you to figure out. Think about it.

The tribal investigator thought about it. *Reed's wife?*

As if by a flash of lightning at midnight, Moon's mind's eye was illuminated for an instant—then blinded by a still deeper darkness.

He didn't like what he'd seen in that brilliant instant. *That's plain crazy.*

Indeed it was. At the very least.

The whisperer snickered. *But is it crazy enough to be true?*

Moon stared at the book in his hand. *What if weird things like that really do happen from time to time?*

The final whisper pierced his ear like an ice pick: *What if weird things like that are happening all the time?*

The images conjured up by this sinister suggestion made Charlie Moon's skin creep and crawl like a tribe of flesh-eating worms were wriggling under his epidermis and tucking napkins under their chins. Don't start nit-picking. Imaginary worms can have chins if they want to.

And napkins, too.

CHAPTER THIRTY-NINE

THE LADIES HE LEFT AT HOME

Before departing for "three or four days," Charlie Moon had directed Sarah Frank and Daisy Perika to call his mobile phone in case of emergency. The unspoken implication was as clear as the grim look on his craggy face—the tribal investigator had some unspecified but serious business to attend to; he would have no time for idle telephone chitchat.

With the most important man in their lives absent, these were lonely days on the Columbine. The younger and the elder dealt with the void Moon had left behind, each in a manner befitting her personality.

From first light until late at night when sleep finally would carry her away from her worries, Sarah mooned and fretted about her absent heartthrob. She also attended classes at Rocky Mountain Polytechnic, prepared meals for herself and Aunt Daisy, washed and dried dishes, got caught up on homework assignments, and generally kept busy and made herself useful. Whenever the young woman had a spare moment, she would pause and stare at a shadowy beamed ceiling or a turquoise-blue sky and wonder where the apple of her eye was *right this minute*, what Charlie was doing, and, most important—*does he ever think about me?*

From time to time, when Charlie Moon wasn't busy making sure that Samuel Reed lived to see the sun rise on the

morning after his wife's thirtieth birthday, he did think
about the winsome Ute-Papago orphan. *I hope the kid's doing all right.* And about his irascible aunt. *I hope Daisy's
behaving like a normal little old lady.* This was more like a
private joke than a serious hope; Moon knew that he might
as well wish for a patch of prickly-pear cactus to produce a
crop of chocolate-coated strawberries.

Unlike the mooning teenager, Daisy Perika had a more
pressing problem to solve. It had to do with her violent assault on Chico Perez, whom she firmly believed was dead. It
wasn't that she was haunted by regrets; quite the contrary.
Not only had it been a matter of self-defense and preventing
a future assault on Sarah—knocking the rascal's head in
with her walking stick had been a gratifying experience. But
life was not all about having a good time, and when the fun
was over, a person needed to settle down and consider the
carnage from a sober point of view. Which was why Daisy
had been thinking about what the consequences might be
when Perez's corpse was discovered. She had no doubt that
when the lurid story hit the newspapers and TV, Miss Muntz
would guess who'd done the deed. *Not that Millie would rat
on me.* Not deliberately. *But that gabby white woman might
let something slip.* And what if someone had seen Miss M.'s
car in the neighborhood that night and told the police about
it? *I bet there's not another old Buick like that in the whole
county.* Cops were like bulldogs; one way or another they'd
worm the truth out of Millicent Muntz. Daisy sighed. *All I
was trying to do was take his wallet back, but I don't have a
single witness to testify that I was fighting for my life. And
now I've not only still got Chico Perez's wallet, I've also got
those other things.* Like so many wacky notions born in the
heat of passion, taking the battle trophies had seemed like a
fine idea at the time. *But if I get caught with any of it, I'm
liable to get arrested.* She sighed. *Try to do the right thing
and where does it get you?* In serious trouble, that's where.
Life just isn't fair.

    After much soul-searching and worrying, the apprehensive old soul made up her mind to dispose of the physical evidence. *And the sooner the better.* But not tonight; the thing must be done properly. *I'll need some time to figure out whether to bury the stuff.* Charlie Moon's aunt concluded that she must do some serious thinking. Which ominous development was, in itself, sufficient to cause spirited mares to kick at their stalls, tough cowboys to tremble in their sleep, and old hounds to awaken with startled snorts.

All of which occurred (respectively) in the Columbine horse barn, beneath the roof of the forty-bed bunkhouse, and under the headquarters porch, where Sidewinder slept.

CHAPTER FORTY

EVENING, JUNE 3
A CLOSE ENCOUNTER IN
GRANITE CREEK

More specifically—on Sand Hills Country Club property, of which institution Mrs. Bernice Aldershott was a member, and where she preferred to indulge in her nightly exercise on the golf course. The middle-aged lady, of sinewy build and iron will, was just short of her three-mile mark when—over Peggy Lee's "I'm a Woman" vibrating the drum in her right ear canal—her left ear detected something out of the ordinary.

The jogger stopped abruptly, lowered the volume on her iPod, and listened intently.

Bernice heard a squeaky creaking. *What on earth is that?*
Now a creaky squeaking.
It seems to be coming from somewhere over there.
(It would be helpful if the lady would be more precise.)
Somewhere near the groundskeeper's toolshed. What were the odds that someone would be working there after dark? Making it about twenty to one, the determined woman set her jaw and set about to investigate the source of all this confounded creaking and squeaking. Approaching the source of the mysterious sounds, she spied a dark something in the moonlight. The myopic woman squinted. *Someone is definitely messing about at the toolshed.*

But who? And for what unseemly purpose?

Like our other natural appetites, Curiosity demands to be satisfied.

The plucky lady pressed ahead. And got a better look.

Bernice's lips made an O. She whispered, "Oh my—someone is attempting to pry the shed door open with one of those whatchamacallits!" In an instant, the nighttime jogger realized that she had encountered Granite Creek's infamous Whatchamacallit Burglar. What a glorious opportunity for a conscientious citizen to do her duty! Within a few heart-beats, she had her trusty mobile telephone in hand, punched in 911, and heard the graveyard-shift dispatcher's snappy response. "Granite Creek Police—what is the nature of your emergency?"

She whispered, "I've spotted the ne'er-do-well who everyone is talking about." *Or is it* "whom" *everyone is talking about?* Doing one's level best to be grammatically correct was *so* trying. "The fellow is trying to break into the shed with his whatchamacallit."

"His what?"

"His *whatchamacallit*, dammit—you know what I mean!" *Why can't they hire people who understand English?*

"If you could describe—"

"Oh, it's one of those long thingamabobs with a hook on the end." Bernice's voice was teetering right on the ragged edge of shrillness.

The dispatcher tried harder. "A hook, huh . . . like an old-fashioned walking cane?"

"Well, I suppose it *looks* like one of those. But that's not what it's used for." Explaining things to slow-witted men was irksome. "Carpenters use them to pry on things, and this miscreant is using his to break into the shed. And it's made of iron."

"An iron shed?"

"No." The irate citizen held her breath and counted to three. "The *thingamabob with the hook* is made of iron."

The light began to dawn on the dispatcher. "You talking about a crowbar?"

"Of course I am!" *I wonder why they call them that.*

"Now would you please send a horde of club-waving constables to take this thieving vandal into custody?"

"Yes ma'am. What's your address?"

"At a time like this, what on earth do you want to know *that* for?"

"Well, so I can dispatch officers to your home and—"

"I'm not at home, you nincompoop!"

"What is your present location?"

"I'm very near the thirteenth hole."

Three heartbeats.

"You're at the golf course, ma'am?"

"Of course." *His brain must be the size of a peanut.*

The dispatcher's tone betrayed his suspicion that the caller was under the influence of a chemical substance. "Uh, what're you doing on the golf course this time of night?"

"Practicing my putting!"

"Oh." Three more heartbeats. "You wearing one of them baseball caps with a little flashlight on it?"

"No, I am not!" The fashion implications alone were horrid. "My remark about putting was an attempt at sarcasm. I'm jogging—or I was until I heard the creaky squeaking."

"Yes ma'am." *There's an off chance she's spotted the perp we've been looking for.* "Hold on a sec."

Bernice Aldershott listened to the alleged Peanut Brain dispatch the nearest of two night-duty police units to the Sand Hills Country Club. *He does seem to be marginally competent. Perhaps I was too hard on him.*

"A unit with two officers is on the way. ETA is about one minute."

"Thank you, young man. I suppose I am a bit nervous; and I do owe you an apology. I'm sorry I called you a nincompoop."

"Don't give it a thought, ma'am. My mother-in-law calls me worse names than that. Now here's what I want you to do. First of all, stay on the phone. And this is very important— don't go near the suspect. You got that?" Silence. "Ma'am, are you there?" The GCPD dispatcher was talking to empty air.

* * *

Officer Eddie Knox pulled their unit away from Chicky's Daylight Doughnuts. His longtime partner, E. C. "Piggy" Slocum, was riding shotgun. (Yes. Same sawed-off twenty-gauge.)

Knox was practically salivating at the thought of nabbing the Crowbar Burglar. "Nobody's being threatened, Pig—so we'll make our approach in stealthy mode. No siren, no lights."

"Okay with me, Eddie." Having just finished off the next-to-last doughnut, Slocum wiped powdered sugar from his mouth onto his sleeve.

Not quite a minute later, Knox eased the lights-out supercharged black-and-white Chevy into the country-club parking lot, cut the ignition, and pointed with his jutted chin. "The toolshed's over yonder, behind that little grove of poplars."

"I know, Eddie. I used to caddie here years ago, when I was in high school. Back then, there was only nine holes and—"

"When I want a history lesson, Pig, I'll let you know."

"Right, Eddie."

Eddie Knox cut the ignition. "You go down the lane, straight in." He checked his sidearm, then opened the car door and got out. "I'll loop around to the back. We'll pen the suspect in."

"Right, Eddie." Slocum checked his sidearm and the shotgun. As soon as his partner was out of sight, he made a grab for the last jelly doughnut.

Bernice Aldershott was tiptoeing toward the shed. *While the police are on the way, I'll see if I can get a good look at the miscreant with the thingamabob. That way, if he should flee before he can be apprehended, I will be able to provide the authorities with a description.*

Highly commendable.

Problem was, the fellow who'd been making the squeaky-creaky noise had spotted Bernice's profile on the grassy ridge. Being too far away to hear the lady's conversation with the police dispatcher, he didn't know whether she had seen him and was summoning the cops or was merely calling home to nag her unfortunate spouse. Until he knew which way the wind was blowing, Crowbar Man thought it prudent to conceal himself behind the shed.

Which was why, as Bernice Aldershott approached that small wooden structure, she was unable to spot the alleged felon. "Oh, rats—he has gotten away!"

The lady should be so lucky.

The closer she came, the more the miscreant with the thingamabob was convinced that . . . *she knows I'm here. And she won't stop snooping around until she finds me.*

What to do? How could he rid himself of this meddlesome pest?

On occasion, even a ne'er-do-well has a great notion.

This one also had a sense of humor.

Oh, double rats! Bernice Aldershott had no doubt that her quarry had fled. *If I hadn't spent so much time trying to explain things to that lamebrain at 911, I'd have caught him red-handed!* The civic-minded citizen stared at the shed door, which had been broken open and was hanging on a single hinge. *I wonder what he intended to steal.* She had no idea what sort of tools the head groundskeeper kept locked up inside. But in the moonlight, by the corner of the modest structure, Bernice spotted something on the ground. *What is that?* The smallish rectangular object looked like a book. *But that's silly; surely a burglar wouldn't be taking time to read. Unless, like everyone else these days, thieves feel entitled to take regular breaks. But what would a common criminal read during a brief respite?* She speculated that the bookish-looking object might be a volume of popular short stories. *But the moonlight is not bright enough to read by.* She cocked her head at the perplexing object. *It looks like my father's old cassette recorder.* But that seemed even more unlikely than a book. It occurred to her that this might be part of the burglar's loot that he'd left behind. *Whatever it is, it will be an important clue.* As the clueless citizen was stretching out her hand to apply her fingerprints to the presumed physical evidence, she heard a low, guttural growl behind her. The terrified jogger turned to encounter a horrifying apparition.

The multitasker concealed under the black sock hat and black raincoat brandished the crowbar with his right hand, thumped his chest with the left, and stomped (alternately) with both feet.

The woman's mind instantly responded with a memory of the ancient *King Kong* black-and-white flick she'd watched on the TV just last week. *It's a gorilla!*

Reinforcing this conclusion, another throaty growl, chest thump, and foot stomp.

Bernice was off like a gazelle. Or, if you prefer—an Aldershott fired from a cannon.

Encouraged by the success of his ploy, the supposed gorilla (as they say in these parts) "took off" after her. But only after retrieving the *smallish rectangular object*, and only for a few strides. The vandal was no world-class sprinter, and had no interest in putting the grab on the jogger.

With every raw fiber of her being, Mrs. Aldershott wanted to scream, but she was determined not to waste the breath. When being chased by a hideous, vicious ape that is armed with a whatchamacallit or thingamabob, the thing to do is to put considerable distance between the horrible beast and yourself. Having aimed her strained face toward the nearest path to the parking lot, she never looked back. By the time the jogger passed the Sand Hills flagpole, she had bested her all-time best one hundred yards by two seconds flat and was picking up speed.

Go, Bernice!

And go she did. A blur herself, the sprinter did not see the plump form of Officer E. C. "Piggy" Slocum until she was within a few strides of him. It was as if the dark, hunched form had materialized out of another dimension.

It's another damn ape!

Hemmed in on both sides of the pathway by prickly hedges of holly, she slowed to a mere trot.

Startled by the sudden appearance of the dark, slender

figure, Slocum assumed that this was the Crowbar Burglar making a run for it. The rotund cop, who had a mouthful of jelly doughnut and a sugary-slippery handful of shotgun, attempted to shout, "Stop right there!" What came out of his mouth was, "Sogg bipe bare!" The flustered cop dropped the shotgun and fumbled for his holstered pistol.

(This was one of those situations that can end badly.)

Convinced that she was hotly pursued by the first gorilla, her escape blocked by a second knuckle dragger, Bernice was trapped in a nightmare. *What can I do?*

What the lady needed was sage advice.

What she got was a premonition of doom from her iPod.

Miss Peggy Lee crooned sweetly in Bernice's left ear: *"It's all over now . . ."*

"The *hell* it is!" Filled with fury at this infestation of the Sand Hills Country Club by hairy primates, the charter member accelerated. Within five strides, she was rolling along like the Wabash Cannonball roaring down the mountain on a full head of steam. *Straight at King Kong Number Two.*

What a woman!

Officer Slocum was bowled aside like a lone tenpin.

Mrs. Bernice Aldershott did not stop until she was inside her house, which residence was almost a mile away.

CHAPTER FORTY-ONE

"I wish to lie where a mother's prayer
And a sister's tear will mingle there.
Where friends can come and weep o'er me.
O bury me not on the lone prairie."

JUNE 4
ON THE EVENING WHEN PROFESSOR
REED IS DESTINED TO DIE

Irene Reed, who was dining with friends, was not expected home until well after dark.

A shadowy precursor of twilight was already thickening the atmosphere when Charlie Moon spotted Scott Parris's black-and-white from the guest-house bedroom window. The Chevy lurched into the driveway and kicked gravel all the way to the guest house, where it skidded to a stop. In six seconds flat, the garage door was up, the squad car was inside, and the heavy door was slamming shut.

The Ute unlatched the upstairs door.

Samuel Reed ascended first, toting four plastic bags of groceries. In passing, he nodded respectfully to his silent bodyguard, then unloaded his burden on the kitchenette's speckled granite countertop.

Scott Parris followed with a mumbled "Hello, Chuck" and placed a man-size backpack and a large canvas suitcase onto the parlor couch. With the exaggerated care of one who dares not damage county property, the cop removed the contents. A pair of GCPD portable radios. A disassembled Remington deer rifle and two full boxes of 6-mm ammo. An infrared 4X SniperScope for the rifle and Japanese photomultiplier/IR binoculars that required only the faintest starlight to illuminate the darkest night. When viewed with either optical instrument, a warm-bodied creature such as a loping coyote, a lop-eared jackrabbit, or a gun-toting biped would light up like electrified ornaments on a Christmas tree.

While Parris mounted the scope and Moon checked out the hardware, Reed prepared a light supper for his solemn companions.

There was no conversation during the meal of jack-cheese omelets, grilled brown trout, and lightly seasoned wild rice.

After the feast, Reed seated himself at his parlor desk and turned on a laptop computer.

Moon and Parris took turns at the windows with the binoculars.

Aside for a comical porcupine gnawing on a tasty cedar, there was nothing to see.

Aside from the balmy whisper of a late-spring breeze, all was quiet.

From time to time, the Ute would slip outside to circle the ten-acre property, then return to report that nothing was amiss.

Which lack of visible threat served to create a nagging stress.

The chief of police began to mutter under his breath.

The stone-faced Ute uttered not a word.

Aware of the increasing undercurrent of tension, Samuel Reed broke the silence by suggesting that the lawmen settle in and relax. "Nothing will happen before eleven o'clock. In the meantime, why don't we pass the tedious minutes by entertaining ourselves?"

His bodyguard-guests acquiesced to this reasonable request.

"Good," Reed said. "I'll begin by telling you fellows a hilarious joke."

Not a great opening.

Scott Parris barely suppressed a groan.

Charlie Moon was already amused.

"There were these two atoms." The scientist was already smiling in anticipation of the upcoming mirth and merriment. "They were walking along the street and about to meet—"

"Which street?" Parris inquired.

"It doesn't matter. The point is—"

"Matters to me," the heckler grumped. "You could at least tell us whether it's a street in Granite Creek."

"Very well." Reed strained to retain his smile. "These atoms are strolling along Seventh Street in our fair city. And before you ask for names, the individual meandering along in a northerly direction is Mr. Indium—"

"Hah—that must be Charlie."

The sidetracked jokester sniffed. "These unseemly interruptions must cease, Mr. Parris."

"Sorry." The cop's silly grin belied his apology.

"Now where was I?" Samuel Reed paused to recollect. "Ah, yes. As it happens, Mr. Indium is about to meet Miss Chlorine, who is clipping along quite briskly on a southerly course. And in point of fact, he does. But, each being distracted by one thing or another, the atoms collide and Miss Chlorine—a relative lightweight—is knocked over a hedge and into Auntie Antimony's flower bed."

"Bummer," Parris said.

"Happily, no harm is done—Miss Chlorine lands in a patch of petunias." The physicist paused to shake his head and sigh. "But sad to say, Mr. Indium is not so fortunate. After brushing pink petunia petals off her plaid gingham skirt, Miss Chlorine calls over the hedge to inquire after his health."

Reed assumed a high-pitched voice that sounded exactly like Miss Lucre: "Oh, dear—are you all right, Mr. Indium?"

In a deeper, masculine tone (not unlike Charlie Moon's) Mr. Indium booms, "No, I am not, young lady. Matter of fact, I have lost an electron."

Shrill Miss Chlorine: "Oh, gracious—are you sure?"

" 'Yes.' (Mr. Indium nods.) 'I am *positive.*' "

Having delivered the punch line flawlessly, the physicist was prepared for an appreciative reaction.

Dead silence from Scott Parris. *What's so funny about that?*

The performer got a respectable chuckle from Charlie Moon, despite the fact that Mr. Indium had heard the joke before.

Though disappointed with this insipid response, Samuel Reed was determined that the entertainment should continue. He suggested that each of his guests contribute an amusing anecdote.

Normally the cowboy humorists would have been pleased to chip in, but witnessing the humiliating failure of a fellow comedian has a marked effect on his colleagues. Neither of the bodyguards was in the mood to tell a joke.

Reed accepted this refusal gracefully, but insisted that the show must go on. He asked the lawmen to relate an interesting story. The chief of Granite Creek police was urged to recall some account from his lengthy experience as a sworn officer of the law, after which the Southern Ute tribal investigator would then do his best to top his friend. "There will no requirement except this—your narratives must be entertaining." Reed added, "The stories can be true, a total fabrication, or a satisfying blend of fact and fiction."

This was more to their liking, and having no better notions for passing the time, Parris and Moon agreed to Reed's conditions. But while one of them was busy spinning his yarn, the other would be keeping watch on the Reed residence from the guest-house bedroom window.

CHAPTER FORTY-TWO

THE TOWN COP'S TALE

After considering any number of anecdotes that might be derived from his adventures in the Windy City, the ex-Chicago cop decided against ancient history and in favor of current events. "I bet you fellas would enjoy hearing what happened at the country club last night."

"Not me." Moon smiled at his image in the bedroom window. "None of my rough cowboy friends mix with that crowd."

"It's a dandy story, Charlie." Parris pointed his chin at their host. "And Sam's a member, so I know he'll want to hear it."

The Ute's likeness grinned back at him. "Go ahead then."

"Okay, here's the short version. A Mrs. Aldershott is jogging along last night on the Sand Hills Golf Course. Lady hears something peculiar and stops to get an earful. Sounds like somebody's breaking into the groundskeeper's toolshed, so the conscientious citizen calls 911. Dispatcher sends Knox and Slocum, then advises the caller to stay on the line and keep clear of the supposed felon—who might be our notorious Crowbar Burglar. But she's already hung up. And I don't have to tell you what happens next."

"No, you don't." Prior to his appointment as a tribal investigator, Charlie Moon had put in a decade as a uniformed cop with the Southern Ute Police Department. "The citizen went to check out the alleged bad guy."

"You know it. And after that, it only gets better." Parris inhaled a deep breath. "Our black-and-white shows up dark and silent. Knox and Slocum split up in hopes of cornering the mischief-maker before he can split."

Moon liked it. "So far, so good."

"According to the jogger, when she gets to the shed where she heard the sounds, somebody has pried the door open. But far as she can see, the perp has hit the road without so much as a 'by-your-leave, ma'am.'"

The tribal cop nodded. "More or less what you'd expect."

"But there's something on the ground."

"Don't tell me—a crowbar covered with incriminating fingerprints."

"Sorry, Charlie—no cigar."

"Don't keep us in suspense, pard."

"Let me see if I can quote the lady from Knox's written report: 'It was a rectangular something. Dark in color. Black, probably. Or maybe navy blue. Could have been royal purple. And' . . ." Parris paused to smirk. "It might've been some kind of electronic thingy, like a cassette tape recorder. Or maybe a toolbox. Or it could've been a book."

"Piece of cake," Moon said to the windowpane. "I got the whole thing figured."

"Amaze us with your awesome powers of deduction, Chucky."

"Alleged felon is actually the country club's innocent night custodian. After checking all eighteen tees and fairways and sand traps for any sign of gophers or other interlopers, Joe Custodian figures he's due a break from his labors. So he saunters over to the toolshed, sits down, and unpockets his pocket-size copy of *The Complete and Unabridged Works of J.R.R. Tolkien*. After reading a few thousand pages, he dozes off."

"Is this going somewhere, Charlie?"

"Patience. After he drifts away into dreamland, our night custodian begins to snore. That's what the lady jogger hears when she thinks somebody's prying on a door. As she approaches to investigate, the country-club employee wakes up, figures it's the boss come to check those nasty rumors that he sleeps on the job. He drops his copy of J.R.R. Tolkien and makes a run for it."

"Then who pried the toolshed door open?"

"Don't expect me to explain every detail, pardner—I've just about shot my wad."

Parris glared at the Ute. "You want to hear what really happened?"

Moon nodded. "As the thirsty hart pants in the desert."

"Okay. According to the jogger, about the time she spots the *rectangular something* on the ground, she hears another sound and turns around and finds herself face-to-face with a gorilla."

"Pardon me, pard—but it sounded an awful lot like you said—"

"Yes I did. And this gorilla made grunting ooga-booga-ooga sounds like them big jungle apes make, and beat on its hairy chest and *shook a crowbar* at the lady."

Moon turned from the window to blink at his friend. "You're kidding."

"Wish I was. You want to hear the rest?"

"My ears are fairly aching for the big finish."

"Faced with this latter-day King Kong, the lady takes off like a rocket."

"Good move."

"At first, the jogger's dead certain the ugly ape's right on her heels—but after a couple hundred yards, she figures she's putting some distance between him and her."

Moon turned his face to the window. "I won't ask why she figures it was a male ape."

"Thank you. Now this is the *good* part." Parris paused for another deep breath of stale air. "She's going lickety-split down the pathway toward the parking lot, when all of a sudden—she encounters a *second* gorilla."

"Sorry, pard. I'm doing my best to keep from laughing out loud—but that's an ape too much." Seeing movement, the Ute raised the binoculars to his eyes. It was a prowler, but not of the biped persuasion. A skinny coyote was trotting across the Reeds' backyard. The canine lifted her long, thin muzzle to sniff at something on tonight's menu. A platter of rabbit, served rare.

"It wasn't funny to the citizen," Parris countered with feigned solemnity. "One big, hairy ape chasing after her—another one blocking her path."

"Okay." The Indian with the IR binoculars watched Ms. Coyote tear out after Mr. Cottontail. "So what'd our hemmed-in jogger do?"

"Ran the second ape down, left him flat on his back like he was so much roadkill."

The rancher made a low whistle. "Tough lady."

"If I ever see her headed toward me on a dead run, I'll stand aside and wave as she passes by." Parris grinned at Sam Reed.

The odds-making Ute couldn't imagine a night runner knocking Eddie Knox down and living to tell the tale. "Must've been Officer Slocum who bit the dust."

"Safe guess. But he can't believe that a hundred-pound woman sacked him like he was a grade-school quarterback." Parris sniggered. "At first, Slocum claimed he'd been trampled by a huge wild animal—most likely a bull elk. After he heard the jogger's story, he decided it must've been one of the apes."

"What about the gorilla at the toolshed—the endangered primate with the crowbar?"

"He got away."

"And took the book with him?"

"Looks like it." Parris shrugged. *If it was a book.*

Moon lowered the binoculars and shook his head. "Gorilla Number One—annoyed at his solitude being disturbed—waves a pry bar at the jogger who interrupted his reading. And depending on who you believe—the lady or the cop—Gorilla Number Two gets knocked on his butt by the fleeing jogger, or one of them hairy apes comes cannonballing along and bowls Officer Slocum over like a spare tenpin. Scott, that's the best danged story I've heard in hours—maybe even minutes."

After listening to Parris's narrative in amused silence, their host was obliged to offer a compliment. "I also enjoyed your tale, Mr. Parris."

"Thank you kindly." The chief of police made a guttural sound that was halfway between a grunt and a growl. "But to tell you the honest, unvarnished truth, I'd like it a lot better except for the ending."

Samuel Reed nodded. "It does leave the critical question unresolved—who or what was this apish, crowbar-brandishing creature who chases ladies off the golf course? If your subordinates had subdued the shaggy rascal and pummeled him mercilessly until he revealed his identity and criminal intentions, your rather disjointed anecdote would at least have some sense of closure."

Scott Parris accepted Reed's constructive criticism in good humor. "Once this story hits the street—and it will—the local rag'll have loads of fun haw-hawing about how us Granite Creek cops couldn't find a six-hundred-pound brass monkey if its momma left it on the GCPD doorsteps, all gift wrapped in a pink satin sheet and trussed up in ten yards of shiny red ribbon."

Moon pressed the binoculars to his eyes. "Got something."

Parris tensed. "What is it, Charlie?"

"Pair of headlights . . . slowing." Two heartbeats. "Turning into the driveway."

Launching himself from his chair, the chief of police hurried to peer over Moon's shoulder.

The Ute focused the night-vision binoculars. "It's Mrs. Reed's Cadillac."

They lost track of the Caddy as the pink GMC earthcraft orbited the far side of guest house. When the gleaming machine reappeared, Charlie Moon fleshed out his report. "Mrs. Reed's driving." In a barely audible whisper to Scott Parris: "No passenger." As the Cadillac approached the residence, the lawmen watched the attached-garage door chinkity-chink its way open, the sleek luxury automobile glide in, a willowy Irene Reed slide out, and the garage slowly close its gaping mouth.

"Ah, my dear wife has returned home." Samuel Reed checked his wristwatch. "And more or less on time."

CHAPTER FORTY-THREE

THE COP HAS DOUBTS

Though it was still early, Scott Parris was haunted by the thought that aside from Sam Reed's payments pumping up his and Charlie Moon's anemic bank accounts, this stakeout was a waste of time. The chief of police could not shake the nagging conviction that by one means or another . . . *Mrs. Reed knows something's up.* He thought it was highly unlikely that she had become aware of Charlie Moon's presence during the last few days. More probably, Samuel Reed had let something slip. And even if he'd kept a tight lip, a wife's antenna can detect a signal from what her husband *doesn't* say, or a blank look on his face when she pouts and asks, "Why do you have to work so late on my birthday?" Sam's pretty young wife was expecting her punctual husband to show up at 11 P.M. sharp, and as the evening wore on, Parris became increasingly confident that the woman had no intent to do her spouse any grave bodily harm. *Not tonight, anyway.* Which meant that the boyfriend wasn't going to show his face on the place.

Scott Parris had a better-than-average track record for guessing right, but every once in a while the experienced lawman's hunches were way off the mark. Which raises the question—

WHAT IS IRENE REED UP TO?

As the chief of police ponders this pressing issue, the object of his suspicions is removing something from her purse.

A shiny something.

A shiny nickel-plated, pearl-handled, .32-caliber something.

Watch the lady make sure the magazine is fully loaded, then expertly inject a cartridge into the barrel. See how carefully she verifies that the safety is in the Off position. Observe how confidently Irene Reed holds the automatic pistol at arm's length, closes her violet-tinted left lid, and uses her pretty right eye to aim the lethal instrument at the back door.

"Bang!" m'lady says. "Bang bang!"

Did her imaginary target fall dead onto the floor?

Evidently.

Her curvaceous lips are curling into a contented smile.

REFRESHMENTS AND ENTERTAINMENT

Samuel Reed brought a tray of coffee, tea, and fixings from the parlor kitchenette into the bedroom and placed it on the mirrored cherry dresser. The fixings included a twenty-four-ounce jar of honey from a first-rate apiary somewhere east of the Mississippi.

After thanking Reed, Charlie Moon poured a cup of coffee for Scott Parris and another for himself.

Reed tasted a cup of strongly spiced tea before lifting it to toast his stalwart companions. "Gentlemen, I drink to you—and your efforts to preserve my life."

The Ute returned the salute, then stirred a spoonful of honey into his coffee.

"You're welcome," Scott Parris said. "And thank you for paying me and Charlie for our time."

Reed insisted that he was pleased to have the privilege.

Moon had not realized that the chief of police was also on Reed's payroll. *If the mayor or DA gets wind of that, there'll be hell for breakfast.*

If Parris was concerned about negative official repercussions, his expression did not reveal it. "Despite what you may've heard—it ain't easy being chief of police." He ripped open three packages of Splenda and poured the snowy contents into his cup. "And the job's pure torment when times is hard."

Moon nodded. "And times are."

Parris took a sip of the steaming brew. "Starving wolf's scratching at the door."

"And gnashing her pointy teeth." The Ute tasted his coffee. *That's good. Would be even better if the honey was from Tulia, Texas.* He added a second helping of the product that was not concocted by Tule Creek's finicky bees. "And like those tough old Ar-Kansas farmers say, it's 'root hog or die.'"

Parris helped himself to one of Reed's ivory toothpicks, unaware that it had been carved from a twenty-thousand-year-old mammoth tusk. "What a man needs these days is a recession-proof profession."

Charlie Moon had been hoping for just such an opening. "I've taken on a sideline." A sip of seriously sweet coffee. "I might even go so far as to call it a new profession."

Samuel Reed seated himself on the bed. "Ah—I do believe Mr. Moon is about to tell us a tale."

He was.

THE RANCHER'S STORY

Scott Parris made a pretense of being interested. "Let me guess. You're gonna buy yourself a beat-up old biplane and make a few bucks dusting crops."

"You're not even close." *But that ain't an altogether bad notion.*

"What, then?"

The reticent raconteur hesitated. "I probably oughtn't to tell you."

"Which is why you will."

"Please do," Sam Reed implored.

Charlie Moon shook his head. "Neither one of you would believe a word of it."

"Don't let that stop you," Parris said. *When you get that funny glint in your eye, I never believe a word you say.* "So what's this profession that's recession-proof?"

For about a while-and-a-half, Moon held his tongue. Then: "Hired gun."

"I like it already!" Reed was perched on the edge of the bed.

Parris arched a doubtful brow. "You gonna be somebody's full-time bodyguard?"

"Even worse than that." Moon avoided his friend's suspicious gaze. "We're talking . . . contract killings."

Charlie's determined to outdo my gorilla story. Parris decided to help his friend along. "Ain't that practically illegal?"

"Only if you get caught with the smoking six-shooter in your hand."

"Maybe so." Parris assumed a disapproving tone. "But ain't it right on the ragged edge of being not entirely ethical?"

The hired gun contemplated this weighty philosophical issue. "Depends on who gets gunned down."

A fair-minded man couldn't argue with that logic. "Well, just be sure you don't assassinate anybody except them that has it coming." The town cop asked the obvious question: "Any prospects so far?"

"There's no flies on me, pard. I've already got my first assignment."

Parris rolled the ivory toothpick to the other side of his mouth. "The money good?"

"Not right off," Moon said.

"What's the goin' rate?"

"Two bits a head to shoot 'em dead."

"That's not a lot," Parris observed. "Considering the risks."

"Beginners like myself has to start at the bottom."

"Lots of experienced assassins hogging the high-paying jobs?"

"Mmm-hmm. It's a matter of seniority." Moon cocked his head. "The way the hired-gun trade is played . . . well, I don't know exactly how to explain it—except to say it's kind of like a union shop."

"Sounds like you'll have to make it up in volume."

"That's the way I see it." Moon's expression was a picture of fortitude and strength. "But my momma taught me to believe in the American Way. If I wash my face and comb my hair and show up on time and work hard and don't complain, sooner or later I'm bound get a promotion, a good medical plan, and an annual increase in pay."

Parris nodded to indicate his approval. "I don't suppose you'd care to tell me who you're gonna kill for twenty-five cents."

"I thought you'd never ask." Moon eyed his friend, then Sam Reed. "Strictly confidential, your ears only?"

"My lips are sewed shut."

"Mine as well," Sam Reed said.

"I might be able to stretch the rules and tell Professor Reed—but not you, pard." Moon managed a wonderfully sorrowful expression. "That file is marked NOT FOR SMALL-TOWN COPS."

"Okay. Keep the victim's identity to yourself." Scott Parris's eyes twinkled like two blue stars in the half-darkness. "I don't suppose you'd care to mention who's paying you twenty-five cents to off this bucket of buzzard guts."

Moon shook his head. "Client identity is also strictly confidential."

"You could tell me." Parris looked hurt. "I'm your best buddy."

"Don't make no difference. Some folks may look down on our line of work, but us guns for hire have a strict code of ethics."

"Oh, all right. Just the same, I wish you'd found a slightly more respectable sideline."

"Me too, pard. But there's not much call for Ute hedge-fund managers with no experience or money to speak of."

Parris nodded. "Times is hard."

Moon agreed. "But they'll get better."

"I sure hope so." The splinter between Parris's teeth had lost its taste. He was not one to complain, but . . . *Sam Reed ought to buy a box of those colored ones that have different flavors, like strawberry and lemon and ginger.* As his wealthy host cringed inside, Scott Parris tossed the chewed ivory sliver aside, and replaced it with a fresh fifty-dollar toothpick.

CHAPTER FORTY-FOUR

THE FINAL HOURS

After his turn as lookout, the chief of police settled into a comfortable armchair. With a satisfying yawn, Scott Parris clasped his hands across his chest and closed his eyes.

Charlie Moon stationed himself at the window that framed a moonlit landscape with the Reed residence as its centerpiece. The sprawling brick house seemed to be waiting for whatever might happen when the eleventh hour tolled. The night was rolling in from the mountains like molten obsidian and the stillness was absolutely crystalline. After a few hundred heartbeats, Moon had almost lost track of why he was here. And where *here* was, on the face of a weary planet that had tired of turning and was gradually slowing to a halt. Presently, it seemed as if Time itself had stopped to take a nap.

By and by the illusion was shattered by a frolicsome wind that drifted in to worry last year's brown grasses and agitate a sedate community of crispy leaves into a swirl of frenzied confusion. Its preparatory work complete, the playful breeze departed to other venues and fresh mischief, but only to be replaced by her older, more serious sibling, who came with gusty huffs. Big Sister's bluffing puffs did not amount to much. A madcap tumbleweed bounced and rolled across Reed's backyard. Spindly bone-white aspen branches flailed with feigned anxiety; newborn leaves chattered with childish laughter.

All this was taking its toll on Charlie Moon.

It was one of those black, bittersweet evenings when a man calls to mind faded images of a long-lost sweetheart; days and opportunities that have slipped away forever. His soul shrouded in inner twilight, Moon listened to sorrowful winds whine and sigh in the pines. The lonely man sighed along with them.

Unaware of the Ute's uncharacteristic angst, and Parris's worries that Mrs. Reed was onto the game, Samuel Reed would have given a week's income for the ability to imitate the steely coolness of this pair of silent men, but he could feel a bad case of the fidgets coming on. What the man of business sorely needed was something to keep him busy, but he found himself with nothing to do but pace. Clear his throat. Check his wristwatch. And, from time to time, mumble incomprehensibly.

Scott Parris cracked the lid of his left eye at the hyperactive fellow. "It's liable to be a long night." The lawmen did not intend to leave before dawn. "Why don't you stretch out on the bed and catch yourself a few winks." *And quit being such a botheration.*

Samuel Reed replied in a tone that was very close to being tart, "Because I am not sleepy." Like a caged cougar perpetually looking for a way out, the edgy man stalked around the bedroom, eyeing every shadowy corner, measuring the height of the walls. Evidently finding no means of escape, he strode across the carpeted floor to the window. Unable to peer over the tall Indian's shoulder, Reed asked, "Do you see anything interesting?"

The Ute nodded.

The curious fellow elevated himself on tiptoes. "What?"

"Rabbit in the flower bed."

"Oh." Withdrawing to pick up a tiny cup of freshly brewed espresso from the bedside table, Reed took a tentative sip before gulping what was left down his gullet. As the overdose of caffeine began to do a buzz-job on his brain, he began to think about his wife with an intensity of interest that surprised him. *I wonder what Irene is doing at this very moment.* Something inexplicable, no doubt. *Probably painting her toenails pink.* Which was pointless, since Mrs. Reed's toenails were naturally pink. *Or plucking her eyebrows out by the roots.* The mystified spouse sighed. *And then drawing fake eyebrows on her skin with a pencil.* Wondering what Irene might be *doing* was not the end of Reed's curiosity; the wealthy man would have given a tidy sum to know what his missus was *thinking* about. Despite being endowed with a remarkable intellect that managed most knotty issues quite well, Samuel Reed shared one characteristic with ordinary men—the minds of women in general and his wife's in particular were an impenetrable mystery to the scientist-turned-entrepreneur. He plopped his butt onto the bed. *What I need is another cup of espresso.* He got up. Cleared his throat again. Checked his wristwatch again. Mumbled incomprehensibly again. Began to pace again. And—

All this motion and commotion was disturbing Scott Parris's catnap. *Enough already.* Something had to be done to terminate this infernal pacing about, bed plopping, throat clearing, timepiece checking, and whatnot—and the chief of police was just the man to do it. For a fellow accustomed to saying howdy to felons with a ham-size fist in the face, Parris was uncommonly gentle. "Charlie, seems to me it's Sam's turn to spin a yarn."

The almost-invisible Ute might have nodded his black John B. Stetson. It was too dark to tell for sure.

"Sorry, fellas—but I'll have to pass." Reed raised his hands in a self-effacing gesture. "I don't know any good stories."

The town cop responded with that eloquent silence reserved for whiners, welchers, and teammates who did not pull their weight.

The amiable Ute offered a helpful suggestion: "You could tell us how you got rich as Fort Knox."

Reed spoke to the Indian's back. "I would be embarrassed to provide a dry account of my investment activities, particularly after the splendid entertainment you two have served up tonight." A chuckle bubbled up from his belly. "I mean, a knuckle-dragging ape chasing a lady jogger across the golf course—and the county's most respected rancher hiring out as an assassin for twenty-five cents per hit. Really, now—how could a stodgy businessman compete with such imaginative tales as that?"

Parris told him how: "You could lie a little bit."

"Oh, I don't know that I could do *that*." Reed frowned, but there was a merry sparkle in his eye.

Charlie Moon stared at the windowpane. "It's not flat-out lying unless you can convince us it's the truth."

Parris nodded. "And me and Charlie promise not to believe a solitary word you say."

The Ute's voice was silky soft. "Think of it as creative fiction."

"I'd like to oblige, really I would." Samuel Reed kicked his toe at a hideous flower that seemed to be growing out of the carpet. *That's what I get for allowing Irene to decorate the guest house.* "But there is simply no way to make a story about myself entertaining." The middle-aged man smirked. "Unless I sprinkled it with lurid sexual exploits and truckloads of gratuitous violence."

"It works on TV," Parris said.

But not for Charlie Moon. "What I had in mind was something that would educate me and Scott. In hard times like this, we could benefit from knowing how to invest any spare dollar we might come across." The lookout watched a cottontail munch at a tender sprout. "We'd be much obliged if you'd give us some pointers."

"Of course. Such as how to place bets on sporting events." Reed ground the offensive carpet-rose under his heel. "And how to predict next week's price of beef."

"That'd be a great help to a rancher like myself." Moon waited for a heartbeat. "And while you're at it, you could tell us why you're so sure that somebody plans to shoot you dead tonight."

Scott Parris was instantly alert. *Charlie's onto something.*

"A successful investor does not share his trade secrets," Reed replied. "Not even with his closest friends."

"Then make up something," the town cop said. "Tell us whatever comes into your head."

Barely aware of Parris's presence in the guest-house bedroom, the canny investor fixed his entire attention on the tribal investigator's back. "I am tempted to have a go at it." He paused for a few heartbeats. "But fiction is not my long suit."

"Take your time," Moon said softly. "I expect you'll come up with something."

Reed's small audience waited.

And waited.

The Indian's still form at the window might have been chiseled from stone.

Parris might have been sound asleep.

Even the wind in the pines had fallen to the merest whisper.

It seemed that the ensuing silence would never end.

Until Samuel Reed cleared his throat. And began.

CHAPTER FORTY-FIVE

THE SCIENTIST-ENTREPRENEUR'S STORY

"I've come up with a first-rate corker!" The edgy physicist seated himself on the edge of the bed. "Forget all about crazed apes that pursue terrified ladies across golf courses and hard-up ranchers that hire out as two-bit assassins—compared to the tallness of my tale, such occurrences are utterly commonplace." He twirled a finger in the air. "I am about to spin a yarn that'll set your heads to gyrating."

If Moon had been a fox, his ears would've pricked at this. They did.

If Parris had been a 'possum, he would've grinned. He did.

The over-caffeinated storyteller got up from the bed and strutted across the dimly illuminated room. "In the interest of complete disclosure and utterly disarming honesty, I shall stipulate right up front that my offering is presented entirely in the interest of entertainment." He cast a sly glance at the Ute. "By no means do I intend to convey the impression that there is the least grain of truth in it."

Sam Reed's glance had not gone unnoticed by Scott Parris. *Something's going on between him and Charlie, and I'd give a week's wages to know what it is.* The wallet in his hip pocket felt paper-thin. *Okay, let's say a day's pay.*

Without shifting his gaze from Professor Reed's upscale

residence, Charlie Moon leaned against the window frame and settled in to enjoy the slippery man's performance. *This oughta be good.*

It oughta and it would.

Clasping his hands behind his waist, Reed began to pace back and forth alongside the bed. "In strictest confidence, I shall reveal the secret of my enviable success as the business world's most remarkable prognosticator." Inordinately pleased with this opening line, the consummate actor helped himself to a deep breath. He expelled it with: "So. How do you fellows like it so far?"

Parris shrugged. Also grunted.

When the taciturn Indian did not respond, Reed paused in midstride. "And what say you, Mr. Moon?"

Silence hung heavily around the Ute, like the atmosphere gets just before a rip-snorting cyclone comes a-whirling over the prairie to yank trees up, roots and all. Moon's response was like a rumble of distant thunder. "I'd say you haven't quite got started yet."

"A fair observation." Reed affected a worried look. "I must admit to some apprehension." Pure, unadulterated malarkey—the narrator was as cool as the evening breeze. "In fact, I am not sure I should continue." Six strong men with a hundred yards of duct tape could not have sealed his lips.

The Ute-thunder rumbled closer. "Why's that?"

"What I have to say is likely to prove unnerving. Perhaps even ruin your day."

"Go right ahead," Moon said.

"Very well, if you insist." He restarted his pacing, paused after three strides. "In this tale, I shall refer to an entirely ficti-tious version of myself. With that fact in mind—and despite my natural modesty—I shall present my compelling narrative in that popular form known as 'first person.'"

"Works for me," Parris muttered.

"Prepare yourselves for a shock." Samuel Reed drew himself up to his full height. "I do not foresee the future—I *remember* it."

The tale-spinner had captured his small audience's attention. Charlie Moon and Scott Parris waited for the narrative's next line. And continued to wait.

Until the white cop had had enough. "Well?" Parris growled.

Reed arched an eyebrow. "Well, *what?*"

The cop added a scowl to the growl. "You tell us you remember what's going to happen, and that's it—the whole shebang?"

"Certainly." The storyteller assumed an innocent expression. "For those present who are not familiar with common literary forms, my nine-word narrative was what is known in the trade as a *short* story."

Moon couldn't help but grin.

Parris's mouth gaped. "Then that's The End?"

Reed pursed his lips. "Just so."

This wasn't fair, and Scott Parris's mild fair-weather scowl was beginning to turn stormy. The cop who'd killed a half-dozen felons and maimed more malefactors than he bothered to recall resorted to the most cruel violence of all—harsh literary criticism: "Well I don't mean to sound picky, but it'd be nice to hear how a human being could 'remember' what hadn't happened yet."

"Yes." Reed sighed. "I am also curious about that point. But unlike highly proficient yarn-spinners who sit on the courthouse steps seven days a week, whiling away their idle hours squirting tobacco spittle from between their lips and whittling pine knots into curious shapes, I lack the talent to fabricate a five-hundred-page novel right on the spot. However, if I should wake up in the middle of the night with nothing important to occupy my mind, I might give the matter some thought." He smiled at the lawmen. "Perhaps on some future occasion, as we three chummy hardcases sit around a smoky campfire chewing on rancid buffalo jerky and sipping cowboy java whilst filtering grounds betwixt the comical gaps in our teeth, I will flesh out my story with a few lines of explanatory prose."

The disgruntled cop shook his head. *What a crappy cop-*

out. Internally, Parris made that rude sound that is known in vulgar circles as "the raspberry." He might as well have expressed his opinion aloud.

Even your hard-boiled storyteller is not without feelings, and Samuel Reed's had every reason to be hurt. The man apparently had skin like a rhinoceros. "Thank you for your kind attention; this little exercise in fiction has been amusing." He glanced at his wristwatch. "But fun does not pay the bills; business must be attended to. Please excuse me for a few minutes while I do." With this, their host withdrew from the guest-house bedroom.

TENDING TO HIS BUSINESS

Samuel Reed seated himself at his desk in the parlor, where he busied himself with his computer.

This activity proved to be both effective and profitable.

The investor contacted a broker in St. Louis and sold two thousand shares of General Electric (it would tumble two dollars by tomorrow afternoon). He also called a gaming agency in Reno to place modest wagers on several sporting events. A Dublin horse race (Danny Boy's Luck would win by a nose), a middleweight prizefight in Chicago (Raymond Dymouski would dance in his corner while LeRoy "Sweet Evening Breeze" Washington took a refreshing nap at center ring, a championship bicycle-polo game in Mexico City (the all-star team from Canada would rout the frustrated Colombians), and so on and so forth and et cetera. The entrepreneur did not rest until all his tasks were completed. All told, Reed's profits during this brief interlude would amount to a mere forty-two thousand dollars and change, but by such modest gains are mighty fortunes made.

While Professor Sam Reed was tending to his business, he was unaware that Scott Parris had taken up the lookout post at the bedroom window. And that Charlie Moon was standing behind him, peering over his shoulder at the computer display.

The Ute poker player, who had placed a few bets on ball games in his days, couldn't help but wonder what it would be like to "remember" who'd won the Super Bowl or the World Series *before* the games were played. An absurd fantasy, of course. And even if a man had an advantage like that, sooner or later his luck would run out. Those hard-eyed, coldhearted fellows who make a living off folks that can't stay away from fancy card tables, spinning roulette wheels, and noisy slots might not be Rhodes Scholars, but neither were they simpletons. One way or another, they'd be bound to find out about a high roller who consistently won more bets than the Laws of Probability permitted. The fact that Sam Reed was still alive suggested that the wealthy man was either extraordinarily cautious or very lucky. Or both. Charlie Moon's interest was piqued when Reed opened a commodities-trends Web site. The cattle rancher naturally shared Reed's interest in a graph that charted the hourly prices of American beef.

When Samuel Reed left the commodities page to peruse Bloomberg.com, Charlie Moon lost interest in the businessman's business. He returned to the bedroom, where Scott Parris was at the window, watching a black owl-shadow slip over the moonlit ground like the dark preview of an upcoming nightmare.

Within a minute, Sam Reed also entered the bedroom. "My business is taken care of." But it wasn't. He paused, blinked like a man remembering something. "Oops, almost forgot. There's one last matter to check on." He punched several keys on a cell phone, then dialed a preprogrammed number. When the process was complete, the investor made a low whistle. "Just as I expected, the market for beef is leveling off." He aimed a questioning gaze at the Ute rancher. "By tomorrow, prices will begin to slip. I do hope you have sold your splendid whiteface cattle."

Charlie Moon nodded. "And I'm much obliged to you, sir. Without your tip, the Columbine would be in deep trouble."

"It was a distinct pleasure to be of assistance." Reed resumed his seat on the bed.

The rancher was mildly amused at his host's duplicity.

Sam Reed checked the beef prices on his computer a few minutes ago, so the telephone call was all for show. But to what purpose? *I guess he wanted to remind me that I'm indebted to him.* Which was probably nothing more than the shadowy side of his host's human nature. But a second possibility made Moon uneasy. What if the wealthy man had some kind of payback in mind?

A WOMAN'S WORK

While Samuel Reed, Scott Parris, and his Ute deputy were preparing for the climax—or anticlimax—to this evening's minor melodrama, Mrs. Reed—all alone in her upscale home—was not idle. Like her husband, the lady was busy tending to business. Irene was putting her house in order. It is rightly said that a woman's work is never done, and it would be impractical to provide a detailed list of her various tasks. Suffice it to say that Samuel Reed's spouse was *arranging* things. What in particular?

Oh, this and that.

A pair of antique coin-silver candlesticks on the purple porphyry mantelpiece.

A selection of white and yellow rosebuds in a delicate Connecticut cranberry vase.

Also schedules, without which a household cannot properly function.

As she arranged, the lady was thinking. About her invariably prompt husband, who was due home at 11 P.M. And about that other, younger man in her life.

As it happened, only about nine miles away as the owl-shadow flies, that *other man* was about to receive the most significant communication in a life that had—especially of late—been filled to overflowing with jarring events.

CHAPTER FORTY-SIX

CHICO PEREZ GETS THE MESSAGE

Times were tough enough already, but what with being un-employed, sleeping in the backseat of his Camaro, and bandaged and aching from Daisy's violent attack, the former assistant golf-course groundskeeper was—to sum it up in a single syllable—glum. In four more, down in the dumps. And no wonder.

Chico Perez didn't have enough cash to fill his gas tank, which had about six gallons sloshing around inside. After three days of dining on bland peanut butter spread onto saltine crackers, he was hungry for something a man could get his teeth into. But, like gasoline, beefsteak wasn't free, and the hard-up fellow needed to find some way of raising enough ready money to feed himself and drive his classic Chevy a long way from Granite Creek, Colorado. Figuring out how to deal with his cash-flow problem would take some serious thought, which was why Perez was doing what he generally did when he needed to think, which was go for a slow drive after dark in some lonely, out-of-the-way place. Which in this instance was Forest Road 1040 in the mountains above Granite Creek, also known by locals as IRS Road.

Mulling over the possibilities, Perez scratched at his bandaged head, which itched like a tribe of hyperactive chiggers had set up camp. *I could pull off a convenience-store robbery.* Any half-wit could manage that, but there was always the risk that some nervous, pimply-face clerk with more testosterone than brains would produce a Saturday-night special and commence to perforate a professional robber's hide until all the ammo was used up. *Maybe I should break into a rich person's summer house here in the mountains and steal some stuff I could sell.* He squinted at the dark, twisting forest lane. *Like expensive jewelry and cameras and computers.* But, from previous experience as a burglar, Perez realized that his prospects were not altogether promising. *Most rich folks didn't get that way by being dopes, so they don't leave much in their second homes that's worth stealing.* On top of that, fencing purloined property in a little burg like Granite Creek would be next to impossible. It occurred to Perez that being a thief was not nearly as appealing as some other vocations, like panhandling in Aspen or Taos or rolling drunk college kids in Boulder for the few dollars they had in their pockets. *Or maybe I should—*

This latest felonious inspiration was interrupted by the mobile phone clipped to his belt. The distinctively harsh warble of a yellow-headed blackbird—which is not unlike the squeaky creaking of a rusted gate hinge—signaled that he had received a text message. Which was Mrs. Reed's preferred method of communication. Chico Perez pulled his Chevy to a stop and read the few words. Like other young men who enjoy being right, he was pleased to see Irene's characteristic salutation and signature.

> HONEY BABE
> IM HOME ALONE
> COME RIGHT OVER
> DONT PHONE
> TXT ME ON MY NEW CELL
> IR

Perez thumbed in his response:

> OK IM ON MY WAY

After making a hard U-turn that startled another young buck (and his equally edgy harem of lady friends), the eager boyfriend was on his way. *This is my chance to make a big score. Irene keeps three or four credit cards in her purse, and I bet she's got a couple of thousand bucks of spare change in the house. Why didn't I think of this before?*

This was a thousand percent better than knocking off a convenience store or burglarizing somebody's fifteen-room "cabin."

I'll hold a knife to Irene's throat until she coughs up all the cash in the house, then I'll snap the rich bitch's neck and hit the road.

Heading downgrade, the young fellow threw back his head and, in a mellow voice that belied his capacity for cruelty, boomed out, "I'll be comin' 'round the mountain when I come!"

GRANITE CREEK'S TOP COP ALSO
GETS THE MESSAGE

As the brutal young bully bellowed at the top of his lungs, Samuel Reed was in the guest-house kitchenette, brewing a fresh batch of high-test espresso while happily humming "Let Me Call You Sweetheart." Charlie Moon had left the comfortable stakeout headquarters to make another round of the Reed property.

Scott Parris was at the bedroom window, eyeballing the Reed residence. Barely a minute after Chico Perez had received and responded to the suggestive text message, the chief of police received a heads-up from Dispatch on his GCPD mobile phone. The subject was a "relevant communication" from Mrs. Reed. *I wonder what she's up to?* His internal query was followed promptly by the text from Irene Reed's tapped cell phone. As he read it, Parris held his breath. *If that ain't the "all's clear" signal for the boyfriend to come over and help her commit a homicide, then I'm a monkey's favorite uncle.* Parris was rereading the text message when

Perez's reply scrolled onto the screen. The cop's mouth formed a silent *Wow!*

There could be no doubt about it now.

It's coming down. Mrs. Reed and her boyfriend plan to do away with Sam Reed tonight. Scott Parris set his heavy jaw like a steel vise. *But it's not gonna happen on my watch.*

CHAPTER FORTY-SEVEN

"For there's another whose tears will shed.
For the one who lies in a prairie bed.
It breaks my heart to think of her now,
She has curled these locks, she has kissed this brow."

THINGS GET TOLERABLY MESSY

The tribal investigator was on the rocky ridge overlooking Samuel Reed's residential property when he took his friend's call on the GCPD portable radio. A virtual shadow-man among the junipers and pines, the Ute listened to Scott Parris's terse report of the text-message exchange. "Got it," Moon said, and thumbed the radio off.

Without saying a word to Samuel Reed about the shady character who was coming to pay a late-evening call on his wife, Scott Parris remained at the bedroom window.

Charlie Moon watched a dead-silent Shadowlane Avenue for almost a quarter of an hour before a big-hatted young man in a Dodge pickup older than he was zipped by at about sixty miles per hour. The aged truck rattled at every rusty joint and the right front fender shuddered like it might fall off at any moment. *Knox and Slocum will put a big ticket on that cowboy if he don't slow down.* Four minutes later Moon smiled at a shiny Volkswagen convertible with the top down—four laughing teenagers were on their way to town. The happy youngsters left an uneasy quiet in their wake.

The Indian's antenna went up when a pair of headlights appeared almost a mile away on Shadowlane. Moon didn't know *how* he knew, but he was dead certain that . . . *this'll be him.* Sure enough, as the vehicle came closer, it began to slow. The tribal investigator watched a sleek, low-slung Chevrolet sedan pull to the curb about fifty yards from the Reeds' driveway. Admiring the profile of the classic Camaro, which had been the automobile of his dreams about twenty years ago, Moon watched the driver emerge and waited to get a better look. The fellow fit the general description of Mrs. Reed's boyfriend . . . *but it looks like the guy's head is bandaged. Maybe he's had an accident. Or . . . he might've been in a fight.* The part-time cop smiled. *I'd hate to see what the other guy looks like.* He thumbed the Talk button on the GCPD radio and pressed the instrument against his ear to hear a corresponding click. "Company coming," he murmured.

Parris's happy anticipation rang in Moon's ear. "Our guy?"

"Big fella. About the right age. And he's driving an old Camaro."

"Blond hair down to his shoulders?"

"I don't see any hair at all, pard—his head's either bandaged or he's wearing a white turban."

"Never mind—it's gotta be Perez." Parris checked his wristwatch. *And right on time.* "The boyfriend's been invited, and he's showed up. Perez is here to help the lady do a job on her old man."

"You sure Reed can't hear you?"

"Sure I'm sure." The cop in the bedroom craned his neck to glance at the entrepreneur in the dimly illuminated parlor, who—apparently oblivious to all else—was busy conducting business. "He's on the phone again, probably making a deal to buy IBM."

As the Ute began making his way down the ridge, he was experiencing a touch of the familiar twisting sensation in his gut. *Something's not quite right about this.* "So we just wait to see what happens?"

"That's the drill."

"Our visitor's headed through the trees toward the back of the house. No . . . hold on. He's stopped now . . . taking a look around." Seemingly of their own volition, Moon's long legs stretched to pick up the pace. "There's still time for me intercept him before he gets there."

"No way, Charlie—we stay with plan A. Let him pass. After Mrs. R. lets him inside, we'll watch the house and see what develops."

I don't like it. "What's plan B?"

"Things get kinky, we'll improvise." Apprehension is a communicable illness and Scott Parris was beginning to feel a little feverish. *It ain't like Charlie Moon to get antsy.* To make sure his deputy didn't go off half-cocked and muck things up, he added in a softer whisper, "Come inside and help me keep an eye on Mr. R.—just in case he realizes something's up and freaks out. We'll watch the show from here in the penthouse." To terminate the discussion, the chief of police shut his radio off.

Samuel Reed pocketed his mobile phone as he entered the guest-house bedroom. "So what's Mr. Moon reporting—someone skulking about outside?"

He's got better ears than I figured. "Just some guy driving by." Parris faked a yawn. "Charlie's coming inside for a spell."

Parris's cell phone played a few bars of "Golden Slippers." *That's Dispatch again.* He snatched the instrument from his pocket and barked, "What?"

Dispatcher Clara Tavishuts told him what.

Parris felt the skin on the back of his neck prickle. "Thanks, Clara." He broke the connection just as Charlie Moon opened the parlor door and stepped inside. As the Ute's lanky form loomed in the bedroom, the chief of police addressed both men. "Mrs. Reed has just placed a 911 emergency call. She claims somebody is attempting to break into the rear entrance of her home." Parris took another look at the Reed's back door. *And there's nobody there.*

Samuel Reed received this piece of news with a cock of his head. "That's rather peculiar, don't you think? I mean—

there's obviously no burglar about or you fellows would have spotted him." The husband rolled his owlish eyes. "Ever since her supposed encounter with the so-called Crowbar Burglar, Irene has been nervous about being home alone. My wife must be hearing things."

Moon and Parris exchanged edgy looks. And thought identical thoughts.

It's a long time before eleven o'clock. Something's gone wrong.

Samuel Reed resumed his pacing and began humming another old tune.

Alerted by a slight jerk of his friend's head, Moon strode to the window. Both lawmen watched Chico Perez's bulky form approach the back door of the physicist's home. The man with the bandaged head did not bother to knock. He fished a key out of his pocket, unlocked and opened the door—and stepped into that final darkness.

A pair of pistol shots popped like firecrackers.

Chico Perez roared like a gored bull.

Simultaneous with Irene's shrill scream—two more shots.

As the wounded man charged the woman, Charlie Moon was racing down the guest-house stairway four steps at a time. Scott Parris was one stride behind.

As Perez got his right hand on Irene's throat, the Ute was on a dead run to the Reed residence.

His .38 snub-nosed revolver ready to conduct serious business, a huffing-puffing Parris was coming on like a steam locomotive—but not quite so close now to the rangy rancher.

What the lawmen found inside was more or less what they had expected.

With several bullet holes in his abdomen, Perez was flat on his back, spitting cherry-red blood that dribbled along his chin and onto his neck. "Crazy bitch!" He coughed and gurgled. "She's gut-shot me—I'm done for." The dying man waved his hand in front of his eyes . . . as if to ward off some horrific vision that only he could see. "No—" he rasped, "stay away from me!"

Crumpled on the floor like a discarded rag doll, her pearl-handled Browning .32-caliber automatic death-gripped in her right hand—Irene Reed was likewise *done for.* Perez had snapped her lovely neck.

The summoned ambulance arrived in seven minutes flat. As her two co-workers were loading the cursing, blood-soaked man into the white Ford van, the tight-lipped EMT consulted her wristwatch and pronounced the adult Caucasian female dead at 10:14 P.M.

While sirens screamed to clear the way to Snyder Memorial Hospital, Chico Perez groaned and moaned away his spirit. He expired as the anxious EMTs rolled the stainless-steel gurney into the ER.

Minutes later, one of the emergency medical technicians who had tended to the wounded man while the ambulance rolled along at seventy-plus miles per hour complained of a headache and knocked off early from his customary 8 P.M. to 8 A.M. shift. The seasoned professional did not withdraw to his lonely basement apartment, wash down a couple of aspirins with ten-dollar-a-liter red wine, and hit the sack. He went to his mother's house, woke the old lady up, and told her about the homicide and how he'd had lots of company on the way to the hospital. No less than a half-dozen "unauthorized passengers" had gone along for the ride, all eager to witness the expiration of the fatally wounded man.

Momma reached out to pat his hand. "Who were they, Sonny?"

"They was all women, Ma—young women." The EMT cleared his throat and, for the first time since he'd walked through the front door—looked his mother straight in the eye. "*Dead* young women."

"Oh, my!"

That should have been sufficient.

But when Sonny turned his face away, his mother heard him say, "One of 'em was that dead lady we found on the floor beside the big guy—the one that shot him."

CHAPTER FORTY-EIGHT

A BRIEF STUDY IN CONTRASTS

The scenes at the Reed residence and at Charlie Moon's home could hardly have been more dissimilar.

At the very *instant* when Irene Reed was perforating Chico Perez's hide with lead slugs, the women in Mr. Moon's life were cleaning off the supper table in the Columbine headquarters dining room.

As the emergency medical technician pronounced Irene Reed dead, Daisy Perika yawned a good-night to Sarah Frank, toddled down the hallway to enter her bedroom, closed the door, turned off the lights, crawled under the covers and— No.

What's this?

Daisy did switch the lights off, but the fragile old soul *never made it to her bed* to crawl under the covers.

Something is definitely amiss.

THE PRONE FIGURE

A few minutes later, as Sarah slips under a colorful Amish quilt in the adjacent bedroom, Charlie Moon's aunt is lying on the floor, in a narrow space between her bed and the oak-paneled wall. She is not moving a muscle.

Is Daisy Perika dead? It would appear so. Perhaps the aged woman has succumbed to a heart attack or stroke. Very sad. We can comfort ourselves with the thought that she went quickly.

But wait. Cup your ear. Do you hear that feeble thumpity-thump? Daisy's heart still pumps.

Is she merely unconscious? Quite the contrary.

The tribal elder is wide awake and extraordinarily alert. She listens.

Listens to what?

Here is a hint: the side of Daisy Perika's head rests on a cold metal vent.

This isolated factoid does not provide sufficient illumination to a murky situation? What one wants is a detailed elaboration?

Very well. Here it is: ducts are commonly installed underneath floors to provide pathways for heated air to flow from the furnace. When not serving that essential but rather noisy function, these conduits are excellent transmitters of sound. Especially between adjacent rooms.

SLY OLD FOX

Daisy Perika waited until all she could hear from the bedroom next door was a rhythmic breathing, not unlike the peaceful sigh of a Hawaiian surf. Convinced that Sarah must be fast asleep, the crafty old woman pulled a canvas grocery bag from under her bed. After turning the floor lamp on, she emptied the fabric sack and placed her collection of Chico Perez memorabilia on the cedar chest of drawers. This was not going to be an easy task. Perez's wallet had no sentimental value, but parting with his more *personal* property would be particularly painful. For the longest time, Daisy shifted her wistful gaze back and forth between the trophies. The more presentable of the prizes was tastefully displayed in a gallon Ziploc bag, and the others (a matched pair) were sealed in a mayonnaise jar half filled with alcohol. *Giving this stuff up will be like cutting off the fingers on my right hand, but if I get caught with it I'll end up in prison sleeping on a rickety little cot with a smelly mattress that's got more fleas and bedbugs than stuffing.* And that was just for starters. *All I'll have to eat will be moldy month-old bread and dirty water from a rusty bucket.* The potential convict could not bear even to think about the toilet facilities.

Daisy had no choice but to dispose of her trophies straightaway. *I'll hide them someplace where nobody'll ever think of looking.* The wallet would also have to go, but not before she helped herself to Perez's cash money. *It's not like he needs it anymore.*

Daisy would not learn until tomorrow that Chico Perez had survived her violent walking-stick assault—only to be shot to death by Irene Reed. As she was removing the greenbacks from the stolen wallet, the pickpocket realized that something was concealed in a space under the slot where Perez kept his Visa card, Colorado driver's license, and Social Security card. Hoping to discover something of monetary interest in this hiding place, Daisy proceeded to investigate.

Sadly, there was no secret stash of folded money.

What she did find was another driver's license, a second Social Security card, and a snapshot of a smiling woman. *Probably another one of his married girlfriends.* Daisy squinted at the picture. *I'm sure I've seen the face before, but I can't remember where or when.* She examined the expired driver's license and the tattered old Social Security card. Neither had been issued to Chico Perez, but the face in the photo on the out-of-state license was a dead ringer for the man Daisy had assaulted with her oak walking stick—except for one detail. In this older picture, the young man's long hair was straight, and black as chimney soot. *But it's Perez, all right.* The name on the concealed ID was different—and as hauntingly familiar as the woman's face in the photograph. *Now where've I heard that name before?* As soon as Daisy posed the question, the recollection bubbled up from the shadowy depths of her memory.

So that's who Perez really was.

It was indeed a small world, and now Daisy understood the *pitukupf*'s sinister warning. *It wasn't Lyle Thoms the little runt was warning me about—it was this Perez devil.* This revelation buoyed her spirits almost as much as pocketing the bad man's money. *Now I'm double-glad the rascal's dead!*

But, intriguing as this new twist was, it did nothing to alleviate the predicament Daisy found herself in. Despite the fact that Perez *had it coming,* the incriminating evidence of her noteworthy accomplishment still must be concealed— which vexed the old soul no end. The tribal elder found a dusty shoe box in her bedroom closet and removed a pair of shiny black shoes she hadn't worn since attending a cousin's funeral. *I'll put everything in this box and then drop it into that old dry well behind the blacksmith's shop.*

A good start. But it is terribly hard to discard testimonials to one's valiant deeds.

It is easy to compromise.

Daisy desperately needed some small memento to remember her adventure by. *I know what I'll do—I'll hold on to the woman's picture; nobody could prove I took that from Perez.* This decision made, she slipped the snapshot into her purse and put the wallet with both sets of ID and the other evidence of her righteous assault into the shoe box. She wrapped the cardboard container in brown paper and secured the parcel with Scotch tape and two yards of white cotton twine.

There, that looks nice. So nice that . . . *it seems like such a shame to toss it in a well.* A melancholy sigh. *But I can't think of anything else to do. . . .*

Yes she could!

Daisy had experienced one of those delightful inspirations that—if she had been a 1950s cartoon character like petite Minnie Mouse or Li'l Abner's pipe-smoking mammy—a hundred-watt light bulb would have flashed on above her head. And the more the plotter turned the notion over and looked at it from this way and that, the more she liked it. Inordinately pleased with herself, Daisy Perika cackled wickedly.

Had a sensitive soul such as Sarah Frank heard the cackle, she might have characterized it as *insanely* wicked. As it happened, the eighteen-year-old girl in the adjacent bedroom did hear the tribal elder's guttural chuckle. Sort of. While she was asleep.

Sarah awakened from a pleasant dream with a startled expression on her face. She sat up in bed wondering what the matter was. Came up with a blank. The girl shuddered and hugged her knees. *Oh—I feel like something awful has just happened!* But (she assured herself) that was silly. *Nothing's wrong.*

And so the innocent laid her head back onto a billowy feather pillow, pulled the handsome quilt up to her chin, and yawned. Within a few heartbeats she was fast asleep.

It was sheer coincidence that the cinematic dream Sarah drifted into was a big-budget production starring Aunt Daisy.

It was pure chance that the vicious old woman was wearing a bloody butcher's apron.

And mere happenstance that the tribal elder—armed with an equally bloody butcher knife—was carving up a sizable side of meat.

Which wasn't beef.

CHAPTER FORTY-NINE

A LONG NIGHT'S WORK

Charlie Moon did what he could to assist his friend.

Scott Parris knew he'd messed up big-time and got ready to take his lumps. He set his square jaw, sucked in his gut, and got right at the awkward duty of briefing a half-dozen astonished GCPD cops and a couple of hard-eyed state-police officers on the clandestine stakeout. Parris did not mention the bet he'd made that he could keep Sam Reed alive until June 5, or the fact that the wealthy man had paid for the dubious services rendered by his bodyguards. There was no concealing the fact that the double homicide had occurred while the chief of police and his Indian friend were close enough to toss a rock at Chico Perez.

As a welcome diversion from this singular humiliation, Doc Simpson showed up "all bright-eyed and bushy-tailed" (as he described himself) and got right to work. After a cursory examination of Mrs. Reed's remains, the county medical examiner pronounced her demise as ". . . primarily due to crushed fourth and fifth cervical vertebrae." The sprightly octogenarian appended an incomprehensible string of medical et ceteras that was pointedly ignored by the collection of cops.

While the ME was occupying center stage, the chief of police was discreetly advised by Officer Alicia Martin that a grief-stricken and dazed Samuel Reed was wandering around aimlessly throughout the premises, mumbling over and over that he could "hardly believe that such a horrible thing could happen in my home." Parris read the riot act gently but firmly to the bereaved spouse. "Your home is an official crime scene, Professor Reed. You'll have to bunk somewhere else for a few days." Officer Martin graciously offered to drive the befuddled man wherever he'd like to go, and made several helpful suggestions.

Sam Reed agreed to be transported to the Silver Mountain Hotel, which thriving enterprise he could have purchased for a tiny fraction of his liquid assets.

Throughout all this frenetic activity, Charlie Moon had little more to do than verify Scott Parris's testimony about the evening's bloody events and provide moral support to his best friend. When, at about half past one, the tribal investigator deemed his duty done, he said good night to Parris and took leave of the official commotion. Moon maneuvered his Expedition out of the guest-house garage and threaded his way through a congregation of official vehicles. The sleek beetles winked and blinked bright red and blue eyes at him.

AN INCOMPLETE METAMORPHOSIS

As he rolled along on the highway toward home, Scott Parris's part-time deputy was gradually being transformed into a full-time rancher—his face set toward greener pastures. The nearer Charlie Moon got to the reality of his vast cattle ranch, the more this night's misadventure seemed like a lurid piece of fantasy. By the time he made a right turn, the bizarre double killing had taken on the surreal aspect of an absurd nightmare.

He slowed, pressed the gate-control button on his key chain, then—*I forgot that the gate's broken.* But, to Moon's surprise, it opened in response to the radio-frequency command.

This blessing was gratefully received.

Maybe my foreman or one of the cowboys got it working again. The amiable rancher felt a twinge of guilt. *I guess I was a little hard on that pushy technician who wanted to sell me a high-tech gate controller.* He smiled at the thought of calling from a telephone in China to open a gate in Colorado. As the creaky gate clanged shut behind him and Moon began to smell the earthy aromas of his home on the range, he decided to put the matter entirely out of his mind.

And almost succeeded.

Somewhere in the multidimensional depths of that vast inner space that clinical psychologists and cocktail-party experts refer to as the *subconscious,* Charlie Moon's brain was hard at work. At about the time the Expedition slipped silently by the foreman's residence, something ugly bubbled up. As the big rubber tires went rattling across the Too Late Creek bridge, Moon began to get a glimmer of a sinister notion. He parked under his favorite cottonwood and fixed his gaze on a bright star. How long he remained behind the steering wheel, watching the illusion of a distant sun slipping through the night sky while the seemingly immobile earth rotated, Mr. Moon neither knew nor cared. He spent the hours before dawn adding things up, fitting together pieces of a puzzle whose misshapen elements might have been created by a demented jigsaw operator.

At about that fine time when first light began to shine like heaven's smile and the warm morning began to flow over the high prairie, the lawman realized that even if he was right, nothing could be done about it—not by district attorneys, juries of peers, or solemn judges. Moreover, Moon could not quite shake off the notion that . . . *this might be one of those times when it's best just to leave things alone.*

Despite this night's bloody history, the dawning morning was filled with sweet mystery. As Moon watched the edge of the sun explode over the mountains to make another day, he smiled as he remembered what his father used to say. When the old man was presented with a knotty problem by the woman of the house, Daddy would lift his chin, grin at little Charlie's mother, and repeat the familiar deferral that had annoyed his wife no end.

Somewhere out there, Daddy's words were forming in the atmosphere.

Sifting through new cottonwood leaves, the early-morning breeze breathed a whisper, which formed between Moon's lips. *I'll have to think on it.*

And he did.

What it finally all boiled down to was, *If it wasn't for Sam Reed, the Columbine would be shut down.* The rancher owed him a staggering debt.

But what do you give a man who can pay hard cash for anything the world has to offer? Something money can't buy. Friendship. But Reed didn't need a week-kneed, fair-weather buddy who'd shrug off what was dead wrong and make feeble excuses like, "In this hard world, a man sometimes has to do hard things." No, what the rich man needed was a stand-up friend who'd do his level best to make things *right*.

Charlie Moon was that man.

CHAPTER FIFTY

7:57 A.M. SATURDAY, JUNE 5
BAD NEWS FOR BREAKFAST

While Charlie Moon slept in, Daisy Perika toddled into the Columbine headquarters kitchen, where Sarah Frank was working at the propane range. Seating herself at the table, Daisy returned the girl's chipper good-morning with a dismissive grunt.

Sarah was tending to a matched pair of black iron skillets. In one, four eggs fried sunny-side up in a shallow pool of olive oil. It its twin, eight strips of bacon sizzled to a crispy finish.

The tribal elder's nostrils barely detected the delectable scents of a hearty meal. *Most mornings, nothing smells better than pork fat frying—but I don't have any appetite.*

Barely audible on the FM radio (so as not to disturb the man upstairs), Flatt and Scruggs were trying to liven up the morning with "Foggy Mountain Breakdown."

Daisy lifted her chin to indicate her nephew's second-floor bedroom. "He's back."

"I heard him come in." The eighteen-year-old flipped the bacon strips. *I wonder what Charlie's been doing for the past few days.*

"There's no point in asking him," Daisy said.

Sarah turned to blink at the unnerving old woman. "Ask him what?"

"What he's been busying himself with." Daisy shrugged. "Charlie hardly ever talks about police business."

The girl barely suppressed a shudder. *She's reading my mind again.*

"You don't have any secrets from me." The sly old crone pointed to a spot over Sarah's head. "I can see your thoughts floating in a white balloon, like you was Little Orphan Annie in the comic strip."

The Ute-Papago orphan thought of a delightfully tart retort, but, being a proper young lady, she settled for: "Do you want your eggs well done?"

The elderly diner shook her head. "I couldn't choke down any cackleberries if my life depended on it."

At this instant, which was, eight o'clock on the dot, Lester and Earl yielded the airwaves to a Rocky Mountain Polytechnic journalism major whose happy task it was to report the local bad news.

Sarah persisted: "How about some nice, crispy bacon?"

Daisy made a hideous face. "Ugh!"

The girl gave up.

Too easily, Daisy thought. "Maybe I could manage a little bowl of oat—"

"Shush!" Sarah said.

To say that Daisy was taken aback would be an understatement worthy of a card-carrying member the tight-upper-lipped British aristocracy. In all the years she'd spent with Sarah Frank, the girl had never so much as raised her voice to the tribal elder. The aggrieved senior citizen glared at the upstart youth.

The object of the glare was turning up the volume on the radio. "Listen!"

Daisy cocked her ear to hear the newscaster's voice.

". . . The victims of last evening's homicide at 1200 Shadowlane Avenue have been identified as Mrs. Irene Reed—a resident at that address—and Chico Perez—a former employee of the Sand Hills Country Club. At approximately ten P.M., Mrs. Reed made a 911 call to report an attempted break-in. Chief of Police Scott Parris and a part-time deputy were on the scene shortly after the incident occurred. We are informed that Mrs. Reed shot Perez—and that before he died

of the gunshot wounds, Perez killed Mrs. Reed with his bare
hands. When we asked GCPD Officer Alicia Martin whether
Chico Perez might be the infamous Crowbar Burglar who
has been terrorizing local citizens, the response was a terse
'no comment.' We expect to have more on this breaking story
on today's *High Noon News*. We'll be back with a weather
forecast after this message from our sponsor." A ditty extol-
ling the virtues of Red Buffalo Snuff blared in the Columbine kitchen.

"Turn if off," Daisy snapped.

Sarah silenced the radio. "Mrs. Reed is that married
woman we followed to the golf course." She lowered the ring
of blue flame under the eggs. "That man she shot must have
been her boyfriend."

"It was him all right." Daisy knew he wasn't actually
Chico Perez, but that's who the dead man would remain to
the tribal elder—who was too old and set in her ways to call
him by his right name. The issue that troubled her was . . .
How could he have still been alive last night? Daisy's brow
furrowed into a disappointed scowl. *I was sure I'd killed him
with my walking stick.* The aged woman remembered previous unfortunates who had not survived her violent assaults.
Thus recollected, her victims paraded by her mind's eye
one-by-one, each fixing the Ute elder with an accusing stare.
A Navajo haunt went so far as to make a rude gesture. Daisy
found this experience immensely gratifying. She sneered at
some, laughed at others. *Every one of you scalawags had it
coming!*

By and by, nostalgia was elbowed aside by an unfamiliar
and unwelcome visitor.

Guilt.

Daisy attempted to comfort herself with the defense that
I'm just a tired old woman. (Listen to her self-pitying sigh.)
*Every once in a while I might make a mistake, but I always
do the best I can.* (Watch the salty tear form in her eye.) *I
can't help it if sometimes things don't work out like I intended.*

But enough of this maudlin whining. As far as Daisy is

concerned, apologizing is for prissy sissies and politicians who get caught with their hands in the cookie jar. The wielder of the oak walking staff was made of sterner stuff. What was called for was cold, hard analysis—looking the facts straight in the eye. *All that Chickasaw lowlife needed was two or three more good whacks to crack his head wide open.* So why hadn't she gotten the job done? *I just ran out of steam.* With the problem properly defined, what one wanted was a solution. The leathery-faced old soul jutted her chin in a bloodcurdling impression of Geronimo about to mount a take-no-prisoners attack on the Tombstone stagecoach. *What I need to do is keep my strength up.* Charlie Moon's determined auntie was just commencing to think that *maybe I ought to take three or four of those One A Day vitamin pills every morning . . .* when she was interrupted by the aforementioned orphan.

"Are you sure you don't want something to eat?" Sweet Sarah Frank patted Daisy on the arm. "I'd be happy to make you some oatmeal."

"Bite your tongue, Little Miss Do-good—you can save those Quaker flakes for another day." Sniffing at the tantalizing aroma of sizzling pork fat, the hungry old carnivore banged knife and fork on the table. "Bring me a half-dozen fried eggs, a pound of greasy bacon, and a stack of flapjacks tall enough to shade me from the noonday sun!"

CHAPTER FIFTY-ONE

MONDAY, JUNE 7
THE SNAPSHOT

Scott Parris and Charlie Moon practically had the Columbine headquarters to themselves. When the chief of police arrived at the ranch, Sarah Frank was leaving for a morning class at Rocky Mountain Polytechnic and Daisy Perika was in her bedroom watching a familiar-looking raven settle onto a tree branch just outside the window. Whatever conversation might have passed between Charlie Moon's enigmatic aunt and the so-called Delilah Darkwing is a matter known only to the Ute shaman and her feathered friend. Which is probably just as well.

Blissfully unaware of the old lady's sinister business, Moon invited his best friend into the kitchen.

Being more or less a member of the Columbine family, Scott Parris didn't wait for an invitation to belly up to the table. Like any sensible Western lawman, the town cop ambled over to his customary spot where he'd have his back to the wall, seated himself, and watched as his long, lean host folded himself into another chair. *Charlie looks like he's got something on his mind.*

Something was brewing besides coffee.

Moon poured himself a mug. *Scott looks like he didn't get a wink of sleep last night.* The rancher passed the blue enamel percolator and some welcome news to his friend. "Fred Thompson over at Cattleman's Bank called just as you pulled up under the cottonwood. He said to tell you that Sam Reed has conceded the wager. You can pick up your winnings when you're of a mind to."

Still high on last Friday night's excitement, Parris had not given much thought to the bet. "Thanks, Charlie." The blue-eyed cop grinned like a little boy with a triple scoop of strawberry ice cream in a chocolate waffle cone. "It'll be nice to thicken up my wallet with Reed's four hundred bucks."

"I imagine it will."

Charlie hates to miss out on a bet. "It's too bad you didn't get a piece of the action. That bet was a sure thing right from the start."

"I had my chance." *And I didn't pass it by.* But the Ute gambler would not be so graceless as to mention his winnings, which would make Scott's four hundred dollars seem like pocket change. Not right away. Somewhere down the road, maybe—on one of those occasions when his friend was getting a bit too big for his britches.

Resting his elbows on the table, the small-time winner leaned toward Moon and whispered, "I s'pose we need to talk about a thing or two."

The Ute nodded. "I reckon we do."

And they were about to, when the old woman who conversed with lonely ghosts, wild and domesticated animals, and a sinister dwarf who lived in an abandoned badger hole, managed to "just happen by." Presumably to tend to a few pressing domestic matters. Such as wiping an imaginary grease spot off the six-burner propane range. Turning off a hot-water faucet that wasn't dripping a drop. All the while, humming "Swing Low, Sweet Chariot." Seemingly oblivious to the lawmen's hastily contrived conversation about the weather, the old lady had both ears fine-tuned for any tidbit of gossip that might come her way.

Amused by her transparent stratagem, Charlie Moon could not allow the opportunity to pass without making a grab for its neck. Assuming his fair-to-middlin' poker face, the tribal investigator lowered his voice just enough to get his aunt's complete attention. He winked at his guest. "Is it true what I hear about you retiring?"

Parris was quick on the uptake. "I was gonna tell you all about it later on, but I guess now's good a time as any." He spoke in a low monotone. "It's set for the middle of next month and that's not a day too soon. I was all wore out before this bad business with Mrs. Reed and Chico Perez, but that double homicide has pushed me over the edge."

Daisy turned and tilted her head, thus aiming her best ear toward the conversation.

Charlie Moon continued the charade. "Is there going to be a surprise party with presents and a great big cake?"

"Sure, the whole works. You can check with Officer Martin; she's setting things up for the ballroom at the Silver Mountain. I'll get a call that there's a holdup in progress at the front desk, but when I show up at the hotel the whole place'll be dark as the bottom of Mud Creek at midnight, and about the time I walk in and holler, 'What'n hell's goin' on here?' somebody'll switch on the lights and I'll be so danged surprised that I'll faint and fall back in it."

Edging her way to the table, Charlie's aunt brushed a tiny crumb off the red-and-white-checkered oilcloth. Daisy also adjusted the salt and pepper shakers just so. She picked up the blue coffeepot and sloshed what was left around as if to estimate the remainder. 'Twas all for naught. To her considerable annoyance, the men clamped their mouths shut. Daisy waddled away to the sink with the percolator, dumped out the grounds, and put on a fresh pot of coffee.

Moon resumed the conversation. "So what'll you do during your retirement, kick back and go to seed?"

"That's what I'd had in mind, but I've been offered another job."

The Ute shot a sideways glance at his aunt. "Doing what?"

"Don't say a word about this, but . . ." Parris leaned close to his best friend and whispered loud enough for the old woman to hear, "A couple of weeks from now, the president of the United States is gonna appoint me to be the ambassador to Ireland."

"Good!" Daisy snorted. "When you get there, send me back a bushel of blarney."

The men enjoyed a good belly laugh.

What a couple of silly-boogers. But, knowing what was expected of her, the butt of their joke presented her standard scowl.

Feeling just the least bit guilty, Scott Parris got up from his straight-back chair and looped an arm around the feisty old woman's stooped shoulders. "How'd you like to hear some honest-to-goodness true gossip?"

She turned down the flame under the pot, which was beginning to make burpity-perking sounds. "Make it worth my while and I'll pour you a cup of coffee that'll take all the enamel off your teeth."

The chief of police leaned and kissed her on the cheek, then addressed Daisy's good ear. "There's been an interesting new development, one that the recently deceased Mr. Perez might have been mixed up in."

Daisy waited to hear what that might be.

So did her nephew.

Returning to his seat at the table, Parris told them. "A woman in town has gone missing." When neither of the Utes asked him "who?" the chief of police told them. "The lady's name is Janey Bultmann."

Never heard of her. Daisy poured coffee into Parris's mug.

"Thank you kindly." He took a sip of the brackish, scalding brew and pursed his lips. *She wasn't kidding.* Parris eyed Moon's deadpan face. "You must've seen Janey around town. She's owner-manager of Bultmann Employment Services."

Moon did recall the testy blonde who always had a cigarette dangling from her lips.

"Her mother called GCPD from Seattle to tell us that Janey—who was supposed to be there about four days ago— hadn't shown up. And Miss Bultmann hadn't called her momma since the day she was supposed to leave Granite Creek on a three-week vacation." Parris tapped a spoon on his coffee mug. "Janey supplied temporary staff to the Sand

Hills Country Club. Not only for the restaurant and cleaning staff—also for the golf course."

The Ute's eyes narrowed. "Such as Chico Perez."

"You got that right." Steeling himself, Parris downed a man-size gulp of Daisy's high-octane coffee. "And before you tell me that's a pretty thin connection, consider this curious factoid—Janey Bultmann hasn't been seen since the day I visited the country-club manager—a stuffy little peacock by the name of Howell Patterson. That was when I ID'd Chico Perez as the guy Sarah saw with Irene Reed. Turns out that Patterson put in a call to Janey to let her know that Perez's services were no longer needed at Sand Hills. From what he tells me, Janey promised to 'remove Mr. Perez from her list of clients.'"

"So you figure the lady who runs the employment agency canned Perez, and he's responsible for her being listed among the missing?"

"It fits." Parris pulled a small manila envelope from his jacket pocket, opened it, and removed a grainy copy of a photograph. "Here's a picture of Janey that was taken sometime last year. Her mother faxed it to me."

Moon took a look at the snapshot. "Yeah, that's her all right." *And she's got a coffin nail in her mouth.* Under the circumstances, a sobering metaphor. And there was more. The longtime lawman had experienced this eerie phenomenon before. Charlie Moon would never have admitted it to his aunt, but about nine times out of ten he could glance at a photo and instantly know whether or not the person that looked back at him was still among the living. This one wasn't.

Daisy Perika peered over her nephew's shoulder. *Why, I know that face.* It took only a moment to remember where she had seen it. *She's that homeless person that smelled so bad. The one I saw outside the candy store, when Sarah and Charlie was inside buying the butter pecan ice cream with my twenty-dollar bill.* Which raised an interesting possibility. *So maybe she isn't dead; maybe the poor thing had a stroke or lost her mind and she's wandering around the streets and alleys and . . .* Alleys? *Oh, my.* Daisy coughed. Cleared her throat. "Where is that woman's business?"

Scott Parris told her the address on Copper Street.

Daisy's fingers and toes were going cold. "Is that any-where near the candy store?"

"Sure. It's right next door to the Copper Street Candy Shop." The curious cop frowned at the enigmatic woman. "D'you know something I don't?"

Such a silly question called for a derisive snort and a tart retort. "That's like asking am I older and smarter than you are."

The beefy cop grinned. "So tell me what's so important about Bultmann Employment Services being close to the candy—" He was talking to Daisy's backside.

Her oak staff tap-tapping on the linoleum floor, the old woman hobbled away to her bedroom as fast as she could go, which was at about a good enough clip to pass a three-legged terrapin who was making his way up Pine Knob.

Parris shot Moon a questioning look. *What's this all about?*

Daisy's nephew returned a shrug. *How would I know?* Charlie Moon wasn't altogether sure he wanted to find out.

The tribal elder turned the latch to lock her bedroom door, found her purse, and rummaged though it until she found the woman's picture. The blond lady's face in the snapshot smiled at her like they were old friends. There was no doubt about it. *That's the same woman I saw on Sunday morning after church. And she was on the sidewalk in front of her business.* There was no need to show the picture to the men in the kitchen. *They already know about the connection be-tween this Bultmann lady and Perez.* Moreover, the pick-pocket didn't care to be questioned about how she had come to have the missing woman's photograph—the only remain-ing keepsake of her violent adventure.

For a few heartbeats, the old warhorse suffered the bitter taste of resentment at the loss of the other items. But Daisy

Perika washed her mouth out with the memory of how she had ingeniously disposed of the dead man's wallet and the treasured battle trophies. As she savored the sweet recollection, Charlie Moon's aunt was immensely pleased with her clever self. A satisfied smile creased her leathery face. *Nobody but me would've thought of doing a thing like that.*

CHAPTER FIFTY-TWO

THE TOWN COP CONFIDES IN THE
TRIBAL INVESTIGATOR

The moment Daisy was out of sight, Scott Parris took another gulp of her heavy-duty coffee and regarded his Ute host with a pained expression. "Something's gnawing at me, Charlie."

"I'm not surprised. Aunt Daisy's brew'll eat the lining out of your stomach."

"It's Chico Perez that's giving me heartburn." The chief of police reflected his Indian friend's faint smile. "There's no doubt that the dead man was the late Mrs. Reed's boyfriend. Three country-club employees and one of Mr. Perez's neighbors have positively ID'd his body." Parris started to take another sip of coffee, hesitated. "The guy's dead as a doorknob and I'd be happy to let the matter rest there. But something's fishy about this Perez character's actual identity."

"You told me some time ago that Chico Perez wasn't his right name."

"There's more to it than that, Charlie." Parris banged his coffee cup on the kitchen table. "We found the registration in his old Camaro and a State Farm insurance card—both documents had Perez's name on 'em, along with his Granite Creek address." He paused to sop up spilled coffee with a paper napkin. "But when Perez showed up at the Reed residence, he wasn't carrying any form of ID. "No driver's license or credit cards. Nada." He waited for the obvious query.

"Nothing at all in his wallet to give you a clue as to who—"

"The guy didn't have a wallet on him, Charlie. And before you ask, it wasn't in his rented house out on Sundown Avenue—or in his Chevy."

"Maybe the guy lost his wallet, or it got stolen." Charlie Moon blinked at his friend. "Did he have any money on him?"

"The so-called Chico Perez had exactly six bucks and fifty cents in his jeans." Parris furrowed his brow. "And I haven't gotten to the *good* part."

NOW, THE GORY DETAILS

Scott Parris got up from the kitchen table to take a quick peek down the shadowy hallway. Relieved to verify that Daisy wasn't listening from that strategic location, he figured this was a good opportunity to reveal some police-ears-only information to his occasional deputy. After tossing back the thick dregs of tar-black coffee, the well-caffeinated cop began to pace back and forth. "I expect you'd like to hear what Doc Simpson found out when he examined Perez's carcass." He shot a sly look at the Indian. "Or maybe you'd like to make one of your famous wild guesses."

"I'm not much interested in the subject of pathology, or making unfounded speculations—but since you're my guest and best buddy, I'll do my best to please you." Charlie Moon cocked his head. "I already know that the man's head was bandaged when he showed up at the Reed residence. So I expect that whatever our favorite medical examiner discovered must've had to do with Perez's skull."

Parris refilled his mug from the percolator. "You're getting warm."

"Are we talking room temperature or high noon in Death Valley?"

The edgy cop eased himself back into his chair. "It was Perez's hair."

"What about his hair?"

"Well . . . it wasn't there."

Moon stared. "None of it?"

Parris nodded. "Except for a little sprig here and there—it was all gone."

"Sounds like Perez was altering his appearance. The fella must've shaved his head too close, then had to wrap some bandages around it."

"His head hadn't been shaved, Charlie—it was more like his hair had been hacked right down to the roots." Parris held his breath. "And that's not the worst part."

Moon assumed a ready-for-anything expression. "Go ahead—get it over with."

"Charlie, I don't know how you're going to take this—you being of the Native American persuasion and me being one-hundred-percent Caucasian—so brace yourself before I pull the trigger."

"Consider me braced, paleface." The Indian grinned. "And take your best shot."

Parris leaned forward and lowered his voice. "According to Doc Simpson, a few days before Mrs. Reed shot him dead—Chico Perez had been . . . well . . . *mutilated*."

The Ute lost his grin. For a long time, he stared at his friend. He didn't dare ask.

Didn't have to. Scott Parris told him.

Moon shook his head. "Who'd do a thing like *that*?"

As if in answer to his query, Daisy Perika toddled into the kitchen.

The lawmen turned to gaze at the wily old lady.

She approached the table. "Seems to me, you two coppers could use a little help."

Her nephew did not like the sound of this.

DAISY DROPS A BOMB

Charlie Moon's aunt placed her thumb on a red square, to rub a small wrinkle from the checkered oilcloth. "It has to do with that missing woman—the one who owned the employment agency." The tribal elder counted three heartbeats before turning to fix her shifty eyes on the chief of police.

"I'm not dead sure about this, but I'd bet next month's Social Security check that you'll find her body where Chico Perez dumped it."

Parris inhaled a deep breath. "And where'd that be, Daisy?"

"In the sewer." Leaning on her oak staff, the old woman wrinkled her nose at the unpleasant olfactory memory. "If I was you, I'd start by looking for a manhole cover in the alley behind her office."

Parris cast a querying glance at the peculiar old woman's nephew.

His face hard as flint, there was a barely perceptible nod of Moon's head.

Enough said.

GCPD's top cop used his mobile phone to place a call to Dispatch. After barking the appropriate orders, Scott Parris got up from his chair and began to pace again. A full six minutes passed without a word being spoken. The brittle silence was broken by Parris's telephone playing a lively rendition of "Turkey in the Straw," courtesy of Charlie Moon and his fine Stelling's Golden Cross banjo. "Talk to me," the cop said.

The dispatcher talked and Parris's already chalky face blanched a shade more pale with every word. "Tell Officers Knox and Slocum I said don't touch a thing and—" He listened again. "Yeah, I guess they wouldn't, at that. Call Doc Simpson. You already did that? Good work, Clara." After terminating the conversation with Clara Tavishuts, Parris pocketed the telephone. "Eddie Knox spotted a corpse under manhole cover number 128, which is located in the alley behind the Copper Street Candy Shop and maybe twenty paces from the rear exit of Bultmann Employment Services." He stared at Charlie Moon's aunt. "Turns out that employees of the candy store have been complaining about a stink of something dead in the alley."

Daisy could have dropped a second bomb by telling Moon and Parris who Chico Perez really was, but she was saving that explosive for an occasion when it would produce maximum effect. Wearing a deadpan expression that any poker player would've envied, Daisy departed from the kitchen for the final time that day. The vain old lady had enjoyed her brief moment in the limelight. And she wasn't done yet.

Neither of the lawmen could think of a thing to say. But again, the men who knew her so well shared more or less the same thought.

If we ask Daisy how she knew where Chico Perez had dumped Janey Bultmann's body, she most likely wouldn't tell us. Then, there was the really scary possibility: *She just might.*

Daisy's nephew had a serious matter to tend to. But the tribal investigator's business could wait until tomorrow. To that end, Charlie Moon asked Scott Parris to stay the night.

The rancher's gracious invitation was gratefully accepted.

CHAPTER FIFTY-THREE

" 'O bury me not...' And his voice failed there.
But they took no heed to his dying prayer.
In a narrow grave, just six by three
They buried him there on the lone prairie."

A RUDE AWAKENING

After enjoying the benefits of a restful sleep and tranquil dreams, Scott Parris awakened in gradual stages of increasing awareness. His drowsy perceptions included the observation that it was still dark outside and that . . . *I'm not in my own bed.* After realizing that he was in the Columbine headquarters downstairs guest bedroom, the reassured chief of police dozed off and on until the first pearly-gray glow of dawn, which he greeted with a soul-satisfying yawn. *Now this is the kind of life a man ought to live.* Parris stretched luxuriously, popping wrist, elbow, and shoulder joints. *A thousand miles from town and good friends all around and fine horses to ride and enough rolling prairie and rivers and lakes and mountains to satisfy a fella right down to his marrow.* He rubbed his eyes. *Guess I ought to hit the floor and get ready for breakfast.* He poked his foot out from under the covers. *This bedroom's cold as kraut and it's nice and warm here under the blankets.* The tough guy yawned again, turned to his other side, and settled in. *I'll take me a little nap.*

Rap-rap!

What the hell was that? Parris sat up in bed, eyes popped like poached eggs. *Sounded like somebody banged on the wall with a baseball bat.*

The solution to the small mystery was provided forthwith.

"Up and at 'em!" Daisy yelled from the hallway. "Breakfast is burning in the skillet, the coffeepot's boiling over, and after you get your belly full there's firewood that needs splitting, rusty fences that need mending, and cow pies that need kicking." The old crone cackled and gave his bedroom door another hearty thump with her walking stick before hobbling off to the kitchen, where Sarah Frank was baking made-from-scratch biscuits and frying sliced Idaho spuds, big slabs of Virginia ham, and mouthwatering pork sausage patties. Also heaps of scrambled eggs.

A SECLUDED SPOT

Best friends have ways of communicating without words. A sideways glance at the window, the merest nod, an eloquent silence—all speak volumes. Before breakfast was over, Scott Parris was informed by several such cues that Charlie Moon had something to tell him—but not where Daisy Perika could eavesdrop on their private conversation. After they had complimented Sarah on the fine meal and Daisy for her top-secret biscuit recipe, the rancher and the chief of police meandered to the parlor with their third cups of coffee, where they had a habit of sitting before the hearth, where famished flames tongued hungrily at select, succulent morsels of split piñon. Not this morning. On this occasion, the wily conspirators crossed the parlor and stepped onto the front porch.

Daisy Perika was watching the sneaky menfolk from the hallway. *That won't do you any good.* The tribal elder smirked at their vain effort to slip away onto the front porch and discuss matters not meant for her ears. *I'll creep over by the window like I always do, and hear every word you say.*

And so she did. (Creep over to the window.)

But she didn't. (Hear every word.)

All Daisy heard was the breeze picking up and the happy chatter of cottonwood leaves. The men who she supposed were on the porch were not present and accounted for. The spy arrived at the window just in time to see Charlie Moon open the door to the new horse barn. She watched the men vanish inside and scowled at having her plan foiled. *What are they going in there for?* To saddle up some horses and go for a ride, she supposed. The meddlesome old soul was right on the mark.

After fording the frigid river and getting soaked from the knees down, the horsemen headed for the hill that had been called Pine Knob in one language or another for centuries.

An amber-faced sun was smiling the chill off the morning when the riders got to the top of the lonely knoll where Charlie Moon had personally laid several bodies under the sod. A well-groomed grave with a simple marker cradled the remains of a young woman whose destitute mother could not afford a decent burial for her only child. One of the unmarked graves concealed the moldering bones of a friend the Ute had been forced to pass sentence of death on—*at the drop of a hat*. But that had happened way back when, and Mr. Moon was concerned with right now.

As it generally did on the summit, the light wind was whining in the pines—except for the dead, lightning-scarred ponderosa that stood atop the hill like a fossilized sentry doomed to stand ramrod-straight at his last post until Time itself had ticked its last tock and faded away. It had no needles for the wind to whine in.

The men sat easily on their mounts, the chill northerly breeze on their backs.

After a suitable interlude of comradely solitude, the rancher stretched his lean right arm and pointed in a southerly direction. "On a clear day, you can just about make out the Columbine front gate from up here."

"Maybe *you* can." *I guess I ought to get me a pair of*

spectacles. The long-in-the-tooth white man sighed along with the breeze.

Moon turned in the saddle and spoke to his companion. "D'you know that if I had a state-of-the-art controller on my front gate, I could open or close it from here on Pine Knob?"

Parris admired all kinds of high-tech gadgetry. "What kind of doohickey would let you do that?"

"One that answers a telephone." Moon watched a dozen or so elk enter a thick stand of willows and aspen saplings along the riverbank. "If I was of a mind to, I could make the call all the way from China, and press two or three buttons on the phone to operate the gate."

"Imagine that." At a sudden gust of wind, the chief of police grabbed the brim of his cherished felt fedora before it took flight for Gunnison or Salida. "What'll they think of next?"

"What's been bothering me is"—the tribal investigator held on to his black Stetson—"what did somebody *already* think of?"

Parris eyed his friend warily. "I bet you're going to tell me."

The elk now lost to sight, Moon directed his gaze at the distant Columbine entrance. "If a man can open or close a gate with a telephone call, he could operate any electrical gadget you might care to mention."

"Okay, Charlie—who's the man and what's the gadget?"

"Sam Reed's the man." As the wind fell off to a gentle breeze, Moon let go of his hat. "The gadget was something that could play back recorded sounds." *Probably a cassette tape player.*

Parris studied the inscrutable Ute's craggy profile. "Recorded sounds of *what*?"

"Wood splintering." The tribal investigator couldn't help but admire Samuel Reed's ingenuity. "Like a burglar would make if he was crowbarring Mrs. Reed's back door open at about ten o'clock on the evening of June fourth."

Parris opened his mouth. Nothing came out.

Moon turned again to look at his friend. "You remember

that phone call Reed made from a mobile phone just about the time Perez showed up on his property?"

Parris strained to recollect. "The one when he checked on cattle prices?"

The Indian cowboy nodded. "But his call wasn't about what beef was selling for." He smiled at the memory of his misunderstanding of Reed's duplicity. "Sam Reed already knew about the beef market from his computer. Five'll get you fifty, that call was when our slippery friend activated the break-in sound effects."

The chief of police was not about to accept the wager.

"Reed could've placed the burglar-sound-effects call while he was alone in the parlor, but the man's a born show-off. I expect it made his day to make his final play with you and me as witnesses." The Ute's keen eye spotted a tiny jasper arrowhead on the sandy ground. "And there's other things a clever man like Professor Reed could do with a mobile phone besides making his wife think the dangerous Crow-bar Burglar was breaking into her back door."

Scott Parris didn't like the sound of this. "Like what?"

"Like sending a text message to his wife's boyfriend and inviting the so-called Chico Perez to come over right away."

"But Sam didn't do that, Charlie—the text message to Perez was forwarded from the tapped mobile phone that he loaned his wife."

"That's right." The Ute was tempted to dismount and pick up the arrowhead. He decided to leave it for someone to find long after he was gone. "But Reed could have borrowed his phone back from her on June fourth."

Charlie can be a real pain in the butt. "Okay. Just for the sake of annoying me, let's say Sam Reed swiped the borrowed phone back from his wife." The cop shifted his aching posterior in the saddle. "But having the tapped phone wouldn't do him any good unless he knew the boyfriend's mobile-phone number. And even if he'd managed that, how could he send Chico Perez a message that'd pass for one from Mrs. Reed?"

"That bothered me for a while, pard. But what if Mrs.

Reed didn't misplace her original mobile phone like Sam told you she did—what if he slipped it into his pocket when she wasn't looking?"

This suggestion stung like a slap on Parris's face.

The descendant of Chief Ouray watched a red-tailed hawk wing her serene way over Pine Knob. Golden drops of sunlight dripped from the tips of her wings. As he enjoyed the spectacle, Moon continued in an easy, conversational tone. "Sam might've suspected that his wife had a boyfriend. Having the phone she'd used to communicate with Perez would've sure put him in the catbird seat."

The tribal investigator's sinister insinuation percolated through Parris's thoughts, and left a bitter aftertaste. *When I hinted to Reed that he should swipe his wife's phone so he could give her one that was tapped, the clever bastard told me she'd already lost it.* A pair of arteries began to thump in the cop's temples. *Sam Reed liked my notion all right, except he didn't want me to know he'd already taken her phone.*

Obviously curious about the pair of horses and riders, Miss Red Tail was circling the lightning-scorched ponderosa.

Time drifts by leisurely on Pine Knob. On occasion, it seems to slow to a dead stop.

As precious moments of his life stole away into the past, Scott Parris sat astride the Columbine quarter horse without moving a muscle or uttering a word. The harried lawman watched the feathery predator land lightly on the tip of the tall pine. When her inspection of the intruders was complete, Parris watched as the hawk lifted off to soar aloft on a thermal and was filled with a melancholy longing. *I wish I could fly away from here to someplace where life was simple and nobody bothered me.* He recalled that they were in a makeshift cemetery. *After I'm six feet under the sod, maybe then I'll get some peace.* He exhaled a sigh and an admission: "I guess Sam could've swiped his wife's phone and found some messages on it between her and Perez." He flicked his bridle at a pesky horsefly buzzing busily about his mount's neck. "And he could've borrowed the tapped phone he gave her back long enough to send a phony message to Perez—and received Perez's reply." The older cop recalled something that would rip a big hole in Moon's theory. "But if that's what happened, how do you account for the fact that I found the tapped phone in Mrs. Reed's purse right after the shooting?"

"How long is 'right after,' pardner?"

"Pretty damn quick." Parris's shoulders heaved a shrug. "Well . . . no more'n a few minutes."

"Sam Reed would've only needed a few seconds to slip the tapped phone back into his dead wife's purse."

"You sure know how to ruin a fellow's day." The town cop glared at his Indian friend. "And you look like you're not done yet."

The Ute seemed about to say something. Hesitated.

"Don't be bashful, Charlie—spit it out."

"Don't know if I should. It doesn't actually prove anything."

"But I bet it's a real hair-raiser."

"I wouldn't go so far as to say that." Moon squinted at the hawk, who was getting smaller and smaller. "D'you remember how, at about the time Chico Perez was making his way to the back door of the Reeds' home—where Mrs. Irene Reed was waiting with a loaded pistol and probably listening to a recording of a crowbar splintering wood—how Sam Reed started humming a tune?"

"No, I don't." *Charlie's pulling my leg now.* "Correct me if I'm wrong, but unless I've missed something in the county ordinances, there ain't no local law against a man *humming.*"

"In an instance like this, maybe there oughta be. I bet you can't guess which famous composition it was."

"A real classic, huh?"

"You bet. One of the great musical accomplishments of Western Civilization."

Parris gave it some serious thought. " 'Cotton-Eye Joe'?"

"Not even close."

"I got it, Charlie—'Pistol Packin' Mama'!"

"No, but I like it."

"I'm all guessed out. Gimme a bodacious big hint."

"Leadbelly recorded it way back in 1932." Charlie Moon

enjoyed a nostalgic memory. *But I like Ernest Tubb's version best.*

"Leadbelly and '32 don't ring no silver bell. Tell me the name of the song."

" 'Goodnight, Irene.' "

CHAPTER FIFTY-FOUR

CONFIRMATION

Charlie Moon received the expected call the following morning. "Hello, pardner." He took the telephone to his favorite rocking chair, which was waiting patiently by the parlor hearth.

Scott Parris was out of breath, not unlike a sedentary man who has just sprinted up four flights of stairs—or a keyed-up chief of police who's found a cassette tape player on a shelf just inside the rear entrance of the Reed residence. A tape player that could have been turned on remotely by the thumb-size telephone controller that was concealed behind it. "Only there wasn't any cable connecting the controller to the player." He felt his temples begin to throb. "Or, for that matter, a cassette in the player." Parris clenched his teeth and waited for the steel fingers to put the squeeze on his aging heart. When the coronary pain did not come calling, the grateful man thanked God.

Unaware that his friend was a candidate for triple-bypass surgery, Moon pitched a chunk of fragrant piñon onto the smoldering embers. "Sam Reed probably removed the connector cable and break-in-sound-effects cassette while you were checking his wife for a pulse." *And I was tending to her wounded boyfriend.*

"Yeah. And I betcha the rascal tossed 'em both into his fireplace a minute later. But there's more, Charlie." Parris inhaled a deep breath that swelled his chest. "A twenty-second call was placed to the controller phone number a couple of minutes before ten P.M. on the night of the double homicide—from the tapped mobile phone Sam loaned to his wife. But we know who placed the call."

The Ute nodded at the crackling fire. "And a few minutes before that, Sam Reed used the same 'borrowed' phone to send the fake text message from his wife that set up the meeting between Mrs. Reed and her boyfriend."

"It all fits. Problem is, there's no way to *prove* he made those calls."

"Looks like he gets away with it." Charlie Moon knew he should be angry. But he wasn't and there was no getting around it.

Scott Parris was furious enough for both of them. "What really burns me is that you and me are Sam Reed's alibi. The slicker was with us when he made both phone calls, and when the homicides occurred. The sneaky bastard *used* us, Charlie!"

"We let him do it, pard." The Ute smiled at the picture his mind painted of Scott Parris's red face. "But what's done is done, so don't go busting a blood vessel over us getting outfoxed. There is a bright side."

"Please tell me what that might be."

Moon settled back into the rocking chair. "The world is lots better off without the likes of Mr. Perez."

"True. But Mrs. Reed ended up dead too."

"Her husband couldn't have foreseen that." *But I wonder if he hoped it would happen.*

The line went dead quiet while Parris thought about it. "I guess you're right. Sam Reed wanted to stir up some trouble, but he had to realize there was a fair chance that Mrs. Reed would recognize her boyfriend when he showed up."

The rancher nodded at his distant friend. "And even if Mrs. Reed thought Perez was a burglar and took a shot at him, she might've just winged him. I expect that would've been more than enough to satisfy her husband."

"Still . . ." Parris's protest tailed off into a wistful sigh.

"You'd like to arrest Sam Reed and charge him with something or other."

"Yeah." Parris allowed himself a half smile. "Like making fools of us."

"It's not the first time somebody's done that." *And not likely to be the last.*

"But Sam Reed *lied* to us, Charlie—and he set up his wife so she'd make those two break-in calls that'd both look like fraudulent reports."

"Not quite. Mrs. Reed was planning to shoot her husband, just like you figured early on. The first emergency call from Mrs. Reed was bogus as a nine-dollar bill."

"How do you figure that?"

"The lady made the initial 911 call quite some time before Sam Reed recorded his break-in sound effects."

"Okay, I'll ask you again—how do you figure that?"

"Well, we know for a fact that Mrs. Reed placed her first break-in call several days before the golf-course jogger was chased by an ape."

This statement made Parris's head ache. "What's *that* got to do with anything?"

"Unless I'm wrong—the ape on the golf course was you-know-who."

"Sam Reed?"

"Sure. The jogger interrupted the professor while he was making a cassette tape recording of the sounds his crowbar made while he pried on the door of the toolshed." Moon enjoyed a few slow rocks and a smile. "But that's just a hunch."

"Charlie . . ." Parris sighed into the telephone. "I hope you won't take this the wrong way. But it'd have helped some if you'd told me about this hunch yesterday."

Moon stopped rocking long enough to toss another chunk of piñon onto the fire. "Didn't want to overload you with too many speculations."

The chief of police laughed into the tribal investigator's ear. "Way I see it, you're a lot like Sam Reed—both of you like to show off."

Charlie Moon's deep voice took on a somber tone. "Here's the bottom line, pard—this business is over and done with. Nobody will miss Mr. Perez. I'm sorry that Mrs. Reed is dead, but sooner or later, one way or another—Sam Reed will pay for what he's done."

Scott Parris exhaled a long, melancholy sigh. "I sure hope so."

CHAPTER FIFTY-FIVE

THE ASSASSIN'S PAYOFF

Daisy Perika was in her bedroom when she heard Charlie Moon's cowboy boots clunk-clunking down the hallway and into the headquarters parlor. He was walking like a man who had someplace to go and something to do when he got there. She cocked her head in the manner of an inquisitive spaniel. *I wonder what he's up to.*

No, the tribal elder was not more nosy than some other folks we know. She was endowed with an inquiring mind and a fervent desire to keep abreast of current events.

Charlie just got home for lunch, so it's not likely he's going out again. She opened the bedroom door ever so slowly.

Not that she was sneaky. The door hinges were squeaky, and the thoughtful lady did not wish to disturb her nephew with an annoying noise.

Miss Manners poked her head into the hallway. *He's opening the west-porch door to somebody.* Daisy squinted. *Probably just some smelly cow-pie kicker.* The practiced spy cocked her good ear. *No, that don't sound like one of Charlie's half-wit hired hands.* Daisy smiled as she recognized the Indian's clipped speech. *Well—I didn't expect him to show up so soon.* But it was a gratifying development. *The old geezer must've figured out who sent him the stuff and he's come all the way from Oklahoma to thank me.* Which prospect was very pleasing. *But I can't go out there looking like this.* Charlie Moon's aged aunt withdrew into her bedroom's private bathroom, where she commenced to wash her face and, one by one, brush her remaining peglike teeth. After inspecting her disheveled image in the mirror, Daisy clucked her tongue. *I look like the wolf that ate Grandma.* She applied a brush to her frazzled hair.

Charlie Moon invited his unexpected guest to sit in the padded leather armchair by the fireplace, which was one of the highest honors the Columbine had to offer.

The head man of the Blue Lizard Clan accepted this favor with the self-assurance of a person who expects nothing less than the very best. After seating himself and placing a fringed buckskin briefcase in his lap, Lyle Thoms curled his lip at the embers. "I wouldn't go so far as to say that's the puniest fire I've ever seen."

The towering Ute smiled down at the Chickasaw elder's graying hair. "It is a little past its prime. But you should've seen it at breakfast time."

"I had my breakfast with Oscar Sweetwater."

"So how's the tribal chairman getting along?"

"Ah, you know Oscar. Grumpy old man complains about most everything." Thoms faked a shiver. "That fire don't put out enough heat to warm a flea's knees."

Moon picked up an iron poker and made several sharp jabs at the dying fire, which responded with a few feeble pops and anemic sparks. He tossed a handful of cottonwood splinters onto the embers, then a resinous chunk of piñon. The newborn flames licked hungrily at the tasty meal. "We're about to have lunch, Mr. Thoms—I hope you've brought along a healthy appetite."

"I could eat a whole he-goat, hoofs, horns, and hide. All I got on my plate at Oscar's place was a couple of sickly poached eggs and some dry toast." He frowned at the disgusting gustatory recollection. "Oscar's getting kinda paunchy, so his woman's put him on a strict diet." *And I had to starve along with Old Fatty.*

"We'll see that you don't go hungry," Moon assured his guest. "Come lunchtime, you'll be looking at the finest pound of prime rib you ever put a fork in. And I won't even mention the baked Idaho spud dripping with hand-churned butter that I buy from a sweet little old lady who keeps some Holstein dairy cows that don't eat anything except the greenest grass this side of the front range."

"That grub sounds like it might be all right." Thoms's mouth was watering.

"In the meantime, how'd you like a cup of coffee?"

"I guess that wouldn't do me any harm." The chilly clan leader held his palms to the fire. "But be sure it's good'n *hot*."

"I'll go start us a fresh pot."

When Daisy Perika had completed her primping (the Chickasaw was a fine-looking man for one of his years), she emerged from her bedroom and entered the parlor with the feigned nonchalance of a lady who believes she is alone in the house. Her entrance was wasted. The men were seated at the fire, sipping mugs of coffee—with their backs to the aged actress. No matter. When one ploy doesn't work, Daisy generally has another up her sleeve. "Oh, excuse me, Charlie. I didn't know you had a visitor." She turned to depart, but not so quickly as to miss her nephew's predictable invitation.

"Don't go, Aunt Daisy." Charlie Moon got up from his rocking chair. "Mr. Thoms has favored us with another visit."

The Chickasaw clansman, who would have preferred to remain seated, grunted himself up from the comfortable armchair. Which wasn't easy, with his briefcase in one hand and a cup of steaming coffee in the other. He focused a steely stare on the confounded Ute female who was responsible for his discomfort.

"Oh, I remember you." Daisy smiled at the hatchet-faced Indian from Oklahoma. "You were here a little while back, with Oscar Sweetwater." Leaning on her oak staff, she approached the guest and echoed Moon's query, but not quite word-for-word. "So how's that nasty old rascal getting along?"

Even among the distant Chickasaws, Aunt Daisy was almost as well known as her renowned nephew. Thoms grinned at the meanest Ute woman ever to draw a breath. "That shifty politician's getting along a lot better than he deserves."

I like this skinny old Chickasaw scalawag. Daisy pointed her walking stick at Thoms's briefcase. "What've you got in there?"

Momentarily discombobulated by this direct query, the clansman took a deep breath and exhaled it to reply: "Something for your nephew."

"Oh." Daisy's face froze. *He must figure it was Charlie that sent him the box.* There was nothing she could do about that. Not at the moment.

"I guess I might as well give it to him now." Thoms unbuckled his briefcase and removed a parcel that—like the one Daisy had mailed to him—was wrapped in brown paper and tied with white cotton twine. Unlike the shoe box that had contained Posey Shorthorse's wallet and ID, his curled, bleached hair, and the pickled body parts in a mayonnaise jar—this package was about the size of Thoms's hand. The old man offered it to his host.

A mystified Charlie Moon cut the string with his Meerkat pocketknife and unwrapped the brown paper. The man with the famous poker face was wide-eyed at what he saw inside.

As was his aunt.

A neatly framed, brand-new quarter dollar.

A shiny *Oklahoma* quarter dollar.

Daisy, who was supposed to be ignorant of the deal between the Chickasaw elder and her nephew, inquired with the innocence of a cloistered saint, "So what's that for?"

Without so much as a glance at Daisy, Lyle Thoms said, "It's private business—between me and Charlie."

Neither man noticed that the old woman was beginning to smolder.

Though initially puzzled at why he was receiving his "fee" for executing Posey Shorthorse, Charlie Moon didn't take long figuring things out. *Somebody must've killed Shorthorse and Lyle Thoms figures I'm responsible.* There was only one thing for an honorable two-bit assassin to do. "Thank you,

Mr. Thoms." He offered the payment to his guest. "But I can't accept this."

Ignoring the framed quarter, the Chickasaw glared at Moon. "Why not?"

"Because I didn't carry out my end of the contract."

Thoms blinked. "If you didn't take care of business, then who did?"

Not caring to pursue this delicate matter in his aunt's presence, Moon hesitated.

Sensing that something was wrong, the Chickasaw pressed on. "If you didn't do the job, then who sent me the package with—"

"I don't see what the problem is." Daisy snatched the payment from Moon's hand. "If Charlie don't want this nice, shiny quarter, I'll take it."

Lyle Thoms turned his glare on the hard-looking old Ute woman. "I'm sorry, Mrs. Perika. That's a special fee from the Blue Lizard Clan for the man who—"

"You don't have to tell me nothing, you sawed-off little Chickasaw rooster! The reward is for the person that put the knife to Posey Shorthorse—who was calling himself Chico Perez—and then sent you his wallet and scalp and pickled ears!"

Charlie Moon might have been slapped in the face three times. *Wallet? Scalp? Pickled ears?* And . . . *Chico Perez and Posey Shorthorse were the same person?*

Unfazed by the startled men's wide-eyed stares, Daisy pressed the framed quarter dollar close to her breast. "I'm going to hang this on the wall in my bedroom." Jutting her chin, she smirked maliciously at the Chickasaw. "Next time you have a job a man can't get done, come and see *me* about it." With this parting shot, she turned and was gone. For the moment.

Thoms turned his questioning gaze on Moon.

The long-suffering nephew shook his head at the Chickasaw. *Leave it alone.*

Daisy poked her head back into the parlor. "I hope you're staying for lunch, Mr. Thoms."

Lyle Thoms scowled at the rude old woman.

Charlie Moon held his breath. *What now?*

"I've got a few pieces of leftover meat in the freezer." Daisy's tone was sweet as honey in the comb; her face radiated the wonderful purity of a sleeping infant. "I'm not saying whether it's pork or venison or something else altogether, but there's about enough for a batch of my secret-recipe posole." Her black eyes sparkled at Lyle Thoms. "I call it Shorthorse stew." The tribal elder made her second departure with a sense of soul-gratifying satisfaction that warmed her all the way down to her marrow.

As it happened, the head man of the Blue Lizard Clan did not stay for a helping of the Ute elder's posole.

The reason for Lyle Thoms's hasty departure remains uncertain, because the taciturn Indian left the Columbine without uttering another word to Charlie Moon. The visitor's healthy appetite may have been diminished by an unexpected gastrointestinal event such as older men are apt to experience. It is just as likely that the busy Oklahoman remembered another pressing appointment. Or it may be that the Chickasaw gourmand—whose taste buds were all primed and ready for Charlie Moon's tasty prime rib—did not care to settle for Daisy's mediocre substitute. Or some combination of the above.

We simply don't know why the famished man chose to pass on Daisy's stew.

But there is a suggestive clue.

Lyle Thoms was seen later that afternoon in Granite Creek's tiny health-food restaurant, which establishment is operated by a stern vegetarian. The ardent meat eater was dining on a triple helping of homemade peach-pecan yogurt.

CHAPTER FIFTY-SIX

JULY 9
HE DITHERS

Since the unpleasantness at his residence, Samuel Reed had gotten accustomed to bunking in the Silver Mountain Hotel's sumptuous presidential suite. After the police investigation of the crime scene was completed and two hundred yards of black-and-yellow tape had been removed from his domicile, the widower would drop by the Shadowlane homestead from time to time to make sure that everything was in order. But, though he had tried, Professor Reed could not manage to stay overnight. Grim memories of the violence that had occurred on the premises haunted the recently bereaved husband, and he was considering putting the place up for sale and moving to warmer climes. The wealthy man was toying with the notion of purchasing a secluded island in the Caribbean. Nothing ostentatious. He imagined a modest and tasteful hideaway that would not attract undue attention. The house should not have more than ten rooms. There must be essential infrastructure, such as a protected harbor with a dock for a sixty-foot yacht. Also a landing strip that would accommodate a Lear jet. He promised himself not to spend more than five hundred million dollars. But finding just the right property would probably take a year or two. In the meantime, he needed something to keep his mind occupied.

Sam Reed was at loose ends. Ennui had fixed its lethargic

eye on him, and for the first time in his vigorous life, the concept of a quiet retirement was beginning to look attractive.

Sadly, Samuel Reed's favorite pastime (making money hand over fist) would not suffice. Ever since the unnerving evening of June 4, he had apparently lost whatever ability he had to "remember the future," which rendered him unable to foresee with certainty trends in the stock market or the outcomes of sporting events. One can imagine his dismay, but despite this handicap and to his credit, Reed did keep his hand in the game. He would spend an hour or two of each day in his office over the Cattleman's Bank. During these quiet interludes, he would pace and sigh and remember splendid days gone by when he had amassed small fortunes in mere minutes. When wearied of pacing, sighing, and waxing nostalgic, Reed would find diversion by surfing Internet financial blogs for rumors of upcoming mergers, hot tips about which major midwestern bank was teetering on the brink of failure, or hints that a certain former Fortune 500 company was looking Chapter 11 right in the eye. From time to time the investor would purchase a few hundred shares of a promising stock or place a thousand-dollar wager on a major sporting event. As often as not, the stocks tanked. But even in his present debilitated state, Reed exhibited a modest knack for prognosticating the outcomes of horse races, baseball games, prizefights, and the like. This was gratifying, but he was unable to regain his former enthusiasm for life. His verve had taken a vacation.

What the man of business needed was some interesting business to conduct, but aside from the mildly entertaining diversion of playing games with his pocket money, Samuel Reed did not have enough work to occupy either his time or his mind. With nothing better to do, he became a familiar figure on Copper Street, which boulevard serves as Granite Creek's main drag and provides most of the goods and services that a finicky nabob might require, including a variety of food and drink in a half-dozen restaurants, Fast Eddie's Barbershop, suitable clothing in Eubank & Son's Men's Fine Apparel, and a variety of essential financial services in the bank below his office. The widower's life was more orderly than ever. And dull as a butter knife.

Even so, there was bound to be the occasional perturbation that would prove jarring to this man who placed a high value on predictability. One such event was about to occur as Samuel Reed approached the customary barbershop for a touch-up, which occurred promptly at 10 A.M. on alternate Fridays.

A DANGEROUS LADY

Though it was barely five weeks after his wife's untimely demise, it was fated that dapper Samuel Reed would encounter a captivating woman who would catch his eye. Just as he glanced at his wristwatch to verify that he would arrive at Fast Eddie's clip joint at precisely 9:59 A.M., a sleek black Lincoln pulled up alongside the yellow-painted curb.

The woman on the passenger side lowered the window. "Excuse me."

As he turned, Reed put on the perfunctory smile that is expected of civilized men who are queried by disoriented tourists who park beside shiny red fireplugs. As he got a gander at the attractive brunette whose eyes were concealed behind rose-tinted sunglasses, Reed's smile began to feel welcome on his face. His left hand got the message and tipped the homburg.

Her matching rose-tinted lips smiled and said, "You must be Professor Reed."

"If I must, then so be it." *But who are you?*

The lady lowered the rosy shades just enough to reveal a pair of stunning blue eyes. "But of course you don't know who I am."

"Alas, no. But I hope that oversight will be promptly remedied."

The woman in the blue pin-stripe suit who emerged from the luxury car was tall, and of the type often referred to as willowy. She offered him a business card.

Reed inspected the rectangle and mouthed aloud what was written thereon: " 'Theodora Phillips, Attorney at Law.' " He lost the smile and arched his left brow by almost a full millimeter. "That's all—no name of your firm. No address. Not even a telephone number."

"My name and profession will be sufficient, Professor Reed." Looping a black leather purse over her shoulder, the elegant lady took him firmly by the arm. "This brief meeting shall be our only contact." As she ushered her captive down the street and away from the barbershop, Ms. Phillips smiled.

Such behavior was more than a little off-putting, but Sam Reed's curiosity was pleasantly piqued and so he went along without protest. Glancing back at the Lincoln—which had a Nevada license plate—he saw an older, tough-looking fellow emerge from the driver's side. The broad-shouldered man, who wore a black shirt, black trousers, and black cowboy boots, could have passed as a lumberjack if outfitted in a black-and-red flannel shirt, faded jeans, and big muddy shoes with cleated rubber soles. *Obviously a combination chauffeur-bodyguard.* Reed treated himself to a mildly supercilious smirk. "Who is that—your law partner?"

Theodora Phillips replied in a coolly professional tone, "Alex is my driver and personal assistant. Not being privy to my business affairs, he will remain at a discreet distance while we drop into that quaint little restaurant"—she pointed her cute, turned-up nose—"where you will be immensely pleased to buy me a cup of tea."

"The Sugar Bowl?"

"The very same. I am reliably informed that they serve Tangerine Orange Zinger, which is my favorite *chai*." She laughed. "You may also treat me to an order of buttered whole-wheat toast."

Being endowed with a sense of humor that leaned toward irony, Samuel Reed did not mind occasionally being manipulated by a forceful woman. But something about this attorney was beginning to make him feel uneasy. Looking for a graceful escape, he checked his wristwatch again. "I have a rather busy schedule this morning. I suggest that you call my office and leave a brief message on my voice mail—"

"Out of the question."

Reed deliberately slowed his pace. "What's this all about?"

As an openly curious passerby walked by them, Theodora Phillips lowered her voice. "I have been dispatched to convey some critical information to you."

"Information?" This couldn't be good news. "About what?"

"A matter of importance."

Reed's left brow arched again, and quite noticeably. "How important?"

The blue eyes behind the pink shades smoldered. "It falls into that category often referred to as 'life and death.' "

"Whose life, my dear?" He smiled at the delightful little turned-up nose, which was liberally sprinkled with tiny orange freckles. "And whose death?"

"Why yours, of course." With a gentle feminine relentlessness that could not be withstood by a gentleman, she maneuvered him to the entrance to the Sugar Bowl Restaurant. "Let's go inside. After I have had my tea and toast, I will explain."

They did and he did and she would.

Theodora Phillips's driver/assistant followed, at a respectful ten paces. While a host took Samuel Reed and the out-of-town lady to a table with a fine view of Copper Street, Alex seated himself at a booth where he was well out of earshot of whatever conversation the pair might engage in.

CHAPTER FIFTY-SEVEN

THE LADY EXPLAINS

Though despairing of the delayed haircut, while Samuel Reed sipped tentatively at black coffee he got a better look at the fortyish woman's face. Outside in the high-altitude sunlight, her features had been soft and alluring as a tree-ripened peach. In the restaurant's artificial twilight, the attorney's finely chiseled features were cold and hard as graveyard marble. The exception to this grim aspect was her lips, which were genetically obliged to curl upward at the edges. Theodora's friends interpreted this perpetual smile as evidence of her vivacious good humor. Not so her current companion, who had inherited a marked tendency toward obsessive suspicion. Unnerved by the persistent smirk, Reed was nagged by the conviction that the attorney was amused by some secret knowledge. Being a thoroughly self-centered man, he had no doubt that the irksome woman was privy to confidential information concerning himself.

Ever so often, a paranoid egoist's suspicions are justified.

As a prelude to taking control of the situation, Reed cleared his throat. "You have your tea and toast and my undivided attention. Now what's all this twaddle about a matter of life and death?"

Theodora swirled a bag of aromatic tea in her china cup, watching the amber whirlpool with intense interest. Then, as if she had just heard his query, the lady looked up. "You have been found guilty."

This was hardly what the hopeful widower had wanted to hear from the attractive woman, especially on what practically amounted to their first date. "I *beg* your pardon."

"Don't bother." Her remarkably expressive lips curved into a genuine smile and her next words sent a chill rippling along Reed's knobby spine. "I am merely a messenger for the Committee, but I can assure you that they do not issue pardons. The Big C conducts thorough investigations, makes final decisions—and hands down sentences. That's it."

"What on *earth* are you talking about," Reed heard himself say. "I mean, what am I supposed to be guilty of?"

"Improper conduct."

"What the blazes does *that* mean?" He glowered at the impudent attorney. "And what in hell is the *committee*?"

"I object to your coarse language." Theodora placed the spent tea bag onto a saucer. "An apology is in order."

"Please forgive me. I am immensely contrite."

"Accepted."

"Allow me to rephrase the query." Professor Reed raised his chin imperiously. "What in *heck* is the 'committee'?"

"First of all, I don't have any notion of who serves on the Committee—that is none of my business. I'm merely a—"

"Yes, I know—you're merely a *messenger*." Reed's hand trembled as he pushed his coffee aside. "I don't know what kind of con you're attempting to run on me, Theodora—but let me assure you that I am not a moron."

"It would never have occurred to me that you were, Samuel."

"And neither am I without influential friends." He aimed his high-caliber steely stare at the aggravating woman. "Among them is the local chief of police—who would no doubt be pleased to meet you."

"A splendid idea." The twinkle in Theodora's blue eyes was barely concealed by her pink shades. "If you're entirely certain that he is your friend, why don't you give Mr. Parris a call and ask him to join us?"

Sam Reed's bulging eyes blinked. "You know him?"

"Only by reputation. But I would be delighted to make his personal acquaintance."

I'll call her bluff and watch her fold. The self-assured entrepreneur produced his brand-new BlackBerry and selected the programmed number for Granite Creek PD.

Theodora mouthed, *He won't be in.*

Reed smirked at the cheeky attorney and mouthed right back, *We'll see about that.* Hearing Clara Tavishuts's voice in his ear, he said, "This is Sam Reed. Please put me through to Scott."

"The chief's not in his office," the dispatcher replied. "He's in a meeting with the DA. Shall I connect you to his voice mail?"

"Uh . . . no. Thank you." The red-faced man disconnected.

"You might wish to call District Attorney Bullet's office." The frisky young mare tossed her dark mane. "Chief Parris had a midmorning appointment with Pug, who is well known to my associates."

Samuel Reed had never before encountered such an unnerving woman. "You seem to be rather well informed."

The lady shrugged under her immaculately tailored jacket. "It's a job requirement."

Their conversation was interrupted by the waiter, who placed the bill facedown beside the gentleman's coffee cup.

After the young man had departed to deliver a similar invoice to Theodora's driver, she said, "The Committee has noticed your remarkably consistent tendency to garner large profits from gaming."

Samuel Reed's arms and legs went cold as a week-old corpse's limbs. *So that's what this is about.* In an attempt to conceal his fears, the flustered man fell back on bluster. "I do place an occasional wager, just like thousands of other men. If I am fortunate enough to guess right now and then, I don't see why that should concern—"

"Oh come now. Don't be so modest." She aimed a slender finger at his nose. "We don't yet know precisely *how* you do it—but you have managed to fleece the firms represented by the Committee of an enormous sum." The attorney wagged the pointing finger at him. "You have been a very naughty boy."

"This is patently absurd. I don't know what your game is, but if you're about to attempt some kind of shakedown—"

"Don't go out of your way to annoy me, Professor Reed. That would not be in your best interests." Theodora removed her pink shades to laser two beams of blue fire at him. "I'm about the closest thing to a friend you've got in this world— and I'm liking you less with every minute that passes."

To avoid the woman's sizzling stare, Reed glanced at the timepiece on his wrist. "Speaking of minutes, I still have time to get a haircut before noon. So let's skip the seamy preliminaries and go directly to the bottom line."

"I've never seen a man so anxious to hear bad news." Watching the nervous fellow fidget, Theodora helped herself to a triangle of buttered whole-wheat toast. After daintily nipping off an acute angle, she washed it down with a sip of tea and licked her lips. "You've messed up big-time, Samuel. My employers will tolerate a high roller lining his pockets every now and then, but you went *way* over the top."

"But—"

"Shush!" She wagged the finger again. "The Committee has decided that you must make amends."

"Amends?"

Theodora nodded. "Call it repentance—a turning around."

Well. *That doesn't sound so bad.* "In the vernacular, I must straighten up and fly right?"

"Either that, or you face certain consequences."

"*Consequences* is a rather off-putting word, Theodora." The gambling man took a sip of coffee that he could not taste. "I would prefer to hear about how I am to make amends for my supposed sins."

"Now that's the spirit!" The lady opened her purse to remove a pale blue envelope, which she offered to her companion.

Grateful that she had not produced a cocked and loaded double-barrel .38-caliber derringer, Reed accepted the envelope between two fingertips. "What's in it?" He winked at her. "A harmless white powder posing as anthrax? Or an insidious toxin derived from the lowly castor bean?"

"The envelope contains a list of several nonprofit institutions. Beside each of them is a sum which you will contribute."

I knew it. A shakedown. Producing a pearl-handled Case pocketknife, Reed used the single slender blade to slit the envelope open. It contained a single sheet of matching blue stationery, upon which the names of eleven organizations were printed. As Reed read, his lips silently formed the words. He looked over the paper at Theodora. "These appear to be reputable charitable organizations; I've heard of several of them."

"Ten of the organizations have sterling credentials for worthy projects. Your contributions to them will be tax deductible and your generosity will feed widows and orphans and help to eradicate illnesses such as cancer, malaria, and diabetes."

"But the eleventh 'charity' is a front for . . . your employers."

"I would not say that, Samuel." The lady shot a warning look. "And neither should you." She added crisply, "But suffice it to say that the eleventh organization will be shut down shortly after receipt of your payment."

The physicist did a bit of mental arithmetic, then swallowed hard. "This adds up to quite a tidy sum."

"As have your ill-gotten gains at fraudulent gaming. I am authorized to advise you that your contribution to charities one through ten can be cut in half by revealing your system." She wagged the finger a final time. "But don't even *think* about lying to the Committee. Our experts are aware of every scam in the book—and a few that are not."

Amused by the irony of his situation, the man who had told Moon and Parris that he *remembered the future* shook his head and sighed. "I have no system—just call me lucky."

"Have it your way, Lucky. If you'd rather pay than disclose your method, that's your choice." Theodora took another nip of toast, another sip of tea. "But I daresay that even without the discount, your contribution will represent only a fraction of your ill-gotten winnings. The Committee's purpose is not to recover the entirety of its members' losses, but rather to put an end to your nefarious activities." The lady had an afterthought. "Which reminds me of the other requirement. For as long as you live, you will not participate in any form of commercial gaming."

Reed arched his left eyebrow to its uppermost limit. "You seem to assume that my cooperation is a foregone conclusion."

"I assume that you are an intelligent man." A pregnant pause. "In those rare instances when the offender is so foolish as to refuse the amendment option, the Committee provides severe penalties."

Droplets of sweat began to bead on Reed's face. "Define *severe*."

"If all financial transactions on the list have not been made in the full amount within five business days—you should have all your affairs in order. The standard execution is three .22 slugs in the head."

"Such a lowly caliber." He tried vainly to smile. "Would a request for 9-mm cartridges be considered unseemly?"

"Given the gravity of your circumstances, flippancy is unseemly." She presented a lovely smile. "Perhaps it will please you to know that the .22 slugs are hollow-points."

"I am suitably impressed, and herewith withdraw my request."

"So noted." Her lips relaxed to the obligatory minimum upward curl. "You will naturally consider flight. I am directed to advise you that any attempt to avoid the Committee's judgment will be futile and against your best interests. Try to hide in the Costa Rican rain forest, the vast plains of Outer Mongolia, or the disease-ridden hinterlands of Timbuktu. You might buy yourself a month or two—but you *will* be found. When you are, your death will be neither swift nor easy. Your grisly remains will be photographed and provided to the supermarket-tabloid news media and bloggers who delight in the macabre. The Committee's policy in instances of flight is to make a gut-wrenching example so that other potential rip-off artists will think twice about crossing them

and then making a run for it." Theodora finished her toast
and downed the last gulp of tea. "I would love to stay and
chat with you, but the secretary of the Committee is expecting
my telephone call. Before I say, 'Goodbye, Professor Reed,'
I would appreciate the courtesy of a response."

He thought about it for a couple of heartbeats, shrugged.
"I'll transfer the funds to the charities." It was galling, but
what else could a man do?

"A prudent decision." As the lady got up from her chair,
her associate in the booth did likewise. "Goodbye, Professor
Reed."

From force of habit, the gentleman got to his feet.

The attorney looped the black leather purse over her
shoulder. "The service in this charming little café was quite
satisfactory. I hope that you will leave a generous tip."

As Samuel Reed watched the long-legged lady depart
with her tough-looking driver tagging along, it occurred to
him that, painful as it would be, making the payoff was much
like getting an abscessed wisdom tooth pulled. The sooner
the thing was done, the better. *I might as well visit the Cattleman's Bank and get things moving.* Slipping the blue envelope into his jacket pocket, popping the spiffy gray homburg
onto his head, the freshly fleeced man set his face like flint
and headed—as they say in these here parts—*thataway.*

CHAPTER FIFTY-EIGHT

COMPARING NOTES

The lawmen placed their orders (grilled almond trout for Charlie Moon, baked lasagna for Scott Parris). They waited until the waiter had closed the door to the Silver Mountain Hotel's bijou private dining room before resuming their conversation.

The tribal investigator kicked the exchange off thusly: "So you told Pug Bullet what we wanted him to know."

"That I did." The chief of police popped the lid on a crystal candy jar and helped himself to a complimentary chocolate mint. "Now, no matter how things turn out, the DA can't complain that he wasn't informed about our mutual suspicions of Sam Reed's . . . ah . . ." The strain of recollection creased his brow. "His *nefarious* activities."

The Indian smiled at his friend's latest conquest. Scott had mastered about a dozen words from his girlfriend's list.

He offered the heavy candy jar to Moon and watched the Indian help himself to a chewy caramel. "Now tell me how things are going with our slippery friend."

Moon commenced to unwrap the sugary treat. "From what Theodora tells me—that was her name today—Sam Reed was more than a little suspicious about her story." He paused to invite the expected response.

"No kidding." *I told him Reed wouldn't go for it.* "The scam was pretty hokey—a lawyer representing a mysterious gambling industry committee that deals harshly with cheats.

Either make restitution or wake up stone cold dead some warm morning." The cop snorted. "Who'd go for a con like that?"

"Sam Reed did." Moon grinned at his friend. "He caved in the end."

The chief of police was goggle-eyed. "He actually bought all that guff?"

"Swallowed the whole boulder, moss and all. My lady friend tells me our big fish turned green at the gills when she explained what'd happen if he didn't make the payoffs to the specified charities."

Being a typical male, Parris hated being wrong. "It was awfully *fortuitous* that he bought that lie about those charities being fronts for criminal elements involved in gambling."

Moon corrected his friend's misconception. "Theodora told him the truth—that with one exception, the charities were on the up-and-up."

The town cop's eyes narrowed suspiciously. "Exception?"

Charlie Moon placed the unwrapped candy on the saucer beside his coffee cup. "The lady has to cover her expenses." *And make an exorbitant profit.*

The county's senior sworn officer of the law wished he hadn't heard that. This business was getting downright *nefarious.* "Where was you when the lady pulled the con?"

"Right there in the Sugar Bowl, in a corner booth behind a couple of potted palms. I watched the whole thing go down."

"I bet that was entertaining."

"More fun than a three-ring circus and all the cotton candy you can eat." Moon popped the caramel into his mouth and chewed for a while.

Parris exhaled a wistful sigh. "Wish I could've been there with you."

"Me too, pard. But somebody had to deal with the DA, and that was your department."

"So what'd Reed do after the lady made her pitch and hit the street?"

"Soon as Theodora took her leave, our bad boy made a beeline for Cattleman's Bank."

"That's great, but . . ."

"But what?"

"I don't mean to sound mean, Charlie." He jutted his chin. "But I wish she'd taken that slippery rascal for everything he owned."

"You don't really mean *everything*."

"Yes I do—right down to his skin!" The vindictive cop grinned. "And left him wearing an iron-hooped wooden barrel, like in the old comic strips."

"That's way too ambitious, pard. When setting up a scam, the secret to success is knowing just how far to push the mark."

Parris picked up a sticky red Gummi Bear. *I don't know why kids like these things.* He returned it to the crystal jar. "You figure Reed'll eventually figure out he's been had?"

"Somewhere down the road, he's bound to get a little suspicious." The rancher shook his head. "But right now, the fella's spooked like a high-strung horse that's just stepped on a timber rattlesnake. Theodora did a first-rate job on him."

Scott Parris could not suppress his natural curiosity. "Where do you know this woman from?"

"Met her on the res, about nine years ago." Moon took some time to enjoy the memory. "I did the shady lady a favor when she and her daddy were arrested for running a gambling scam on our Southern Ute casino."

Parris found a coffee-flavored truffle in the jar. He undressed the red-foiled sweet straightaway. "Sounds like crime runs in this family."

"Yeah. Today, Poppa was her driver."

The cop chomped down on the tasty treat. "Ware's er mobba?"

"Theodora's momma's doing five to seven in an Illinois clink. Sweet little old lady took a big fall for real-estate fraud."

"Sub fabbly." Parris swallowed.

The Ute nodded. "Crooked as a bucket of corkscrews." Moon's smile wouldn't go away. "But I like 'em."

"Well, it's all over and done with. Still, I wish there was some way to make Sam Reed pay big-time for setting up his wife and that . . . that *nefarious* Chickasaw." Parris searched the candy jar for a sweet delectable and found it—another truffle, this one with raspberry crème filling. "Aside from the killings, he made us look like dopes."

"Let's not be too hard on Professor Reed. Don't forget that he gave me that insider tip about the hoof-and-mouth outbreak down south of the equator—and that you're four hundred bucks the better from that wager he paid up on." Moon's winnings, in the five-figure range, were also a considerable consolation to him. But this was still not the proper time to mention this enrichment to his buddy.

"I haven't forgotten about that, Charlie. But Reed didn't make the bet or drop the cow-disease tip to help me and you." Parris popped the truffle into his mouth. *That is de-lish!* After properly savoring the treat, he completed the thought. "That was all part of the bastard's plan to get us on the stakeout, so—in case he was suspected of doing something underhanded in connection with what was going down—he'd have a couple of highly respected—practically *legendary*—local lawmen to provide him with an iron-clad alibi."

Moon was amused by his friend's overheated self-esteem.

"I'd like to see him suffer a little more." Parris licked his fingers. "But I guess hoaxing him into donating a chunk of his fortune to widows and orphans is enough to even the score."

"I wasn't trying to even a score, pardner. Way I see things, we did him a big favor."

Parris squinted to see Moon's point. "By discouraging his gambling habit?"

The ardent poker player shook his head. "That part was his punishment."

"Then what was the big favor?"

"Maneuvering the rich man to give away money he doesn't really need to desperate folks who don't have two thin dimes to rub together."

"Excuse me, Charlie—but I don't believe Sam Reed would consider that an act of kindness on our part."

"Not today, maybe. But I bet that he'll end up feeling mighty good about what he's done."

I bet. The two magic words. "How long before this transformation happens?"

Moon: "Oh, let's say by this time next month."

"Even money?"

The Indian nodded. "Let's say a U.S. government engraving of Tom Jefferson."

Scott Paris did not have a two-dollar bill, but common copper pocket change was legal tender for all debts, public and private. "You're on."

"Sucker bet," Moon said with evident pity. "By this time next week, all ten of those charities will be letting Sam Reed know how much good he's doing in the world."

Parris produced his characteristic snort. "Which is just another way of saying they'll be filling his mailbox with requests for more donations."

"They'll also be showing him pictures of skinny little children who've got enough to eat, and sick people who're getting effective treatment." The Ute Catholic ended his sermonette with: "Good works are habit-forming."

Parris was about to make a snappy comeback when their conversation was interrupted by a barely perceptible thumping on the dining-room door.

"Wa-hoo!" the hungry cop hollered. "Bring on the grub!"

Charlie Moon shared neither his friend's enthusiasm nor Parris's assumption that the waiter had already returned with their food. The Ute had recognized the distinctive request for admission, which was more on the order of—

A gentle rapping.

A mere tappity-tapping.

CHAPTER FIFTY-NINE

THE UNINVITED GUEST

In the hallway outside the private dining room, someone announced his presence with a tentative "ahem."

"C'mon in," Charlie Moon rumbled.

The door opened a crack, to reveal a vertical slice of Samuel Reed's face. "Excuse me, I hope I'm not interrupting."

"You're excused," Scott Parris grumped. *Now hit the bricks.*

Moon gestured the man in. "Have a seat."

With a wary glance at the chief of police, the uneasy man eased himself inside. "I won't be a moment."

"Help yourself to a piece of candy." Parris pointed at the jar. "If you're still here when the food shows up, you can pay for the eats." He regarded the party crasher with frank suspicion. "How'd you know me'n Charlie was here?"

"I'm living at the hotel nowadays." Reed leaned his ivory-knobbed cane in a corner, hung his homburg on a hatrack, and slipped into a chair beside Charlie Moon's. "One of the employees told me you were having a meal in the Paiute Room."

"And you figured you'd drop by." Parris gave him the gimlet eye.

"Well, yes." Reed met the cop's hard gaze. "I hope you don't mind."

"Speaking of minds," Moon said, "what's on yours?"

Unsure of how much he should reveal to the lawmen,

Reed thrummed his fingers on the dining table. After considering several options, he decided on the minimalist approach. "I have recently had an unsettling encounter with an attractive lady that I'd never laid eyes on before today. I thought I'd ask whether either of you two know anything about her."

Each of the men instantly assumed his best poker face, which was world class in Charlie Moon's case and fair to middlin' in the instance of Scott Parris.

"Her name is Theodora Phillips," Reed said. "She represents herself as an attorney."

Parris waited for his friend to take the lead.

Which Charlie Moon did in about 250 milliseconds. "Is *she* in town?"

"She was." Reed blinked owlishly at the Ute. "The lady left a few hours ago."

"That's *fortuitous*," Parris said.

The man who'd been royally flimflammed looked from one steely-eyed cop to the other. "Is Ms. Phillips a disreputable person?"

Parris rolled his eyes.

Moon scowled but held his silence.

"Well tell me!"

The Ute looked at the white cop.

Parris sighed. "You tell him, Charlie."

Moon did. "Don't *ever* mess with Miss Phillips." The period at the end of this bottom line was the size of a cast-iron skillet.

Reed's mouth gaped. "That's it?"

The tribal investigator nodded. "End of story."

"But you can't just leave me hanging—"

"Sure we can." Parris's eyes twinkled. How brightly? Like a couple of two-for-a-dollar sparklers on the Fourth of July.

Moon should've left it there, but the merry Ute couldn't help himself. "It's what's known in the trade as a *short* story."

Reed's lips went thin. "Gentlemen, this is not funny!"

"Neither's that lady lawyer," Moon said. "And don't tell

me and Scott what kind of business you were conducting with her."

Parris shook his head. "We don't want to know."

"Forget you ever heard of her," the tribal cop warned.

Reed's face paled to a chalky white. "The people she is associated with—are they as dangerous as she suggests?"

The lady's dangerous associates exchanged knowing looks.

"Some folks who've crossed paths with 'em might say so," Moon said.

Parris added, "Those few who've lived to talk about it."

"But I expect their reputations are puffed up some." The Ute's eye-twinkle was more like a pair of fireflies at five hundred yards. "All of 'em together probably haven't personally maimed and killed more than a dozen men."

Parris agreed with Moon's estimate. "I've met tougher guys at Methodist Church socials."

It appears that my fears were justified. Reed thrummed his fingers on the table again. "Earlier this afternoon, I donated a significant amount of money to several worthy charities."

"Did you, now?" Charlie Moon was already feeling two dollars richer.

The wealthy man nodded. "For the very first time." He stopped finger thrumming long enough to slap his palm on the polished wooden surface. "And do you know what?"

The Ute shook his head. But he knew.

Scott Parris held his breath. He knew, too.

"It felt *good*!" Reed commenced to thrumming again. "From this day forward, I intend to contribute ten percent of my earnings to those who are less fortunate than myself."

Parris's mouth twisted into a sarcastic grin. "There're plenty of us around."

"Tithing is a time-honored practice and good for the soul." Moon looked down his nose at the novice philanthropist. "But are we talking gross or net?"

The man of business thought it over. Thrummed harder. "Gross, by golly!"

"Now that's the spirit!" Moon shot his friend the Look. *It's payday, pard.*

Scott Parris stuck his hand into his pocket and came up with eight quarter dollars.

"Thank you kindly." Moon arranged the shiny coins into a neat stack. "Looks like some local official has been knocking off parking meters."

"Consider it advance payment for assassinating eight local lowlifes of my choice." Parris aimed a finger at the Indian, cocked it. "I'll give you the list tomorrow." *And Sam Reed's nefarious name will be right at the top.*

"What's this all about?" The object of Parris's ill thoughts hated being left in the dark.

"Nothing important," the Ute said. "A small debt Scott owed me. Which reminds me—you still owe the both of us."

The recently fleeced citizen blinked. "Owe you what?"

"The rest of your story."

Reed arched both brows. "Story?"

The chief of police scowled at the paneled wall. "This danged room has an aggravating echo problem."

Moon patted the wealthy man on the back. "You never finished your short story."

"The one where you *remember the future.*" Parris put on a mocking smile.

"Oh, that." Samuel Reed cleared his throat in preparation for a flimsy excuse that never got past his lips.

"Here we are." Moon made a sweeping gesture that encompassed the occupants of the exquisite little hotel dining room. "Three chummy hardcases sitting around a smoky campfire."

"Chewing on rotten buffalo jerky," Parris added.

Moon aimed a reproving look at his friend. "That's *rancid* buffalo jerky."

"Oh, right." Parris took a moment to grind his molars on the imaginary rancid flesh. "Thanks, Charlie."

"Don't mention it, pard."

"This past-its-sell-by-date buff jerky's not half bad," Parris said. "But ain't we washing it down with some genuine campfire coffee?"

"You betchum." Moon tipped an imaginary tin cup of black coffee. "We're sipping cowboy java whilst filtering the grounds between the gaps in our teeth."

"That is *betwixt* the gaps." Reed smiled at the cheerful cops. "And I believe you two comedians have quite made your point."

The taller and leaner of the comics set the make-believe hot beverage aside. "Then it must be about time to hear the rest of your story."

"If you insist." Reed turned up his nose and sniffed. "But you will not like it."

The Ute allowed himself just a hint of a smile. "That's what you said that night during the stakeout."

A peculiar expression began to creep its way over Reed's face. Like a dead soul staring into the abyss and preferring blindness to what he saw there, his eyes seemed to glaze over. "I do have a tendency to repeat myself." As he withdrew from his unsettling vision, the scientist's mouth curled into a slightly lopsided grin that suggested a mild stroke. The situation was far more bizarre than the clever lawman could possibly have imagined. *Every word I utter simultaneously passes through countless lips.*

A madman's thought? Hard to say.

Moon's faint smile had slipped away. *Reed's right. I won't like it.*

Scott Parris: *This'll be off-the-scale creepy.*

Both assumptions were correct.

But if he had tried with all his might, Samuel Reed could not have cared less what they thought.

CHAPTER SIXTY

PROFESSOR REED'S TALL TALE

Prior to his life-changing encounter with Ms. Theodora Phillips, Samuel Reed would not have considered offering such an outrageously unbelievable anecdote—particularly to a couple of hard-nosed cops who might not take kindly to being trifled with. But a soul who has discovered that it is indeed more blessed to give than to receive has enjoyed a foretaste of true freedom. The experience was exhilarating for a man who has been entangled with the dubious pleasure of amassing a fortune. Reed's partial release from his worldly entanglements was delightfully intoxicating; he was now capable of saying and doing all manner of things that would amaze those who were acquainted with his former self.

The recently emancipated sinner got right to the heart of the matter without so much as batting an eyelash. "My ability to peer for a few hours or days into the future is not what is commonly called precognition. On the contrary, it has to do with slipping backward in time. From today to yesterday; from this month to the one before."

Charlie Moon was not surprised. His eyes had seen what was between the covers of the book in Reed's guest-house bedroom.

Scott Parris's mouth drooped into a distasteful scowl. "Sounds like science fiction." He preferred Westerns set in the late 1800s, with big six-guns belching lead and smoke as bodies of bad guys thudded onto the saloon floor.

The scientist who had taught university-level physics classes found the tone of the cop's remark off-putting. But Sam Reed was not entirely displeased; no pedagogue worth 10 percent of his inflated opinion of himself can pass up an opportunity to explain an incomprehensible phenomenon. Particularly to one whom he considers his intellectual inferior, a category that typically includes about 99 percent of the earth's adult population. But let's listen in; Professor Reed is puffing up his chest for the task.

He delivered his opening blow in the crisp tone of one who is *in the know*. "Time is a fantasy, a figment of our imagination." Enjoying a favorite private joke, the successful investor generously decided to share it. "Which, since Time is Money, calls into question the reality of dollars, pounds, and francs—not to mention yen and rubles." Confronted by Parris's blank stare, the professor realized that humor was wasted on this knuckle dragger. "Can you tell me the time of day?"

Parris consulted the Timex on his hairy wrist. "About twenty minutes past five."

"Well done. Now, pretend that you do not own a time-piece."

Parris shrugged. "Okay."

"Under that constraint, how would you find out what time it was?" Reed waggled a disapproving finger when the shrewd fellow eyeballed a Seth Thomas clock mounted on the dining-room wall. "You are not allowed access to any manner of man-made chronometer. Nor do you have any means of communicating with those who do."

The beefy cop was reminded of one of his favorite pas-times. "Like I'm off somewhere in the mountains hunting a bull elk?"

"Precisely so. And because elk season ends at six P.M. sharp, you naturally wish to know what o'clock it is."

Parris raised his gaze to the plastered ceiling and watched a tiny eight-legged creature that was suspended on an invisible thread. Ever so slowly, the crafty creature lowered herself toward the brass chandelier. "If it wasn't too cloudy, I'd check out the sun."

"Of course. And if your elkish rendezvous was scheduled for midnight, you might consult the moon."

Parris cocked his head. "So what's the point?"

"The point," the scientist said in a condescending manner, "is that the fourth dimension, which we homo sapiens refer to as 'time,' is merely a human invention to keep track of changing physical events, particularly those of a cyclical nature. Such as the rotation of the earth, which produces the illusion that the sun is passing overhead. The phases of the moon. The annual circuit of our rocky planet around the nearest star." Reed tapped his chest. "And the thumping of the pump that circulates blood through our soul's fleshly abode."

"Everybody knows that," the sensible cop said. "But time wasn't invented by people; it'd still be here if everybody on earth was dead and gone."

"An excellent exposition of an almost universal misconception." *This is somewhat more difficult than I had expected.* Reason having proven ineffective, Reed resorted to authority. "To paraphrase Professor Einstein—time is an illusion, although a very persistent one."

"I don't care who said it." Parris jutted his chin. "Any way you slice it, it's still baloney."

Reed paused for a sigh, a roll of the eyes. "I should not expect to relieve you in a moment of an error that you have embraced for a lifetime. But just to raise a healthy doubt in your mind, I shall pose what scientists and philosophers refer to as a thought experiment."

The cop's expression reflected his increasing uneasiness.

"This won't hurt a bit, and you might even enjoy the process." Samuel Reed was obviously enjoying himself. "First, imagine a vast, boundless universe that is entirely empty." *Much like the space between your ears.*

Parris sensed a trap. "Why would I want to do that?"

"Merely to humor me." Reed cracked a genuine smile. "That, and I'll give you something special that I have in my jacket pocket."

The intransigent pupil was instantly won over. "This empty universe don't even have a speck of dust?"

"Not a solitary atom, electron, or quark." A first-rate scientist is able to imagine impossible things. *And unlike the so-called vacuum of our outer space, its immense emptiness is a true void. There is no energy. No matrix of space to warp. No virtual particles popping into existence, only to vanish immediately.*

Parris closed his eyes and tried to imagine Nothing.

Professor Reed regarded his slow student with amusement. "Are you there yet?"

The reluctant scholar grunted. "Close as I'm gonna get."

"Excellent. Now, let us place a single particle in this vast, vacant space."

"A particle of what?"

"Never mind." Reed's eyes narrowed imperiously. "Just do as I say."

"Okay." The cop imagined a teensy-weensy black speck. "Got it."

"Excellent. This is a very special particle, Mr. Parris. It has no component parts and it neither vibrates nor spins."

"Okay by me." His sunburned brow furrowed. "How big is it?"

"The question of size has no meaning, as there is no meterstick in this imaginary universe to measure our lonely particle with."

Maybe so, but this was Parris's imagination. The infinitesimal speck grew to the size of a BB like the ammo he'd loaded into his childhood Red Ryder air rifle. Little Scotty was about to pull the trigger and shoot the sphere across the empty universe when—

Sam Reed added another constraint. "And as vast as its home is, this particle cannot move to another place."

Bummer. "Why not?"

The physicist turned his head to address the silent Indian. "Would you like to make a guess, Mr. Moon?"

The Ute shook his head.

The haughty pedagogue returned his attention to the Caucasian cop. "With only a single particle, there are no *places* in this universe, Mr. Parris—no reference points. The concept of movement or velocity has no meaning whatever." *Inertia is another matter, but that subject is beyond the scope of this cartoon universe.* He drew in a deep breath. "What we have is a rather simpleminded example of a perfectly static universe. As there is no possibility of change, the concept of time is meaningless. Thus, the temporal illusion in our own universe is unmasked for what it is—a mere artifact of physical alterations. Planets spinning. Satellites circling. Molecules vibrating. Automobiles passing mile-marker signs along the highway."

"So you say." Parris opened his eyes and shot a wry glance at the Ute rancher. "So what does that have to do with the price of beef next week?"

"Ah, I should have expected that you would get right to the point. Here it is. As the seasons and moons wax and wane, your wristwatch tickety-tocks, and my noble heart beats, I am approaching a significant mile marker. For the purposes of this discussion, I shall call the little green signpost on my life's highway 'June fourth.' Quite unexpectedly, I encounter a Mack truck. Head-on."

Like his Ute colleague, the Granite Creek chief of police had examined enough twisted wreckage and mangled flesh to last for several lifetimes. "Sounds to me like you've cashed in your chips."

"An astute observation, and entirely correct—as far as it goes. My earthly husk is as deceased as a fossilized sunflower seed, and before many days pass it will be planted beneath the sod." The scientist's eyes assumed a dreamy glaze that was more appropriate to a visionary or poet. "But this is not the end of my story."

Parris waited for the punch line.

Also Moon.

"When my death occurred on June fourth, that ineffable essence of myself which contained my iron will, sparkling personality, and astounding memory—my humble *soul* if you prefer—found itself back at an *earlier* mile marker. I refer, of course, to May third."

Parris was beginning to get the gist of it. "The day before

you showed up in my office with the story that somebody was gonna murder you."

"Yes, but again you get ahead of me. The relevant issue is that this is not the first occasion when my consciousness has taken the reverse journey along that illusory pathway which we refer to as *time*." Reed frowned at his distorted reflection in the jar of colorfully wrapped candies. "I have no doubt that time-slips are occasionally experienced by practically everyone, though the vast majority of us are either unaware of the peculiar phenomenon or dismiss it as a mere product of the imagination. In my case, the experience has become a frequent occurrence. The slippage may be as little as a few minutes to several months, and though a jarring emotional event sometimes initiates the adventure, there is not always an evident trigger for it." He turned his gaze from the multicolored candy to Parris's ruddy face. "Shortly after the most recent event, all that I could recall of my future were isolated bits and pieces. Such as leaving the candy shop with a box of chocolates tucked under my arm. Getting into my Mercedes in the bank parking lot. Driving for two or three blocks. After that, nothing except the evening's highly unpleasant climax—being shot dead. I didn't know where the horrific event had occurred. But a few days after the transition, I gradually began to regain a more complete memory of the critical half hour prior to my death. Within a week, I recalled virtually everything—including the fact that I was gunned down as I entered my home."

Scott Parris posed the obvious question: "Did you see the shooter?"

The storyteller shook his head. "It was too dark." He hesitated. "My final recollection was stepping into the rear entrance of my residence, seeing the flash of a gunshot, the sensation that a boulder had struck my chest, feeling the bullet tear through my flesh." Sam Reed paused to compose himself. "I concluded that it was almost certainly my wife who had shot me. Irene had the classic motives: the significant difference in our ages—and an enormous fortune to inherit. But later, when she made the 911 call about a break-in,

I was greatly relieved. I initially concluded that this was the prelude to a future error on my wife's part. I theorized that on the evening of June fourth of my previous life, Irene had mistaken me for a burglar." He frowned and shook his head. "But the next day, I learned that the police officers had found no evidence that anyone had been prying on our back door. That, and the troubling fact that that my spouse was expecting me home at eleven on the evening of the shooting—which was precisely when I had arrived—made it appear far more likely that my spouse's emergency call was a phony; the coldblooded groundwork for a homicide that would be excused as a tragic instance of mistaken identity. Dear Irene was planning my untimely demise." The intended victim smiled wanly under his thin mustache. "A birthday present for herself, as it were."

Scott Parris went for a sucker punch. "So how'd you find out about the boyfriend?"

Reed's face stiffened, but it had been a glancing blow. The widower's smile was as bitter as the taste in his mouth. "When I expressed an interest in how Irene was spending her spare time, several of our closest country-club friends were only too happy to drop heavy hints about my wife's infidelity. One of the gossips took me aside and identified Mr. Perez as the object of Irene's adulterous affections."

Charlie Moon had been watching Samuel Reed's remarkably expressive face. *He's either the best storyteller in Colorado or the man's suffering from a severe case of self-delusion.* The Ute poker player couldn't quite make up his mind. Too many tells can be tougher to read than a face sculpted from stone.

CHAPTER SIXTY-ONE

AUDIENCE RESPONSE

His performance completed, Samuel Reed addressed the lawmen. "So. What do you fellows think of my story?"

How palpable was the silence?

You could have carved off slices of hush with your Buck pocketknife, rolled the chunks up between your fingers, and used them to caulk logs in the cabin wall.

The performer was wide-eyed with contrived surprise. "What, no applause?" Reed assumed an equally false expression of injury. "I did not expect big cowboy hats tossed into the air, raucous hoots of approval, and thunderous boot-stomps demanding an encore performance—but this is faint praise indeed! The very least you owe me is a measure of constructive criticism." The fastidious man arched an inquisitive eyebrow at the Indian. "What say you, Charles?"

Charles Moon did not respond.

"Oh, come now—tell me what's on your mind. Did you find the notion of reverse time-slipping somewhat disconcerting?"

"I can take it or leave it." *So long as you don't try to make me believe it.*

"Fair enough." Turning away from the taciturn Indian, the teller of tales presented an expectant expression to the chief of police.

"Sorry, Sam." The cop shrugged dismissively. "Your tale's a mite too *Twilight Zone* for me." And, for reasons Parris did not care to share, a little scary. "It'd be easier to believe that Charlie was grazing a herd of pink unicorns on a crop of purple prickly pears."

"A colorful metaphor. But allow me to remind you that my whimsical anecdote about how *I remember* the future— while based upon widely accepted tenets of modern science— was presented for the sole purpose of entertainment. I never suggested that you should *believe* a smidgen of my tallish tale; I merely hoped that you would enjoy it." Reed's lips curled into an impish smile. "When you spun your fantastic yarn about a ferocious ape chasing a terrified lady across the golf course, and Mr. Moon made his extraordinary claim about executing ne'er-do-wells for the princely fee of twenty-five cents per lowlife—did I protest that either of you was attempting to deceive me? I will eat my hat if I did!"

"Okay." Parris eyed Charlie Moon's candidate for the golf-course gorilla. "It's an awfully queer story, though. Somebody shoots you dead on June fourth, and you wake up healthy as a floppy-eared hound puppy on May third. And then you recall what's gonna happen during the next several weeks." He shot a sly glance at his rancher friend. "Like ups and downs in the price of beef."

The tribal investigator was distracted by a whispering in his ear. And those pesky flesh-eating worms were beginning to wriggle under his skin again. Charlie Moon knew he shouldn't raise the issue, but some things just have to be said. "Your story's okay as far is it goes." He paused as if puzzling over just how to make his point. "But there's one thing that bothers me."

"Only *one*?" Reed laughed.

Moon regarded the wealthy man with a quizzical expression. "I've been thinking back to May fourth, when you showed up at Scott's office. And I've been trying to imagine how I'd be spending my time if I believed somebody intended to murder me."

Reed returned a solemn look. "Let me assure you that such a circumstance tends to concentrate one's attention."

Charlie Moon nodded. "A man in your shoes would have

plenty of serious business to take care of. No time for the small stuff."

"Most definitely."

"That's what made me wonder why you did it." Moon waited.

Sam Reed was literally on the edge of his chair. "Did what?"

"With all your problems, you took a stroll down Spruce Lane and paid a call on Leadville Lily."

Scott Parris blinked. *I must've missed something here.*

The stunned man stared at the tribal investigator. *So it was you who followed me to the tattoo parlor that morning.* Needing a moment to organize his thoughts, the deadpan scientist held his tongue.

Scott Parris could shatter any annoying silence he happened to encounter. "I don't get it, Charlie. What's ol' Tattoo Lily got to do with Sam's weird story?"

"Now that's the question, pard." Moon's gaze did not waver from Reed's frozen face.

The object of the Indian's intense scrutiny managed to find his voice. "Do you have an answer to this hypothetical question you pose?"

Moon responded in a monotone, "Thought I'd leave that to your imagination."

"Oh, I see." Evasion having failed, Reed resorted to a pretense of misunderstanding Moon's insinuation. "Your introduction of a tattoo-parlor visit does present a worthy challenge to my ability to improvise." To purchase a few more seconds, he coughed. Hummed a few bars of "Jack of Diamonds." Thrummed his fingers again on the table. Finally: "I'm trying to think of a way to weave this unforeseen element into my story line."

The lawmen waited.

The chief of police with a puzzled look. *What'n hell is Charlie up to?*

The tribal investigator with a wry twinkle in his eye. *I bet this'll be good.*

It would.

Samuel Reed had come to a difficult decision. *I shall tell them the unvarnished truth.* That would be the last thing a couple of cynical cops would expect, and was certain to create confusion. He cleared his throat and began. "I paid Leadville Lily fifty dollars to tattoo an identity mark on my left forearm."

Surprised at the man's candor, Charlie Moon nodded. "Like a brand on a steer."

"Indeed." Reed flashed a smile at the rancher. "But let's amend that to 'bull.'"

Bull works for me. Parris glowered at the shifty customer. "Don't you carry a driver's license in your wallet like ordinary folks?"

"I certainly do." Reed regarded the lawman with an expression that suggested infinite patience. "And that plasticized card would prove useful to the authorities in the instance of my untimely death—say in a horrendous motorcycle accident where my handsome face was obliterated. The authorities could immediately determine that the grisly remains were those of Samuel Reed, Ph.D., who formerly resided at 1200 Shadowlane Avenue in Granite Creek, Colorado." *Go ahead. Ask the obvious question.*

Parris's eyes narrowed to suspicious slits. "So why d'you need your name tattooed on your skin?"

"I do not."

"What?"

Samuel Reed removed his jacket, unbuttoned his cuff, and rolled up his shirtsleeve. "Behold."

CHAPTER SIXTY-TWO

SAMUEL REED'S BRAND

The lawmen leaned forward to examine this example of Leadville Lily's art.

What they beheld on the pale skin of his forearm was a mere number.

24

Scott Parris barked like a an irritable old dog, "So what the hell's *that* good for?"

As he rolled his sleeve down, Samuel Reed returned Parris's glare with a cold stare. "If I tell you, you won't believe a word I say."

"I might," Charlie Moon said.

"Yes, I expect you would." Reed rebuttoned his cuff. *You must've been onto me for some time.* "Each morning when I wake up, I check my left forearm. If I see the proper number on my skin, I know that my conscious self is occupying the same body it did when I drifted off to sleep the night before." He shrugged into his jacket. "If my skin is a blank slate, so to speak—or if I see a smaller number—I realize that I have slipped backward in time and into another version of my strikingly handsome fleshly self." He fastened three buttons on his jacket. "When I have made a slip, I am able to *remember the future*. If the slippage amounts to at least a few days, I am able to profit thereby by buying low and selling high."

The chief of police stared dumbly at this cool-as-ice customer who had engineered the deadly encounter between his wife and Chico Perez. This did not compute. For the moment, it was if the trillions of tiny gears in Parris's brain had jammed.

Likewise, Samuel Reed seemed to have *had his say*.

The Indian cop broke the brittle silence with a compliment. "Well done."

"Thank you, Mr. Moon."

The effort to wrap his mind around all this balderdash was making Parris's forehead ache. "What'n hell are you talking about?"

Having entirely recovered his composure, the storyteller addressed the town cop with a supercilious curl of his thinly mustached lip. "I have done my best to provide a lucid explanation of the means whereby I have amassed a fortune." He cast a wry glance at the Ute. "Perhaps Mr. Moon would like to give it a try?"

Mr. Moon was pleased to, and directed his remark to his friend. "I believe that our scientist-magician has just pulled a couple of dozen parallel universes out of his hat."

Parris was more puzzled still. "Parallel *what*?"

"The subject is far too complex to explain in a few words." Reed exhaled a weary sigh. "Suffice it to say that the concept I have utilized to account for an alleged visit to a tattoo parlor has to do with the cosmological theory that you, Charles, myself, and everyone else—all exist in an enormous multitude of worlds. Some of which are very similar to this one, while others differ strikingly."

The chief of police's head felt like a toy balloon that was about to float away. "What does *that* mean?"

"Merely that there are other, parallel realities wherein we live out our respective lives." Raising his hands to fend off a growling protest from the bearish cop, the physicist continued. "I do not propose to offer a detailed explanation, but I could refer you to several excellent books on the subject which are intelligible to the intelligent layman." *A little flattery does no harm.* "What it all boils down to is that whenever a human consciousness—or a copy thereof—leaves one body to occupy another, it likewise departs from one universe and enters another."

Having nothing to say to *that,* the presumably intelligent layman stared at Reed.

The Ute smiled. *He should try writing some science fiction.*

The scientist inhaled a refreshing breath. "I am glad that I have told you fellows about this strange business while I can still recall it. My memories of the recent shooting of Samuel Reed Number 23 and my subsequent slippage in time are already beginning to seem more like a fantastic dream than an actual occurrence. Within another month or two, I will retain only vague recollections of these events." The teller of tales paused to flash a counterfeit smile at his small audience. "There, what do you think—was that not a commendable display of on-the-spot improvisation?"

The cops stared at the enigmatic man, each occupied with his own thoughts.

Charlie Moon: *Reed's either a first-rate slicker or . . . or something else altogether.* Just what that *something else* might be was an issue the Ute did not care to pursue.

Scott Parris: *Am I looking at the one-and-only Sam Reed who makes up dopey stories? Or has this guy not only come back from the dead—but from some other world that's practically just like this one?*

Increasingly uncomfortable under this intense scrutiny, the uninvited guest got up from the chair, popped the spiffy homburg onto his head, and retrieved his elegant walking stick, which began to twirl in his hand like the blades of an electric fan. "Please pardon me for intruding on your private meal." He tipped the hat. "A good evening to you both." As Samuel Reed was opening the dining-room door to depart, he encountered a uniformed hotel employee carrying a silver tray that was heavy with delicious victuals.

An instant after the waiter had unloaded the tray and

departed, Samuel Reed reappeared in the doorway, tapping the ivory-knobbed cane against his shoe. "Please excuse me." He flashed a foxy smile at Scott Parris. "I was in the lobby when I remembered my promise to give you something special." His left hand removed an object his jacket pocket and placed it onto the dining table by the cop's platter of lasagna. "I thought you might like to have this small memento of our shared adventure. I found it in the magazine rack by the parlor couch, where Irene apparently lost it."

The cop who had searched every nook and cranny in Reed's home stared dumbly at the pink telephone. *Charlie was right again. Sam had it all along.*

"You will no doubt be interested in a number of text messages stored on my spouse's misplaced mobile phone."

The furious chief of police turned his wolfish gaze on the liar's face. "Messages exchanged by Mrs. Reed and her boyfriend?"

"Yes." Reed reached into the pocket again. "I also have something for Charles." The hand emerged with a smallish object.

Moon watched the wealthy widower place a cassette tape beside his linen napkin.

"I hope this is not an imposition," Reed said. "But when you have the time, I would be obliged if you'd have a listen."

The Ute could not unfasten his gaze from the gift. *This has to be the tape he recorded the break-in effects on.* Did the fellow actually have the brass to literally lay the evidence on the table—and dare them to implicate him?

No. Even the brash Samuel Reed would not go *that* far. Prior to this morning's recording, the tape had been carefully erased. But there was just a hint of a prankster's mischievous smirk as he said, "I hope you will not think me absurdly presumptuous." He pointed his ebony stick at the cassette. "This amounts to shameless self-promotion; a devious means of securing an audition with your highly regarded bluegrass band."

The leader of the Columbine Grass turned a puzzled look on Samuel Reed.

"You are already aware that I am an enthusiastic member

of the local barbershop quartet." The gifted tenor smoothed the slender left wing of his mustache. "But you may be surprised to discover that I am also a fair hand with the mandolin."

"I'll give it a listen." Moon slipped the cassette into his shirt pocket.

"I'm not quite ready for a raucous gig at a smoky honky-tonk where rowdy cowboys fling long-neck beer bottles at the performers, but I'd love to hit a few hot licks with you and your lively crew." Reed winked slyly at the Ute musician. "If you like my performance, perhaps you will invite me join your group during some upcoming jam session." He gave his cane its final twirl for the day. "And now I will leave you fellows to enjoy your delicious food." A courtly bow. "Good evening, gentlemen."

Parris scowled at the heavy door the clever man closed behind him. "He lays the phone he swiped from his wife right on the table, knowing there's no way I can use it to prove how he set up his wife and her boyfriend. And he gives you the cassette tape the 'ape' made the break-in sound effects on. That barefaced bastard is determined to twist our tails!"

"It does look like Professor Reed enjoys the last laugh." *But what's done is done. And he did it with style.* Charlie Moon enjoyed his final smile for the day.

CHAPTER SIXTY-THREE

SCOTT PARRIS RAISES
THE CRITICAL ISSUE

One of the allegedly legendary lawmen was already chowing down on a full pound of grilled trout.

As the other picked listlessly at his lasagna with a silver fork, he addressed his friend in the morose tone of a diner who has lost his manly appetite. "Charlie, d'you mind if I ask you something?"

The famished Indian kept his eye on the platter. "Would it matter if I did?"

"No."

"Then go right ahead and ask."

"This stuff about Reed slipping backwards in time—d'you figure there might be any truth to it?"

"No." Charlie Moon paused to return the trout's flat-eyed gaze. "I don't think so."

Parris laid his fork aside. "But you're not absolutely certain."

"The things I'm absolutely dead certain about, I can count on the fingers of one hand." As he slipped along toward tomorrow on the presumably illusory arrow of time, the practicing Catholic counted all four of them.

The chief of police started to say something, then decided to let it ride. At least until Charlie had finished his meal.

A REFLECTION ON LIFE'S MYSTERIES

After dessert, Charlie Moon was ready to settle back and let recent events recede into the past.

Not Scott Parris. The man who could never leave well-enough alone felt compelled to broach a worrisome subject. "Charlie?"

Uh-oh. Moon reached for the last cookie. "Don't do it."

"Do what?"

"Whenever you say 'Charlie' in that tone of voice, you generally end up ruining my good mood."

"All I wanted to say was . . . well—I don't know how to account for the fact that a smart man like Sam Reed believes the strange things he does."

Moon didn't agree with the premise of his friend's concern. The fellow who'd outsmarted both of them was smart enough and then some, but what the fellow actually believed was hard to pin down. As far as the Ute was concerned, Reed's story was a tall tale and that was the end of the matter. "Maybe Professor Reed's *too* smart."

"What does that mean?"

The rancher bit off half the cookie and took his time enjoying it. "When a man's IQ gets beyond a certain point, sometimes he slips off the deep end."

That was an interesting notion. "You figure Reed's a genius who's also a nutcase?"

"Let's just say that he's an overly clever fellow who occasionally lets his imagination run away with him." Moon pointed the half cookie at his friend. "Don't ever let that happen to you."

"You figure I'm that smart?"

"Nope. I figure you for the other type."

"What?"

"Gullible."

"That's not a nice thing to say, Charlie."

"Okay, consider it unsaid. How about 'highly impressionable'?"

"That's better." *But not much.*

"So let's forget all about Sam Reed dying in June and coming back in May."

Parris nodded. "And ending up in world that was more or less like the one he left, and remembering his future."

"Yeah, forget about that too."

"I'll try." A pensive sigh. "But it ain't as easy as you think, Chucky."

"I hope you'll notice that I'm not asking 'why?'"

"Well, because that tale Reed told us kinda got me to thinking."

"That's *your* problem, pard—don't go giving me heartburn."

"I can't help it." Parris belched and felt the sting of acid in his throat. After crunching a Tums, he explained, "Since Sam Reed told us all that weird stuff—I've recalled about a half-dozen peculiar things that've happened to me over the years. Any one of 'em could be explained by me slipping back and forth between this universe and another one like it."

"I don't want to hear a single, solitary word about it."

"Okay, here's a f'r instance. About a year ago, I woke up one morning with a mole on the back of my right hand. One that wasn't there the night before."

"Maybe some moles are like tomatoes, pard—they grow fastest at night."

"This was a great big one, Charlie. Size of a nickel."

"That's a whopper all right."

"You haven't heard the really creepy part."

"And I don't want to."

"The very next day, that mole was gone—I mean there wasn't the least sign it'd ever been on my hand. Now explain how that happened."

"I don't have to; it wasn't *my* mole." Glancing at the clock on the wall, Moon began to unfold his slender frame from the chair. "Discussing your skin blemishes is great fun, pardner—but I've got to be rolling on down the road toward home."

Parris was gazing at his unfinished meal with a glassy-eyed expression. "One morning when I was a kid, I was fishing for catfish in Pigeon Creek and I fell asleep. When I woke up I was a good twenty miles away."

"Maybe you got abducted by undocumented aliens."

Parris shook his head. "I was in Aunt Minnie's house in Midway and it was the *day before yesterday*."

Charlie Moon didn't try to conceal his surprise. "There's a Midway in Indiana?"

"Sure." Parris blinked. "It's midway between De Gonia Springs and Richland City."

"Sounds like a nice spot. I'll check it out next time I'm in the neighborhood."

Charlie's trying to make me forget what I was talking about. "You oughten to make sport of me."

"Why not, pard?" Moon reached for his hat.

The displaced Hoosier jutted his chin. "Because some fine morning . . ." He turned a blank stare on the candy jar.

The happy man flicked a fleck of white fluff off the brim of his Stetson. "Some fine morning *what*?"

Parris elevated his gaze to glower at the tall, thin man. "Some fine morning, you're liable to wake up and find out you're *somewhere else*. And in another time."

As the rancher donned his handsome black hat, he thought about that. "I hope it's on a nice beach in Tahiti in 1950, and pretty girls in grass skirts are bringing me pineapples and papayas and whatnot." The Ute saluted his best buddy in this universe. "See you later."

"Drive careful." For quite some time after his Indian friend had departed, the chief of police tarried in the private dining room. After taking a tentative taste of the cold lasagna, the famished man commenced to consume samples of every treat in the candy jar except for the Gummi Bears. While absorbing about three thousand sugary calories, the lawman contemplated his conversation with the tribal investigator. *I guess it's a good thing that Charlie's so down-to-earth and levelheaded.* But Scott Parris's grunt suggested that a "but" was in the offing. *But every once in a while, he sure does go against the grain.* The discomfited soul comforted himself with the hopeful thought that *sooner or later, Mr. Moon's gonna get his comeuppance.*

Sooner.

CHAPTER SIXTY-FOUR

"And the cowboys now as they roam the plain,
For they marked the spot where his bones were lain,
Fling a handful o' roses o'er his grave
With a prayer to God his soul to save."

A TRIVIAL DETAIL

As Charlie Moon was making his way to the Silver Mountain Hotel parking lot, he was smiling about his conversation with Scott Parris. *I guess I spurred Scott a little too hard.* The semirepentant offender unlocked and opened the Expedition door. *I'll find a way to make it up to him.* As he eased himself onto the driver's seat, something caught Moon's eye. Something that *wasn't there*.

What? Why, a facsimile of a spider on the windshield, of course.

This doesn't make sense?

Patience. All will be explained.

What the driver was surprised *not* to see was the break in the safety glass where—just last month—a chunk of gravel had made a pit. Over the past week, the thing had grown eight little legs.

Moon inspected the windshield with considerable care. Didn't help. *It just ain't there.* He continued to stare at the unbroken glass. There had to be a simple, rational explanation. But try as he might, Moon couldn't think of one. *That spider break was there this afternoon when I parked the car, so unless somebody replaced the windshield while I was inside having supper with Scott . . .* But even that outlandish explanation wouldn't work. *This windshield isn't a new one, not by a long shot.* The glass was dirty, and the lightly sandblasted surface still had the wiper marks from a rain days ago. *And the sticker from the last oil change is still in the upper-left-hand corner.*

Well. What does a man make of a weird thing like that?

As he pulled out of the parking lot and aimed his trusty automobile in the happy direction of hearth and home, Charlie Moon made up his mind to forget about it. *Every once in a while, something peculiar happens.* Like the big mole that showed up one morning on the back of Scott Parris's hand, only to be gone the next morning. And little Scottie going to sleep beside the creek and waking up twenty miles away and two days earlier in Aunt Minnie's house in Midway, Indiana. Like those inexplicable conundrums, the missing break in the windshield fell into that category of *sleeping dogs* that a sensible man leaves alone.

And so he did, with the aid of a musical distraction.

When Granite Creek was about mile and a minute behind him, Charlie Moon plugged Reed's audition tape into the dashboard cassette player. The leader of the Columbine Grass was impressed as he listened to the rich man sing and finger the strings. *Sam Reed has a fine tenor voice and he sure knows how to make that mandolin sing.* Moreover, the member of the Velvet Frogs barbershop quartet had selected a fine old song for a lonely man to listen to around about sundown.

As the Ute rancher rolled along on the darkening high plains, his consciousness slipped backward in time to *away back then* when the dying cowboy had begged his friends not to bury him out here on the *lone prairie.*

EPILOGUE

LOOSE ENDS

CONCERNING THE SO-CALLED
CROWBAR BURGLAR

To date, this particular pest has been neither identified nor
arrested, but it is gratifying to report that the troublesome
felon no longer plagues the peaceable folk of Granite Creek.
His chosen vocation was abruptly terminated during a break-
in on a balmy August evening when a sweet little eighty-six-
year-old retired schoolmarm got a bead on the center of his
belly with her single-shot Remington rifle and popped a
.22-caliber projectile into his Coors belt buckle. Upon hearing the metallic ping of a lead slug on brass and the thug's
startled yelp, the shooter made the following observation:
"Thunder and damnation! I did so want to gut-shoot the foul
miscreant!"

Alas, before the lady was able to reload, the startled in-
truder had vanished like a dandelion puff in a stiff breeze,
and has not been seen or heard from since. Chief of Police
Scott Parris opines that the undesirable element has found a
more congenial place to settle down and pursue a less-stressful
vocation.

Which he has.

Among his other transitory enterprises, the habitual criminal is using the Internet to sell Idaho real estate. We are

talking prime shoreline lots on Lake Colette, which is located approximately six miles east of Taffy Creek.

Potential buyers who bother to consult a map will conclude that both the lake and the creek are entirely fictitious.

ONE LAST DETAIL

An inconsequential postscript. Hardly worth mentioning.

But in the interest of fair play, it must be reported that Charlie Moon was mistaken in his suspicions of Samuel Reed. We do not refer to the golf-course-ape escapade, where the tribal investigator's speculation was right on the mark. Reed did indeed make his break-in recordings at the groundskeeper's toolshed, and he was the "gorilla" who chased Ms. Bernice Aldershott.

Moon's wrongful suspicion has to do with the investor's uncanny prognostications. The wealthy man never made a dime on insider information. Moreover, Samuel Reed was convinced that he slipped between parallel universes, and he firmly believed his assertion that there were as many otherworldly copies of Charlie Moon and Scott Parris as himself. And for that matter, *yourself.*

Speaking of whom—brace yourself for some serious bad news.

That's right. Professor Reed's enormous multiverse is also populated by gazillions of Daisy Perikas. Each copy, no doubt, up to malicious mischief specific to her peculiar circumstances. The mind reels, boggles, and so forth at the contemplation of such a calamity. (Parenthetically, let us say multiuniversal calamity.) Notwithstanding the fact that in many of these worlds Miss Daisy would have clubbed Chico Perez (aka Posey Shorthorse) to death. In which instances, Mrs. Reed might well have lived happily ever after.

But enough of this pseudoscientific twaddle.

Let us dismiss all that does not lead to bliss.

Good night.

May you sleep in perfect peace and dream visions of multihued autumn hills, rainbow fields of wildflowers, and crystalline mountain streams wherein speckled trout dart about.

And just on the off chance that Professor Reed is right, may these same blessings be enjoyed by all your hypothetical counterparts, doppelgängers, doubles, and whatnot.

Wherever they might be.

And whenever.

Read on for an excerpt from

Coffin Man

The next Charlie Moon mystery by James D. Doss—
available soon in hardcover from Minotaur Books!

CHAPTER ONE

THURSDAY MORNING
CAÑÓN DEL ESPÍRITU

Daisy Perika has resided at the mouth of Spirit Canyon for
more bone-chilling winters than she cares to remember.
Since the tribal elder now spends about nine days out of ten
at her nephew's vast cattle ranch northwest of Granite Creek,
her home has become a place to spend a day or two in now
and then. During these occasional visits, Miss Daisy begins
by making sure that nothing is amiss, such as an odorous
skunk that has taken up residence under the hardwood floor,
a pair of frisky squirrels raising a family in the attic, or a
broken window where the dry west wind blows dust in. Charlie Moon can be counted on to deal with such problems
forthwith, and when all has been made right, Daisy enjoys
sleeping away a peaceful night in her own bed, cooking
breakfast on her six-burner propane range, and taking long,
soul-satisfying walks in her canyon.

Yes, *her* canyon.

It matters little that the shadowy space between miles-long
Three Sisters Mesa and the lesser promontory known as Dogleg is owned by the tribe. As long as Daisy Perika has lived in
this remote location, hardly anyone besides herself ever sets
foot inside Spirit Canyon but those lonely haunts that *Cañón*

del Espíritu is named for and the dwarfish *pitukupf* who allegedly resides therein.

But enough about local geography and Daisy's thousand-year-old neighbor, who will make his presence known if and when he is "of a mind to." What currently commands our attention (and excites our olfactory senses) are the tantalizing aromas drifting out of Daisy's kitchen. Ahhh . . . sniff a whiff of *that*!

(Nothing smells quite so appetizing as burning animal fat.)

On the left half of a massive Tennessee Forge skillet, plump pork sausages are sizzling deliciously. On the opposite side, strips of bacon pop grease hot enough to put out a bronze statue's eyeball.

And that's not all.

In a matching black cast-iron cooking implement, fresh eggs, sharp cheddar cheese, presautéed Vidalia onions, and Hatch green chili are being stirred by Sarah Frank into an exceedingly tasty scramble.

In a blue enameled pot, tar-black coffee percolates with seductive *plickity-plocks*. This high-octane concoction is guaranteed to knock off your socks.

In the top of the oven, Daisy's secret-recipe, made-from-scratch biscuits are slowly baking to a golden-brown perfection. On the shelf below that, a tray of delicious cinnamon-bun confections are swelling with justifiable pride.

One is tempted to drop in and tuck a napkin under the chin. Sadly, Daisy's dining table is set only for four.

BREAKFAST IN DAISY'S KITCHEN

After busying herself importantly around the stove—where Sarah Frank was doing all the real work and graciously accepting sage advice from the tribal elder—Daisy Perika decided that her assistant was doing a fairly competent job for someone who was only half Ute. The senior cook took the coffeepot to the table and filled all four cups with steaming brew. This done, the lady of the house seated herself and waited for the girl to bring on the victuals. Daisy knew precisely what Sarah would put onto her plate: two strips of crispy bacon, one patty of sausage, one biscuit, and a just-so helping of scrambled eggs.

As the hungry fellows bellied up to the table, Sarah began to deliver the food on preheated stoneware platters.

Charlie Moon offered a heartfelt cowboy compliment: "That looks good enough to eat."

Nodding his agreement, Scott Parris upped the ante: "That and then some."

So much for original conversation when breaking fast; the taciturn menfolk got right at it with knife and fork.

Daisy buttered her biscuit, added a dab of Kroger strawberry preserves, and took a bite. *I can't hardly taste that.* But even an old body needed nourishment and . . . *I have to keep my strength up.* This being so, she chewed and dutifully choked it down. Being of an analytic and morbid inclination, the old soul reviewed the highlights of her decline. *First it was my hearing.* A second dab of jam on the biscuit. *Then my eyes started to get cloudy.* Another halfhearted bite, followed by feeble mastication. *Now I can't hardly taste anything I put in my mouth.* She supposed that aged people were much like rusty old pickup trucks or antique sewing machines: sooner or later, various parts were bound to wear out. Daisy figured her brain would go next. *Some morning soon, I'll wake up and wonder what my name is.* In search of something more pleasant to think about, she looked across the table at Sarah, who was gazing at Moon with big cow eyes. *Sooner or later Charlie'll have to tell this silly little half-Papago girl that he don't intend to marry her because he's old enough to be her daddy.* The senior member of the gathering helped herself to another mouthful of buttered biscuit and jam. *That tastes a little better—maybe my mouth just needs more practice.*

Scott Parris reached for a jar of Daisy's homemade damson-plum preserves. While spooning a generous helping of the fruity treat onto his second biscuit, he cast a glance at Sarah. "What classes are you taking at Rocky Mountain Polytechnic?"

"Computer Science, History of Western Civilization, and Statistical Analysis." The young woman, who had avoided both meats and the bread, pecked at her modest portion of scrambled eggs. "Oh, and Social Studies."

"That's a pretty heavy load," Moon observed.

"It keeps me busy." The slender little scholar shrugged under her blue polka-dot dress. "In Social Studies, I'll be doing a research project on indigent persons in Granite Creek."

His mouth full, Parris was obliged to suppress a snort. After swallowing, the stocky white cop offered this observation: "We got plenty of those characters hanging around town."

Sarah Frank took a sip of coffee. "My professor suggested that I find my subjects in U.S. Grant Park."

Taking on the role of a concerned uncle, the chief of police eyed the orphan sternly. "Don't you get caught in the park after dark. Most of those so-called 'indigent' folks are wild-eyed dope addicts, whiskey-soaked alcoholics, or flat-out howling-at-the-moon lunatics." He took a hard look at his biscuit. "Some are all three."

A smile played at the edges of the girl's lips. *He's so sweet.*

"Pay attention, Sarah." Charlie Moon used his Buck sheath knife to deftly slice a pork patty into four equal pieces. "Scott knows what he's talking about." He speared a quarter section with the tip of the blade. "Some of those unfortunate folks are downright dangerous."

"I'll be careful." Sarah flashed a pretty smile at Moon. "I'll do all of my research in the middle of the day."

The lawmen grunted their approval; even Daisy seemed pleased with the girl's prudence. And so it went. A delightful breakfast.

No one present could have imagined what was about to happen.

When the morning meal was completed, the eldest of the diners opened her mouth to let out a long, satisfying yawn. *I feel a nice nap coming on.* The tribal elder withdrew to her parlor without a word to her guests or the least concern about who would clean off the table, wash dishes, and so on and so forth. The sleepy woman wedged herself into a creaky old rocking chair and settled in there with her feet on the bricked hearth. A second yawn began to slip between Daisy Perika's lips. She was asleep before her mouth had time to close.

A brief siesta is generally beneficial after a meal, especially for those citizens who are older than eighty-foot-tall pink-barked ponderosas. This was not an appropriate time for a nightmare, but the morning's sweetest dream occasionally walks arm-in-arm with her sinister midnight sister.

CHAPTER TWO

THE OLD WOMAN'S VISION

As with so many misadventures, Daisy Perika's nap-dream began innocently enough.

Like a tender brown bean shelled from its dry hull, something forever young was set free from the prison of her old, tired body. As it slipped away into a velvety-soft twilight, this essence of her soul (or so it seemed) prepared to take flight. Her spirit floated effortlessly up from the rocking chair to pass through the beamed ceiling and into the attic. Daisy was intensely aware of every detail in that musty, dusty space. She counted eleven spiders on eleven webs, examined every knot in every pine two-by-six, frowned at a nail that an inept carpenter had bent, and spotted a hickory-handled Ace claw hammer the careless fellow had left behind. But the dreamer did not tarry there; she penetrated the roof as if that sturdy assembly of planks, plywood, and shiny red Pro-Panel was merely a misty figment of her Lower World imagination.

Up—up—up she rose, ever faster—and spread her strong young arms to soar among those proud hawks and eagles who ruled this airy underbelly of the earthly heavens. As if hours were minutes in this singular dimension, the cerulean sky began to darken with a ferocious rapidity. Roiling blue-black clouds inflated with explosive intent; thunder began to rumble over those big-shouldered mountains that would not be named after San Juan for centuries. Lifted by the sighing winds,

Daisy drifted effortlessly over Three Sisters Mesa, gazing down at the sandstone remnants of those Pueblo women who had fled to escape the horror of a marauding band of painted-face, filed-tooth cannibal terrorists from the south. Though the atrocities had occurred more than a millennium ago, Daisy's dream-eyes witnessed the slaughter of the remnants of the Sisters' tribe—those unfortunates who had attempted to hide in the shadowy depths of Spirit Canyon.

But like her feathered comrades who drifted over the scene with serene indifference to the problems of wingless human beings, Daisy's heart was likewise hardened to the suffering and death unfolding below. Her experience was like watching a moving-picture show about the horrors of some long-ago calamity where nameless innocents were slain. The dreamer was so far removed from the carnage that it seemed more like lurid fiction than tragic history.

But, as so often happens with those of us who have no empathy for the suffering of others, the shaman's experience was about to become extremely personal—and take a sudden turn for the worse.

Though Daisy did not fall from the sky like a stone, her majestic, soaring form was abruptly diminished to something resembling a tiny, wing-flapping sparrow. No longer the peer of bald eagles and red-tailed hawks, the shaman darted a few yards over the floor of *Cañón del Espíritu*—pursued by a rapacious predator. The fleeing dreamer did not see the creature that was intent upon eating her alive, but her spirit eyes did perceive a huge owl shadow slipping quickly along the canyon's sandy bottom.

DAISY'S JARRING AWAKENING

The kitchen now shipshape and squeaky clean, the menfolk and the Ute-Papago girl were almost ready to leave Aunt Daisy at home alone.

After taking a final swipe at the shining dining table, Sarah Frank withdrew to the guest bedroom that she used when staying overnight with Daisy Perika. She opened the closet door to take her dark-blue coat off a plastic hanger, reached up to a shelf for her nifty cowgirl hat—and during the process knocked off a shoe box, which fell to spill its contents onto the floor. The girl knelt to gather odd bits of this and that, which included the chubby snow-white leg of an antique china doll (a brown shoe was painted onto the tiny foot), a jet-black 1940s-era Sheaffer fountain pen with the nib broken off, a red plastic flower, and—something else that was folded in a piece of gauzy tissue paper.

Sarah picked it up, her smooth brow furrowing as she unwrapped it. *What's this?*

Hers was a rhetorical question.

The thing she held between finger and thumb was quite obviously a feather. And not a particularly distinguished member of that category of covering that had first sprouted on the nimble limbs of smallish proto-dinosaurs. Perhaps three inches long, its sorry excuse for color resided somewhere in that dreary neighborhood between mouse brown and slate gray. The tip of the feather appeared to have been scorched, and a hint of odor remained that was similar to the unpleasant scent of burned hair. Sarah wrinkled her nose. *I wonder why Aunt Daisy is keeping this old thing?* She immediately smiled at her silly question. One might as well ask why the old woman had stashed away a doll's leg, a broken fountain pen, and a plastic rose. *They all mean something to her, I suppose.* Still, the girl was curious about the feather. *I'll ask her about it.* If there was not a good story behind this unlikely artifact, the tribal elder would feel obliged to make one up.

After restoring the other objects to the shoe box and returning it to the closet shelf, Sarah donned her coat and wide-brimmed hat. Entering the parlor, she gazed at the old woman who slept in the rocking chair. *It seems like a shame to wake her up.* She twirled the feather between finger and thumb. *But we can't just leave her here all alone and asleep without saying goodbye.* Not wanting to awaken the sleeper too abruptly, she whispered, "Aunt Daisy?"

No response.

Feeling more than a little whimsical—very nearly mischievous—Sarah thought: *I ought to use the feather to tickle her nose.* But for whatever reason, that was not precisely what she did. The girl stroked the feather ever so lightly over the old woman's left eyelid, the bridge of her nose, and across the other closed eye.

The sleeper shuddered; both eyes popped open to glare at Sarah. "What'd you do?"

Startled by the suddenness of the awakening, Sarah stuttered. "I . . . tick-tickled your . . ." By way of explanation, she showed the old woman the feather.

"Silly girl." Daisy snorted. "If you want to wake me up, just let out a big war whoop and tell me the 'Paches are riding in to massacre us all—or shoot off a big pistol by my ear!"

Relieved, the nervous youth giggled. "I'm sorry. It's just that we're about to leave, and—"

"We're about to leave?" Disoriented by her awakening, the old woman blinked. "Where're we going?"

Sarah Frank was saved from the pain of explaining when Charlie Moon and Scott Parris stomped into the parlor to announce their imminent departure.

Sarah offered the face tickler to Daisy, who waved it aside. "What would I want with *that*!"

Not knowing what else to do with the offending feather, Sarah stuck it into her hatband. "When do you want me to come back?"

The old woman frowned. "Come back for what?"

"To take you back to the Columbine."

"Oh . . . sometime next week, I guess." Rubbing the residue of sleep from her eyes, Daisy got a grip on her oak staff and pushed herself up from the rocking chair. "I'll call you when I'm ready." She followed Sarah and the men outside, where her small family commenced with the standard rituals of departure.

The old woman received a big hug from Charlie Moon and the usual suggestion that she should stay close to her house until Sarah returned. Which was Moon's way of advising his reckless relative to resist any temptation to stray alone into *Cañón del Espíritu*. A lot of good such advice from her nephew would do.

Scott Parris bear-hugged Daisy, too, and warned, "There's always black bears and hungry cougars and a few two-legged varmints roaming about, so you'd best be on the lookout." Breathless from these manly embraces, Daisy was unable to respond with her usual tart remark that if any furry varmints or wild-eyed outlaws came skulking around her place, it'd be *them* that'd need to be on the lookout because she had a double-barrel 12-gauge shotgun in the closet that was loaded with buckshot and she knew how to use it. But the white cop knew what Daisy was thinking and she knew that he knew and that Charlie Moon did too.

The final hug, a light embrace such as might be made by a fairy queen in a little girl's dream, was administered by Sarah Frank. This expression of affection was accompanied by a pair of surprises that quite took the old woman's breath away—two tender expressions that Charlie Moon's aunt had not experienced in decades.

The sweet girl whispered in Daisy's ear, "You're like a grandmother to me."

This was more than sufficient to strike the old woman dumb.

Sarah whispered again, "I love you." And kissed Daisy's wrinkled cheek.

Overkill.

If Daisy Perika was not literally bowled over by these tender endearments, they created a peculiar sense of disorientation. The woman with the barbed tongue and quick wit had not even the *urge* to make a sarcastic reply. Indeed, a salty tear appeared in the corner of her left eye. Daisy promptly blinked it away. *Now what did Sarah do that for?*

To those tender souls who appreciate occasional displays of fondness, Daisy's querulous query might seem peculiar. But the woman who had suffered multiple huggings—and even being *kissed*—felt like one who has been deprived of some essential strength. And not the mere weakening of muscle or intellect; it was as if the tribal elder had been robbed of some precious inner possession . . . an essential secret weapon.

Daisy Perika scowled at her departing friends as if one of them were a thief. *Or maybe it's all three.*

Any fair-minded person who is acquainted with Charlie Moon, Scott Parris, and Sarah Frank will be appalled and insist that Daisy's unspoken accusation is without the slightest justification. The old woman—always prone to unseemly excesses—has finally become completely unhinged.

That possibility cannot be ruled out.

But bizarre as Daisy Perika's conviction may seem, this much may be stated with absolute certainty—a vital arrow was suddenly missing from the shaman's quiver.

Even so, did someone really purloin the pointed projectile?

Despite Daisy's dark suspicions, a deliberate theft seems unlikely.

But it is equally improbable that the tribal elder has mislaid her treasured weapon—or that the missing arrow has bent a metaphoric bow and set *itself* aflight.

So what the dickens *is* going on here?

Those intrepid souls who raise such questions might be well advised to exercise a degree of caution. Ignorance, if not always bliss, is occasionally preferable to knowing what's going on.

CHAPTER THREE

CONCERNING THE VISUALIZATION OF DEAD PEOPLE AND THE PERCEPTION OF THEIR VOICES

As Scott Parris drove away in his aged red Volvo, Charlie Moon's Expedition was close behind. Sarah Frank waited in her freshly washed and waxed red F-150 pickup until the dust had settled, then waved at Daisy Perika as she left.

The very instant when the departing vehicles were out of sight, Charlie Moon's aunt locked the front door of her house, got a firm grip on her walking stick, and set her wrinkled face resolutely toward her intended destination. Within the minute, the canyon's gaping mouth had swallowed her whole.

As she trod along slowly, the tribal elder wondered how many times she had followed this sinuous deer path into the solitude of *Cañón del Espíritu*. A thousand? No. *More than I could count on the fingers of a thousand hands—and here I go again.* And she entered therein with the comfortable certainty that today's journey into this inner sanctum of her soul would be witnessed by a multitude of curious characters. Daisy could already *feel* the cunning animal eyes watching her from their various concealments. (Her observers included a pair of prairie rattlesnakes, several cottontail rabbits, a gray squirrel, and a harem of shy mule deer.) Daisy was confident that the gossipy raven would show her face, and that Delilah Darkwing would to bring her up-to-date on the latest gossip concerning the occupants of Spirit Canyon.

Thus far, her feathered friend was nowhere to be seen. The feisty old woman particularly looked forward to a contentious conversation with the venerable *pitukupf*. She supposed that after a light breakfast of wild honey and piñon nuts, the dwarf was probably napping in his snug underground home. (He may have been; we have no reliable information on the Little Man's current whereabouts.)

But even if Daisy encountered neither her diminutive neighbor nor Delilah Darkwing, there was one constant in the Ute elder's pilgrimages into these shadowy spaces between the canyon's sandstone walls—the dead people who dwelled there. Like flitting bats who appeared with soft twilight and fuzzy moths drawn to flickering candlelight, the haunts were bound to show their faces—and several of these disembodied souls would bend Daisy's ear with pleas for one thing and another. Among the recently deceased, the most common request was for information about friends and relatives who remained among the living. Once in a while, a vindictive apparition would (with considerable relish) inquire whether old So-and-So had finally died yet, and express the hope that his death had been painful. Some long-dead phantoms would announce their presence with sinister grunts and horrible groanings, and one of these ancients might utter unintelligible mutterings in a language that had died ages ago with his long-forgotten tribe. Most of these dead folk were unpleasant to behold, but Daisy had grown accustomed to empty eye sockets, withered limbs showing gristle and bone, and skin that hung in tattered shreds. Unique among the residents of *Cañón del Espíritu* was an Apache skin-walker whom Daisy had (with malice aforethought) personally dispatched to his present condition. Evidently chagrined, her victim delighted in making dire threats against the Ute elder's person, to which the shaman would reply in like kind. The irascible old woman enjoyed such interactions, and most of her encounters with the ghosts of Spirit Canyon were stimulating social events. Though she would not have admitted it, the old woman looked forward to the hideous apparitions' predictable appearances.

To her dismay, on this day they did not.

Appear, that is.

Oh, the haunts were *there,* all right.

Daisy could hear the voices of several wandering souls. A recently dead quilt maker from Ignacio asked how her unmarried daughter was getting along. An Anasazi sorcerer who evidently considered the shaman a kindred spirit whispered urgently into Daisy's ear. She could not understand a single syllable of what the dead magician said. A lonely old prospector who'd panned the stream almost two centuries ago inquired about the current price of gold. An 1870s Fort Garland soldier who'd died within sight of Three Sisters Mesa pleaded with the old woman to find his resting place and see that he got a decent Christian burial.

Though she usually enjoyed conversing with the dead, the Ute elder did not utter one word in response.

Her Apache victim (presumably waiting at the end of the queue) muttered several obscenities. He also threatened to sneak into her bedroom some dark night, suck all the blood from her veins, and vomit it into her water well. This aggravation was sufficient to loosen her tongue. "Come right ahead," the feisty old woman said. "Try to put the bite on me and I'll sew your nasty lips shut so tight that you won't be able to say a four-letter word or suck sour stump water through a straw!" Under ordinary circumstances, this threat-counterthreat entertainment would have brightened up her morning. But not on this occasion.

Daisy was distracted by a totally unforeseen development. For the first time ever, the shaman could not *see* a single one of those dead people who hovered so closely about her.

It was unnerving.

So much so, that without a thought to the friendly raven who was gliding down to land on a nearby juniper, or the cantankerous *pitukupf* whom she assumed was napping in his underground den, Daisy Perika turned as abruptly as one of her advanced age can and set her haggard face toward the open end of *Cañón del Espíritu.* As she pegged her way back along the deer path with her sturdy oak walking stick, a dismal thought hovered about her like a noxious vapor rising from a fetid swamp: *I'm losing my powers.* From Daisy's unique perspective, this was equivalent to admitting that her vital life forces were ebbing. *Sure as snow melts in May and cottonwood leaves fall to the ground in November and rot right on the spot—I'm dying.*

Are Dr. Daisy's self-diagnosis and bleak prognosis accurate? Perhaps. The truth of the matter remains to be discerned.

But of this much we can be certain: even as the old soul trodeth steadfastly toward hearth and home, Charlie Moon's despondent aunty is not alone in this world of troubles. Other problems are always brewing in other pots, and one in particular is about to boil over that will—in one way or another—*scald every member of the tribal elder's inner circle.*

When and where?

Tomorrow morning in Granite Creek.

For those who hanker for a higher degree of specificity, the epicenter of this localized eruption will be—the Wanda Naranjo residence and its environs.

You've never heard of the place?

That lack of familiarity shall be immediately remedied.